Praise for *A Season on the Wind*

"What a delight Suzanne Woods Fisher's latest novel is! *A Season on the Wind* is multifaceted and thoroughly enchanting. By the time I finished the first chapter, I was cheering on each of the central characters, was invested in their goals and secrets, and was anxiously turning pages to see what happened next. I've always loved Suzanne's distinct, relatable voice. She has a gift for enabling readers to feel like they're part of the story—so much so that they don't want to leave the world she's created. *A Season on the Wind* is everything a novel should be—engaging, heartfelt, bold, and charming."

Shelley Shepard Gray, *New York Times*
and *USA Today* bestselling author

"Sparks fly in a lively tale about the Audubon Christmas Bird Count in Amish country. *A Season on the Wind* overflows with warmth and conflict, laced with humor, and the possibility of rekindled love."

Amy Clipston, bestselling author of *The Jam and Jelly Nook*

"*A Season on the Wind* is a compelling read, an enjoyable volume that entertains on a quiet evening, or under a shade tree on a warm spring afternoon. Suzanne Woods Fisher calls our attention to the lives of bird-watchers and birds, both rare and common, that grace the pastoral hills of Pennsylvania. An endearing visit with our Amish friends, with a side order of birds and human nature."

Cheryl Harner, president of the Ohio Audubon Society

"*A Season on the Wind* by Suzanne Woods Fisher is a great Amish tale. . . . This book is a must-have for all Christian and Amish fiction readers!"

Urban Lit Magazine

"*A Season on the Wind* is Suzanne Woods Fisher's newest Amish fiction book, and it truly is a wonderful read!"

Interviews & Reviews

"This is a delightful Amish story . . . one of love and forgiveness and discovering one's true self. You will be uplifted and inspired in the reading."

Evangelical Church Library

Anything but Plain

Novels by Suzanne Woods Fisher

Anything but Plain

SUZANNE
WOODS
FISHER

Revell

a division of Baker Publishing Group
Grand Rapids, Michigan

Published by Revell
a division of Baker Publishing Group
PO Box 6287, Grand Rapids, MI 49516-6287
www.revellbooks.com

Printed in the United States of America

Library of Congress Cataloging-in-Publication Data
Names: Fisher, Suzanne Woods, author.
Title: Anything but plain / Suzanne Woods Fisher.
Description: Grand Rapids, MI : Revell a division of Baker Publishing Group, [2022]
Identifiers: LCCN 2021061038 | ISBN 9780800739515 (paperback) | ISBN
    9780800742232 (casebound) | ISBN 9781493438822 (ebook)
Subjects: LCGFT: Novels.
Classification: LCC PS3606.I78 A85 2022 | DDC 813/.6—dc23/eng/20211217
LC record available at https://lccn.loc.gov/2021061038

Baker Publishing Group publications use paper produced from sustainable forestry practices and post-consumer waste whenever possible.

22   23   24   25   26   27   28   7   6   5   4   3   2   1

"Walking the beans" is an old-fashioned farming term for weeding by hand. Walking the beans isn't just meant for the fields. It's a way of saying that a man, or a woman, should pay close attention to all that the Lord has given them. Their family, their children. The work of their hands.

—Bishop David Stoltzfus

Meet the Cast

Lydie Stoltzfus—Single Amish female, age nineteen, daughter of the bishop. Has trouble holding down a job.

Nathan Yoder—Single Amish male, age nineteen. Boy next door to Lydie Stoltzfus. Nathan lives at Black Gold Farm, land that has been in his family for five generations. Has a keen interest in organic farming. Encouraged by the bishop, he steps into the role of market manager for the first Stoney Ridge Farmers' Market.

David Stoltzfus—Amish bishop to the little church in Stoney Ridge. Father of Lydie Stoltzfus, husband to Birdy, son to Tillie Yoder Stoltzfus.

Tillie Yoder Stoltzfus—Known by her grandchildren as Mammi die Nasiche. *Mammi the Meddler*. Mother to the bishop (a role she takes very seriously), grandmother to Lydie. She's come from Ohio to help her son better manage his work, church, and family. Never mind that he did not ask for help.

Birdy Stoltzfus—Wife to David, stepmother to Lydie, mother to two little boys.

Dok (Ruth) Stoltzfus—The only doctor in Stoney Ridge. Sister to David, daughter (estranged) to Tillie, wife to police officer Matt Lehman. While in her teens, Dok left her Amish upbringing to pursue higher education. Her mother has never forgiven her.

Walt Yoder—Father to Nathan and Mick, husband to Sarah. Has managed his wife's family farm, Black Gold Farm, since his father-in-law passed away. Has absolutely no interest in his son Nathan's keen interest in organic farming. Just the opposite.

Mick Yoder—Single Amish male, age twenty-one, older brother to Nathan. Leans toward his father's methods of agriculture and far, far away from his brother's methods. Has no interest in organic farming whatsoever.

Sarah Yoder—Walt's wife, Nathan and Mick's mother. Inherited Black Gold Farm from her parents.

Patsy Glick—Single Amish female, age eighteen. Known to others as Perfect Patsy. Also known as Sie hat's Garaiss. She is very much sought after.

Owen Miller—Not Amish. (Not anything.) Young adult male, works with his father, Frank Miller, as a chemical rep to aid farmers with man-made treatments of pesticides, insecticides, and fertilizers.

Fern Lapp—Older Amish widow. First introduced in *The Keeper*. She has a knack for setting straight the younger generation.

Hank Lapp—Needs no introduction. You'll hear him coming.

Edith Fisher Lapp—Hank's wife. Best to stay out of her way.

1

Something was always happening to Lydie.

She was never quite sure how such mundane moments, such tiny and insignificant choices, could snowball into circumstances that could go so terribly wrong.

Take today. Lydie had been late to work this afternoon, which was unfortunate because today was her first day on the job and Edith Fisher Lapp was not a terribly understanding employer. Edith had hired Lydie to do some sewing and mending for her because, she explained, her eyes weren't what they used to be. As Lydie smoothed out Edith's new dress that needed a shortened hem, her husband, Hank, burst in the room on a desperate hunt for scissors. Lydie set aside Edith's dress to give Hank the scissors. While she waited for him to return, she picked up another dress that needed its hem let down. She put that one down to find Hank and get the scissors. Long story short, when she finally returned to her task, she mixed up the two dresses. When Edith tried on one dress, the hemline hung just above her knees.

Hank burst out with laughter at the sight. Laughing so hard

he lost his hat, slapping his hands on his knees, punctuated by big, loud guffaws. "My EDDY has a MINI-skirt!"

Lydie smiled. Hank Lapp's normal talking voice sounded like he was shouting into the bottom of a well. She looked at Edith to find her frowning. Edith was always frowning. Lydie's smile faded.

Edith pointed to the other dress. "And I suppose that hem will drag the floor."

"Well, um . . . you see . . ." Lydie's mouth suddenly went dry. It wasn't easy to keep her thoughts together when Edith Fisher Lapp was giving her a beady-eyed look through large, smudged glasses. She wondered if this was how a field mouse felt when spotted by a raptor. Her mind was wandering again. She bit her lip, trying to remember what Edith had just said.

"Do you think this is funny?"

Looking at Edith's face, Lydie rather thought not. Even Hank tried to settle down, though his shoulders were still shaking with laughter.

"Never mind." Angry red stains began to trickle up Edith's round cheeks. "I only hired you as a favor to Birdy. Everyone says you're an accident waiting to happen. I should have listened."

Lydie cringed. Such a small thing! But no doubt the whole town would know about the incident before long. She shuddered to think of how the story would fly and grow with each of Edith's retellings.

On the walk home, she pondered how to tell her dad. This was her fastest dismissal yet. She couldn't bear seeing the look of disappointment on his face. Such soul-wrenching sadness.

"Lydie."

Startled, Lydie had been so preoccupied that she hadn't realized she was passing by Black Gold Farm. Passing by Nathan Yoder.

"What's wrong?" He closed the door on the phone shanty to

approach her, peering down at her with his warm, concerned blue eyes. As blue as a bluebird. As blue as the ocean.

She had to look away from those beautiful blue eyes. "Oh, I just had a tiny sewing mishap with Edith Lapp."

"Can it get straightened out?"

An interesting choice of words! She hadn't dared tell Edith, but the way-too-short hem in the back of the dress was also crooked. Lydie had to swallow a smile. "I don't think so." Other than having to tell her dad and Birdy about the mishap, Lydie wasn't terribly disappointed. "I like to sew, but not *that* much."

A laugh burst out of Nathan. "You just say whatever pops into your head, don't you?"

Oh, yes, she did. Regrettably, yes.

Nathan didn't speak unless he had something important to say—something Lydie had a hard time understanding, because it was the opposite of the way she was. Often she didn't know what she was saying until it was said.

The fondness in his eyes as he looked at her reminded her of the way things used to be, before everything had changed. He took a deep breath as he pushed his hat up his forehead. "I've sure missed you, Lydie."

And just like that, the comfortable feeling between them slipped away. Under his steady gaze, she could feel the color building in her cheeks, so she pulled her eyes away from his again. *Just friends, just friends, just friends.*

"I was hoping that maybe I could take you home from Sunday's Singing."

Her eyes came back to his, and something queer started happening to her stomach. She backed away a step or two. Away from those blue, blue eyes. "I'm sorry, Nathan." This was one of the reasons she had to leave. "I should go. I'm . . . late. I'm always late. I should have been gone by now." Long gone. A few months ago, she had realized that she needed to leave Stoney

Ridge, leave her family, her church, but she wasn't quite sure where she would go or what she would do. Nor did she have any money saved up. So here she was, early April, still in Stoney Ridge. Soon, though, she would leave.

Nathan looked away. "Mick, I suppose, will be taking you home." There was something a little tight about the way he said it.

She opened her mouth to tell him a lie, to spare him the truth, but she was the daughter of a bishop, after all. She couldn't tell a lie. "It's best if we just stay friends, Nathan." Her words came out shaky.

They stood there a moment, a weird heaviness between them. He rested his hands on his hips.

A stillness came over him, though a trace of color rose under his fair skin. "But it's different with Mick?" He clamped his lips together after he'd asked the question, like he wasn't sure he should've said what he was thinking.

Mick was Nathan's brother, older by two years. They were neighbors and schoolmates, she and Nathan and Mick, and there'd hardly been a day without one or the other finding a reason to run through the hedge. It seemed strange, now, that they could've been so close, because the brothers were so very different. Mick, quick to laugh and just as quick to anger, reckless to a fault. Nathan, careful and cautious, and maybe just a little too restrained.

He waited for her to give him an answer. The silence between them took on a prickly tension, the very air seemed to crackle and snap around them.

"Ja. It's different with Mick." That was the truth, though she knew that Nathan would hear it in a different way than how she meant it.

The look he sent her was one of pure frustration, but then he swept his hand over his face, and when he was done, he looked like his normal self again. His gaze wandered past Lydie to his family's farm, beyond the small creek lined with weeping willows, beyond the sheep grazing with their lambs in the low-lying pasture. It was as if Black Gold Farm was beckoning to him, reminding him of where he belonged. He tipped his hat and headed toward his driveway. Back to his father who couldn't forgive Lydie for a mistake she'd made.

Watching Nathan go, her heart hurt. There was a time when they would stand at the hole in the hedge that bordered their families' properties and talk until the dinner bell rang. They used to be *friends*. She missed him terribly. She let out a puff of air. This was why she had to leave soon. She didn't want him to love her only to have her leave. She wasn't worth all that.

The sound of an approaching horse at full gallop made her spin around and bolt out of the way. Dashing past was a horse and driverless buggy. *Oh no. Oh no, no, no, no, no!* She knew that horse! It was Old Jim. Her dad had let her take him to the Lapps' because she'd been running so late this afternoon. And in the upset with Edith, she'd left the Lapp house, completely forgetting Old Jim.

<hr />

All winter, Nathan had fought a building desperation. The longing he felt for Lydie was becoming all-consuming. He couldn't make sense of the distance she'd put between them, and any time he tried to get her to talk about it, she clammed up. He had a hard time believing that she had chosen Mick over him.

Nathan loved his brother. But he also knew him. And Lydie knew Mick just as well. He was always running after what he couldn't have. He chased a new girl each week, tiring of them quickly when they returned his interest. It was impossible to believe that Lydie would be drawn to Mick when she had always disparaged his dallying. And yet, that's what she'd been telling him.

So maybe he was the fool. He was the one who couldn't bear to accept the truth.

But was it the truth? Wouldn't he feel it, deep in his bones, if Lydie were truly in love with Mick? Nathan knew in his soul that he and Lydie were supposed to be together, but he didn't know how to make her know it too. He clenched and unclenched his hands, then took off, heading up to the orchard, his favorite place on the farm to go to quiet his soul.

In the center of the orchard, he turned in a circle to study the trees. Apricots always bloomed first, blossoms appearing in April, with cherries right behind them. They were cold-hardy trees, prolific bloomers, the first to waken the honeybees with much-needed nourishment.

The delicate pink blossoms were here, right on schedule, but there was a noticeable lack of buzzing. The bees had gone missing. Hardly any birds in the trees. The entire orchard just didn't radiate a vitality, not the way it should or could or once did. Then again, as his dad would say with a sneer, they weren't living in the garden of Eden.

No, they weren't. But Black Gold Farm had once been a thriving, robust farm. Its very name came from its rich, dark soil; prime land that had been passed down through five generations of his mother's family. Yet now it seemed to be dying and he had to do something to save it.

He heard the dinner bell clang and left the orchard to walk to the farmhouse. Up on the porch, he sat on the top step to pull off his boots before heading into the kitchen. His mother was a stickler for "leaving the barn in the barn." Inside the kitchen, he heard Mom struggle with another coughing fit. "Just allergies," she would say whenever Nathan, or Dad, or Mick tried to get her to see Dok Stoltzfus.

When he saw his father's buggy roll in, he paused from unlacing his boots and walked over to meet his dad. "The bees, Dad."

Climbing down from the buggy, Walt Yoder handed Nathan the reins to tie to the hitching post. "What about them?"

"There's hardly any bees in the orchard. This morning, I checked the hives and the queens are gone again." Last month, Nathan had realized the beehive boxes were missing their queens. He resupplied them with new mail-order queen bees, but they'd flown off.

His father grunted, which could have meant anything, and walked to the house.

Fewer bees, fewer birds. It grieved Nathan that his father didn't seem to understand the significance of their absence. His father couldn't change, couldn't pivot, even when the need was right in front of him.

If it were up to Nathan, he would've had a cover crop planted by now throughout the orchard, with hopes to attract pollinators. If it were up to him, he would've rotated crops to disrupt the life cycle of pests—something his dad should've been doing for years now. And if it were up to him, he would've canceled the chemical treatment contract Black Gold Farm had with Frank Miller and his son Owen.

This farm had once been considered some of the best real estate in all of Stoney Ridge. Eighty acres that were abundant with natural resources, slopes and ridges in just the right places, a creek winding through the farm that ran with clear water all year long. It was hard to explain the feelings Nathan had about the land and the farm. They were part of him and he was part of them.

As a small boy, Nathan remembered walking through the fields with his grandfather, his mother's father. Grossvati had made him stop to breathe in the smell of the farm. "Know that scent," he had told Nathan. "It smells of new life." Now a young man, Nathan had learned enough to know there truly was an aroma that healthy plants gave off.

In January, Nathan had attended an organic farming conference in Lancaster and heard a speaker describe a breakthrough belief that plants have an immune system similar to people. The plants produced compounds to defend themselves from insects and disease attacks. But each time the plants were sprayed with a fungicide or pesticide, it actually weakened the plants, affecting their immune system, in much the same way as a human being's immune system could be weakened, making the plant susceptible to more diseases. When he came home from the conference and tried to explain to his father all he had learned, Walt Yoder shut him down. "Dummes Zeug," he called it. *Stupid stuff.*

Eight years ago, Grossvati passed suddenly, and Black Gold Farm fell entirely under his son-in-law's management. Immediately, Nathan's father made sweeping changes, reducing livestock and converting pastures into fields. Simplifying the process, he called it. He turned the entire eighty acres into primarily a one-crop farm of feed corn, with plans to sell excess grain to other farmers.

Walt Yoder had been influenced by Frank Miller, a chemical sales rep who was expanding his territory into Stoney Ridge and had taken a special interest in Black Gold Farm. Frank had talked Walt into trying no-till farming for just one year and watching the results.

That first year brought in a higher yield than ever before on Black Gold Farm. So did the second year, third, and fourth. But the fifth year was flat. The insects that had survived the assault of chemicals now had a resistance to pesticides. For the last three years, the crops on Black Gold Farm were riddled with fungi and pests that chemical treatments did little to reduce.

Over the last year or two, Nathan had searched fervently for solutions. After studying the principles of organic farming, he was sure he'd found it. It would mean not only returning the farm back to his grandfather's traditional methods but taking it a step further by completely eliminating the use of chemicals. The need for them. He wanted to replace lost nutrients to the soil, to restore health to the land. But Walt Yoder refused to make any changes.

Tonight, as Nathan entered the house, he slipped into his seat at the table across from Mick, and paused, waiting for the moment when his dad's gray head bent in silent prayer. He followed suit, along with his mother and brother, and offered thanks to the Lord for the blessing of this meal.

Nathan waited until his father had eaten most of his meal before he repeated his worry over the missing bees again. "We've got to do something. Soon."

"Call the chemical rep," Dad said. "Get him back here with something."

That was Walt Yoder's answer to everything. Nathan's name for Frank Miller, under his breath, was Mr. Chemicals. His dad believed everything Frank Miller told him, hook, line, and sinker. So did Mick. Nathan wasn't buying the chem rep's song and dance, not any longer. "Dad, I keep telling you. I think the chemicals *are* the problem."

"And here goes the professor again," Mick said, his brown eyes full of mockery. "Immer das alte Leid singing." *The same old song and dance.*

Nathan slanted a look in his brother's direction. "I think there's a better way. Frank Miller wants you to dump more and more chemicals on the plants, but I'm convinced they're doing more harm than good."

Dad's fork made a soft clink in the quiet. "We've just had a streak of bad luck, that's all."

Nathan shook his head. "We've created that bad luck. The soil is depleted. There's nothing left for the plants. They can't defend themselves."

Mick burst out with a laugh. "Like they're soldiers."

"In a way they are," Nathan said. "Like soldiers without weapons. The natural predators of pests can't flourish when the plants are weak. And the plants are weakened when the soil is deficient."

"Right," Mick said, an edge to his voice, "and you know the soil is bad because . . ."

"Through analysis," Nathan said. "I sent a sample off to the county." Out of his pocket, he pulled an envelope and set it on the tabletop. "It's missing important trace minerals."

"You did that without letting me know? Without my permission?" Dad's eyes drilled into him. "You think organic farming doesn't have risks? It does. It's costly. And yields are lower."

"Lower, yes," Nathan said, "but more substantial. More beneficial in the long term."

Dad tossed his napkin on the table. "Nathan, I've heard enough of this nonsense."

"Why?" Mom was pouring coffee into Dad's cup from a battered, blue-speckled pot. "Walt, why can't you give him a chance?"

Dad looked up at her, startled. "Sarah, you think there's something to this . . . Quatsch?" *Foolishness?*

Mom set the coffeepot on a metal stand on the table. "All I know is that for the last three years, you've been having more and more problems with the crops. Why not try it Nathan's way? Look what he did last summer with my garden. Best garden I've had in years."

Dad picked up his coffee, then set it down again. He stared at his wife, his face settling into deep lines. Mom didn't push back at Dad very often, but when she did, she held her ground. A silence drew out between them, until a coughing jag started up and Mom hurried off to the other room. Dad watched her go, a worried look on his face.

"Don't you ever wonder if the chemicals are making her

sick?" As soon as Nathan voiced his concern aloud, he regretted it.

His father's thick eyebrows met in the middle with a deep furrow. "You're saying I'm making my own wife sick?"

"Not that you mean to, nothing like that. But last week, it seemed like right after spraying that new fungicide, Mom's coughing got worse."

Dad pointed his fork at Nathan's plate. "Why don't you stop your jabbering and finish your meal."

In the other room, Mom kept coughing, a dry hack that hurt Nathan to hear it. For a long moment Dad said nothing, did nothing. Then he set down his fork with a sigh. "All right. Here's what I'm going to do. Split the farm in two for this year's harvest. Each boy takes forty acres."

Nathan was stunned silent. This was the closest his father had ever come to admitting that something was wrong with Black Gold Farm. The closest he'd ever come to admitting *he* might be wrong. Pride ran deep in Walt Yoder.

"Fine with me," Mick said. "I choose the southern forty. Nathan gets the north."

"Nein!" *No.* Nathan snapped into action. "I need those southern acres. I need the elevation."

"Why?" Mick said. "It's more of a slope than much of an elevation."

"It's enough elevation for pesticides to run off or drift on the wind."

"Excuses, excuses." Mick rolled his eyes. "Hold on." He cocked his head, eyes narrowed. "The south side gives you the greenhouse."

"I need the greenhouse. It provides a buffer zone."

Mick shook his head. "Not fair." His voice was serious for once.

"Mick, you've hardly ever stepped a foot into the greenhouse."

"Maybe I will now."

Nathan lifted his palms in the air. "Mick, I want that greenhouse. It's the one place where I can control the entire environment. Nothing but dirt and water and seedlings. No chemicals." He turned back to his father. "I'm going to need three years."

"For what?"

"Three years to get rid of the chemicals so I can get Black Gold Farm certified organically."

Dad's gaze went back and forth between Mick and Nathan. He let out a deep sigh, like he was tired of the topic, tired of the farm, tired of the bleak and discouraging situation. "One harvest. That's all you get. By year's end, whoever ends up with the best yield on their crops gets the whole kit and caboodle."

Nathan and Mick exchanged a shocked look. "You can't be serious," Nathan said. "You're turning this into a contest to win the farm?"

Dad turned toward him, all stiff and stern again. "Das ist das Ende vom Lied." *That's the end of the matter.*

His father's patience had a short limit these days. Nathan lowered his head. The rest of the meal was eaten in silence.

～～

The rattle of the buggy wheels over the metal grate sent off an unnerving sound. Or maybe it was just how he heard it. All day, David Stoltzfus couldn't shake an odd sense of uneasiness, as if stuck in the moment between a lightning strike and the thunderclap. But he couldn't put his finger on the cause of his anxious feelings. Maybe it was the visit today from Roman and Barbara Fisher—another young family planning to leave Stoney Ridge because they couldn't make a living here. Rome loved to farm, yet had to travel long distances to sell his produce at farmers' markets. Their departure troubled David because it seemed to be a developing trend. The church had lost two other young farming families over the last year. The Fishers made three. But it wasn't unexpected news to him.

His daughter Lydie's face suddenly swam into view. Maybe she was the reason he felt as if something dreadful was about to happen. She often was, but this felt different.

David's sister, Ruth, known to everyone in Stoney Ridge as Dok Stoltzfus, had come to see David at the Bent N' Dent yesterday to ask if Lydie could fill in while her receptionist was away for a month or more. "Birdy happened to mention," Dok had said, "that Lydie is between jobs right now."

That was one way of putting it. David thought his wife, Birdy, had been kind. She hadn't wanted to admit that Lydie had yet to hold on to a job longer than a few weeks. A few days ago, she'd managed to do some sewing for Edith Lapp only for a few hours before she was sent home.

"I need a friendly face to sit at the receptionist desk and I thought of Lydie. I've never had much time alone with her—whenever I've been with your family, Lydie, Emily, and Molly were together. Now that Emily and Molly are married, it occurred to me that Lydie must be missing her sisters, and I thought working for me would give us a chance to get to know each other better. Look how well it worked out with Ruthie."

Dok had a demanding job, and she and her husband, Matt, were in the middle of remodeling a fixer-upper. David worried that working with Lydie might not . . . work. "I think Lydie would be delighted to work for you—"

"Excellent," Dok said. "Have Lydie drop by the office tomorrow at closing time, around five o'clock, and I'll go over her responsibilities."

"But—"

Dok was already at the store's door. "Remember to let her know it's just a fill-in position. Temporary. Just a month or two." She rocked her hand back and forth in the air. "Maybe three." And she was gone.

But—David had been trying to say—Lydie wasn't anything like her sister Ruthie.

Now, he glanced at his watch. Fifteen minutes after five and there was no sign of Lydie. He'd stayed at the Bent N' Dent until five o'clock, hoping he could have seen her scooter down the lane to Dok's office. It wasn't far from the store.

At ten minutes after five, he'd left for home, hoping to see Lydie on the way. So far, no sign of her.

Frustrated, he snapped the horse's reins and it lurched forward.

Well, this was just a temporary position. A friendly face to sit at the desk was all Dok said she needed. Low expectations. What could go wrong in a month or two?

Plenty.

David worried about Lydie. Despite the fact that her sisters and most of her friends had joined the church last fall, she had chosen not to be baptized along with them. He hadn't put any pressure on her to do so. Unlike many other ministers, David felt strongly that no one should join the church unless their heart and soul were wholly settled on the matter. The church didn't need half-Amish members. So he respected Lydie's choice in the matter, though he prayed she would have a change of heart. Sooner rather than later. What parent wouldn't have a similar prayer?

He wondered if it was a mistake to have Lydie work so closely with Dok. Putting aside his concern for Dok, he worried that it might not be wise for his daughter to spend so much time with an aunt who'd left home when she was Lydie's age. Not just any aunt, but one who was greatly admired and respected, by Amish and Englisch alike.

Lydie didn't have an understanding of how difficult it had been for David's sister to leave. All she knew was that Dok had chosen to leave the church to pursue a medical career. There was much more to her abrupt departure than higher education—something their mother, Tillie Yoder Stoltzfus, had yet to accept.

He shook off troubling thoughts of his mother and turned back to troubling thoughts about Lydie. He hadn't felt worried when Ruthie started working for Dok, but she was so very different from Lydie.

Ruthie had a strong sense of herself, a keen enthusiasm to face whatever was set before her, and the determination to see things through. Lydie could be impulsive, easily distracted, always eager to move on to the next thing. Act first and think later. Lydie's life in a nutshell.

How many times had Birdy tried to tell him that Lydie needed something . . . more. More what? Even Birdy, who loved her stepchildren and had a way of making each one feel important, had no answer to that. They'd encouraged Lydie to try different jobs in the community. Helping Izzy at the Stitch in Time shop, working as a maid at the Inn at Eagle Hill, hiring out as a mother's helper. She'd start strong, then her interest would fizzle out, or something would go terribly wrong. And David knew it wouldn't be long until she'd be let go.

That's why Lydie was in between jobs right now. There were no jobs left among the Amish for a young woman like her. She always expressed regret and a determination to do better next time, but things never changed. Everyone loved Lydie, felt as if she lit up a room with her lighthearted personality, but no one wanted her to work for them. At least not for very long.

He hoped Lydie wouldn't disappoint Dok. He also hoped she wouldn't be swayed to leave the Amish by working for his sister. He reminded himself that it could be a chance to examine the world beyond the Amish while under the protection of Dok.

And he felt encouraged when he remembered that Nathan Yoder was an important person to Lydie. David had always been especially fond of Nathan. There was just something special about him, even as a boy. Solid as an oak tree.

Last week, Nathan had come into the Bent N' Dent to pick up a few things for his mother, and somehow, in what started as just a passing "What have you been up to lately?" conversation, he started telling David all about a plant's nutritional needs. David wasn't inclined toward the farming life, wasn't even particularly interested in how a plant grew, but he found himself fascinated, drawn in by the young man's enthusiasm.

"You see," Nathan started, as if David had asked, "plants have an immune system much like you and me. Their immune system is dependent on well-balanced nutrition, the same way as our own is. When plants are given what they need to defend themselves, pesticides can be avoided. Natural predators of pests are able to flourish."

The more David pondered that curious thought, the more he realized the same could be said of people too. When church members prioritized their spiritual nutrition, when they ate and drank deeply of God's Word, when they prayed and worshiped, then they were better able to defend themselves against enemy attacks. Pesticides—as detrimental as a visit from the deacon, as uncomfortable as sitting on the sinner's bench, as unnerving as being put under the ban—all those could be avoided. Wouldn't it be wonderful if his church members understood that their souls were as needy as their stomachs?

The Lord never gave up on his people, and neither should David give up on Lydie, his dearly loved, thoroughly frustrating daughter. His spirits lifted at the thought. He looked out the buggy window, at the blue sky, and offered a thank-you for the reminder of God's steadfast love.

He let Old Jim slow to a walk as the horse pulled the buggy up the long, steep driveway that led to his home. Usually, at this time of day, there were signs of life spilling out all over the little house. His two boys were often on the swing set, toys littered the yard, the enticing scent of supper would be cooking in the air. Today, there was nothing. As if something had happened to blow out a candle's light. Stifle the life. Back flooded the uneasy feelings he'd fought against all day.

There was only one reason his entire household ever went into hiding.

"David! There you are!"

Automatically, David threw his shoulders back and sat up straight. *Oh no. Please no.* He searched the yard for signs of her. *Please, please, please, no.*

From an upstairs window, his mother's capped gray head appeared.

2

On the way to the barn, Nathan shivered against a gust of cold wind. Though the sun was shining, though the calendar said spring had arrived, the wind still had winter's bite to it. After his father's unexpected decision to split the farm, he wasn't sure if he wanted spring to hurry or not.

Only one harvest. Six short months. *Man.* Time was going to fly.

In his mind, he went through steps he'd studied toward converting acreage into organic fields. Start with the cleanest field. That was another reason he was glad Mick gave in and let him have the southern forty acres. Those fields had been treated with fewer chemicals last year. He wished there was some way to convince his father to let him convert all of Black Gold Farm. A farm shouldn't be chopped up, shouldn't be managed in separate pieces, but considered as one whole, living organism.

In the tack room of the barn, Nathan cleared off the workbench to serve as his desk. He wanted to plot the organic conversion of the forty acres without Dad or Mick sticking their nose in it. Out of a box, he pulled a thick file of notes about conversion that he'd taken during the January conference. The speaker warned the farmers to expect it to be a painful process, likened to boxing with one arm tied behind your back. Flipping through the pages, he huffed a sigh. Yeah, this was going to be a long, hard, painful process. He smiled. Well worth it, though.

He heard the barn door slide open and recognized the footfalls of his mother. "Sis Zeit fer's Nachtesse!" *Time for supper.*

"Back here!"

Sarah Yoder came to the doorjamb of the tack room and poked her head in. "I rang the dinner bell."

"Did you? I didn't even hear it."

She rubbed her hands together. "It's cold in here."

He hadn't noticed that, either. His mind was thoroughly absorbed with the conversion of the fields. "Mom, thank you. For pressing Dad to let me farm my way." He tapped his pencil on the desk. "At least forty acres, anyway."

"I saw what you were able to do with my kitchen garden last summer. I can't wait to see what you'll do with those forty acres."

"It's not gonna be easy."

Leaning her back on the doorjamb, she smiled. "Nothing worth getting is ever easy." She took a step to leave, then turned back. "I believe in you, Nathan. I have a good feeling about this summer."

As she walked back down the long barn aisle, he heard her cough start up. That dry hack, worse than ever. She'd always been prone to winter colds that lingered, but this seemed different. Ominous.

Dok Stoltzfus had said Mom's cough should clear when the weather warmed up. At least, that's what Mom reported after her recent visit to Dok. But he wondered. As soon as he thought it, he shrugged that worry off. He knew better than to borrow trouble.

He scooped up the papers and put them back in the box.

Later tonight, he'd work on plans to start mapping out his crops.

As he crossed the yard, the wind hit him in the face, stinging his eyes. A horse whinnied in the pasture, and he turned to see a scooter going way too fast, and Nathan knew Lydie was on that scooter even before he saw her. He stopped to watch her tear down the country road, heading toward town, wondering what the hurry was. Then again, Lydie was always late for something. Always on to the next thing, impossible to pin down. She could be the most exasperating girl on this planet.

Man, he missed her.

~

As Lydie rode her scooter along the road that bordered Black Gold Farm, a colt in the pasture let out a loud whinny. Nathan was crossing the yard from the barn, heard the whinny, and looked over at the road. When he saw her, he did a double take that made her heart sing. She quickly snuffed it out. *Just friends, just friends, just friends.*

Besides, she needed to focus on the task at hand. She was on her way to her new job! A temporary job, while Dok's receptionist was helping her mother recover from some kind of awful-sounding surgery. Judging by the look on her dad's face, this job was a serious matter. A doctor's receptionist, he said twice, had to be reliable, dependable, nondistractable—all qualities that had never once been attributed to Lydie.

Dad had told her to meet Dok for training at five o'clock when the office closed for the day. Lydie was late, but not so very late. She could've been early, but her grandmother, Mammi, had arrived that afternoon at the house—*without any warning!*—and she couldn't leave Birdy without reinforcement. She waited until her dad got home and then rushed over to Dok's office. She hoped Dok might not notice how late Lydie was, but she did, and she made a point to stress punctuality as she reviewed the job description. "The office opens at nine in the morning. You must *not* be late. Not ever."

On a paper pad that Dok had given her to take notes, Lydie wrote in big letters, *Don't Be Late.*

"This is your desk. This is where you'll be, ninety-nine percent of the time. Your job is to arrive on time to open up the office, welcome patients, let me know they've arrived."

Lydie had her own desk. Her own little kingdom. She eyed the phone. So different from the one in their phone shanty. So modern. So sleek. Which got her to thinking . . . if the Amish could use telephones, why did they have to use phones that looked to be antiques? Couldn't they update from the rotary dial style?

"Are you sure you're getting all this?"

Oh no! Lydie's mind had been wandering while Dok was talking. What had she been saying? It was too embarrassing to have to ask her to repeat herself. "Sounds pretty doable."

"It is. Answer phone calls, schedule appointments, take messages on this pad of paper, and that's pretty much it."

"That's all?" Sit at the desk, answer the phone, schedule appointments, welcome patients, let Dok know they're waiting. It didn't sound terribly difficult. Lydie smiled. "What could be simpler?"

Dok gave her a tour of the back of the office—two exam rooms, a supply room. Lydie followed behind her, noticing how small and petite she was. As a child, Lydie had always thought of Dok as nearly larger than life. Her hair, which Lydie had always loved because it was strawberry blond, thick and wavy, was held with a clip on the back of her head and had strands of white in it. When had this happened? When had Dok gotten older?

The tour ended in Dok's private office. "We'll start small, and then your responsibilities might increase in time."

"How so?"

"I might have you do small tasks for me."

"Draw blood?"

"No." Dok shook her head vehemently. "Nothing medical. You must not provide any medical procedure, nor give out any medical advice. None. Not even to recommend a tissue to wipe a nose. Remember that."

Well, that was disappointing news.

Dok eyed her, a tad suspiciously. "What I meant by adding small tasks . . . things like . . . run over to the Bent N' Dent and get some supplies."

"I can do that. No problem there. No problem anywhere. I can handle this job." She snapped her fingers for effect. What could go wrong? "Easy peasy."

"There's something else, Lydie. Everything that goes on here—and I mean everything—is confidential. Everything. No patient information leaves this office."

Lydie marked CONFIDENTIAL down on the paper pad in big letters. "Do not worry. I am a vault."

"And one more thing." Dok pointed to a cabinet on the wall of her office. "That remains locked at all times. I'm the only one who goes in and out of it. I keep pharmaceutical drugs in it."

"Got it." Lydie flipped the lid on the pad of paper.

But Dok wasn't done. She emphasized the need to keep the front door to the office locked up when no one was there. She repeated it three times. "Even a saint is tempted by an open door," Dok said, and Lydie wondered if she knew just how Amish she sounded when she said it.

As Dok walked her back to the receptionist's desk, she said, "Lydie, I wouldn't ask you to do the job if I didn't think you could handle it."

It was seldom for Lydie to hear such a vote of confidence in her abilities and she appreciated it. "Everything will be fine!"

Dok gave her a long look, then handed her a key to the office. "Yes," she finally said, "yes, and it's just temporary."

After supper, before the sun dipped too low on the horizon, Nathan walked out to the southern acres—his fields. At least, his fields for this summer. He felt protective of this land and wanted to do right by it. He went to the fence that bordered the road and sat on the rail with his pad of paper and pencil.

After studying the county's assessment of Black Gold's soil, he knew the fields would need tremendous amounts of amendments to reverse the damaging effects of chemical fertilization. And it was already April! He should've spent January tilling the fields with composted manure to amend the depleted soil. He should've started fava beans in the greenhouse, so they'd have been ready to transplant into the fields in February. By now, he should've tilled those fava bean plants under so they would add needed nitrogen into the soil as they decomposed. By May, the fields would finally be ready to plant corn, wheat, and oats.

Time was not on Nathan's side. He had less than a month to amend the soil. Less than a month to plant. Discouraged, he let out an exasperated puff of air.

"I heard your dad split the farm in two."

Nathan nearly fell off the fence at the sound of Lydie's voice. He twisted awkwardly to face her. She was standing a few feet away, one foot still on her scooter. He hadn't even heard her approach. Her cheeks were pink from the cold and her blue eyes were bright with happiness. *Beautiful.* She was so beautiful. She always was, but he hadn't been prepared to see her, and the sight of her struck him dumb.

"Mick told me. He dropped by earlier today."

Of course. Mick spent a lot of his spare time lately over at the Stoltzfus's home. And he always seemed to have a lot of spare time on his hands. If Nathan were a better man, he would've asked him how things were going with Lydie. But he wasn't a better man. Plus, he didn't want to know.

"So you're taking this section and Mick is taking the other?" She squinted, looking past him to the fields. "I'm surprised. I wouldn't think you'd want the hilly side."

She'd been thinking about him. *Pull yourself together, man!* He cleared his throat. "I don't, but I can't risk runoff from Mick's fields contaminating my crops. His fields are lower than this side. I need the elevation, and I need the buffers of the house and barn and greenhouse."

She stared out in the distance. "I could never figure out why your dad made rows that went up and down the hills."

"It's a time-saver. Easier on the horses to sow seeds in a straight line."

"I suppose so. But it seems like you're fighting the way the land just wants to be. The way it was made. Why not just accept the crookedness of the land?"

He coughed a laugh. "Accept the crookedness?"

"Like this . . ." She took his pencil and pad of paper. She drew a hill, then drew rows that swirled into the hillside. "Follow the curves. Plant rows *around* the hills. Not up and down them. So that you work with the crookedness instead of against it."

She was so close to him that he could smell the lavender-scented shampoo from her hair. He remembered the first time he'd held her in his arms, so close that he could breathe in the scent of her. They'd been at the bonfire at Blue Lake Pond with their friends. Mick had been telling creepy ghost stories, getting all the girls scared. As if Mick had cued it, a great horned owl flew right past the bonfire and the girls screamed. Even Lydie. She clung to Nathan, and he wrapped her in his arms to comfort her. Ever since, he'd loved owls. And he loved the scent of her hair.

Suddenly he realized that Lydie had been waiting for him to see what she had drawn. He blinked, then looked at the pad of paper she held out to him. "Oh! You mean contour strips."

"Is that what it's called?" She lifted a shoulder in a half shrug.

34

"I'd better go. Mammi has come for a visit." She pulled a face, her eyes round and worried, and he couldn't help but laugh, which made her grin. The bishop's mother had a reputation for rattling everyone's cage. Even Walt Yoder steered clear of Tillie Stoltzfus.

Briefly, things felt normal again between Nathan and Lydie. Easy and comfortable, the way they'd always been. The way they could look at each other across a room and read what the other was thinking. Two separate people, but of one mind. One heart.

"Lydie," he said softly.

Color flashed in her cheeks. She was so fair she could never hide a blush.

"Lydie," he said again. "What's gone wrong between—"

"I'm late." She hopped back on the scooter. "Gotta go."

He watched her until she disappeared around the bend. These unexpected encounters left him with such an unsettled feeling of loss that he almost wished their paths didn't cross as often as they did. Almost, but not really.

With a sigh, he twisted back around on the fence to stare at the sloping acreage of Black Gold Farm, at the many peaks and dips. Contour strips. Hmm.

While at that organic farming conference, Nathan had attended a workshop touting the benefits of contour farming. The speaker said that contour farming was one of the tools a farmer needed to consider to build soil health. He said that there'd be less soil erosion, better capture of rainfall.

Nathan's mind started spinning. What if he followed the contours of the land to plant the crops? For the highest area, a small section of an extremely steep slope gradient, he could consider terracing.

Changing row directions to follow the contours would be backbreaking work, but on the plus side, he'd be tilling at the same elevation. And during rainless stretches, his crops would have the advantage of less runoff. The rows in contour farming acted almost like mini-dams, holding water in. For the first time since his father had divided up the land, he was thankful he had only forty acres to worry about.

It would be risky. If he failed, he would be the laughingstock of Stoney Ridge, the butt of all jokes. Then again, farming was all about mistakes and uncertainties.

And what if it worked?

Ideas started to take shape, one after the other, like corn popping on a skillet. He bolted across the field and hopped the fence, sprinted toward the barn and went straight to the tack room, yanking his site plans out of the drawer. He flipped the pages until he came to an old contour map of Black Gold Farm that his grandfather had once drawn. Leaning his palms on the workbench, he examined it for several long moments, studying the gradations of the slopes.

He straightened, flung his hat onto a trunk, and took in a big breath. How had Lydie thought of contour farming when she didn't even know what it was? It made perfect Lydie-sense. She could see things in a way no one else could. It was one of the things he loved about her.

He wiped his brow and struck a match to light the wick in the lantern. He had a lot to do tonight. He had a new plan for his forty acres.

❧

At the base of the steep driveway that led to her home, Lydie jumped off the scooter to push. Despite the climb, she liked the hilltop location of their home. The views, especially, were breathtaking. And while the property was small, her dad wasn't a farmer, so the little house on the hill suited their family nicely. Halfway to the top of the driveway, she stopped and turned, hoping to see if Nathan might still be sitting on the fence, drawing on a pad of paper, pondering his forty acres.

Now, *he* was a born farmer. He held an almost poetic view of tilling the earth. Sometimes she wondered if the way Nathan felt about farming might have been the way Adam had once felt when the Lord God brought him to life in the garden of Eden. Like he couldn't imagine a better life for a man.

She saw no sign of Nathan, so she resumed pushing the scooter up the hill. Lydie had always liked watching him unobserved. In church last Sunday, he'd sat in an aisle seat directly across from her and sprawled his long legs out, crossing one booted ankle over the other. She tried to find one new thing about him that she hadn't noticed before. It was a game she'd played for years, and she always discovered something new. Last Sunday, it was his socks. One couldn't stay up, and it kept bothering him. He would lean over and yank it up and, slowly, it would sink down again. It was far more entertaining to watch than listening to the ministers preach their long sermons, even if one of the ministers was her dad, whom she loved dearly.

Tonight she had noted how his dark brown hair curled up from under his black hat. He was lean and not terribly tall, different from the big, stocky, muscular farmers in her church. But then, everything about Nathan was different. His facial features were finely chiseled, with such intelligent, thoughtful eyes under those dark brows.

She heard a door slam shut and lifted her head to see her stepmother, Birdy, at the clothesline, bringing in the day's clean laundry. She hurried the last few yards, dropped the scooter, and crossed the yard to help. "Did I miss supper?" She grabbed a towel off the line.

"No. Mammi insisted on waiting until you returned. She has a surprise for us."

"A surprise?" Lydie's voice sounded flat, even to her own ears. Her grandmother's surprises were never good. She was known by her grandchildren as Mammi die Nasiche—Mammi the Meddler. A domineering woman who felt she knew best how to run everyone's life. Her visits to Stoney Ridge wore the family out, especially Dad. She relished her role as the mother of the bishop. Though he never asked for help or advice, Mammi provided both. "What do you think her surprise could be?"

"I didn't dare ask." Birdy tossed some rolled socks into the basket. "Mick stopped by while you were at Dok's."

"Mick?" Lydie glanced over at Black Gold Farm. "What did he want?"

"Something to do with the shed. He said you'd told him he could use it."

Had Lydie? She didn't remember. Mick was a talker. He said a lot of things that she didn't pay any attention to. "You don't mind, do you?"

"No. As long as the boys stay far away from it."

Birdy's warning came from an incident Lydie wished everyone would just forget about. It had happened last summer. She'd been babysitting the boys for Birdy, and they'd been playing ball outside until the ball got kicked down the hill and landed near the shed. Just at that moment, Lydie heard Hank Lapp bellow from the front yard, looking for someone, and Lydie yelled back to let him know where she was. Hank, being Hank, didn't hear and kept on bellowing. So Lydie told the boys to stay put and she ran around the house to find Hank. He was all bothered about a foxtail caught in his mule's tail and Lydie stopped to help untangle it. By the time she returned to the backyard, the boys had disappeared. She heard their cries and followed the wailing to the old shed, where the boys were bawling their eyes out. Apparently, after they had fetched the lost ball, curiosity led them into the old shed, where the door had jammed shut and they couldn't get out. They had nightmares for a week. One boy would start to cry and he would set off the other. High-pitched screaming in the middle of the night. *Awful.*

See? Some things were best forgotten.

Birdy unclipped a pair of little-boy trousers. "Nathan doesn't seem to be coming around much anymore. Only Mick. He comes a lot."

"Oh?" Lydie bent over the laundry basket to fetch a sock she'd dropped.

From the porch came a high, loud, tinny voice that caused a shiver to run down Lydie's spine. "I warned you about being so friendly with those two brothers. There'd come a day when three was a crowd."

Lydie straightened to find her grandmother peering down at her from the porch, an eagle eyeing its prey. "How does Mammi hear so well?" She hadn't intended to say it out loud. She must have, though, because Birdy snorted a laugh.

"Lydie, I've heard some distressing news about you—" Mammi started, but before she could finish her thought, a crashing sound came from the house, followed seconds later by a child's cry.

Birdy dropped the trousers in the laundry basket and bolted up the porch stairs. "Tillie, you said you'd watch the babies."

Mammi jumped out of her way. "Hardly babies," she said, though Birdy had vanished through the door. She turned back to Lydie. "In my day, children knew to stay put. Those boys can't sit still."

There was some truth to that. Birdy's two little boys, Timmy and Noah, were in constant motion. But Lydie wasn't going to stick around for Mammi's focus to turn to her. Whatever distressing news she had heard . . . well, Lydie just didn't want to know about it. How did her grandmother hear so much gossip, anyhow? She lived in Ohio, but she was more up to speed with Stoney Ridge than Dad and Birdy were. "I just remembered that I should fill up Old Jim's water bucket." She tucked her chin as she marched to the barn, her capstrings lifting by a gust of wind and bouncing against her shoulders. She could feel her grandmother's eyes drill into her back, watching her. *Forget her, forget her, forget her.*

She did wonder, though. Just what had Mammi heard about her? And just who had told her? Edith Lapp, probably. Or maybe Martha Glick. The busybodies of Stoney Ridge. Lydie's fists clenched. For the thousandth time, she wished her dad wasn't the bishop. Her sisters didn't seem to mind being known as the bishop's children, even her twin, Emily, but Lydie had always felt as if she lived in a glass fishbowl, under constant scrutiny. Tested and found lacking.

Had Mammi heard rumblings of Lydie's unfortunate job terminations? The Englisch clothing she kept tucked between her mattress and box springs? Her doodle pad hidden in the trunk in the little barn? The Saturday night parties at Blue Lake Pond?

She didn't drink at the parties. She wasn't anything like Mick and some of his friends who kept their water bottles full of vodka, masked with grape soda. They claimed the all-day buzz helped when they spent their days plowing behind the back end of horses.

Maybe Mammi was distressed because she'd heard that Lydie had no plans to join baptism classes next fall. Dad and Birdy had never once asked if Lydie was considering attending baptism classes. Dad wanted young people to join the church only if their whole heart was in it. "The worst thing of all," he preached more times than Lydie could count, "is to be half Amish."

Mammi felt that once you turned sixteen, you got baptized. It wasn't about waiting for that prompting from the Lord, like Dad implored young people to do. It wasn't about feeling ready to take on a lifetime vow. It was only about turning sixteen. And Lydie was nineteen now. Mammi cornered Lydie over it each time she came to visit. The topic of baptism found its way into every single conversation.

Imagine Mammi's distress level if she knew that Lydie was planning to leave the church. Because she was, she really was. As soon as Dok's receptionist returned, she would go. It was the only path forward for her. As hard as it was to think of leaving, it was even harder to think of staying.

Lydie dug out her doodle pad in the little barn to draw a picture of Mammi on the porch, arms akimbo, with two little boys' faces squawking at the window. Time escaped her, and suddenly a half hour had passed. Rushing to the house, she burst into the kitchen and made a beeline to the sink to wash her hands. She could sense Mammi's narrowed eyes following her progress to her empty chair at the big table. She slipped into her seat and whispered "Sorry to keep you waiting" to everyone and no one in particular, then dipped her head in a quiet prayer of thanks.

Mammi waited until Lydie finished her prayer before she dug into her. "So, Lydie, earlier this afternoon, where exactly did you scoot off to in such a hurry?"

"Me?" Lydie swallowed a mouthful of spring carrots. She glanced at her dad, who lifted his eyebrows in a slightly pleading way. She got it. "I, um, had to talk to someone." Dok was that someone, Mammi's only daughter whom she pretended didn't exist simply because she had chosen to leave the Amish church to pursue an education.

And starting Monday morning, nine o'clock sharp, Lydie would be working for Dok. Better to let her dad deliver *that* news to Mammi. She reached out for a bread roll and took her time buttering it. She knew Mammi was still watching her, but she avoided her eyes, preferring to ponder what Dok must have been like at her age.

"Now that your sisters are married," Mammi said, "you're needed to help with Birdy's children."

Lydie saw Birdy shoot a narrow-eyed look at Dad, whose head remained bowed, eyes hidden. He seemed preoccupied with cutting his carrots with great precision.

"Tillie, the boys belong to David too," Birdy said. "They are his sons, after all."

Mammi took no notice.

Timmy, the older of the two little boys, was using his finger to spread butter on his bread, while his younger brother, Noah, was stuffing green peas into his nose. Lydie reached over to grab Noah's hands before Mammi could spot him. Mammi had noticed Timmy's butter spreading and swatted his hand away from the butter dish.

Ouch! Lydie knew how that felt. She felt sorry for her little brother, watching tears spring to his eyes as he rubbed his hand.

While Dad, Dok, and Uncle Simon had been growing up, did every supper radiate with Mammi's disapproval? It certainly seemed to be the norm, at least as long as Lydie could remember. She had always felt she could never do anything right in her grandmother's eyes. Too noisy, too forgetful, too everything. As hard as Lydie tried to live up to Mammi's ridiculously high expectations, something would invariably go wrong. Emily was Mammi's favorite—meek as a lamb, dutiful, submissive, obedient. Those qualities, Mammi said often, were the quintessential Amish woman. Never mind that Mammi shared none of them.

Birdy handed Lydie the dish of green peas. After noticing that some had gone up and down Noah's nose, she passed.

"Your grandmother's been waiting to share her surprise," Birdy said.

Ohhh. Lydie forgot about that surprise. She lifted her eyebrows at Mammi and forced a smile. "I'm all ears."

Mammi, seated where Birdy normally sat next to Dad, straightened her back and lifted her chin. Lydie hadn't noticed her wattle before, or perhaps it hadn't wiggled as much as it did now. She was wondering why old people got wattles in the first place when Mammi made her announcement. "I'm planning to stay on in Stoney Ridge. Indefinitely."

Everyone over the age of four froze. Shocked into silence.

"I have given the last two decades to help my son Simon with

42

his family. Laura and Abigail are married with families of their own. It's your turn now, David."

Lydie shot a glance at her dad and saw color drain from his face, like a stopper pulled from a full sink. His grip on his fork tightened until his knuckles turned white. "What, uh, do you mean by that, Mom?"

"Yes, whatever do you mean?" Birdy's voice trembled as she said the words.

Mammi smiled, delighted by the rapt attention she was receiving. "I'm not blind to the demands on the two of you. Two little boys who haven't been taught to listen to instruction. The Bent N' Dent store, I have no doubt, is in disarray again. I'll see to that. And then there's Lydie."

Lydie's eyes went wide. *Me? What about me?*

Dad broke the silence. "Well, now. That's quite a big surprise, Mom. Perhaps we could discuss this after supper."

"There's nothing to discuss." Mammi's glance swept the table with a smile, as pleased as a cat in cream, then she returned to her supper.

Dad sat there, fishmouthed. Birdy kept her eyes on her untouched plate. Lydie wondered if there was a chance Dok's receptionist might return sooner than later.

The two little boys, seated on either side of Birdy, kept on eating. Blissfully ignorant. They didn't realize that life, as they knew it, was over.

3

The sun shone bright on Saturday morning. Yesterday's wind had died down, and the chill morning air quickly warmed up. Emily had come to the house to help prepare Birdy's garden for spring planting. It was the sisters' annual birthday gift to Birdy, a tradition that had started during a year when her birthday landed close to Easter, and Dad had been unable to take time away from the church to work the garden. Normally, Molly helped too, but she'd gone out of town for a few weeks.

While Mammi had Emily captive in the kitchen, Lydie slipped out and started to hoe around perennial plants she knew that Birdy wanted to keep. An hour later, Emily came out to join her. "Sorry! I kept waiting for Mammi to take a breath so I could interrupt and excuse myself."

Lydie straightened, put her hands on her hips to stretch her back. "I'm just glad you're here to share Mammi's gift of attention."

"Where did Birdy and the boys go? And where's Dad?"

"Dad had something of great importance to do at the store. As he started out the door, Birdy suddenly remembered she had something she had to deliver *right now* to Fern." She threw her arms in the air. "They scattered!"

Emily smiled, then bent down to study what Lydie was hoeing around. "Why don't you just pull that weed?"

"Because it's not just any old weed," Lydie said. "It's milkweed. It attracts monarch butterflies. Birdy's been worried about the butterflies. They're not as common as they used to be. Fewer butterflies mean fewer birds. That's what's really worrying her." She stopped and looked at her sister. "Monarchs are pretty unusual, as butterflies go. Did you know they migrate all the way to Mexico?" Amazing, when you think how they bobbed and bounced and never flew in a straight line. Dizzying.

"No, I didn't know. But I am glad we have some time together today. We haven't talked in a while. I've missed you."

That was nice to hear. Sometimes Lydie felt as if Emily and Molly were so thoroughly absorbed in their newly married life that they never thought of anyone else.

"Lydie, can we talk about Nathan?"

"What? Why?" She returned to hoeing, a little harder.

"You never told me what happened between the two of you."

"Nothing happened. We just aren't as close as we used to be."

Emily gave her a long look. "Does it have something to do with Mick? Birdy said he's here a lot."

"Mick? No! He's only here because he's using the shed."

"The shed? What's he doing in that old shed?"

"Not really sure. But I didn't think Dad would mind. No one uses it anymore." It was practically falling down the hillside. That's probably the real reason Birdy didn't want the boys near it. That, and those terrible nightmares they suffered. Everyone suffered.

"Lydie!"

She jerked her head up.

"I've been talking to you and you haven't been listening."

"Sorry! I was thinking about something else."

"Were you thinking about Nathan?"

"No."

"I was saying that if Nathan did want to court you, you'd say yes, wouldn't you?"

"No."

Emily frowned, hands on her hips. "Why not?"

"Because . . ." Because she couldn't possibly say yes. "Just because."

Emily sighed. "I'd always thought the two of you would end up together. I had hoped that all three of us would've gotten married last year. Then we'd all live near each other and have babies in the same years."

Lydie cringed. Emily and Molly were always doing this. Expecting her to follow their lead. Trying to jam her into their mold. She didn't fit! Why couldn't they see? "Nathan and I were childhood friends. But things have changed." He had changed. He'd grown up. And she couldn't seem to.

"Don't you like him anymore?"

Lydie did like him. Quite a bit. "Of course. But as a friend."

"From what I hear, you're the only girl he talks about."

When Lydie didn't respond, Emily started hoeing. A few minutes later, she stopped and said, "I just don't understand you, Lydie."

That was nothing new. Lydie could hardly understand herself. She and Emily might be twins, but Emily and Molly were more alike. Emily was everything Lydie wanted to be, wished she were, but just couldn't be.

Weird sounds filled the sky. Lydie and Emily froze, looking at each other. Then Lydie dropped her hoe and ran to the edge of the hill to where the sounds were coming from. Something inside the old shed was creating popping sounds, as loud as fireworks going off on the Fourth of July. Emily came up behind her. Added to the popping was the sound of glass breaking.

"Oh, Lydie," Emily murmured. "What have you done now?"

David was on his way back from the Bent N' Dent when he heard a series of explosions coming from the direction of his own home. He slapped the reins to spur Old Jim into a canter. By the time the buggy neared the house, a terrible smell, like the inside of old boots, filled the air. Beer.

He walked into the house to find his mother and Lydie seated at the kitchen table. His mother's lips were puckered up like she'd been sucking on a lemon. Lydie's hands were clenched tightly together on the tabletop. "Son, we've been waiting for you." As David eased into a chair, his mother turned to Lydie. "Would you like to explain yourself?"

David's head jerked. "Lydie? What do you mean? What do you have to do with this?"

"Not me! Not exactly." Lydie swallowed. "You see, Mick asked if he could use the old shed. I didn't know why he wanted it, but we really don't use it, so I told him I thought it would be fine but I would need to ask Dad first. Then I forgot all about it, and Mick, being Mick, heard the 'thought it would be fine' part. I didn't know he had built a still, I promise I didn't! Not until, well, until I heard the . . . boom."

Blast was more like it. Like a bomb went off. David sat back in his chair, stunned.

Lydie glanced over at him. "I'm sorry, I really am. I never meant for this to happen."

His mother clapped her palms on the tabletop. "You never mean anything. Not everything can be fixed by being sorry."

"But I *am* sorry it happened!"

"And yet things keep on happening!" She wagged a finger at Lydie. "You're not just anybody. You're the bishop's daughter. And if bishop's children just went around doing whatever they wanted, then what on earth would this world come to? You're supposed to be setting a good example."

David cringed. "Hold on, Mom. This isn't about being a bishop's daughter. Let's stay focused on the problem with the shed."

"There *is* no more shed! Because Lydie let that boy blow it up to smithereens!"

Lydie's eyes went wide. "I didn't! Not intentionally, anyway."

His mother wasn't listening. Her finger was wagging at Lydie. "What you need, Lydie Stoltzfus, is to start buckling down and applying yourself. To think past one day at a time. You have got to start taking your life more seriously. You're not a child anymore. You have to start trying harder!"

"I know. You're right. I will. I'll try harder." Lydie quietly said, "Please excuse me." She slipped out of the kitchen before his mother could object.

He heard the front door close behind her.

"David, wann die Alde die Yunge net ziehe, ziehe die Yunge die Alde." *If parents don't train their children, the children will train the parents.*

Oh no. He wasn't going to remain here for a lecture on his flaws as a father, of which there were many. David leaned in toward the table to address his mother. "I'm going outside to see the shed."

He stopped on the threshold as a rank smell assailed him. Down the hill, he walked around the shed, or what was left of it. He couldn't *believe* it. He just could not believe it. Mick Yoder had created a beer brewery. There were so many things wrong with this situation that he didn't know where to start. Typical of Mick, he had no idea what he was doing. He bottled the homebrew too soon, before the fermentation process had finished. Overcarbonated, the bottles exploded. David's shed was a wet, sticky, stinking disaster, full of slivers and shards from broken bottles.

And Lydie, his own daughter, had given Mick permission to do it.

To make matters worse, as he walked around to the front of the house, he saw a mule leading a cart up the steep driveway. In the cart was Hank Lapp, a man who always turned up when he was least needed. When Hank slowed his mule to a stop halfway up the hill, David realized that Walt Yoder was on the driveway. He hopped in the cart with Hank, and the poor mule struggled to climb the rest of the hill to reach David. When the cart came to a rest, the men hopped out, breathed in the stale air, started to chuckle, then doubled over in laughter.

"The bishop is running a brewery!" Walt said, laughing so hard he had tears running down his cheeks.

"WHO would've THUNK it!" Hank said, slapping his knees.

"David," Walt said between rolls of laughter, "haven't you ever heard that if you're going to drink beer, do it quietly?"

That set them both off in another peal of laughter.

David watched them, disgusted. Two grown men, giggling like schoolgirls. Over this? The smell of the beer lay heavily over the yard, probably floating downwind so that everyone in Stoney Ridge would get a whiff. "You might not feel quite so amused when you hear that your son Mick is the mastermind behind this."

Walt's laughter slowed to a stop. "Mick?"

"Yes, Mick."

Walt shook his head hard, as if he weren't hearing right. "Couldn't be Mick."

"Lydie said he had asked to use the shed for a project. He's been coming over nearly every day for a while. I should've realized he was up to something."

That information sobered Walt. "Now, David," he said, his voice turned conciliatory, "you were a boy once yourself."

"I DOUBT IT," Hank said. "I think our BISHOP was BORN all GROWED UP."

"Mick is not a boy," David said. "You can't keep excusing this kind of adolescent behavior."

Walt waved that off. "Better for boys to get this kind of thing out of their system before they bend at the knee. Everybody knows that. Besides, no harm was done. You never used that old shed. It's nothing but an eyesore."

"You're overlooking a few things."

Walt frowned.

"It's pretty bold to start a brewery on the bishop's property."

"Oh, David, come on. Mick doesn't see it like that. We're neighbors. You're making too much of this. No one was hurt."

For one brief second, David set aside the crisis at hand as it occurred to him that Walt sounded like the old Walt. He used to be relatively affable, not the crotchety old man that most now thought of him. The changes in Walt had been so gradual that David had hardly been aware of them—not until this very moment. He wondered what had caused Walt to grow sour, if it had to do with his failing farm, but that line of thinking would have to wait. He had to deal with Mick Yoder and the blown-up shed. "It was only God's goodness that no one was hurt. What if my little boys were playing nearby?"

"But they weren't." Now Walt was growing peeved. Back to the old Walt. "See here now. Mick will build you another shed."

"Yes, he will. But before he does that, he needs to clean up the mess. Find him, now," David said, surprised by the hard tenor in his own voice, "and send him over." As he walked back toward the house, he dropped his chin to his chest, wondering how this day had started rather nicely and ended up shattered into pieces, much like his shed.

No matter how hard Lydie tried, she always managed to make a mess of things. As soon as she saw Walt Yoder, half-way up the driveway, get in Hank Lapp's mule cart, she darted across the yard, slipped through the hole in the hedge that bordered Black Gold Farm's property and the Stoltzfus's yard, and sprinted down to the barn. If Mick was at the farm, that's where he could usually be found. Fussing over his animals.

As she ran, she brushed tears away. As frustrated as she was by her grandmother, it was the look of reproach in her dad's eyes that really stung. She wished he'd lecture her like Mammi did and get it over with, anything but sit there quietly, disappointed in her.

She opened the barn door and paused, waiting for her eyes to adjust to the dim lighting. She followed the sound of Mick's whistle and found him in a horse stall, brushing down a gray gelding. "Mick! Didn't you hear the explosion?"

He popped his head up to look over the horse's mane. "Something happened?"

The horse pricked its ears and tossed its head, more alarmed by Lydie's question than his groomer. Mick went right back to brushing that horse's mane like it was the most important thing a man could do.

And then it dawned on Lydie that Mick knew exactly what had just happened and why. That's why he was here, hiding in the barn, instead of over at her house with his dad. "Why in the world would you think it would be all right to have a brewery in our shed?"

Mick kept his head tucked low. "You said it'd be fine. Your dad never used the shed, you said."

"Mick, I had no idea what you had in mind!"

"Not true." He held the horse's brush in the air. "I told you I had something experimental in mind."

Something experimental? Good grief. Did he really tell her that? She did remember the start of that particular conversation. They were standing near the hedge that separated their families' properties. It was a nippy day for March, windy, with a sky so very blue, full of big puffy white clouds that floated by. As he was talking, she noticed an Eastern bluebird fly past, and realized it was the first one she'd seen this year, and she wondered if it was building its nest, and where, and suddenly Mick was saying, "So what do you think?"

And she was so embarrassed that she didn't know what he was talking about, all she said was, "Fine, just fine."

She'd done it again! Totally blanked out when someone was talking to her. Emily said she was getting worse. She was!

In fact, she was doing it right now. Mick looked at her for a long moment. She put her hands on her hips, irate. "I have too many things on my mind! Starting work for Dok and everything."

"Dok? You're working for Dok? You?" Mick hooted the words as if he couldn't quite believe them.

"Yes. I'm filling in for her receptionist. I'm starting on Monday." She frowned at him. "Stop laughing."

He sobered, trying hard to keep a straight face. "Didn't you just get fired from a knitting shop?"

"Fired? Izzy and I . . . we came to a mutual decision."

He started chuckling again. "And now you're at a doctor's office?"

She frowned. "What's so funny about me working for Dok?"

"I guess, it's just that a doctor's office is such a serious place. The last receptionist acted like she was Dok's guard dog. You're the total opposite."

"Not the *total* opposite. Part of my job is to make sure Dok's time is well spent. I'm supposed to keep track of her appointments. And I need to be there during office hours when she's not there. Open and lock up."

"If she's not in the office, why be there?"

"To answer the phone and take messages. And then on account of the drugs."

"Drugs?" His two bushy eyebrows met in the middle, and for a split second, he reminded Lydie of his father with those caterpillar eyebrows. "Dok keeps drugs in her office?"

"Of course." Dok didn't elaborate on the drugs. *Do not ever touch this pharmaceutical cabinet* were her exact words.

He walked around the back of the horse to where she stood at the open stall door, a serious look on his face. "Lydie, I need your help with something."

"Not happening."

"Hear me out. I invited Patsy Glick somewhere and she turned me down flat."

"Where'd you invite her?"

"To party at Blue Lake Pond."

Lydie didn't know where to begin. "Mick, what makes you think Patsy Glick would be interested in partying with you at Blue Lake Pond?"

"Just a hunch."

"So wrong. Patsy doesn't party. Patsy doesn't do anything she's not supposed to do." Patsy Glick was perfect.

"See, now that's where I think you have the wrong idea about her. People can surprise. I think there's a wild streak inside the buttoned-up Patsy Glick, and I aim to find out before we leave town."

So, so naïve. Lydie took a deep breath. "Maybe you should set your sights on some other girl."

"Nope. Patsy's my target. She's stolen my heart." He crossed his arms over his heart in a corny gesture. "Thing is, for some reason, she has the wrong impression of me. Doesn't take me seriously. So I had a brilliant idea. She'll listen to you. You can talk her into going out with me."

Lydie slapped a hand against her chest. "Me?"

"You're just the right one for this. You know me better than most anyone. Patsy'll believe what you tell her."

"I don't think it's a good idea, Mick. You're not her type." Not that Lydie knew Patsy's type, but she was absolutely, 100 percent confident that Mick was not her type. He was the opposite of Patsy Glick in every way.

"Come on, Lydie. Do this for me and I'll do something for you."

She shook her head. "There's nothing you could do for me."

He wiggled his eyebrows. "What if I were to tell you that I've found jobs for us after we leave Stoney Ridge?"

Except for that. She chanced a sideways look at him.

"My mom has a cousin over in Williamsport, Maryland, who runs a diner called the Clam Shack. They had a long chat on the phone the other day. Mom said she wondered if she knew of anyone looking for jobs this fall. Someone who worked hard and liked clams."

Actually, Lydie didn't like clams at all. The look of them, the taste of them, even the smell of them made her stomach turn. But Dok's job would end in a few months, and she would have money saved up, and she had promised herself that when the old receptionist reclaimed her job, then it would be the right time to leave. Where to go and what to do, that was the tricky part. That was the piece of the plan that kept eluding her. Maybe the Clam Shack was the answer she'd been waiting for. "You're still planning to come with me?" She wasn't quite sure to believe Mick. He had a habit of saying one thing and doing another.

"Of course! Think I want to watch corn grow for the rest of my life? I'd leave now, but I want to stick around this summer to beat my little brother." He clapped his hand over his heart. "And to get to know another side of Patsy Glick."

Patsy Glick had no other side. She was one-dimensional. That's why everyone called her Perfect Patsy. Lydie let out a sigh. "Okay. I'll do what I can to encourage Patsy to go out with you. But no promises."

"Sweeeeeet." His face lit in a broad smile. "I'll take it from there." He stretched his palms out wide. "This is me we're talking about, after all."

That garnered her a tiny smile—Mick's ego was as big as the sky—but the smile didn't last long. "Hold it. I came over because you blew up my dad's shed. Why'd you want to make beer?"

He went back to brushing down his horse. "A friend makes

his own beer and said it's easy to do. He let me have some of his supplies." He shrugged. "So I figured I'd give it a try."

"Well, you need to tell my father that I didn't know you were using the shed to brew beer."

"Yeah, yeah . . . I'll head over there now to offer my sincerest apology." He tossed the horse's brush in the box and closed the stall door. "You coming?"

She hesitated. "Your dad's over there now. I think I'll go pay a visit to Fern." Opposite direction.

"Lydie, you shouldn't let my dad intimidate you. I sure don't." He passed by her and headed for the barn door.

Intimidate? That wasn't exactly the word she would use to describe the tension between her and Walt Yoder. Animosity was a better description. Hostility. Mutual distrust.

And Lydie knew exactly when it had happened and what had caused it.

Last fall, she'd been in between jobs, so her dad asked her to fill in at the Bent N' Dent. She didn't enjoy working at the store—so slow! such tedious, boring work—but she wanted to help her dad out. One of her tasks was to tidy up the store each afternoon after closing. The area near the woodstove, where the old men gathered, was always a mess. Newspapers covered the rocking chairs, peanut shells littered the ground. The old men would try and toss the shells right into the woodstove's opening but almost always missed. Next to the woodstove was a big basket full of old *National Geographic* magazines. The old men in rocking chairs would read through the magazines on quiet winter days. Hank Lapp, for one.

When Lydie picked up the *National Geographic* magazines to put them back in the basket, she noticed their stiff bindings felt funny. Loose. She glanced through a few magazines and realized pages had been torn out. It bothered her that someone would do such a thing. After all, those *National Geographic* magazines were almost like books. The next morning, she scolded the old men for tearing pages out of the magazines, but their faces went blank. Even Hank Lapp's. "WE'D NEVER DO SUCH A THING!" he said, looking hurt. And she believed him.

Then came a chilly afternoon when the store was empty but for Lydie. She had gone into her dad's office to drop the mail on his desk when she heard the jingle of the front door as it opened. She poked her head around the doorjamb and saw that Walt Yoder had come in and sat down in a rocker by the warm stove. His back was to her. She saw him pick up a *National Geographic* to flip through it and she decided not to say hello. To anyone else, she would have, but Walt wasn't very friendly, not like he used to be when she and Mick and Nathan were children. In the last couple of years, Lydie could tell he seemed annoyed whenever she popped through the hedge to visit Nathan or Mick, or bring something to Sarah. "Too much," she'd heard him mutter. "That girl is just too much."

So Lydie went back to her dad's desk to toss out the junk mail. A ripping sound broke the peaceful silence in the store, and she popped her head back around the doorjamb. Vertically, Walt held up a double-spread page torn from the *National Geographic*. She tiptoed into the main room and stood behind the counter. From there she could see it was a foldout of native women with bared breasts. Her first thought was that he was going to toss the pages in the stove's opening to burn, but Walt only stared at the pages for the longest while. Then he folded them carefully and tucked them in his pocket. He rose from the rocking chair, and when he turned, he startled. Visibly jerked. He hadn't realized Lydie was there. Hadn't realized she'd been watching him.

He took a step toward her, then stopped abruptly. "I'm only protecting others from such . . ." Beard bristling, he waved an arm around the small sitting area. "From such rubbish." But his voice was shaky. He pivoted and left the store quickly.

That was the source of the antagonism between Lydie and Walt Yoder. He knew that she knew. And he didn't like what she knew.

4

On Monday morning, Lydie had given herself plenty of time to arrive at Dok's office early, and was congratulating herself because she had remembered the key to unlock the office door's deadbolt. Frankly, she was feeling pretty good about life in general, despite the fact that she'd hardly slept a wink, thanks to Mammi's all-night snorefest. Lydie's room shared a thin wall with Molly and Emily's old room, where Mammi was sleeping. As soon as Lydie got home from work tonight, she planned to move her bed across the room.

The key turned the lock and Lydie walked into Dok's office, set her lunch on her official desk—she had a desk!—and then she saw the number 15 flashing on the telephone. Flashing over and over. Fifteen messages!

She tried to recall which button Dok had said to push to listen to messages. But there were so many buttons on this phone. The message machine in the phone shanty had only one button to press to retrieve messages—on or off. Patting her apron pockets, she wondered what she had done with her notes. *Think, think, think.* She was supposed to . . . supposed to . . . oh, why hadn't she paid better attention to Dok? She squeezed her eyes shut. What had Dok said?

Speak with a smile in your voice.

Welcome the patients. Let Dok know they're here.

Avoid giving out medical advice.

Right. She remembered all those instructions, but what was she supposed to do to retrieve messages? She picked up the receiver and pressed one button. Nothing happened. She pressed another. And another. Finally, she pressed the right one and a woman started talking. She grabbed a pad of paper and wrote: *Patsy Glick, ear infection. Wants to come in right away.*

Lydie knew of two Patsy Glicks in their church and wondered which one was the one with the ear infection. The old Patsy Glick, she decided. The young Patsy Glick wouldn't dare allow infection to get near to her ears.

No sooner had the old Patsy finished than a dearly familiar voice began and Lydie relaxed. Fern Lapp needed her eczema prescription renewed.

Poor Fern. When Lydie dropped by Windmill Farm the other day, Fern couldn't stop scratching her forearm. She was wondering if Fern had tried rubbing apple cider vinegar on her arm and thought she might stop by on the way home to suggest it, when Sadie Smucker's worried voice came on. Sadie's five-year-old had stuffed gum so deep into his ear canal that she couldn't get it out and what should she do? The messages kept coming, one right after the other. Lydie couldn't figure out how to stop the machine to give her time to catch up. She scribbled down messages as fast as she could, but she still missed one or two. Or three. She tried to find a button for repeat, but unfortunately, she ended up erasing the messages. All of them.

She cringed. If this mishap got her fired, it would be her fastest dismissal yet. She couldn't lose this job. She couldn't bear seeing the look of disappointment on Dad's face. Such soul-wrenching sadness. She couldn't let him down. Not again.

They'd call back if they wanted appointments with Dok, wouldn't they? Probably not. Dok had made a big deal about those messages.

Hold on! She thought she recognized the voices of those last three callers. She thought she'd heard those same voices while working at the Bent N' Dent. She closed her eyes. Faces started to emerge in her mind's eye. She grabbed a pad of paper and doodled one face, then another. And another.

When Dok arrived, Lydie told her what had happened and braced herself for a reaction of upset.

Dok's eyes went wide in alarm. "Lydie, I need to know who those callers were. Don't you remember their names?"

"I don't. But does this help?" She handed Dok the pad with her doodles.

Irritated, Dok glanced at the pad, took a second look. Then a longer look. "Mary Smith has big thick glasses, and she always wears a big thick headband. And the one with the unibrow—I wonder if that's Milo Weaver. And the fellow with a nose like a crow's beak and those rather pronounced ears, that's got to be Pete Peterson." She wrote down a name under each face. "Lydie, look up their phone numbers and bring this to me. I'll be at my desk." She started toward the door that led to the back of the office. "Next time, please don't press the red button. That's the one that erases messages."

"Got it," Lydie said, relieved. *There*. She patted the paper pad. In the past, doodling had gotten her into some trouble. But, happily, not today.

Lydie had been doodling ever since she could remember, from the time when she first held a pencil in her hand. It came naturally, a way she'd found to take all the busy thoughts that bounced around in her mind and bring some order to them. One year, she had learned a painful lesson. During Thanksgiving of that year, Mammi had found Lydie's doodle pad, full of sketches of Mammi that were not particularly flattering, and she raised the roof with her ire. Dad didn't punish her, but that was the first time Lydie remembered that now familiar look of deep disappointment on his face.

Yet she still doodled. She just had to. But she kept them better hidden.

Two years ago, in the *Stoney Ridge Times* newspaper, she happened to read a request for illustrations. On a whim, she had sent in a doodle of a horse and buggy, captioned it "The Yoder Toter," and it was chosen to run in the newspaper. But Lydie hadn't included her name or address, so no one knew she held the pencil behind the drawing. Since then, she'd sent in multiple drawings, added witty captions, and they were almost always published. They were full of insights about the Amish life, gentle ribbings from the inside out. Mostly gentle. Every now and then, Lydie drew a doodle with a caption that some might consider to be a jab. But, if so, it was a well-deserved one. Happily, her identity remained completely anonymous.

Until one time.

It happened last September at the fellowship meal following a Sunday church service. Lydie had been serving coffee to a table full of men. The meal was a time of discussion, as well as food. The women always served the men first and ate separately afterward.

The men had fallen into a serious discussion about the recent snowstorm that had just blown through Stoney Ridge earlier in the week. Their Englisch neighbors were still without power. Lydie was pouring coffee into Walt's cup as he raised his fork up high, his face in a sneer. "Heh, heh. Sorry your electric is out!" Startled by the men bursting into raucous laughter as if Walt had made a hilarious joke, Lydie spilled coffee on Walt's raised hand. As she wiped it up, she thought the whole scene—minus her coffee spill—might make an amusing caption for an illustration. And so it did.

But she acted first and thought about it later, a warning her dad was always giving her. She had made a number of mistakes. The Amish man she drew was a dead ringer for Walt Yoder—thick and shaggy caterpillar eyebrows, and a scar running across one cheek that looked like a zigzag stitch. And the missing tip of an index finger, seen as he held his hand up in the air. All three of those characteristics identified Walt. Everyone recognized him, and remembered when he said it, and soon it became the talk of Stoney Ridge. Could it be the unknown illustrator *was* Walt Yoder?

An Englisch newspaper in Lancaster saw the cartoon and republished it. And so did other newspapers that shared both Amish and Englisch communities—as far west as Indiana and Ohio.

Walt Yoder enjoyed the attention he was getting from the cartoon, perhaps a little too much. Bragging a little too much. The church leaders, including Lydie's dad, felt that Walt was not displaying a "love thy neighbor" attitude toward their Englisch friends. Walt was told to sit on the sinner's bench in church and ask forgiveness. That was a very hard pill for Walt Yoder and his pride to swallow.

Then things grew worse.

It happened last December while Lydie had been between jobs and was helping out at the Bent N' Dent. One afternoon, she was alone in the store. Bored, she'd started to doodle on a piece of scratch paper near the cash register. Just an Amish man and woman, holding baskets of apples. She heard the bell on the door jingle and looked up, startled. Walt Yoder had come in to purchase some charcoal, he said, and Lydie had to go to the storeroom to bring out a bag.

As she returned, Walt held up the scratch paper and waved it at her. "You!"

"Me?" Her voice came out like a squeak.

"I remember! You were serving coffee at the table when I made that joke. You spilled coffee on me. Nearly burnt me! I remember you were there!"

What could she say to that? It was true, all true. So she said nothing. Walt leaned over the cash register until she could feel his hot breath propelling his words. "Du hot mich yuscht fer en Narr ghalde." *You made a fool of me.*

Maybe she had.

But if Walt Yoder told her dad that she was the one who had submitted those illustrations . . . oh, she couldn't bear to see that look of disappointment on his face. Lydie would have to look him in the eyes and admit to what she'd done. Imagine if Mammi heard about it! Lydie shuddered. Mammi had less of a sense of humor about herself than Walt Yoder.

They stood in silence for a long, painful moment. Walt's mouth kept that tight, stern grimace. Then he pulled on his beard, and his eyes hardened. "I won't tell your dad what you been up to with them drawings if . . ."

"If?" Lydie said.

"You stay away from my Nathan."

"Nathan?" Had he known they'd been growing close?

"Ja, my boy Nathan." He wagged his finger at her, as if she were a child who needed scolding. "He's worth two of you, my Nathan. You need to leave him alone. You'd only cause him a lifetime of misery. If you really care about him, then let him find a girl who'll be a true partner to him, not one who stirs up troubles like hornets at a picnic." On that note, he left the store, not even bothering to take his bag of charcoal.

If Walt Yoder had warned her away from anything or anyone else, she might not have minded. But she understood what he was telling her. Deep in her heart, she'd always known that Nathan deserved better.

Tears had blurred Lydie's eyes and filled her throat. She had to swallow them down before she turned and went back to stocking a shelf full of bags of dried beans. She'd never thought seriously of jumping the fence, of leaving the Amish, her home, her family. Not until that moment.

5

Somehow this wasn't how Nathan pictured his farm. The gray, cloddy soil he was breaking up was even more compacted than he had thought it was. With help only from a team of borrowed mules, he brought wagonful after wagonful of composted manure, purchased from Beacon Hill Dairy down the road, to spread generously over his fields until they looked like stripes of umber interlaced with gray. He ended up adding three times as much compost as he had originally planned.

Then, he tilled the manure into the cloddy soil, over and over and over. Each time he turned the team to go back to till the same row, he reminded himself that this was for the soil's benefit, to give the plants all the nutrients they would need to grow strong and fend off disease and pests. Once he was satisfied with each row, he went over the fields again to pour a line of soil amendments onto them. Each had to be poured separately—alfalfa meal, soft phosphate, ground mussel shell, kelp meal—then tilled in. One by one. Every time he turned the team around, he would stop and look over his fields, and let out a deep sigh of satisfaction. The soil looked less of a drab, lifeless gray and more of a loamy dark brown.

After the sun set, Nathan would head to the greenhouse, working under a pool of lantern light until midnight, when he would call it a day. He outfitted the sides with additional horizontal shelving, maximizing every square inch of space to soon hold cartons of seedlings. He thought about running the idea past Mick, but his brother never bothered with the greenhouse. Nathan couldn't even remember the last time he'd stepped foot into it.

Dividing the farm in two had the effect on Mick and Nathan of setting a match onto gasoline. They steered clear of each other, hardly speaking more than a word. The last year or so, they'd drifted apart, especially after Mick had buddied up with Owen Miller. But this was different. Last night, Nathan had overheard his mother ask his father why he tried to make rivals of his sons, and he told her, "It'll make men out of them."

I wonder. What did competition have to do with manhood, especially when it meant that someone would win and someone would lose? Why couldn't a family work together, help each other? A family, to Nathan, should be like the farm—one whole, living organism. Like the farm, it shouldn't be split up. Two brothers shouldn't be competing against each other.

Try telling that to Walt Yoder. He would scoff.

Sometimes Nathan wondered if the real competition between the two brothers was trying to win, not the farm, but their father's love. If that were so, what would it take? Nathan had no idea.

The ironic thing was that Mick didn't even like to farm. Not the dirt-and-plants side of farming, anyway. He did like animals, though. For such a tough guy, Mick babied the small collection of livestock on Black Gold Farm like an overprotective mother. He mourned when a fox visited the henhouse. He stayed up all night to nursemaid a sick cow, or keep company with a maiden mare as she delivered a foal. Nathan had seen Mick run through the fields so hard his hat flew off, screaming at the top of his lungs to chase off vultures from a dead lamb.

This was the side of his brother few saw. The side of Mick that Nathan loved. Rubbing his tired eyes, he had a hunch that was the side that Lydie loved too.

∽

It was late. David locked up the Bent N' Dent, knowing his mother would be irritated he had missed supper again. As he hooked up his horse to the buggy traces, he noticed lights on over at Dok's office, though no cars were in the parking lot. He sighed. *Lydie.* She must've forgotten to turn the lights off.

Driving down the lane, he wondered how things were working out for her at Dok's office. Or not working out.

He knew firsthand how exasperating Lydie could be as an employee. Now and then, when he was shorthanded at the Bent N' Dent and if she were between jobs, he would ask her to fill in. But last fall, this last stint . . . was the last time he'd ever ask.

After forgetting to lock up the store too many times to count, after being late more often than she was on time, after losing invoices from deliveries so that payments ended up in arrears, after misplacing cash from the day's receivables more than once, then came the last straw when—out of the blue—she burned all the old *National Geographic* magazines that the graybeards liked to browse through. She gave no reason for it other than she was tidying up. The graybeards were outraged. After that, David gave up. He told her that she wasn't needed at the store any longer. It pained him to let her go, his own daughter.

He turned past Black Gold Farm and stopped the buggy under a large canopied tree to look out over Nathan's fields, letting the sight fill him. It had become his favorite spot to linger each evening. The worries of the day slipped away and calm returned as he paused here. Maybe it was the way the freshly tilled rows contoured the land so gracefully, like a finger from Above had drawn them. Or maybe it was the fact that, with the right combination of care and attention, these weary fields were recovering. Even to David's nonfarming eyes, he could see that what had been tired gray dirt now looked like lush, dark, nutrient-rich soil.

Or maybe . . . he just didn't want to go home and face his mother.

❧

During her lunch break, Lydie scootered over to the Sweet Tooth Bakery to see if there were any cinnamon rolls left. Those chewy, flakey rolls were Mammi's one and only vice. She hoped Mammi might forgive her for this morning's . . . unpleasantness . . . if she brought home a cinnamon roll to her tonight. While Lydie was showering before work, she spilled way too much conditioner from the bottle into her hair and it took a long time to get it rinsed out. Apparently, she had used up all the hot water, so Mammi had to suffer through a cold shower. On a chilly day too. Not a good start to the morning.

As Lydie waited in line at the bakery, she noticed Patsy Glick was one of two girls working behind the counter. Although Patsy was a year younger than Lydie, they'd gone through school together, and yet Lydie still didn't think Patsy remembered her. She remembered Patsy, though. There was never a time when Patsy spoke out of turn, or forgot an assignment, or even acted silly. Not only was her behavior blameless, but her face was just as flawless, as beautiful as a July morning. High, sculptured cheekbones; wide-spaced blue eyes with thick, long lashes. Straight blond hair that never seemed to stray from its pins. Lydie had sat directly behind her in sixth and seventh grade, and spent an inordinate amount of time wondering how Patsy had been able to keep her hair in place, all the time.

"What can I get you?"

Lydie hadn't realized she'd been staring at Patsy. Startled from her musings, she stiffened. Patsy had that effect on people, like they'd been caught doing something they shouldn't, even if they weren't doing anything.

"A cinnamon roll, please. It's for my grandmother. She loves them."

Patsy peered down into the case, then made her face go sad. "They're all gone." Then she lifted a finger in the air. "Be right back." She disappeared through the door to the kitchen. When she returned, she held out a small white paper bag. "Take this. I was going to bring one home to my mother. You can have it."

How nice! Maybe Patsy did remember her, after all. Lydie handed her a few dollars, but Patsy wouldn't accept it. "My treat."

"Oh. Well, thank you."

Patsy came around the corner of the case and threaded an arm through Lydie's. "And now I'd like to ask you for a favor."

"Me?"

"I'd like a little help getting the attention of a certain neighbor of yours."

Her neighbor? Oh. Oh good! This was going to be easier than Lydie had thought. "I'll do all I can to help. Mick is a wonderful guy. A real peach." Pretty much. He had his shortcomings, but he'd been a good friend to Lydie. Other than blowing up the family shed with a hidden beer brewery.

"Mick?" Patsy's face clouded in confusion.

"Mick Yoder. My neighbor."

Patsy shrugged. "I hardly know him."

"But he's part of our church. He was a few years older than us in school, but Mick's hard to ignore." A big, big personality.

"My mind was focused on school, not on boys."

Now *that* sounded like the Patsy whom Lydie had sat behind. "Mick's very good-looking. Surely you must've noticed."

"All I remember about Mick Yoder is that he was in trouble all the time."

"See? You do know who he is."

"Why are we talking about Mick? I want to talk about his brother."

Lydie stilled. "Nathan?"

She leaned so close that Lydie could smell the scent that was uniquely Patsy: lavender soap, like she'd just stepped out of a shower. It's why Lydie switched her shampoo and gloppy conditioner to the one Patsy used. "I'd like to go out with Nathan Yoder."

Lydie swallowed. "You want to go out with Nathan."

Patsy tilted her head. "That's what I said."

To hear that Patsy Glick was interested in Nathan was no surprise. What girl in Stoney Ridge wasn't mildly besotted with him? They all were. He had a way of keeping himself slightly aloof from girls, never showing much interest, which added to his intrigue and only made him more of a catch.

"Everybody knows that Nathan listens to you, Lydie. Being neighbors and childhood friends. You're like a sister to him." Patsy smiled.

A sister. A *sister*?

"So can I count on you to put in a good word for me with Nathan?"

Lydie stared at Patsy. Walt Yoder's angry words circled in her head. *"Nathan's worth two of you. You need to leave him alone. You'd only cause him a lifetime of misery. If you really care about him, then let him find a girl who'll be a true partner to him."* Someone who wouldn't complicate his life. Someone like Patsy Glick.

Patsy Glick would be perfect for Nathan. Absolutely perfect.

It would be the right thing to do—the last thing Lydie could do for her dear friend Nathan, before she left Stoney Ridge. It would be nice to know that he had someone in his life, someone like Patsy Glick, who would be a wonderful partner to his . . . wonderfulness.

Slowly, Lydie nodded.

Owen Miller had struck Lydie as the friendly type when he checked in for his allergy appointment at Dok's office. He was tall, with short-cropped hair, sharply angled cheekbones, and a long, thick neck with a pronounced Adam's apple. He sat down and his phone rang, and while he was talking, Lydie started to doodle him on her paper pad, exaggerating that Adam's apple. Dok had posted a large sign on the wall to remind patients to turn off their cell phones. The room was empty, so Lydie didn't really object to the call . . . not until Owen's voice changed. It rose in volume. He grew angry, then started to use unrepeatable words, sputtering in fury. So scharf as Essich. *As sharp as vinegar.*

When he ended the call, he stared at the phone and muttered, "You're going to be sorry for this, Yoder."

Owen must have sensed Lydie's eyes were on him, because he jerked his head up to give her a cold hard stare. All friendliness was gone. He shook his phone in her direction. "That's what's wrong with you people. You're still living in the Dark Ages."

She found herself in a staring match with Owen Miller, as they sat there assessing each other.

He lost.

Most of the females in Lydie's church avoided eye contact with Englisch men. If ever spoken to, they would defer to their husbands or brothers, let them do the talking for them. It was just the Plain way. But being the granddaughter of Tillie Stoltzfus, Lydie had grown accustomed to those glinting stares.

The door that led to the examination rooms opened and Dok appeared. "Owen Miller?"

He rose to his feet and gave her a hard sideways glance. As he passed by her desk, he spewed a thick glob of tobacco juice right into her wastebasket. She held his gaze, watching him until the door closed.

Owen Miller didn't intimidate Lydie. She did, however, feel sorry for the person on the other end of the phone. There were dozens and dozens and dozens of Yoders in the greater Lancaster area. Whoever it was, she wondered if he realized he should be waiting for the other shoe to drop.

6

Nathan set the phone down in its cradle. He felt shaken, shocked by the ugly words that had come out of Owen Miller's mouth. He'd called to cut the order for Black Gold Farm in half and Owen reacted with fury. He became even more furious when Nathan explained why—that he was converting forty acres into organic.

It baffled Nathan that the chem rep had taken the order cut so personally. It was as if Owen thought Nathan had set out to offend him. Owen's dad, Frank, had always been friendly, going above and beyond the call of duty as a salesman. Whenever Black Gold Farm called with a problem, Frank would drop everything and drive out to see how to solve it. He'd kept them informed of new products and offered them first dibs at ordering. He would walk the fields with Dad, Mick, and Nathan, suggesting solutions from his company to handle pests or viruses. All chemical solutions. While the time spent with Dad always ended up with increased sales for Frank, he had seemed to genuinely care about Black Gold Farm.

His son Owen had started working for his dad, coming along with him on visits to the farm. Mick and Owen had become friendly, spending time together, but Nathan kept his distance. Not that the two ever included him in their weekend adventures. They didn't. But that wasn't what bothered Nathan about Owen. It was the way Mick acted whenever he was around Owen. Like he was trying to impress him.

Take last summer. The weather had been extraordinarily wet and humid, and earworms threatened the corn crop. Frank and Owen had driven out to Black Gold Farm to examine the problem. Mick had sprayed the corn just two days earlier and Nathan could still smell the chemical treatment. It permeated the air.

He had covered his nose and mouth with a bandanna, turning in a circle to study the corn. "I think the earworms have grown impervious to the chemicals."

Frank pulled out a brochure. "I'm carrying a new line of plant-health products that'll knock those earworms out."

Nathan coughed a laugh. "You're joking, right? Plant-health pesticide? Isn't that an oxymoron?"

Owen had given him a look as if he had sprouted horns. "You worry about the planting and plowing and leave the thinking to us."

Whoa. That was no way to talk to anyone, especially a customer. Nathan expected Frank to say something to his son. But Frank turned his back on Nathan and spoke only to Dad and Mick. "Tell you what we need to do. Aerial spray. My boy Owen here just got a plane. A Cessna, a real beauty. Aerial spraying is the best chance we've got so we don't lose this corn crop."

Nathan stepped into the circle to be included in the discussion. "Hold it a minute. Aerial spraying . . . are you talking about crop dusting?"

"Crop dusting, barnstorming," Frank said. "Those are old-fashioned terms."

Owen grinned. "Bomb the living daylights out of those bugs."

"You can't be serious," Nathan said.

"Plenty serious," Owen said, laughing.

"Bomb 'em," Mick echoed, laughing along with him. The two started at each other with elbow jabs like they two thirteen-year-old boys, not twenty-year-old men.

Nathan looked to his dad. Surely he would dismiss the idea of aerial spraying.

His dad was rubbing his forehead, a sign that he was uncertain. "I don't know . . ."

"Today's technology is spot-on," Frank said. "The wings on Owen's Cessna are engineered so the spray is kept in a tight pattern. A drift detection system will tell him if there's any danger of wind carrying the spray beyond the field. Low-altitude flying allows for precision. It'll take care of the problem, Walt. You know as well as I do, the healthier the plants, the bigger the yield."

When Dad still hesitated, Owen quickly added, "No charge."

Now Owen had spoken a language Dad understood—free of charge. Never mind that aerial spraying was not part of traditional Amish farming methods, never mind that he should've run it past the bishop first.

And never mind that it hadn't worked. The earworms won last summer's battle with the corn crop. Black Gold Farm, for the first time in its history, had to purchase feed for its livestock from the Hay & Grain. His grandfather would turn over in his grave.

Today, Owen's furious reaction to the cut in Black Gold's order made Nathan all the more determined to see this organic conversion through, to do everything he could to prove this was the best way to care for the land, to nourish it, revive and sustain it. He held out hope that, eventually, all eighty acres could be converted. First, he had to convince his father and brother, and the only way that would happen was through success.

On the way home from work, Lydie passed Black Gold Farm just as Nathan was getting the day's mail from the large mailbox at the end of the driveway. His head tipped downward as he flipped through the mail, as if deep in thought.

A few feet from him, she let the scooter roll to a stop. "Isn't it a beautiful day?"

He turned around, mail in hand, a startled look on his face. "What?"

"I was just saying what a nice day it is. The sky so blue, and the birdsong so sweet."

He looked up at the sky as if he hadn't thought to notice, but that couldn't be right. Nathan was an astute observer of nature. He noticed things that never occurred to Lydie. The way the clouds could foretell the day's weather, or if a summer day had gotten so hot that insects stopped flying.

Dressed in a blue shirt with sleeves rolled up, he looked . . . tired. "Is anything wrong?" she asked.

He pulled his attention from the great outdoors to look at her, brows risen. "Wrong?"

For a long, awkward moment, a stillness came over them, and they just stared at each other. They were friends; conversation was supposed to come easily. It used to. They used to tell each other everything. "You just seemed . . . preoccupied."

Nathan took his hat off and ran a hand through his hair. "I had to cut the order with the farm's chem rep because of the conversion, and he . . . well, he blew up at me."

So it was *Nathan* whom Owen Miller had been talking to. "He was in Dok's office today. I think I might have overheard the conversation he's had with you." She tipped her head. "He seemed angry. Really angry."

"Owen's a hothead. He'll get over it."

Would he? Lydie wasn't so sure. "I'm impressed that you're not letting anything stop you from going organic. Or anyone." Even creepy Owen Miller.

Nathan put a hand on her arm. "You're the reason I kept pressing Dad to make the conversion to organic."

"Me? What did I say?"

"It's not what you said. It's what you did. Last year, when you decided you weren't ready to be baptized, even though Emily and Molly were getting baptized. You didn't let them pressure you, and I know they tried. I know your sisters. It got me thinking about standing firm, even when you're under pressure. That was when I first started talking to Dad about taking the farm organic. And even though I could only get him to agree to converting half the farm this summer, it's a start in the right direction."

He smiled a slow smile, which started at one corner of his mouth and worked its way toward the other, and it made her feel as if her insides were melting away.

"You did that for me, Lydie. You gave me the boldness I needed."

No matter what she did, Nathan seemed to think she was wonderful. Why couldn't he realize that she wasn't good enough for him? He deserved so much better. She wiggled her arm so he'd release his hold on her. "Patsy!"

"Patsy?"

"Patsy Glick. She's such a . . ." How to describe Patsy? "Saintly girl. Devout. Almost holy." That sounded weird. "And she's beautiful! Have you noticed?"

He shrugged, looked down at the tips of his boots, and his cheeks went a little pink.

So, he'd noticed. "Have you thought of asking to take her home from the Singing this Sunday? She would say yes, Nathan. I'm sure of it."

He looked at her for one long moment, his eyes clouded in puzzlement, before he turned away. "Why do you do that?"

"Do what?"

"For months, you've pushed me away. Now you're pushing me to someone else."

"I'm . . . just trying to be a good friend." *To you. To Patsy.* She jumped back on her scooter. "I'd better get home." She pumped one leg along the road to pick up speed, eager to get on her way.

Leaving would be a gift to him, even if he didn't realize it at the time. He might be a little sad at first, but soon he would love someone else and forget all about Lydie. Probably Perfect Patsy Glick. The very thought of it made her feel nauseated.

∞

On a rainy morning, David sat at his desk in his office at the Bent N' Dent and pulled out his Bible. Two weeks had passed since his mother had moved into his household. Two weeks since Lydie stepped in as a temporary receptionist at Dok's office. He couldn't shake a sense of impending doom on the horizon.

Gratitude. Praise. He knew that what he didn't turn to praise could turn to problems. He believed his mother had come to Stoney Ridge with the best of intentions. She truly wanted to help his family.

And yet, she had a knack for creating strife. Things were off-kilter with Birdy, who had no choice in the matter of his mother taking up sudden residence. He knew Birdy was disappointed in him for not having more of a backbone with his mother, and he didn't blame her at all. He turned into a spineless coward whenever he was around Tillie Yoder Stoltzfus.

Just this morning, Birdy and Timmy and Noah were watching a hummingbird chase off other hummers at the feeder, and the boys had started to act out the fiercely territorial bird, which got everyone in the kitchen chuckling. All but David's mother. Stoney faced, she sat at the table—in *Birdy's* chair—coffee in hand, with an owl-like look on her face. "Wammer de Kinner Schtrick gebt, daerf mer net glaage, wann die em Druwwel mache" was her only contribution to the morning. *If you let your children have their own way, you must not complain when they give you trouble.* Joy left the kitchen and David slipped out right behind it to head to the Bent N' Dent.

Their home was not large by Amish standards, and David's children were talkers. Loud and noisy, his mother complained. It was something he and Birdy had never minded, the noise. Unlike the severely strict households they had both grown up in, they wanted their children to talk. At meals, while working together, during family devotions, at bedtime. He paused and ran a hand over his beard. A trimmed beard, something his mother had already pointed out in disapproval, as if keeping a trim beard was a sign of vanity.

Gratitude. Praise. A worshipful attitude could chase away all thoughts of worry, of distress. He needed to seek things to be grateful for, something Birdy was always reminding him of. Search for them like a lost coin, she would say, because his mind didn't naturally go to gratitude. Most people's minds didn't, but Birdy's did. It was one of the things he loved about her, and what drew him to her, years ago, when he felt ready to love again. And when he took Birdy's advice, it always made a difference. Whatever circumstances he happened to be facing at that time might not have changed, but he had changed.

He opened his Bible to the book of Proverbs and hunted for a verse he vaguely remembered: "Yea, if thou criest after knowledge, and liftest up thy voice for understanding; if thou seekest her as silver, and searchest for her as for hid treasures; then shalt thou understand the fear of the LORD, and find the knowledge of God. For the LORD giveth wisdom: out of his mouth cometh knowledge and understanding."

The Lord would give him answers if he searched for them as for hidden treasures.

Okay. Okay then, Lord, he prayed. *Please open my mind to the gifts of my mother's presence.* He looked up at the ceiling, as if the answers might drop down. And he waited. He smelled the brewed coffee from the pot he'd made when he'd first arrived at the store.

There was one!

His mother was an outstanding cook. Birdy did not like to cook. *There.* One gift for which he could thank the Lord.

Lydie had made it through two weeks of a new job without getting fired. That, too, was a gift worthy of praise.

And then there was his mother's assumption that Birdy needed help managing the household. He felt pinpricks of guilt over leaving his mother in Birdy's care all day long, but still, it kept his mother at the house instead of starting her assault on reorganizing the Bent N' Dent.

Just as David was starting to feel a little cheered up, he heard a rapping on the store's front door. It was only a little after nine and the store didn't open until nine thirty. He left his chair and went to answer the knock.

His sister, Dok, stood under the overhang, shaking her umbrella of water. "Got a minute to spare?"

He moved aside so she could pass. She set down her umbrella by the door and walked in to sit in the rocking chair by the cold woodstove.

"Coffee?" David asked.

"No time," Dok said. "And you're not supposed to have coffee, anyway. Not with your ulcer."

For the most part, he appreciated his sister's directness. Not so much when it came to his own health. David sat down across from her. "How's the remodel coming?"

"Slow. Matt's doing most of the work, but he's had a lot going on at the police station. Someone's selling drugs to minors at the junior high school and he's on a team trying to figure out who's behind it." She put her hands on her knees. "Look, I'll come straight to the point. Have you ever noticed that Lydie seems different from your other children?"

David braced himself. "Yes," he said slowly.

"When did you first think so?"

"I suppose . . . from the very start. She was a fussy baby. Didn't like to sleep or be held much."

Dok nodded, as if she had thought as much.

David had a hunch where this conversation was headed. "So. The job's not working out."

"I wouldn't say that. Though I don't deny that there's been some bumps."

"Bumps?" When David had asked Lydie how working at Dok's had been going, her answer was "Splendidly." But then, she never seemed to realize that she was not performing as an employer had expected. Her "releases" often came as a surprise.

"Nothing catastrophic, mind you, just mildly annoying. For every project she completes, she seems to leave two unfinished. Her desk is a jumbled mess. She arrives late and leaves early."

"Those are the bumps?" David wasn't at all surprised. Those sounded like life with Lydie.

"No. Those are just her work habits. Here are the bumps." Dok ticked off her fingers. "Day one. She erased phone messages left by patients for the day's appointments. Day two. She went into town to pick up some supplies for me and returned to the office without the supplies but with a kitten she'd found abandoned along the road. Day three. She settled Hank Lapp in an exam room and told him I'd be in soon, but forgot to tell me, and forgot all about him. He fell sound asleep on the exam table. Day four—"

David lifted his palms in the air. "Say no more. I get the message."

"Do you? Because . . . I'm a little confused."

"What do you mean?"

"While there've been a few bumps, there've also been some wonderful moments. Lydie makes everyone feel welcomed, as if she'd been hoping they'd come by. I've had receptionists who scare patients off. Lydie performs well under pressure. She's a quick thinker, and I've seen her come up with unusual solutions to problems."

"Such as . . ."

"Well, for one, I was out on a call when Luke and Izzy Schrock came into the office with their baby. Their toddler had knocked over a cup of tea, and the hot liquid spilled on the baby's foot."

"I remember that. It happened here in the store. I sent them right over to you."

"Right, but since I wasn't in the office, Lydie broke off a part of an aloe vera plant and applied it to the baby's foot. It did the trick."

"But . . . surely you don't want her treating patients."

"Of course I don't. And I spoke to her about that very thing. But in this case, the burn was quite mild. Aloe vera was an appropriate way to handle it. Mostly, it was Lydie's calm, clear thinking in a crisis that impressed me. Other times she can seem to be . . ."

"Daydreaming?" Or as a teacher once said, spacy. Not terribly intelligent, said another.

Dok nodded. "Then there was another time when a patient was rather rude. I'm not exactly sure what had happened—a phone call had set him off and he ended up saying something anti-Amish at Lydie. She held her ground without saying a word. Any other receptionist would've burst into tears or would've responded in anger."

It was true that Lydie was not easily offended, not like his other daughters. Not like his mother. Lydie was quick to assume the blame, even if something wasn't her fault. In fact, she was always apologizing. "So, are you trying to find a way to let her go?"

Surprised by the question, Dok shook her head. "No. Not at all."

"Isn't that what you're trying to say?"

"Goodness, no."

Relief flooded David.

"All I'm saying is that . . . Lydie's an interesting person. She's just not your typical cookie-cutter Amish girl. And that's exactly what I like about her."

"That's exactly what worries me about her."

Dok laughed and pushed herself out of the rocker. "Lydie mentioned that your mother has come to live with you. That she invited herself."

David leaned back in the chair and folded his hands behind his head. "She's your mother too."

"But Tillie Stoltzfus isn't living with me. Or talking to me." Amusement filled his sister's eyes.

"Don't look so smug. I've been praying that now might be just the time for the two of you to reconcile your differences."

Dok walked to the door. "As long as she holds fast to the shunning—"

"There was no shunning. You were never baptized."

"But that doesn't matter to Tillie Stoltzfus. You leave the Amish?" She snapped her fingers. "You leave the family." She closed the door behind her. The door had barely latched when she popped her head back in. "Lydie's doodles. They're pretty impressive." And then she was gone.

Her doodles? David knew Lydie had never stopped doodling. He cringed. What if his mother happened upon any of those doodles, like she'd done during that one Thanksgiving? He squeezed his eyes shut and shuddered. It was a year before his mother dropped the topic. It wasn't just Lydie's fault, it was his fault for parenting her so poorly, and Birdy's fault for tolerating it. On and on and on.

David sat in the chair for a long while after Dok left, thinking about his mother, about how he loved her yet felt overwhelmed by her strong personality, by the conflicts she brought along with her. His thoughts wandered to Lydie, his lively, irascible, exasperating daughter. Katrina, his eldest, had gone through a difficult stretch, as did his son, Jesse, and his second daughter, Ruthie. But with those three, it was just that—fairly common adolescent behavior. Lydie had been a challenge from the start. Her days and nights mixed up, quick to learn to walk but slow to learn to talk. Complaints from schoolteachers about the need to apply herself to her task. Molly and Emily had been exceptionally easy, as if they felt a little apologetic about their sister.

The *clip-clop* of a customer arriving in a horse and buggy shook him out of his musing. He glanced at the clock, surprised to see it was already past nine thirty. He got slowly to his feet, feeling suddenly old and achy in all the joints of his bones. He unlocked the door and flipped the sign from CLOSED to OPEN.

Then he froze. His mother had arrived, driving Birdy's horse and buggy, with a grim look on her face.

7

Any time David's mother wanted to go somewhere, she took Birdy's only means of transportation. It seemed grossly unfair to Birdy to be unable to count on using her own horse and buggy. He supposed that he should consider buying his mother her own horse and buggy, but wouldn't that be a signal of permanence? Of assuming that she would never leave?

He should say something to his mother, but how to say it? She offended so easily, and her reaction was a long and cold silent treatment—the very reason David turned into an insipid milquetoast of a man around her. How could his mother be so insensitive to others, yet so sensitive about herself? It was why she had such few friends. Why, her own children and grand-children avoided spending time with her. She really had no one in her corner, other than him. He felt incredibly sorry for her.

As David's mother came up the store's steps, he noticed how she needed to hold on to the railing. She was aging, and the realization brought a sadness, a tenderness that had been lack-ing in him. "Hello, Mom. I was just opening up."

"I've come to discuss Lydie." His mother walked right past

him into the store. "I've given her a list of things to do and she hasn't done a single one." She sat down in Hank Lapp's rocking chair, breathing heavily. "I believe I've discovered where the problem lies. Wammer'n Schtee zu schwer is, loss ich ihn yuscht leie." *If a stone is too heavy, I'll just let it lie.*

The tenderness David had been feeling for his mother evaporated.

"She's lazy. A result of poor parental discipline. I don't blame you. Not entirely. I see Birdy's lack of discipline and how it affects everyone. Perhaps if Anna hadn't passed away—"

David held up his hands. "Stop right there. First of all, Lydie is a lot of things, but she's not lazy. Second, Birdy is a wonderful mother. Third, the Lord took Anna home in his perfect timing. End of discussion." It irked him when his mother made herself sound fond of Anna, his first wife. She'd been every bit as hard on Anna as she was now on Birdy. He walked to the door and held it open. "If you'll excuse me, I need to get to work."

Clearly offended, his mother drew her lips tight. She pushed off from the rocker and went to the door in a huff. The rain had stopped but David's gloom had returned.

❧

There was nothing quite so appealing as the scent of a roasting chicken. Even with the wind blowing hard enough to skin the bark right off the trees, Nathan could smell supper as he walked in from the barn. He washed up at the kitchen sink and glanced around. The chicken was on the table, Dad and Mick were waiting for him, but Mom was missing.

His dad read his mind. "She had to go and lie down. Not feeling well."

The three men bowed their heads in silent prayer. As soon as Dad lifted his head, they all dug into the platters of food. Nathan watched Mick as he grabbed a bowl of mashed potatoes. "So, I noticed that Frank and Owen Miller paid a visit today."

Mick scooped one spoonful of mashed potatoes onto his dinnerplate, then two. "Frank has a miracle seed. Guaranteed to be resistant to pests like earworms."

Nathan had heard *that* line before. "Tell me more."

"He says it's supposed to be the best thing since sliced bread. Ein Wunner." *A miracle.*

Nathan set down his fork, chewed and swallowed hastily. "Hold on a minute. Is the seed genetically modified?"

Mick shrugged. "I don't know. All I know is that Frank guaranteed a crop this year like we've never seen before."

"Mick," Nathan said, "corn is wind pollinated."

"So?" Mick said, chewing.

"I was planning to grow corn too. Your GMO corn will contaminate my fields. I can't get organically certified if my crops have been affected by GMO plants. I can't even use the same tools that have been used on a GMO plant. It leaves residues."

"That, little brother, is your problem."

Nathan looked to his father. Walt Yoder seemed unconcerned as he pulled a drumstick off the chicken. "You have nothing to say?"

His father wiped a smear of butter off his face with his napkin. "You each have forty acres to farm. What more do you want?"

"I want a fair shot at growing organic crops."

Mick grinned. "And I want a fair shot at growing *my* crops."

Nathan stared at him. Was he serious? "But I'm not sabotaging your fields."

"In a way, you are, little brother. Your fancy-pants organic farming is going to hurt Black Gold's overall yield this harvest."

Walt raised his hand, heaving a loud sigh. "That will be seen, come autumn. For now, eat."

Nathan and Mick stared each other down for half a minute, then turned back to their suppers. The kitchen fell back into silence, but for a clink of forks on plates. Now and then,

Nathan could hear the dry coughs of his mother, coming from her bedroom.

As soon as supper ended, Nathan drove the buggy over to the hardware store to buy a second set of tools that would have to be kept separate from Mick's tools. He slapped the horse's reins to hurry it along. Why did it have to be this way? Why couldn't Mick and Dad look at the farm as a whole, living thing? Such a tension-filled home was so frustrating. It was not the way a family should be.

Ten minutes later, in the hardware store, he walked down an aisle to pick out a shovel and hoe.

"New tools?"

He turned to see the bishop coming down the aisle toward him. "Hi there, David. Yes, I'll definitely be needing some new tools this spring. A whole new set."

A few feet from him, David stopped. "What's wrong?"

Something about the kind, concerned look on the bishop's face made Nathan crack open. Everything poured out—the splitting up of the farm, Mick's use of GMO seed, all the frustration he felt in trying to restore Black Gold Farm to the thriving farm it once was. He held nothing back, and David listened carefully, offering mm-hmms and uh-huhs at just the right places. He wasn't sure why the bishop had that kind of effect on him. He had an avuncular attitude toward people—loving, interested, supportive, with just the right amount of detachment.

Arms crossed against his chest, David waited until Nathan had completely finished his rant. "So let me see if I have this clearly understood. You can't grow corn in your acreage if Mick is growing corn in his acreage?"

"That's exactly right. Not corn, not wheat, not oats."

"And you said that's because those crops are wind pollinated." David rubbed his forehead, as if he was trying to remember something. "But isn't that true of most crops?"

"No, other than nut trees. Most plants are self-pollinating, or insect pollinated. Pretty much anything grown in a garden would be vegetation pollinated. Tomatoes, peppers, zucchini, herbs."

"So . . . potatoes?"

"Yeah, potatoes would be a good example. Carrots are another. And most crops that are grown for its leaves, like lettuce."

"Kale?"

"Yeah. Kale's an example."

"Pretty easy to grow, isn't it?"

"It is." Nathan tipped his head. "Why?"

"So what if you grew only those crops that your brother wouldn't grow?"

Poor David. He knew even less than Nathan thought he knew about farming. "Because the livestock on Black Gold Farm need corn and wheat and hay for the winter."

"Eighty acres' worth?"

Nathan wasn't quite sure where David was going with this question. "No. I suppose not . . . if Mick's miracle seed performs like the chem rep promised it would."

"So . . . what if you took your forty acres and grew produce to sell directly to the people who would consume it? For example, at the farmers' market?"

Nathan was careful to keep his voice from sounding patronizing. After all, David was a shopkeeper, not a farmer. "Well, you see, to be a standholder at the Lancaster Central Market requires carrying an insurance policy of over a million dollars." He happened to know that fact because he'd read an article about it in last week's *Stoney Ridge Times*. The Lancaster Central Market was the oldest farmers' market in the country, running three days a week. He'd read that too.

David smiled. "What if you sold produce at the Stoney Ridge Farmers' Market?"

Puzzled, Nathan hesitated, not quite sure how to respond.

David grinned. "I know what you're thinking. There is no Stoney Ridge Farmers' Market. But there could be!" He slapped Nathan on the shoulder. "For years, there's been talk in town about starting one so that folks buy produce grown locally rather than having to drive all the way into Lancaster's Central Market, or even other towns that offer a farmers' market. People want food that's been grown five minutes down the road. There's no reason why people who live in Stoney Ridge need to go elsewhere for their food. There's enthusiasm and support for the venture, there's even a councilman who offered to help get the permits, but so far no one has stepped up to organize it."

"Why not? If there's been all this interest, why hasn't it happened?"

"Two reasons." David ticked off one finger. "Time. Most farmers are just too busy." He ticked off a second finger. "And most farmers have no sense of marketing. They need someone young and enthusiastic. Someone committed to farming, like you are."

Nathan listened, nodding, and slowly it dawned on him, from the way that David's eyes drilled into him, that he was talking about *him*. David wanted Nathan to start the Stoney Ridge Farmers' Market. "Wait a minute." He slapped his hand against his chest. "Me?"

"Think about it, Nathan. The Lord has given you only forty acres to manage, not eighty. You've got the time."

Time? He'd barely slept in the last two weeks!

"You're just the one to organize it. Be the market manager."

"Organize it? Market manager?" Nathan's voice rose an octave. It ended on a squeak.

"Yes. You'd be doing it for your own sake as well as for the town. Getting a farmers' market up and going is a way for us to help our own people, to keep the young families from moving away. And it's a quiet, purposeful way of helping the whole town of Stoney Ridge, a way to build bridges with our Englisch neighbors."

"But David . . . I'm Plain." Which, of course, he knew. But Nathan could just imagine his father's reaction to this idea. David Stoltzfus was highly respected as their bishop, but some church members felt he was worldly minded. Too interested in building bridges.

"Yes, we are Plain. And farming began in the garden of Eden. The Lord gave us the work of being stewards of the earth. Food is a life-giving necessity. No task is more essential. There will always be a need to have someone grow and provide food to nourish a community."

Put like that, a farmers' market sounded noble. But Nathan knew that the reality of it would be a ton of work. "I wouldn't even know where to begin."

"That's why it's a good idea to start small this summer."

"But, David, I really don't know the first thing about farmers' markets—"

"You know enough. And you're a quick learner. I wouldn't ask if I didn't believe in you. And like I said, there's a lot of support for this. You're not in it alone." David backed up a few feet. "We can talk more about it later."

David started to walk away, but Nathan wasn't quite done with his doubts. "Wait . . . what about my father?" He couldn't see his father supporting this endeavor.

The bishop turned, waited a moment, then said, "There's a saying among our people, Nathan. 'You can never say no to the bishop.' Leave your father to me." He grinned and lifted his hand in a wave as he turned the corner.

A little later, Nathan drove home with his new tools, full of new emotions. Conflicted ones. First off, maybe David was on to something about planting crops that Mick had no interest in growing. Mick's fields would be full of what had always been grown in them: corn and wheat and oats. The soil was riddled with fungi and pests that chemical treatments did little to reduce. The soil was beat.

Maybe Nathan should go in an entirely different direction: carrots, radishes, lettuces, tomatoes, kale, peppers, potatoes, herbs. Lots and lots of herbs.

A tiny glimmer of excitement began in his belly. The farmers' market idea sounded like a crazy amount of planning, incredibly overwhelming, but a part of him—a big part—was pleased that David thought he was the one who could do it. Nathan felt, well, honored by the bishop's confidence in his abilities. So opposite of how his dad made him feel.

And then he started to dream. Imagine how much he could learn from talking to other organic farmers. Imagine if the Stoney Ridge Farmers' Market, one day, might be entirely organic? Imagine how it could start to influence farmers who used agricultural methods that brought lasting harm to the environment.

He could do this. He wanted to do this. Let Mick plant all the corn he wanted.

On an impulse, he turned right instead of left and drove down to Blue Lake Pond. It had always been his favorite thinking spot. He tied the horse to a tree and walked down to the lake. Signs of spring's awakening were all around him. Bright green leaves unfurled on the trees, birds darted everywhere, and a mallard couple flew in and landed on the lake, disturbing the mirror-like surface.

At the water's edge, he stopped, breathing in deeply of the pond's clean smell. It was almost like a cathedral, this place, though he'd never been in one. But something about this spot filled him with reverence, and awe. And memories.

He hadn't come here since the first of January, just a few months ago. The trees had been bare, the lake was frozen, and snow covered the rim. There was a beauty in the barrenness, and the day had started so well. It ended so badly. And he was the one who had caused it.

Nathan and Lydie had gone ice-skating on Blue Lake Pond with a group of friends, but the friends never showed up. Even Mick. Too cold, he said, and it was. In the low twenties. Nathan didn't mind, not if Lydie didn't.

They had the entire lake to themselves. He taught Lydie how to skate backward, and she taught him to do figure eights, and finally, their ankles were aching and their faces felt frozen from the nippy winter air. On the shore, Nathan built a fire and they warmed up beside it, sipping hot cocoa from a thermos. She spilled some cocoa on her coat, and as he reached over to help mop it up with his glove, they bumped foreheads. Then something came over him and he leaned in to kiss her. The best kiss ever. He'd never kissed a girl before, but it felt like fireworks had gone off. When the kiss ended, his common sense left him and he told her he loved her. That he'd always loved her and always would. That she was the only girl he'd ever love. All those heartfelt words poured out of him after that mind-blowing kiss.

In return, she stared at him, wordlessly. The color left her face, even the pink of her cheeks disappeared. "But . . . what do I tell Mick?" she finally said.

In that moment, it dawned on Nathan that Lydie didn't have the same feelings for him. That she had those feelings for his brother.

It was odd how such clear, insightful thoughts could race through a person's mind, even when his stomach was turning inside out and his heart was pounding, and he wanted desperately to rewind the last few minutes. He wondered how much damage he'd done, if they'd still be friends. If his one-sided feelings would be too much to bear.

Strange, how those thoughts had been prescient. Things had changed from that day on. With Lydie. With Mick. And it weighed heavily on him that nothing would ever be the same again.

The sun was starting to set, so he strode back up to the dirt parking lot where his horse stood patiently waiting.

By the time he returned to Black Gold Farm and led the horse into his stall, he learned from Mick that the bishop had come and gone. David had done Nathan a favor in that. His father couldn't object, couldn't ridicule, couldn't refuse Nathan the time it would take to manage the farmers' market. As David had said, you just didn't say no to a bishop. Not even Walt Yoder would contradict a bishop's request.

On the other hand, Mick had plenty to say about it. Nathan went straight to the tack room to work on his ever-evolving plans for his fields. Mick sauntered in, jumped to sit on the workbench, and folded his arms across his chest. "Why in the world," Mick said, "did you agree to start a farmers' market?"

Nathan glanced at him. "It's something the community needs. David said there's been talk of it for years, but no one stepped up to take the lead."

Mick scoffed. "Until you volunteered."

"Volunteered? Not hardly."

"Then why do it?"

Nathan looked up to face his brother, head-on. "Aren't you ever going to understand what it means to be Plain?"

Mick was the first to break their staredown. He jumped off the bench. "You're making this contest too easy for me, little brother." He patted him on the back. "Just like everything."

Like Lydie, he meant.

8

Lydie had gone out to the little barn after supper and stayed. She told Mammi she needed to clean out the horses' stalls, but the real reason was to get far away from her grandmother's incessant critiques. She didn't know how Birdy stood it! Mammi had "helpful" suggestions to Birdy and Lydie about, well, just about everything.

Sitting on the trunk, she flipped through her doodle sketch pad. She paused when she came to one drawing. A doodle of Nathan that she would never, ever show him.

It was dated the first of January. She'd just returned home from ice-skating with him on Blue Lake Pond and felt so badly about botching everything up between them that she couldn't go inside and face anyone. Not yet. Instead, she went straight to the little barn and drew.

She wrapped her arms around her knees, thinking back to that wonderful, awful day. When Nathan had told Lydie he loved her, right after he'd kissed her—while her mind was still fuzzy from his unexpected kiss—she bit the inside of her cheek so hard she tasted blood. Her mind raced for a way to respond. She couldn't tell him the truth. He didn't need to know it. She couldn't tell him how she truly felt, for lots of reasons, all triggered by his father's warning to stay far away from him. Added to that warning, she couldn't stop thinking about that one remark made by his father. If Lydie truly cared for Nathan, she'd want him to be with someone who was good enough for him.

She *did* care about him that much.

Back in December, after Walt's warning to stay away from Nathan, she had confided to Mick that she was thinking of leaving. She needed his help to figure out how and when and where she should go. Mick was smart like that.

"I'll come too," he said, like it was no big deal.

"You can't come. You have the farm."

"I hate farming. I'll come. We'll both go. Leave it all to me, Lydie. It'll be a hoot!"

A hoot. That's not exactly how Lydie considered it—torn away from the family she loved dearly. From Nathan.

But it would be easier to go with a friend, and Mick was a good friend to her. He was good company too. Besides, she had no idea what to do next. She just knew she had to go.

And so, the only thing she could think to say to Nathan, as he sat there waiting for her to say something—anything—back to him, was, "What do I tell Mick?"

Such a *stupid* thing to say. Mick and Nathan competed over *everything*. Without meaning to, she had just added fuel to their ongoing rivalry.

But it worked.

The look on his face . . . it nearly made her break down and tell him everything. He quietly put out the fire, helped her to her feet, and they went back to the buggy. The ride home was deathly quiet. In an odd way, it was appropriate. Something *had* died that day.

That hurt look in his eyes, that was what she had tried to draw. She wanted to remember that moment. Whenever she felt as if she didn't have the courage to leave, she looked at this drawing. She never wanted to hurt him again. If she stayed, she would end up disappointing him, like she was always disappointing Mammi. And Dad. She had to leave.

~

A few days later, David arrived home earlier than usual to find Birdy waiting for him outside the house. She walked to the buggy and he braced himself for bad news. "Good day?" There was hope in his voice.

She climbed in on the other side. "Let's sit for a moment."

"Is anything wrong?"

Birdy settled herself on the buggy bench. "No, not wrong, not exactly. Katrina called and said the doctor has put her on bed rest until the baby comes."

Katrina was David's eldest daughter, married to Andy Miller. Last year, they had moved to an Amish settlement in Kentucky, where they could buy good land at cheaper prices than in Lancaster County. "She'll be all right, won't she? Both she and the baby?"

"She's been getting some contractions and the doctor wants her to hold tight until the baby is at least thirty-six weeks along." Birdy inhaled. "She asked if I might come and help. She wants me to bring the boys."

"I don't know, Birdy. Isn't Katrina only six or seven months along? You and the boys might be gone a long time, especially if you plan to stay after the baby arrives. Maybe it's possible to hire a mother's helper to help her out."

Birdy took her time answering. "Perhaps. I can keep a lookout for someone once I'm there. But for now, well, it seemed like . . . good timing." She glanced at the house. "It's very small, our house."

It was. Way too small to include Tillie Stoltzfus, who was not only a large woman but had an even bigger presence. "I had . . . hoped that my mother's visit would pass quickly."

"Like a summer storm?"

A laugh burst out of him. "That's one way of putting it. To be honest, I thought Mom might change her mind about living with us after staying for a week or so, and then life could go back to the way it was." Then he had a brilliant idea. "What if we sent Mom to help Katrina?"

Birdy gave him a look.

He got it. She didn't have to say anything more. The last thing a pregnant woman stuck in bed needed was to have Tillie Stoltzfus move in, with all her complaints.

Birdy kept her gaze fixed on the buggy's windshield. "While I'm away, I know you'll seek the Lord's guidance to find an ideal solution to your mother's living situation."

Ah. Now he understood. This was Birdy's gentle way of saying the current situation was unsustainable.

Here David was, having lived over a half century on this earth, and his backbone still turned to jelly whenever his mother appeared. Last time she had moved in with them for a lengthy period, he ended up in the hospital with an ulcer. He glanced at Birdy, at his wonderful partner, who often saw things he couldn't see.

"Birdy, my mother . . . her intentions are good. But I know she can be . . ."

She put her hand on his. "I know. You don't have to say a word. But she also raised a wonderful man, and for that I am grateful." She squeezed his hand. "I'm sure you'll find an ideal solution. You always do."

He shifted on the bench to turn toward her. "I thought you seemed a little too happy to be leaving home."

Her eyes lit with amusement. "We're packed and ready to go. Bus leaves at six o'clock."

His eyebrows shot up. "Today?"

She smiled.

Not a minute too soon, was what she was thinking. He knew.

He leaned over to give her a kiss, right on her lips. "Birdy, you'll come back, won't you?"

She returned his kiss. "I'll be back."

He just had to figure out what to do with his mother first.

"I know you'll find the perfect answer, one that works for everyone."

Because she wasn't coming back until he did. He knew that too.

～

Walking slowly through the Lancaster Central Market, Nathan compared vendors and their produce. He'd read a book David had loaned him about successful farmers' markets and took note of two things in particular: Variety was essential. So was specialty produce, which was the key to help small-scale farmers, like himself, earn a decent living. But what *was* specialty produce?

Today, he was going to find out. He passed by a lot of arts and crafts stands—wooden whirligigs, birdhouses, wind chimes. Interspersed were artisanal cheese makers—something he doubted could be found in Stoney Ridge—and tempting baked goods. Then he noticed one particular vendor, an older woman with wiry gray hair held in two long braids. "Are you selling specialty produce?"

"Does the sun rise in the east?"

Nathan assumed she meant yes. "So . . . those bags of tiny lettuce leaves would be considered specialty produce?" For four dollars a bag? It looked to him like lettuce that had been harvested too early.

"That bag of tiny lettuce leaves is what we call baby lettuce."

"And it sells?"

"Baby lettuce, baby arugula, baby kale, baby pea shoots. Baby anything. Baby sells, honey."

Nathan tilted his head. "You grew the lettuce?"

"From seed. Right in the greenhouse under grow lights. Tricks 'em into thinking it's summer. I hand cut everything last night to get it all ready for today's customers."

"But . . . why?"

She opened the twist tie and handed him a few lettuce leaves. "Try that."

He did. It was less bitter than mature lettuce. Far sweeter. It was . . . quite tasty. But still, four dollars for a small bag? "And customers want it?"

"Pile it high and watch it fly."

"Customers like it more than mature lettuce heads?"

"You betcha. It's fresher, more nutritive. Any and all baby produce is highly sought after by the foodie crowd. Anything you can't get at the grocery store. Same with heirloom veggies. I try to provide things that grocery stores don't . . . or can't."

Nathan had never heard of the foodie crowd.

"Why can't you get baby produce and heirloom vegetables at the grocery store?"

"They're too hard to package commercially." She held the bag of lettuce out to him with one hand. She held her other hand, palm open out to him. "You know what they say."

"What do they say?"

"Farmers' markets are the taste of the home garden." She smiled. "That'll be four bucks."

Nathan hadn't planned on buying baby lettuce, considering his greenhouse had dozens of leafy greens just starting to sprout, plants he had intended to transplant into his mother's kitchen garden once the true leaves appeared. But he felt as if he owed this lady with gray braids a thank-you. *Farmers' markets are the taste of the home garden.* That could be a motto. He handed her a five-dollar bill and told her to keep the change. She'd given him quite a lot.

As soon as he returned to Black Gold Farm, he went straight to the greenhouse. He walked up and down the rows, studying each tray of seedlings. His mind was spinning, pivoting. He realized he'd already started seedlings of many of the plants that the gray-braids lady sold as baby produce. Tiny little sprouts filled trays of lettuce, arugula, kale, broccoli, Swiss chard, spinach, carrots, mustard greens, radishes, herbs. As soon as he could get to the Hay & Grain and buy more seed, he'd add new ones that he tasted today—microgreens, watercress, endive, bok choy.

The other half of the greenhouse held trays of plants that he would get into the fields after night temperatures rose—tomatoes, zucchinis, pumpkins, radishes, peppers, celery, beans, peas, cabbage, turnips, cucumbers. When matured, those could be added to his produce at the farmers' market.

He thought often of advice that his grandfather had given him: You really couldn't be a farmer without optimism, patience, and keeping the long view in mind. Ironically, today—with quick-growing baby greens from the greenhouse—the short view was the answer Nathan needed.

He just hoped the foodie crowd would come to the Stoney Ridge Farmers' Market.

With Birdy away for an indefinite amount of time, Mammi's role expanded. She took full charge of the household, which included only Lydie and her dad. They were now the uncomfortable recipients of Mammi's full attention. *Awful.*

Lydie did her best to avoid her grandmother, which wasn't easy. She stayed away from home as much as she could and, when she was home, tried to find things to do outdoors.

Meals had changed quite a bit. Pre-Mammi, there used to be conversation and laughter, and antics from the two little boys. Dad used to try and get home in time for supper, but lately his time was absorbed with either store-work or bishop-work. Or maybe he was trying to avoid Mammi too.

But the food had improved, Lydie had to give her that much. Mammi was a top-notch cook. Supper tonight was pot roast and potatoes, with carrots and turnips and butternut squash, of course, and a thick gravy that had no lumps. Lydie's gravy always had lumps. It was because she added the flour too soon, Mammi said, and that didn't surprise Lydie. Patience was not something she had in abundance.

A wagon rolled up the driveway, and Lydie jumped from the table to see who had come calling. Her chair made a loud grating noise in the quiet room as she pushed away to go to the window.

"Lydie, sit down," Mammi said. "For mercy's sake, you're like a jackrabbit."

"It's Mick," she said over her shoulder. "He's bringing a wagon stacked full of lumber. To start rebuilding the shed."

When Mick bolted into the kitchen without even a knock and gave a merry salute, Mammi slowly turned her head and looked at him as if she wondered where he'd come from. She laid her fork down gently on the plate and patted her lips with the napkin that had been spread over her lap.

Mammi was trying to make a point. She didn't like Mick, didn't want him here, didn't want him bothering them at suppertime. She hadn't forgiven him for staining her-son-the-bishop's reputation with a hidden brewery in the shed. Not until the time came for communion, she said. Then and only then would she give some thought to forgiving Mick.

"Hello there, Tillie, Lydie," Mick said, his voice dripping with honey. He considered Mammi's frostiness toward him as a personal challenge and was determined to thaw her out. Good luck with that, Lydie had told him. "I brought over the lumber to start building a new shed to replace the old one. It'll be such a fine shed that you'll be glad the old one is gone."

Mammi shot him a wary look. "Hmmph."

"Tillie, I must say that particular shade of brown is quite fetching on you."

Lydie dipped her chin to hide a smile. Mammi's particular shade of brown happened to be the same dull brown in all her clothing. It was the preferred color for the very conservative church in Ohio, and she wasn't budging from it.

"Something smells delicious," Mick said, peering at the table with a look of longing. "I could smell it all the way down to the road."

"You, on the other hand, have brought a peculiar aroma into this house."

Lydie couldn't believe she said that. "Mammi!"

"He smells like he's come from a factory." Mammi wrinkled her nose.

It was true that Mick did have a strange stink about him. Still, Mammi's bluntness was rude.

Mick took no offense. He lifted his arm to sniff and gave a nod. "Ja, you're right. Partly me, partly the chems. I spent most of today spraying the fields to get 'em ready for planting." He leaned over the table to peer into the big pot. "So what's cooking?"

Mammi's brows rose. "I'm sure your mother expects you home."

"She's not feeling too well today," Mick said. "We three men are having to make do." He sniffed the air. "Tillie, you sure are a fine cook."

Mammi said nothing, only shifted her glare from Mick to her plate.

Lydie rolled her eyes. "Well, it seems to me that we have more than enough to spare."

Mammi breathed a deep sigh. "Finish unloading that wagon. And then, if there's anything left, you can take a plate. To go."

Exasperated, Lydie set her napkin on the table. There was enough pot roast and potatoes to feed half the town. "I'll help Mick unload."

Mammi gave her a stony look. "No, you won't. He got himself into this mess and he can get himself out."

"Your grandmother is absolutely right," Mick said magnanimously. "Do not worry, ladies. I've got everything handled."

Mammi waved a hand as if to dismiss him. Surprisingly, Mick took the hint. With an exaggerated flourish, he took off his hat and bowed, backing out of the kitchen like a humble servant.

Lydie couldn't help but smile as she watched him through the window. He had pulled fresh lumber out of the wagon and heaved boards on his shoulder. How big a shed was he planning to build? It looked like he had enough wood for two sheds. When he disappeared from view, she turned her attention back to the table and realized Mammi was staring at her. "I'm sorry. What were you saying?"

"I was saying that it's time we had a talk."

"About what?"

"Tell me about Mick Yoder."

"There's nothing to tell."

Mammi sighed, a heavy sound. She frowned. She was always frowning. "Schee is wer schee dutt." *Handsome is what handsome does.*

Lydie's eyes narrowed in perplexity. What was Mammi getting at? "Clearly you don't think much of Mick Yoder."

"I don't. He'll be caught in a sin one of these days. You just watch and see if I'm not right." She sighed. "I had a hope you'd end up with that brother of his. But it's time to face facts."

"What facts?"

"According to Edith Lapp who buys her eggs from Martha Glick, there's something brewing between her daughter Patsy and Nathan Yoder. She's planning to be baptized this fall." Again, she sighed. This time it was a sigh aimed at Lydie's unbaptized condition. "No doubt we'll be seeing rows upon rows of celery in the Glicks' garden this summer."

Lydie opened her mouth, then shut it. Where had Mammi heard such a thing? She wondered if it were true.

"Edith thinks highly of Patsy Glick. Everyone does, she says, especially the boys. Sie hat's Garaiss." *She is very much sought after.*

"That, she is."

With yet another deep sigh, Mammi said, "I can certainly see why a serious young man like Nathan would prefer a girl like Patsy. She's quite . . ."

"Perfect." Lydie was well aware.

"No one is perfect but our Lord and Savior." Mammi surprised Lydie with a short laugh. "I suppose, though . . . Patsy is closer than most."

Then it was Lydie's turn to exhale a sigh, flat and aching. So, if news was trickling around town about Patsy and Nathan, it probably meant Nathan had taken her advice and offered to drive Patsy home from a Singing. Mick would end up with injured feelings, but he was nothing if not resilient. Patsy had never been right for him. Lydie hoped Mick would still help her get the job at the Clam Shack in Williamsport. All that was stopping her from leaving now was Dok's temporary job, and the threat against Nathan by the chem rep. She hadn't figured out what to do about that quite yet, as she had no proof, just a gut feeling that trouble lay ahead.

She looked down at her plate. Suddenly, she'd lost her appetite.

"Oh fine. You might as well help him unload that wagon. Otherwise he'll be here until the cows come home." Mammi put down her fork and gave Lydie a long look. Then she took in a deep breath as if she needed extra courage. "I suppose a boy like Mick Yoder will keep a girl's life full of the unexpected. I suppose that's . . . something." She tried on a smile of resignation, but Lydie could tell she didn't mean it.

Why bother to try and explain? Mammi would never understand. She rose from the table and made a dash toward the door.

"Lydie, wait!"

But she kept going. Waiting was what Lydie'd been doing for far too long.

On Saturday morning, Nathan walked the downtown section of Stoney Ridge. Location, location, location. He'd heard that word over and over at the council meeting this morning. The right location would be critical to the success of the nascent farmers' market. It should be in a high-traffic area and include a parking lot. Oh, and it should come without any fees. The council members were fully supportive of the farmers' market, convinced it would be good for local business and keep locals shopping in Stoney Ridge rather than elsewhere—but no one could agree on where it should be held. He was handed the task of finding a suitable spot as soon as possible.

Other than the location, much had been decided at this morning's meeting. David had been right about the enthusiasm and support. Council members were so pleased someone was willing to spearhead it that they eagerly volunteered to help with specific tasks: filling out paperwork for the permits, seeking vendors, doing advertising and promotion. There was even a councilman who had experience with health and safety requirements, something Nathan and David hadn't even considered. But if done right, they could include vendors with canned fruits and vegetables, and baked goods.

They agreed on a start date of May 15, an end date of October 1, and holding the market only on Saturday mornings. Nathan was relieved by that decision. He could afford to give up one morning a week, but any more than that and he was worried his own fields would suffer.

Everything was getting nailed down other than where to locate the market. So far, nothing seemed to check all the boxes.

He walked to the end of Main Street and then back again, slowing as he drew near the Sweet Tooth Bakery, enticed by the scent of cinnamon in the air. Suddenly ravenous, he made a beeline to the bakery. He opened the door to a whoosh of warm cinnamon-scented air, and he took a place at the end of the line. And then he suddenly heard the unmistakable sound of her laugh. Lydie's laugh.

9

Standing a few places in line ahead of Nathan at the bakery were Lydie and Mick. He watched them, wondering what Mick had said that made Lydie laugh. Around the nape of her neck were tendrils of curls. He thought back to their school years, when her thick strawberry-blond hair hung down her back in two long braids. He remembered the day when she came to church with it pinned up, tucked under her prayer kapp. She'd been so pleased at how grown-up she looked, and he remembered feeling a little sad. He didn't want things to change.

The door opened and a loud voice called out, "LOOK WHO'S HERE!"

Hank Lapp.

Lydie whirled around, noticing Hank, and then Nathan. Their eyes met briefly, met and held, and then Nathan felt Hank's hand grasp his shoulder. "I HEAR you're STARTING a FARMERS' market. I WANT a STAND."

Two conflicted feelings arose whenever Nathan was confronted by Hank Lapp—either a desire to laugh or to run to the nearest exit. But the face Nathan turned to Hank wore a polite expression. "What is it you'd want to sell?"

Hank lifted his eyes to the ceiling. "Well . . . I DON'T know. But I'll THINK on it some."

Overhearing Hank—who couldn't hear him?—Lydie slipped out of line to join them at the end. "Everyone in town is talking about the farmers' market."

Nathan felt his cheeks grow warm.

Mick joined them in time to add his two cents. "Sure. Who wouldn't want to be known for selling frou-frou arugula in little baggies, listening to vendors gripe about the rain."

Rain! Nathan hadn't even considered a location that could protect vendors from inclement weather. Mentally, he added it to his growing to-do list.

Lydie frowned at Mick. "Well, I think it's a great idea." She turned to Nathan. "Is everything getting figured out?"

"Maybe. I don't know. I hope so." Nathan motioned that they should move along in the line. "We don't have a location nailed down yet."

"Oh?" Lydie lifted her head to look at him. "Have you thought of having it at the public school?"

"The school?"

"The junior high school. It has that new pole barn close to the parking lot."

"Hold on. It's kind of an open-air pavilion, isn't it?" Now that she'd mentioned it, Nathan remembered he'd seen it getting built. He'd even stopped and watched a crane lift the trusses from the truck and onto the roof. Transfixed by the sight, he couldn't help comparing the building process to an Amish barn raising. Those roof trusses had been built elsewhere and trucked in. Getting them to fit to the frame of the building took a long, long time. He remembered because he had gone into town to pick up some tools at the hardware store and on his return trip, he stopped again to watch. He wondered what those construction workers would think of an Amish barn raising, where trusses were custom built on the spot, and slipped on like a glove.

"Lydie," he said, "you just might be onto something." She had a knack for solving problems, for seeing things he couldn't see. He smiled, and she smiled, and he felt that wonderful sense of being in sync with her, a feeling they'd always had . . . until the day he ruined it.

"What can I get you, Nathan?"

Startled, he realized they had moved all the way to the counter and there was Patsy Glick. She was behind the counter, smiling up at him in that mysterious way she had, as if she was here but her mind was elsewhere. Patsy made him nervous. She always had, as long as he'd known her. And now she was waiting for him to respond. "Uh . . ." His mind went blank. Completely wiped out.

Mick stepped into the vacuum. "I'll take five cinnamon rolls while my little brother tries to make a decision." He gave Patsy his most charming smile, but she barely glanced at him. Her coolness only made Mick try even harder. "Whatcha got planned for this weekend, Patsy?"

She completely ignored him. He could've been telling her the sky was blue. He had to repeat himself two more times.

"Oh, this and that," Patsy finally said, filling a pink box full of cinnamon rolls.

Nathan couldn't understand why Mick would dare flirt with Patsy Glick when he held the heart of Lydie Stoltzfus in his hands. He glanced at Lydie, wondering what she thought about Mick's flirting. She didn't even seem to notice Mick as he practically drooled at Patsy over the counter. Lydie was absorbed by Hank Lapp's loud and lengthy commentary over each bakery item. Apparently, he'd tried them all.

Lydie ended up choosing a cinnamon roll. She and Mick paid and left the bakery while Nathan remained at the register, with Patsy watching him. Carefully. Like she was studying him. Nathan felt a bead of sweat roll down his back. "Have you decided yet, Nathan?"

He cleared his throat. "Are the cinnamon rolls gone?"

"All sold." She leaned across the counter and whispered to him, "Hold on. I'll check in the back." She disappeared and returned a moment later with a box. "The baker had set a few aside. But as a special favor to me, he said you can have them."

"That's not necessary, Patsy."

"I don't mind." She gave him an enigmatic smile.

For just a brief moment, he found himself caught in Patsy's mysterious aura. Then a customer cleared his throat behind him in that impatient way, and Nathan snapped together. He handed over a ten-dollar bill for the cinnamon rolls. She put her hand over his and squeezed. "My treat," she whispered. "A small thank-you for all the work you're doing to get the farmers' market up and going. Everyone's so excited about it."

Her hand felt warm, and so soft, and time suddenly stopped. Until Hank Lapp noticed. "WELL, ain't THIS a CHARMING sight! LOVE at the SWEET TOOTH BAKERY."

Nathan yanked his hand from Patsy's and put the bill into the tip jar, scowling at Hank and his big mouth. He left the store as quickly as a man could make an exit, avoiding the eyes of customers in line. When he reached the outside, he saw a buggy head down the road, with Mick and Lydie inside.

Flustered from Hank, Nathan had forgotten to take Patsy's box. He glanced through the door and saw Hank at the counter, pointing to baked goods in the glass case. The box of cinnamon rolls was right there, still on the counter. Should he go back in to get them? Face loud Hank? Risk his childish innuendos? Look like a moonstruck adolescent to Patsy?

She sure was pretty. Lydie was right about that. As beautiful as a summer day.

He opened the door and went back in.

Lydie listened carefully to a frantic mother on the phone. Her toddler had been bitten by a poisonous snake. She put the woman on hold and interrupted Dok with a patient to give her the message.

"Find out what kind of snake she thinks it was."

"I asked. She's sure it was a water moccasin." Lydie held out a piece of paper. "Here's her address."

Dok jumped from her stool so fast that the patient, a middle-aged woman with diabetes, looked startled. Lydie followed Dok as she rushed into her office to unlock the pharmaceutical cabinet. Her eyes went from shelf to shelf as she muttered, "Anti-venom, anti-venom. Why haven't I organized this cupboard? Oh . . . there it is." She grabbed the vial and picked up her medical bag. "Cancel all my afternoon appointments. I'm going to take the child to the emergency room. I'll check in with you later today." She raced out the door. The patient she'd left behind stood at the open door with a surprised look on her face.

"I'm sorry," Lydie said. "I'll reschedule you for first thing in the morning." She spent the next hour apologizing to everyone in the waiting room, rescheduling them, then calling to cancel and reschedule all afternoon appointments. She was feeling rather pleased with herself for accomplishing so much for Dok in such a small amount of time. She even felt proud of herself for not feeling guilty because everyone was annoyed at her for being inconvenienced. One woman asked what was so important that Dok had to reschedule, and when Lydie said she couldn't tell her due to patient-doctor confidentiality, she hung up in a huff.

The door opened and she turned to start her spiel of explaining Dok's absence, but it was only Mick, with a broad grin on his face. "Lydie! Big party this Saturday night. I'll meet you at the usual place."

The good feeling Lydie had started to fade. She was his designated buggy driver. "Mick, don't you ever get tired of the Saturday night parties?"

"Tired of 'em? Why, I wish each night were Saturday. I wish every day was a summer day."

"What about your fields?"

"That's the beauty of it. Just planted the seed. Now it's time to let them do their thing and grow. When the time is right, I'll harvest."

Such a Mick answer. He'd always made farming sound like child's play. An image of Nathan in the fields filled Lydie's mind. She'd passed by Black Gold Farm this very morning and saw him walking through rows of small green plants, bending over now and again to study them closer.

Mick cleared his throat, and she snapped her head up. He'd been waiting for her to respond.

"I can't go. Not this weekend."

"You gotta go. You gotta bring Patsy. You promised."

"I never made such a promise."

"Sure you did. If I promised to get us jobs at that Clam Shack in Maryland, you promised to help me get together with Patsy."

Ugh. She sorta did agree to something like that. "Patsy's never going to want to go to your type of parties, Mick."

His face fell. "Ever since your grandmother arrived, you've lost your sense of fun."

Had she? Maybe so, but it wasn't just because of Mammi. Or if it was, it was because Mammi kept pointing out that it was high time Lydie grew up. She was trying! She just couldn't figure out what that meant. "Dok was called out on an emergency and I've had to do a lot of rescheduling. I'm hungry too. I forgot my lunch on the kitchen counter and was hoping Dad might have brought it with him to the store." He usually did.

"I'll stay. You go."

"I can't go. Dok keeps telling me to clean my desk." It was a bit . . . disheveled.

"I won't touch your desk."

Still, she hesitated. "I'm supposed to stay at the office when Dok's gone."

"The Bent N' Dent is right over there. I'd offer to go for you, but I'm laying low around your dad after the, uh"—he winked and pretended to guzzle a beer—"shed incident."

She hesitated. "I really shouldn't." But she was so hungry! She'd slept late and only had time to wolf down a bowl of cereal for breakfast.

"How long you gonna be? Five minutes? Go." He gently steered her to the door. "I'll sit right at your desk and answer the phone."

"No! Don't answer the phone. Let it go to messages." After a month at Dok's office, she had finally mastered that complicated phone.

"Gotcha. Now go."

She ran over to the Bent N' Dent and hurried to the back office. But her dad wasn't at his desk. Mammi was!

Lydie pivoted on her heels. "I was just stopping in to say hello."

"Hold it! Wait just a moment, Lydie. Since you're here, I want to discuss something with you."

Whenever Mammi started a sentence like that, it meant a long lecture followed. Lydie had to cut her off at the pass. "Could we talk when I get home tonight? I'd better get back to work."

"It'll only take a moment. Come in and sit down."

Trapped. She was trapped. She stayed by the door, though, with her hand on the doorjamb, ready to flee.

"This morning, you left milk on a pantry shelf and a box of cereal in the refrigerator."

Oh. That. "I guess I was in a hurry."

"I wish I could say that it was a unique situation, but it has happened three times since I've come."

"I'll try harder."

Mammi sighed. "Your bedroom . . . it looks like a hurricane blew through."

Not now! "I'll straighten it up tonight. First thing. Just as soon as I get home. And I'll try harder tomorrow."

"You must do more than try harder, Lydie. You must apply yourself to your task. You're not a child any longer. Alt genunk Verschtand zu hawwe." *You're old enough to know better.* "Sit. You can't be still for longer than a tick at a time."

Tick. Time! She glanced impatiently at the wall clock. Five minutes had already passed. "Mammi—"

"It's all right, dear," Mammi said, in that maudlin voice she used for pets, small children, and Hank Lapp. "I've come to realize that the Lord has brought me to Stoney Ridge for a specific purpose. I knew I was needed here, but I didn't know why. Your father has always carried extra burdens as a church leader, and Birdy is so easily overwhelmed. I thought perhaps I was meant to come and relieve them of some of their responsibilities. But now I know better." She pointed a finger at Lydie. "You."

Lydie clasped her palm over her heart. "Me?"

"You. You're the reason I'm here." Mammi smiled. "You're going to be my special project. We are going to fix you."

"Fix me?" Lydie's voice sounded shaky to her own ears.

Mammi clapped her hands together, a thing decided. "First thing, you must slow down. So flink as e Katz." *You're as quick as a cat.*

Lydie had to bite her tongue to stop from snapping at Mammi. *Slow down.* As if she hadn't heard *that* her entire life! *Slow down. Sit still. Try harder. Get organized.*

As if it were all just a matter of willpower! As if she could make herself act different, move different, think different. If it were that easy to change, wouldn't Lydie have done so? She didn't want to be the way she was. She just . . . couldn't help it.

She heard the bells on the front door jingle as a customer came in and it reminded her of the time. She glanced at the clock. Ten minutes had sped by. "Mammi, I really, really need to get back to Dok's."

Mammi reached down and held up her lunch bag. "You left this on the counter. Consider it to be the last time you forget your lunch because you're rushing around like your hair is on fire. Today, Lydie, is the start of a new life for you."

If Lydie weren't so hungry, she would've spun around and left the lunch with Mammi, just to have the last word on the subject. But she was *that* hungry. Almost absurdly slowly, just to make a point that she had been listening, she reached out for the lunch and left.

When she returned to Dok's office, Mick was sitting in her chair, his feet on her messy desk, with a pleased look on his face. "What took you so long?"

"My grandmother. Any calls?"

"None."

"Good. Now get your feet off my desk and be on your way."

"Well, that's a fine way to say thank you for covering your bum."

"My grandmother just told me that I'm going to be her special project. She said she is going to fix me." She squeezed her eyes shut. "I need to be alone."

He held up his hands in the air like she was holding a gun to him. "Say no more. I'm off."

After eating, Lydie felt much better. So much better, she even cleaned up her desk. When Dok finally returned, she seemed pleased with the calm atmosphere in the office. Unfortunately, that lovely peaceful feeling lasted for only a few minutes.

Dok emerged from her office with a shocked look on her

face. "Lydie, something is missing from the pharmaceutical cabinet."

A terrible feeling came over Lydie.

She walked up to Lydie. "What's gone on here while I was away?"

Lydie weighed the risk of saying something against the risk of saying nothing. One thought kept coming to mind, like bright lightning strikes flashing over and over in her head: she'd messed up—again.

❧

David dropped his chin to his chest, astounded by what his sister was telling him. How could this have happened?

Dok settled back into a chair. They were in David's office at the rear of the Bent N' Dent. "It's not quite as serious as it might seem, David. I'm partially to blame. I was in a hurry and left the cabinet unlocked. Wide open."

"You should be able to trust your employee."

"I do. It wasn't Lydie who rifled through the cabinet. It was Mick Yoder, and he only took one thing." She explained that Lydie had run over to the Bent N' Dent to get her lunch and let Mick remain at the office. "Thankfully, I've been running low on supplies and forgot to call the rep to come through. There wasn't much in the cabinet—some vials of anti-venom antidotes, some bottles of aspirin, an asthma inhaler. And then . . ." She started to grin. "I shouldn't laugh, but it's almost amusing. I had a jar full of baking soda in the cabinet that I keep handy for insect bites. And that's the only thing that Mick took."

"Baking soda? But why?"

"He didn't know what it was. It comes in a box, but I can't shut the cabinet because the box is too big. So I've gotten in the habit of pouring the baking soda into a jar. It wasn't labeled." David must have had a funny look on his face because she quickly added, "I know, I know. A bad habit. But I'm the only one who's in and out of that cabinet, so I didn't think it was really necessary to label it."

"But why would Mick want baking soda?"

"Most likely, he assumed it was cocaine. It looks like it, especially to a novice. Users snort it through a straw."

David's eyebrows lifted. That sounded awful. "Could the baking soda hurt him?"

A slow grin started on Dok's face. "It'll just give him a sore nose."

That was some relief, David supposed. "Still, Lydie shouldn't have left the office in Mick's care."

"No. That's true. She shouldn't have. She knows that and she feels terrible. But she did a lot of things right today. She managed an emergency for me, she handled upset patients whom she had to reschedule, and she told me the truth about leaving Mick alone in the office. That counts for a lot."

David rubbed his forehead. "Are you going to fire her?"

"No, no. Of course not. I like Lydie. Patients like her. She adds . . . a lightness to the office. One patient called her a mood lifter. I agreed. She's always happy."

"All that is true, but she also makes some horrendous decisions." Lately, it seemed, more than ever.

Dok nodded. "And I think I might know why." She paused for a moment, as if to gather her thoughts. "Are you familiar with Attention Deficit Hyperactivity Disorder? It's referred to as ADHD."

"I've seen pamphlets about it at the Mountain Vista Rehab Center. I don't know much about it, though."

"It's not something that's commonly observed among the Amish. Most likely, it goes undiagnosed."

"Mick Yoder isn't thought of as hyperactive. Lazy, maybe." Like his father. "But not hyperactive. Just . . . sorely lacking in common sense."

"I don't know Mick very well. But I have gotten to know

Lydie these past few weeks." Dok leaned forward in the chair. "I think she should be tested."

"Lydie?" That astounded him. "But she's not hyperactive."

"Females tend to be misdiagnosed because they don't usually have the hyperactivity behavior. More often, it gets described as character traits. Dreamy, spacy, forgetful. Inattentive, impulsive."

David thought of the many complaints teachers had made about Lydie through the years. Daydreamy, preoccupied, absentminded. He remembered a school event around Christmas, when parents came to hear the children sing. Emily and Molly were singing their hearts out. Lydie stood beside her sisters, hardly singing. She kept getting distracted by a bright red cardinal at the window behind her. Confused by its reflection, the bird kept bonking its head on the window.

"Look, David. The more time I spend around Lydie, the more I see myself in her. Especially knowing ADHD can have a genetic link."

He snapped to attention. "Wait a minute. What do you mean by that?" Was she thinking *he* had ADHD? Did he?

"After decades of struggle, I was finally diagnosed."

Hold it. "You? You have this . . . ADHD?" How had she never told him?

She nodded. "Matt was the one who encouraged me to get tested. It's made such a big difference to me to know why I felt so frustrated all the time."

David was having trouble processing this news. "But you and Lydie—you're very different."

"Yes and no. ADHD isn't a one-size-fits-all diagnosis. While Lydie has symptoms of distractibility, I had more of what's called hyperfocus. When I was Lydie's age, all I could think about was getting to college. That single-minded devotion steered me like a runaway horse. Looking back, I think having ADHD actually helped me get through medical school." She lifted a hand in the air. "Don't get me wrong. I love my life. I feel called to medicine. But I know I caused a lot of damage along the way. Nothing mattered but what I wanted. I'm sure you remember the fights between Mom and me. She was as determined to keep me under her thumb as I was determined to get out from under it." She let out a soft laugh. "Personally, I think Mom has ADHD too. More like mine. A hyperfocus . . . but on people. Fixing them." A text came in on Dok's phone and she stopped to answer it. Then she tucked her phone into her pocket. "So how do you feel about getting an assessment for Lydie?"

Oh no. David stiffened. He wasn't in favor of that. Slapping a label on a child seemed like the world's way of handling behavior problems. The Englisch way. He preferred to think of each individual as fearfully and wonderfully made in the eyes of God. Those in their church with unique needs or handicaps were called "special children." Their lives were gifts, bringing opportunities to a family to build patience and empathy. "I don't like it."

"Hear me out on this. A diagnosis of ADHD is an explanation, not an excuse. But left undiagnosed and untreated, it can only lead to more difficulties. It can interfere with work, with home, with relationships. Don't you think life must feel frustrating for Lydie? Haven't you noticed? She thinks everything is her fault. She magnifies her mistakes."

An all-too-common refrain of Lydie's came to David's mind: *I make a mess of everything.*" And the sad thing was that she often did. But not always. He had to agree with Dok that Lydie did take on more blame than she should, and downplayed the responsibility of others.

"You mentioned that she has had trouble holding down a job. I've noticed that she seems to lose track of the passing of time."

David nodded. "Yes, she has trouble with time. And that ends up in a lot of procrastination."

"Have you ever noticed that maintaining friendships can be difficult for her?"

David thought of Nathan Yoder, and how the two had been such close friends up until a few months ago. He thought of how exasperated Emily and Molly often were with Lydie. Birdy too. Lydie borrowed their things and forgot to return them. She made promises she didn't keep.

His face must have showed his thoughts because Dok burst out with a laugh. "I know, I know. Too much, too soon. I can tell you're trying to absorb all of this. Plus, I'm meddling in your daughter's life. I think I inherited that trait from Tillie."

Meddling. An apt description. David found himself squeezed between his mother and his sister. "This morning Mom told me that she's on a mission to fix Lydie."

"Fix her? Oh wow." Dok sighed. "That sounds like a disaster waiting to happen."

"I guess that lately—"

Another beep came out of Dok's phone, interrupting his thought as she reached into her pocket to look at the face of her phone. "Rachel Fisher is in labor. I'd better go. She delivered her last one in less than an hour." She slipped her phone back into her pocket. "David, I know you want Lydie to reach her full potential. If I'm right, if she does have ADHD, then you'll have a better understanding of how to help her get there. She'll know what her weaknesses are. And her strengths too. There are a lot of strengths that come with this diagnosis. ADHD is simply a difference in the way a person thinks and acts. In some ways, an advantage."

Was it? David wondered. It seemed like a life sentence would be handed to Lydie. "But what would change if she were given this diagnosis? You mentioned treating it. I don't like the idea of medication. I've been around Mountain Vista Rehab Center enough to know the saying—pills don't teach skills."

"Slow down. I never said anything about medication. Treatment can include lots of different options. I'm all for finding nondrug methods and practices. For example, cognitive behavior therapy is proving to be very beneficial. But let's leave all that for a later conversation."

He ran a hand through his hair. "Maybe Mom's right. She says Lydie reminds her of Jesse. She thinks if she would just slow down—"

"Lydie *can't* just slow down. She's not the same as Jesse, or any of your other children. Her brain is wired differently. She reminds me of a butterfly, floating in the air, looking for a place to land. She wants to find a place to belong in this world. But right now, I don't think she's finding it." She reached into her purse and pulled out a book. "Read this. Then we can talk more."

He looked at the title: *Living with Adult ADHD.* "I'd like to think this over. Time to pray about it."

"Of course. Take all the time you need." She started to get up from the chair, then stopped and sat down again. "Being Amish is a wonderful thing when you fit in. It's a hard place when you don't. And it's a cold, dark place when you leave. My ADHD might have helped me through college and medical school, but it caused a lot of trouble in almost every other area of my life."

David glanced at his sister. They rarely spoke of that painful time.

"What worries me is that if Lydie doesn't get some help and guidance, she'll end up leaving the Amish."

"What?" David felt heat rise up his cheeks. This was the unspoken fear that had kept nipping at his heels these last few months. Lydie had never said a word about leaving, but the worry kept circling through his mind. He thought about it every day. "Has she said something to you?"

Dok opened her mouth, then closed it, as if she decided not to say what was on her mind. She pulled a folded paper out of her coat pocket and handed it to David. He opened it to find a

121

page full of Lydie's doodles. Different doodles were connected by arrows, with captions underneath each drawing. A Stoney Ridge bus led to Williamsport Clam Shack, underlined with the caption "A job!" The Williamsport Clam Shack arrow led to a little house, with "A place to live!"

This was how Lydie's mind worked. He'd found so many of these doodles over the years, but he'd never given them any thought. Never paid any attention to them, except for that Thanksgiving when his mother found the ones about her. It hadn't occurred to him before, but now he wondered if Lydie's doodling was a way to bring structure to her busy mind. A way of expressing her feelings. Her thoughts. And now her plans.

So, David realized with a drop in his stomach, she really was thinking of leaving. Preparing to leave.

Dok reached out and took the paper from his hand, folded it up, and slipped it back into her pocket. "Look, I don't want Lydie to leave the church. Honestly, my hunch is that she doesn't want to leave . . . she just wants to stop disappointing everyone . . . especially you. She's been trying to fit into the very defined role of an Amish woman and she just can't do it. No doubt she thinks that life would be easier for her outside of such rigid conformity, but the truth is she'd find herself in many of the same situations wherever she goes." She clapped her hands on her knees. "I get it. That's how I felt as a teenager. I could never measure up to expectations."

Their mother's expectations, she meant. "And so you left."

"And so I left." After a long moment, Dok added, "And I'd better get going now too." She rose, grinning. "Best of luck dealing with Mick Yoder and his father."

David's chin dropped to his chest.

10

It rained off and on all day. Just the kind of day Nathan needed. He had spent most of it in the greenhouse, preparing soil to sow seeds, moving trays from one row to another to adjust for direct sun exposure, watering, fertilizing with a compost tea he'd made, organizing, cleaning up. All the while, his mind was focused on preparing for the upcoming farmers' market. Opening day was only a week away.

Through the greenhouse glass, he saw the bishop drive up and park his buggy in front of the house, tie his horse to the post, and head to the house in a purposeful way. Then David paused at the bottom step of the porch and dipped his head. Nathan had seen him do that very thing often enough that he wondered if he was stopping to say a prayer. Just as abruptly, David lifted his head and went up the porch steps to knock on the door, but it opened before his fist could fall. His father must've seen or heard David's buggy. The two sat down on the porch bench.

Nathan had been planning to stop at the house to get a raincoat before he went to the fields but changed his mind. He had a funny feeling about the bishop's visit, and figured it was best to make himself scarce. As he walked out of the greenhouse, his dad's loud voice floated on the wind, something about Mick and Dok's office. No, something about Mick *in* Dok's office. Nathan stopped short when he heard his father mention Lydie's name.

Had Mick tangled Lydie up in some kind of trouble? A terrible feeling came over him, a feeling he struggled to deny, for it wasn't right to feel pleasure over someone's failings. But the feeling was there, nonetheless. Nathan felt relief. Maybe now, finally, Lydie would realize that Mick wasn't worthy of her. His fists fell to his side. Shame swept in for thinking such thoughts about his own brother, especially knowing what his father would have to say to Mick when he returned home. His father had no tolerance for failure. No forgiveness for mistakes.

Lydie, on the other hand, was far too accepting of others' shortcomings. Yet Nathan also admired that quality in her too. Once he'd asked her why she was so quick to give others the benefit of the doubt. "How could I not?" she'd answered. "How could I not when I have had so many shortcomings myself?" Such a humble response astounded him. Lydie was always surprising him like that. Convicting him, but without the sting. She made him a better man.

He wished Lydie realized how special she was, how unique. He wished she saw herself the way Nathan saw her.

But he also wished she held Mick to a higher standard than his brother held for himself. He wished she wouldn't excuse Mick so much. He let out a sigh. Frankly, he wished a lot of things for Lydie. He turned and went back into the greenhouse.

He wasn't sure how much time had passed when he realized his father stood not far off, waiting for him to notice he was there. He lowered the watering can and turned to him.

"Where's your brother?"

"I'm not sure," Nathan said. "I think he went to town on errands."

"Did you know that he's gone and got himself involved with drugs?"

"Drugs?" Now, involved with the drink, yes. Gsoffe. *Drunk*. Quite often. But drugs? Nathan shook his head. He didn't think Mick would go that far. But Owen Miller, he would go that far, and he had a strong influence over Mick. There'd be no point in telling that to Walt Yoder, though.

His father walked up and down the greenhouse aisle. He stopped to peer at young zucchini plants. "Those should be in the ground by now."

"Soon. I want to make sure the ground is warm enough for some of the heat-loving plants."

"Your brother's already planted his crops. All of them."

Yes, Nathan knew.

His father went to the greenhouse door and gazed out at Nathan's neatly tilled fields. Many of the rows held small green plants. Spikes of onions and leeks, small balls of cabbage, bush beans, carrot and radish tops. But many of the rows remained empty, waiting for plants. All part of Nathan's plan to give his fields a head start. When the night temperatures didn't dip below fifty degrees, then he'd get those heat-loving vegetables out of the greenhouse and into the rich soil, with all conditions ready to thrive. His dad had never said a word about the work Nathan had done to prepare his fields. Not a word. Never offered to help, either. Nathan wasn't really sure what his father was doing with his surfeit of spare time this spring. His dad just seemed restless and irritable lately, like he had a toothache. Like everything and everyone bothered him.

His dad shifted slightly to look at the path that led up to the Stoltzfus's home and made a grunting sound. He turned to lock eyes with Nathan. "Lydie Stoltzfus. She's the one to blame for this."

"Lydie?!" Nathan looked at his dad in disbelief. "How in the world do you figure that?"

"She's been working at Dok's office. No doubt she tempted Mick to the ways of the world."

Nathan shook his head, hard. "You've pegged her all wrong. She isn't like that."

Dad's long, wiry beard shook. "You and your brother—you both stay away from that girl."

Nathan knew that his dad had never been fond of Lydie, but lately his dislike had turned to downright hostility. He had always complained whenever she popped over to their house for a visit. She was too much for him. Too talkative, too fast moving, too quick to laugh.

All the things Nathan loved about Lydie.

⁓

Early Monday morning, Lydie startled awake to the sound of someone clapping hands over her bed, loud and insistent. Her eyes popped open. FIRE!

No. Only Mammi.

"Wacker warre! Wacker warre! Sie is allfatt schpot wacker warre." *Wake up! Wake up! You always wake up late.*

Groaning, Lydie pulled the pillow over her head. She'd had trouble getting to sleep last night, her busy mind swirling with thoughts about the day.

"Today is the day we start the Lydie Stoltzfus Improvement Project." Mammi yanked the pillow away and clapped again. "Today is Finish What You Start Day."

Lydie blinked a few times. "Finish What You Start Day?"

"Not me. You. Have you ever noticed how often you start things and never finish them?"

Lydie slipped her feet off the bed and started toward the bathroom, but Mammi stopped her.

"First, make the bed."

"But . . . I have to . . ."

Mammi gave a firm shake of her head. "I've been observing you."

Lydie's hands curled into fists. "Observing me?"

"Once you leave the bedroom, you realize you are running abysmally late, so you dash back and dress for the day, rush downstairs, grab a piece of toast, and dash off to town."

Now that Lydie thought about it, Mammi was right. She had just described a typical morning.

"The bed remains unmade, cupboards are left open, the knife and butter are forgotten on the counter. You leave chaos in your wake."

Lydie rubbed her eyes. This was a lot to take in before the sun had even risen.

"I have woken you an hour early, so there is plenty of time for you to calmly finish morning chores, sit with the family to eat a nourishing breakfast, and leave for work without acting as if your hair is on fire."

"That's how I act?"

"Every morning is an ongoing crisis."

Lydie returned to her bed to pull up the covers and fluff the pillow. She glanced at the clock, expecting to feel that familiar hitch of panic. It was only five o'clock in the morning. There was plenty of time.

"I'll return in ten minutes. You need to dress and make the bed before you leave this room."

Lydie quickly dressed. She turned to the bed and noticed a layer of dust on her small alarm clock and reached for the tissue box on the nightstand to wipe it down. There were no tissues. She was reading a book with a sad ending last night and used the last tissues to wipe away her tears. Why in the world did she bother reading such sad stories? She never slept well afterward. This one was about a girl who loved a boy who loved another girl. For some reason, her mind kept supplying an image of Patsy Glick as the other girl. Maybe it was because the author described the eyelashes of the other girl as thick fringe. Patsy had thick, dark lashes. They reminded Lydie of the family's beloved dairy cow, Moomoo, who died a few years back. Patsy, though, was no cow. Lydie headed to the door to get a new box of tissues from the hall closet. As she opened her bedroom door, there stood Mammi, standing guard, arms folded across her ample chest.

Mammi pointed past Lydie. "The bed!"

Lydie looked over her shoulder at it. "What about it?"

"You haven't finished making it."

"I will. I just thought I'd get a fresh box of tissues."

Mammi let out a loud sigh. "What is today?"

"Monday. Isn't it?" She thought it was. Yesterday was an off-Sunday, she knew that much. A yawn escaped from her.

Mammi's eyes closed briefly, as if she was sending up a prayer for patience. "Yes, it is Monday. But today is also FINISH WHAT YOU START Day."

Good grief. Mammi spent way too much time around Edith. She was starting to sound as loud as Hank Lapp.

"*That's* the problem with you, Lydie. You start something, then get distracted by something else, and you never return to finish what you start. It's a terrible habit. It must be stopped. Today. Whatever you start today—any little thing—you must finish."

Lydie returned to the bed to pull the bedspread up, tucking it under the pillow. She smoothed out wrinkles and stepped back to examine it, satisfied. "There. Perfect."

"Not perfect," Mammi said, as she smoothed out another wrinkle. "Nothing is ever perfect."

Nope. Not where Mammi is concerned.

"But good enough for day one. Now you may have breakfast."

Lydie darted out the door and down the stairs, bolting through the front door without stopping for breakfast. She dreaded facing Dok this morning after the baking soda incident; she was sure she was going to be fired. But if she had to choose between Mammi and Dok, she'd rather face Dok.

If you'd asked Nathan two weeks ago what worried him most about starting a farmers' market, he would've said finding vendors to fill the booths. As it turned out, that was astonishingly easy, largely because David had recommended limiting the number of vendors to twenty for this summer. That had been especially helpful information to have when Owen Miller stopped by Black Gold Farm early Monday morning, found Nathan in the greenhouse, and told him he wanted a booth.

"Why?"

"To provide information about what my dad and I have to offer the farmers." He handed Nathan a brochure. It listed all the pests that the Millers promised to eradicate from the land. The planet.

"I'm sorry, Owen. The booths are all spoken for."

"Name your price. We'll pay."

"It's not about money. All vendors are providing food that's locally grown. Fresh or preserved. That was a decision made by the committee."

Owen didn't like that answer.

Hank Lapp didn't like Nathan's response to his request for a booth, either. He wanted to sell junk he'd found in the attic. "Hank, this is a farmers' market. Not a flea market."

That offended the old man. "ONE man's JUNK is another man's TREASURE."

"Whatever it is you call it, it's not edible."

Hank didn't like being left out. The next day he arrived at Black Gold Farm with another pitch. "I'm PLANNING to sell my EDITH's prickly pear PRESERVES. We SEEM to have an ABUNDANCE in the PANTRY."

Nathan had to look away to hide his grin. Edith Fisher Lapp was known for her prickly pear preserves and not in a good way. First off, they tasted terrible. Second, after years of making the preserves and giving jars away to friends (who fed the preserves to their hogs), she never seemed to catch on to the irony. *She* was the prickly pear.

"Hank, here's what I'm going to do. All the booths are taken. But if you want to set up a card table, you can sell Edith's jars." He could try, anyway.

"DONE!" And Hank left happy.

Everything David had said about the ready support for the Stoney Ridge Farmers' Market had been spot-on. It just needed someone to get the ball rolling. Nathan felt downright embarrassed when others complimented him on the hard work of setting it up, because all the vendors lent a hand, all did their part to ensure a successful market. So far, Nathan felt blessed by saying yes to the bishop's request.

He hoped that sense of blessing wouldn't fade after the market's rapidly approaching opening date. All Nathan needed now was to keep his plants growing, thriving, producing . . . without chemicals. One thing he had come to realize: there was no way Nathan was going to be able to outproduce Mick's GMO corn. No possible way. But if he did well by selling baby produce and heirloom vegetables, he hoped to bring home cash. A lot of it. And that would get his father's attention. Money always did.

Lydie could hardly believe that Dok wanted her to keep working as her temporary receptionist. She had fully braced herself to be fired. She deserved to be let go! "Dok, why aren't you firing me? I really blew it." Worse than usual.

Dok's hands were on her medical bag, but she paused. "You made a mistake by letting Mick stay in the office unattended. But it was Mick who blew it."

Still, it was Lydie who had given Mick an opportunity to blow it.

On her way home that evening, she spotted Mick's buggy in front of the hardware store and went inside to find him. He was in the back, looking at hammers. He looked up when he saw her.

"I got you in trouble, didn't I?"

"Nah," he said, shrugging it off.

"I told Dok it was you. Dok told Dad. Dad told your father. And now you're not only having to sit on the sinner's bench next Sunday, but you're getting baptized and joining the church. And all because you stole baking soda!"

"How'd you hear about the baptism?"

"Your mom came in for an appointment with Dok today. She mentioned it. She seemed pleased." Overjoyed, actually. Sarah Yoder wasn't one to show much emotion, but she struck Lydie as practically giddy over the news.

"It was one of two options. Dad said I could get baptized now or he would hand over the entire farm to Nathan, lock, stock, and barrel." He lifted his shoulders in a careless shrug. "Getting baptized makes Mom happy. So why not?"

Why not? Lots of reasons. "But, Mick . . . why would you rifle through Dok's pharmaceutical cabinet?"

Mick lifted his palms in the air. "Stupid thing to do, I know." He clapped his hands together. "On a cheerier note, are you making any progress with Patsy?"

"Patsy?"

He frowned. "I figured you'd forgotten your promise. Look, there's another party on Saturday. I thought you could, you know, grease the wheel for me this week. Put in a good word."

Lydie's jaw dropped open. "Wait just a minute. Doesn't getting baptized mean anything to you?" It meant so much to her! So very, very much. That's why she hadn't done it.

"Sure it does. It means I have to be"—he tapped his forehead with his finger—"far more clever."

"What about the Clam Shack in Maryland? What about leaving?" *What about me?*

He grinned. "That was before I was handed the golden opportunity to beat my brother out of Black Gold Farm."

"You don't even like farming."

"Livestock's not too bad. At least sheep and cows have some personality. Vegetables aren't exactly the life of the party." He turned somber, for once. "Farming is all I know."

Lydie heard someone in another aisle mention the time, and she remembered Mammi's complaint that she was always late for supper. She was! "I'd better go." She started down the aisle toward the front door until she heard Mick call out her name. She pivoted.

Mick bounced his bushy eyebrows. "Talk to Patsy. Put in a good word for me. Convince her to say yes when I ask her to the party."

She threw up her hands. "Patsy is not a party girl!"

Mick didn't listen. He never did.

By the time Lydie reached home, Mammi was at the kitchen table, an unhappy look on her face. "You're late."

"Sorry." She didn't even bother to explain. She washed up at the kitchen sink, dried her hands on a towel, and slipped into her seat. "Where's Dad?"

Mammi gave a deep sigh. "Delivering a death message to Edwin Miller. His eldest sister passed away today."

"Whoa! Edwin Miller is so old. Imagine how old his sister must've been."

Mammi scowled at her. She didn't like discussing old age. She dipped her chin in a silent prayer and Lydie followed suit. When Mammi lifted her head, she handed Lydie a platter of pork roast. As Lydie forked a slice onto her plate, Mammi said, "On Saturday morning, I'm going to a Comfort Quilting at

Edith Lapp's house. You'll come too. It will give you a chance to improve Edith's impression of you."

Think, think, think! Lydie's eyes landed on the bowl of apple-sauce. "Oh, I so wish I could . . . but I can't." Just as Mammi opened her mouth to object, Lydie added, "I need to help Dad at the farmers' market. Grand opening this Saturday, you know." She hadn't given any thought to going, but now she definitely planned to be there. In fact, she would plan to be there every week. Each Saturday, until she left Stoney Ridge for the Clam Shack in Maryland . . . which felt a little less of a sure thing after talking to Mick at the hardware store. A lot less.

11

⁂

I t was five in the morning. The sky was just starting to lighten
when Nathan heard the first birdsong of the day. He'd been
up since three a.m., working away in the greenhouse, snip-
ping baby greens into plastic bins. His hands were raw from
the repetitive action of the scissors, but he was pleased to see
that there were few, if any, bugs on the greens. Still, he would
give everything a once-over look as he scooped the greens into
plastic bags to sell at today's market. Quality counted. Pretty
food, the lady with gray braids called it. If he could sell each
bag for four dollars, he didn't care what it was called.

By seven o'clock, Nathan had arrived at the site of the Stoney
Ridge Farmers' Market. The grand opening. While waiting for
other vendors to arrive, he unpacked bins of produce from his
wagon and stacked them on top of his farmstand. So maybe
calling it a farmstand was a generous description. Nathan had
been too busy with the fields and the market to think about
his own stand until this morning, when it dawned on him that
he needed some kind of tabletop. He grabbed two sawhorses
from the barn and found an old door in an empty stall used

for storage. He set the door on top of the sawhorses. That was the extent of his stand.

As other vendors arrived and set up their booths, he tried not to beat himself up for how feeble his stand looked in comparison. Most of the vendors had brought portable canopies to frame their booths, complete with foldable tables. He also noticed that most vendors had signage near or on their booth. He had nothing. He found a large piece of cardboard near a trash bin, and with a borrowed permanent marker, he wrote BLACK GOLD FARM. He set it against one sawhorse and stood back to see how bad it looked. Pretty bad.

Then he heard Lydie's voice. He spun around. She was over at Hank Lapp's card table, helping him set out his jars of prickly pear preserves. He'd known her most of his life, but sometimes out of nowhere the sight of her could snatch his breath and make his chest hurt. She turned toward him, as if she sensed she was being watched, and their eyes locked for a moment, before he lifted his hand in a wave. "I didn't think you'd be here."

Still holding a jar of preserves, she walked toward him. "Thought I'd come and help out. Plus, it gives me an excuse to stay clear of Mammi."

He smiled. "Is your dad around?"

"He's here somewhere. Shall I go get him?"

Nathan shook his head. "No, I just figured he'd be here." Unlike his own father, who showed no interest in the farmers' market.

"Exciting, isn't it?" Lydie smiled, and it seemed like the sky grew a little brighter. "I hope today is a great success and everyone sells out before quitting time."

"Pile them high and watch them fly." Seeing the confused look on her face, Nathan explained. "That's what an experienced vendor taught me. Pile your produce high and watch it fly out of here."

She looked past him to his door on the sawhorses. "Where's your price list?"

D'oh! He slapped his palm against his forehead. He should've thought about that kind of stuff. All he'd thought about was preparing his baby greens. "I forgot to make a list."

"But how are you going to differentiate yourself from any other booth?"

"Oh, that's easy. A couple of ways. My vegetables are pesticide free. Not organic certified, but as close as you can get. And I'm selling a lot of baby produce."

"Baby produce?"

"Bagged salad. Four dollars a bag."

"But how will buyers know?" She slid a telling glance at his cardboard sign. "From that?"

Nathan tipped his hat back. "The market doesn't open until nine. I have time to make some improvements."

"Maybe I could help."

"That would be great. Just great." He reached up to straighten a capstring that had twisted on her shoulder, and as he did, his fingers grazed her neck. They were standing so close together that he could see a muscle twitch in her cheek.

"Lydie! Come on. I need you down here."

The sound of his brother's voice broke the intimacy of the moment. Mick was standing at the far end of the long row of stands, waving to Lydie to join him. She turned to look at Mick, and as she turned, she backed away, out of Nathan's reach.

"Go," he said. "Go on. I'll figure something out."

For a split second, she hesitated, then she left him to go meet up with Mick and see what he wanted. Mick wanted *her*, that's what he wanted. Anything Mick wanted, he got.

Nathan felt foolish, watching the two of them, and turned back to his pathetic cardboard sign.

Five minutes before nine o'clock, after helping vendors unload boxes of produce from their cars or buggies, helping others find the location of their booths and set them up, Nathan hurried back to his own stand to finish setting up his produce. Ten feet away, he faltered to a stop. Someone had set out a large chalkboard on an easel and written BLACK GOLD FARM ALMOST-ORGANIC PRODUCE in large, bold lettering. He walked up to the easel and noticed a list of the baby greens for sale. Then he lifted his head and saw that all his clear plastic produce bags had been stacked on the ledge that rimmed the interior of the stand. The whole thing looked . . . pretty professional. As professional as a door on top of two sawhorses could look. He'd had no such concept in mind for his own stand. Frankly, he had nothing in mind for his stand other than trying to sell his bags of baby greens. He was a routine guy. Creative thinking wasn't in his box of tools. But he knew someone who oozed creativity.

Lydie. He knew it was Lydie.

He almost didn't feel the touch of a hand on his shoulder, so light it was, so tentative. He turned, thinking he'd find Lydie, but there was Patsy Glick. She was pressing her fingers to her lips and widening her eyes. "It's just what you needed, don't you think?" She held a piece of chalk up in her delicate hand.

"You?" Patsy? She did this for him?

She lifted her eyebrows in that mysterious way. "People shouldn't be buying from you out of pity."

Pity? Ouch. Nathan swallowed once, then twice.

Suddenly David Stoltzfus was coming toward him. "Nathan! It's nine o'clock. Time for the market manager to open the market. Customers are waiting."

People were milling everywhere, more than he had anticipated. Lots of bonnets and beards, but lots of baseball caps too. That's just what David Stoltzfus had hoped for—to bring the Amish and Englisch communities together.

David laughed. "Nathan, you're the market manager. Go ring the bell."

Me! He meant me. Wow. I'm the market manager. Nathan

sprinted to the bell at the front of the market and rang it loudly. The first day of the Stoney Ridge Farmers' Market had begun.

Nathan's booth was tucked at the end of a long row of the U-shaped market. He had let other vendors choose their location, which meant he ended up with the one that no one else wanted. Unfortunate. He saw customer after customer load up their baskets or bags and turn to leave before reaching his stand. He also regretted letting Hank Lapp set up his rickety card table as his kitty-corner neighbor. Hank kept yelling at people to come and sample his prickly pear preserves and the opposite happened. His voice was so loud that he made children cry. Dogs barked. Customers fled.

Or maybe it had something to do with the vendor on the other side of Hank's card table. She called herself Chatty Kathy, an apt name. He noticed customers started veering around her booth. Chatty Kathy felt compelled to tell her entire life story to each person who strolled by.

Whatever the cause, Nathan spent the first hour of the farmers' market without a single customer. Not one.

And then a shift occurred, and Nathan started to wonder if there might be a rhythm to farmers' markets. Early-to-arrive customers knew exactly what they wanted. They found it and left. But then another group arrived. The lingerers. Or maybe these were the foodies whom the lady in gray braids talked about. In no particular hurry, they wandered from booth to booth at a leisurely pace, slowly making their way around the entire U-shaped market, interested in what each booth had to offer. Even Hank Lapp's wobbly card table full of unsold jars of prickly pear preserves, though Hank had lost interest during the first hour and wandered off. When the lingerers came to Nathan's booth, they would pause to sample his baby greens. After a taste, they would ask him questions.

How was it grown? Organically, though his farm was in the

process of getting certified. No pesticides, no fertilizers other than natural locally sourced soil amendments.

Where was it grown? Three miles from town out at Black Gold Farm.

When was it picked? Just hours ago.

Who grew it? Nathan pointed to himself. "I'm the farmer who grew these greens."

Satisfied, they would buy a bag or two. And then they would tell their friends. By eleven o'clock, miraculously, there was a small line forming in front of his stand. By noon, before ringing the bell to announce closing time, he had sold out.

Sold out! On the very first day.

Lydie hadn't planned to spend the entire morning as Fern Lapp's personal assistant at the farmers' market, but Fern needed someone to help sell her jams and jellies. She'd gotten a little hard of hearing lately, and her booth had a line snaking down the wide market aisle. Hank Lapp came over to see what was stealing his customers (his words), and he ended up staying, sampling each jar, offering his opinion on each flavor in a loud voice. Happily, he loved each one. "FERN, you are a MASTER in the KITCHEN." His lip-smacking proclamations only brought in more customers, curious to see what the ruckus was all about. Fern's line grew longer.

And suddenly, the market bell rang for closing time.

"LYDIE! FERN! HERE'S a JOKE for you. Why shouldn't you TELL a SECRET on a farm?"

The two women stopped packing up unsold jars in a box to look at Hank. "Why not?" Fern said.

"Because the POTATOES have EYES and the corn has EARS!"

Fern did not find Hank's little joke as entertaining as he had hoped, but Lydie gave him a mercy laugh and that was all he needed. She glanced over at his card table, full of prickly pear jam jars. She had a hunch he hadn't even sold one, especially after he put samples of it out for people to taste. "Maybe you should sell jokes."

Hank hooted. "There's an IDEA!"

Lydie turned around to see if Nathan was still at his stand . . . if you could call it an actual stand. It was barely an improvement over Hank's wobbly table. She wished she'd thought to help him make a booth. She should have known that would be the last thing on Nathan's mind. So was claiming a good location for his stand. He'd let the other vendors have their pick, she knew he did. He was unselfish like that.

When Lydie saw that awful cardboard sign leaning against the sawhorse, she wanted to fix it, to find a better table and maybe even a canopy and a wooden sign that was worthy of his wonderful greens. She nearly said as much but bit her lip and said nothing. Mammi had told her to stop making promises, at least not unless she knew she could keep them. If she'd had more time, she could've done more, but in less than an hour before the market opened, there was no way she could do much more than scribble on the chalkboard easel she'd run to buy at the hardware store and straighten up his bags of greens. It was something, at least.

Mick sauntered up the aisle and Lydie waved him over. "Can you help us get these boxes into Fern's buggy?"

"I'll do that," he whispered, "while you talk me up to Patsy. She's coming your way." He took a box in his arms and headed toward the parking lot, where Fern's buggy lined up beside other buggies. The tethered horses stood patiently waiting under a large shade tree.

Someone called Lydie's name and she whipped around to see Patsy Glick. All five foot two of her. Not just short, she was thin and as cute as a proverbial button. "Lydie, thanks for letting Nathan think I made the Black Gold chalkboard sign for him. You're the best."

"You? He thinks you made it?"

She held up the piece of chalk Lydie had used on the chalkboard easel. "Isn't that why you handed the chalk to me and told me to wait right there?" She smiled. "It had just the effect on Nathan that you'd planned. You're a true friend."

No, not really. She'd had to help Fern for a minute but planned to hurry right back to put some finishing touches on Nathan's sign. And then she completely forgot all about the sign, and all about Patsy.

Right at that moment, Nathan walked by them with his plastic bins—now empty, Lydie gathered, from the way he held them in one hand—and did a double take when he saw Patsy. "Thanks again. That sign made all the difference today."

"It was just what your stand needed, Nathan." Patsy gave him her most charming smile.

Lydie's eyes went wide. *Seriously?*

"Patsy, I was thinking, it'd be nice to have another chalkboard easel right at the entrance of the market. Welcoming folks, maybe state the hours. I'll buy everything you need." He handed Patsy a slip of paper from his coat pocket. "I was thinking that this might be a good motto for the market."

Patsy read aloud: "Farmers' markets are the taste of the home garden." She held the slip of paper against her chest with a sigh. "It's an ideal motto. Nathan, you are a wonder. I'll be happy to take care of this sign for you, if you don't mind bringing the chalkboard over to my house one day."

"I'll bring it over this afternoon." He blushed, and Patsy batted her eyelashes in return, and Lydie choked back a gag.

His eyes lifted over Patsy's head to look at Fern. "Each time I looked your way, I saw a long line."

"Those little baby green bags of yours were the talk of the town. No one around here ever thought to eat baby produce." Fern walked over and gave him a motherly pat on his arm. "We all owe you a thank-you, Nathan. This market wouldn't have happened without you." She pointed to a *Stoney Ridge Times* reporter who'd been wandering the market, taking photographs and talking to vendors. "I told him that very thing. He couldn't believe you were selling a bag of baby lettuce for four dollars."

Nathan's Adam's apple bobbed above his open collar. He glanced at Lydie, dropped his head in a brief nod, looking embarrassed by the compliment, then went on his way.

Patsy sidled up to Lydie and whispered, "Come to my house this week to make the sign."

"Me? You told him you'd do it."

"No. I said I'd take care of it. I'm doing just that." She squeezed Lydie's forearm. "Remember your promise."

"It wasn't a promise," Lydie said, but Patsy had scurried off to catch up with Nathan.

Fern's eyes narrowed. "What's that all about?"

Lydie turned to her. Fern's hard of hearing–ness was surprisingly selective. Before she could think of how to answer, Hank Lapp bellowed for Fern to sample a taste of Edith's prickly pear preserves. He held up a spoon and an open jar. "Why aren't FOLKS buying this fine combustible?"

Fern sighed. "For that very reason."

Lydie leaned forward. "I think you meant to say condiment."

"What DID I say?"

"Combustible. It means flammable."

"NO KIDDING?" He twisted his head to look down the aisle at his card table. "Blast that Mick Yoder. HE'S the one who TOLD me to use that word. He even WROTE it OUT for me."

"Serves you right for asking Mick Yoder to help you with advertising." Fern turned her attention to the reporter as he ambled by. "I'm going to go tell him that Nathan sold out of everything. He should be sure to write that up in his article." She took two steps, then pivoted, a question on her face. "That doesn't sound prideful, does it?"

"Not if you just state the facts," Lydie said. "Besides, you're only trying to encourage folks to come to the market."

Fern spun around and hurried after the reporter.

Hank watched her go, his hands on his hips, then slowly turned back to Lydie. "I WONDERED why a fellow asked if it could SUBSTITUTE in a pinch for LIGHTER FLUID." Then he brightened. "Maybe that's the way I can get rid of this stuff. We've got jars and jars of it in the basement. Next week, I'll promote it as BBQ Starter!" He laughed and went back to his table to pack up.

Lydie's mind was spinning on a doodle of the scenario. She couldn't wait to find a piece of paper and a pencil.

12

Hindsight is always 20/20. Lydie was well aware of that adage, but it held new meaning for her on Wednesday of the following week, when the edition of the *Stoney Ridge Times* was published and delivered.

Last Saturday, instead of going home with her dad after the farmers' market closed, she decided to stay in town. She went to the Sweet Tooth Bakery and sat in the corner, doodling a sketch of Hank at his wobbly card table, eagerly selling jars with flames coming off their lids. The caption read "Jam for sale! Doubles as lighter fluid!"

If only she had made herself wait a day or so before popping it into the *Stoney Ridge Times* mail slot. Maybe she would've thought to disguise Hank's very recognizable wild-haired appearance. She might've thought to not make it a jar of jam but something else, something that didn't point so obviously to Edith Lapp's horrible prickly pear jam.

If she'd waited a few days, she might not have even submitted it. She might have considered how much attention the brand-new Stoney Ridge Farmers' Market would be getting in this week's edition of the newspaper—after all, it was big news for a little town—and she would've realized that, of course, the doodle would be positioned alongside the story, right beside photographs taken of the market.

But she didn't do any of those things. Instead, she finished the doodle, carefully folded it, and left the bakery to head home. When she passed by the *Stoney Ridge Times* mail slot, she remembered that she'd run out of postage stamps at home and Mammi had asked her to buy more when she was in town, but she'd forgotten. Envelopes too. So, thinking only of the fact that it would be Monday before she could get to the post office, she popped the doodle into the slot. And then she forgot all about it.

It wasn't until Wednesday, after the newspaper was printed and distributed, and patients in the waiting room were laughing over the cartoon on page 12, that she realized submitting the doodle might have been a bad idea.

David was in the phone shanty, waiting for Birdy to call for their Wednesday evening catch-up. As he waited, he skimmed today's copy of the *Stoney Ridge Times*, particularly interested in the article about the debut of the farmers' market. It was remarkably positive, almost over the top, especially about the spearheading of the market by young Amishman Nathan Yoder. The rest of the article focused mostly on Nathan, noting that his baby greens produce was unique to the other vendors, that the greens tasted remarkable, and that he sold out before closing. And then the article shifted to the growing interest of consumers to eat locally grown food, including organically grown produce, and the ability of farmers' markets to meet consumers' demands. It carried over to page 12, but when David turned to it, the page was missing.

He wondered about the quality of the newspaper's printing service, but then the phone rang and he forgot all about the newspaper and the farmers' market as he spent the next hour getting caught up with Birdy. He missed his wife.

∽

Apparently, Patsy Glick didn't trust Lydie to remember to come to her house and draw a chalkboard sign for Nathan. It was just as well, because Lydie had completely forgotten about it. On Monday afternoon, Patsy arrived at Dok's office at five o'clock, plunked Lydie's scooter in the back of the buggy, and ordered her inside.

"I really should go home first," Lydie said, feeling as if she'd just become a hostage to this petite blond kidnapper. "My grandmother is expecting me." Sadly.

"Not to worry. I stopped by your house to tell your grandmother not to expect you home until late tonight."

"Late? Why? The sign shouldn't take me much time."

"Signs." Patsy gave her a smug look. "Loads of signs. Nathan dropped off twenty chalkboards. One for each vendor. No, twenty-one. He wants one for the entry to the market."

"What?! How did that happen?"

"I guess one vendor talked to another and another, and they all loved the sign I did for Nathan. They want one too."

Lydie's eyebrows shot up. "The sign *you* did?"

"Now remember, you promised to help me capture Nathan's heart."

But I never did! "Patsy, that's not what I—"

"And these signs are just the thing." She handed Lydie an unsealed envelope. "In that is the information that each vendor wants on their chalkboard. Nathan wants all of them in a different font. Do you know what that means?"

With a sigh, Lydie nodded.

"I have all the chalkboards set up behind the barn so my folks and little brothers won't see you. And I even bought you a new package of chalk. Colored chalk."

From the look on Patsy's face, Lydie got the impression that she expected to be thanked.

Nearing the Glicks' driveway, Patsy slowed the buggy to drop Lydie off on the road. She pointed to a small path that led to the barn. "Don't forget the chalk."

Lydie hesitated. "Patsy, I haven't eaten much today." Hardly anything. She'd forgotten her lunch and only ate a stale granola bar she'd found in her desk.

"I'll sneak something out to you." Patsy tucked a curl under her cap. "If I can."

Lydie made her way up the steep path and found twenty-one chalkboards in a row, propped up against the barn's foundation, just as Patsy had said. She kneeled in front of the first one. Reading through Nathan's instructions, she wrote out: WELCOME TO THE STONEY RIDGE FARMERS' MARKET. SATURDAY MORNINGS, 9–12. Underneath she added: FARMERS' MARKETS ARE THE TASTE OF THE HOME GARDEN.

Satisfied, she got up and went to the second one. She decided to do the easiest ones first, like Fern's—she only sold jams and jellies. Lydie spent time doodling an open jar with a spoon in it, then added plump red strawberries around the base of the jar. Next she drew Hank's two-in-one prickly pear jam, adding bursting firecrackers in the top corners. She became so absorbed in doodling, she didn't even hear a small boy come up behind her until he sneezed and she startled. One of Patsy's little brothers? She had quite a few. Patsy was the eldest and had no sisters, which was a pity.

"You made a mistake," he said.

Yup. Definitely Patsy's brother. "Did I?"

"You put an extra L in jellies."

So she had. She picked up the corner of her apron and wiped it away. "Aren't you supposed to be having your supper?"

"Yes, he is," Patsy said, coming around the barn. "Benny, you keep quiet about this."

He lifted his palm. "It'll cost you a dollar."

Scowling, Patsy handed him a dollar. "Not a word to anyone." Benny pocketed the dollar and disappeared around the corner of the barn. "I brought you an apple."

One measly apple?

Patsy examined the chalkboards. "Only three are done? You'd better hurry before you lose sunlight." She hurried off without another word.

Lydie sat cross-legged on the ground and ate the apple, which was disappointingly mushy. She moved down the line to the fourth, to the lady who talked your ear off but sold beautiful vegetables. Inspired, she drew a border of vegetables just inside the frame, then colored them in. A purple eggplant, bright orange carrots, green spears of asparagus.

"WHAT? You're only on the fourth one?"

Lydie jerked at the sound of Patsy's voice. She hadn't even heard her sneak up. Patsy stood behind her with fists on her hips. A mini-Mammi.

"You're taking too long!"

"I'm trying to make each one unique to the vendor." And the more she thought about the vendor, the more elaborate her doodling grew.

"All Nathan asked for was a different font."

"I'm pretty sure he'll be pleased." She knew he would be.

Frowning, Patsy said, "Well, you're just going to have to come back tomorrow night and finish." She let out a huff. "I left your scooter down by the road. You should get on home before it gets any darker." She waved her hand like she was dismissing a servant.

Lydie looked over at the sun, which had disappeared behind a fringe of treetops. Night was fast approaching. How did time go so fast? She had no idea. But she did have fun.

The next day at five o'clock, Patsy was waiting for her outside of Dok's office. "Get in," she ordered. "You were right.

Nathan stopped by today and said he likes the direction we're going with the signs."

"*We're* going?"

"So you can take all the time you need as long as they're done by Saturday morning. I'll come and get you when you're done at work each afternoon so we can maximize the sunlight."

There was that *we* again. "Sounds like I'm going to be missing supper each night."

"Don't worry. I told your grandmother that you're helping me with an important project. She was very pleased that we're spending time together." She smiled. "Your grandmother thinks I'm a wonderful influence on you. She said so."

I'll bet she did, Lydie thought.

⁓

Locking up the Bent N' Dent for the day, David kept thinking about the earlier conversation he'd had with Fern Lapp. She had dropped in the Bent N' Dent to stock up on spices. She casually mentioned that Lydie helped her sell jams and jellies at the farmers' market last Saturday. "We make a good team," Fern said. "She did just fine, as long as I didn't leave her on her own. Lydie reminds me of a helium balloon that can drift away in the wind." Her eyebrows met in the middle. "I suppose that makes me the weight that keeps her pinned down." Fern wasn't trying to be caustic, but David felt the sting, nonetheless.

He heard a car pull in the parking lot and turned around. Dok had arrived. He walked down the porch steps to say hello.

Instead of returning his hello, she said, "Have you changed your mind about getting Lydie tested for ADHD?"

He backed up a step. Maybe he shouldn't have bothered to say hello.

"David, when someone has ADHD, it's like a carpenter without tools. A farmer without a horse. They're missing some key components to manage the big picture."

He frowned. He definitely should've stayed in the store.

"Here's another way of thinking about how Lydie's mind works. Imagine a cook in the kitchen, making a pot roast. She has an hour before dinner will be served. She has ingredients but no recipe. She dashes around the kitchen to find the salt and pepper, then remembers the meat is in the freezer and requires six hours to defrost. She forgets to preheat the oven until the very last minute. She has everything she needs to succeed, but everything she does is out of sequence. Can you see?"

"Yes. Dinner isn't going to happen on time." He let out a sigh. Okay, he was starting to get the point his sister was driving home. "In fact, dinner might not happen at all."

"Yes! Exactly. And yet she desperately wants to get that pot roast on the table, right when everyone arrives to eat. She just can't manage the whole thing. Not without some help."

"I'm not disagreeing with your assessment. Just on how to help her."

"Well," Dok said, "have you read the book I gave you?"

"Not yet."

Dok frowned. "If you want to help your daughter, start there."

⁓

Thanks to the newspaper article that featured the opening of the farmers' market, the second Saturday brought in double the customers, like bees to blossoms. And it was good timing, because early summer produce was starting to show up. At least, a lot of it was on display at Chatty Kathy's booth.

Hank Lapp was suspicious, convinced that she was schlepping in produce from a Southern state. "NO ONE has RIPE STRAWBERRIES in MAY in Stoney Ridge."

Chatty Kathy dismissed him with a wave of her hand. "You just stick to your . . . whatever it is you're selling, and I'll take care of mine."

It did give Nathan pause to see the colorful bounty on Chatty

Kathy's stand. The market was set up to benefit local farmers, and it was unlikely that most of her produce would be ripe by now, even if she grew them in a greenhouse. Like tomatoes, this early in the season. Cantaloupe, watermelon, cucumbers for pickling. How did she do it? Still, customers were delighted to get a hint of the coming summer. Nathan decided to let it go this week but to have a conversation with Chatty Kathy after the closing bell. Better still, let David talk to her about where her produce had been grown.

When he returned to his humble stand, he winced. The only new produce he had to add to his stand this week were baby carrots with their fernlike tops. Well, give it time. He'd planted the rest of his forty acres this last week, and things were looking promising. The weather was warm but not hot, and there'd been light rainfall each night.

In his mind's eye, it wouldn't be long before he'd be harvesting bushels of melons, heirloom tomatoes, cucumbers, celery, basil and parsley, squash, peppers, radishes and carrots, and, of course, flowers. He wanted to cover the whole alphabet, from asparagus to zucchini, all ripening at the same time . . . which he knew was impossible but, still, a farmer could dream.

Sun or rain, Nathan loved every minute of the market. He recognized customers from last week. During slow moments, he mentally divided people into categories: There were those who had to touch everything before they bought. There were frazzled moms pushing strollers that blocked the aisle. Bikers, too, who thought nothing of pushing their bicycles through the crowds. There were older ladies with those purse dogs—little dogs in actual clothing. There were pretend shoppers who came for free samples. And then there were his favorite type: those who intentionally sought out organic produce, examined it, and applauded him for growing such fine-looking greens.

The vendors were also easy to categorize. Most farmers loved growing things but couldn't care less about selling them. But there were a few, like Chatty Kathy, who seemed a little too slick to be a farmer. A little too savvy. The most successful combination, Nathan decided, was a Mennonite couple named Mose and Martha Lehman. Their booth was right at the market's opening, something they'd paid extra to secure. Mose was the curmudgeonly type, a man of few words, though his finely displayed produce spoke volumes. His wife, Martha, couldn't be more congenial. She greeted each customer like a long-lost friend. Their booth had a lengthy, enviable line. Watching them behind their stand, for one split second their faces blurred, then reappeared as Nathan's and Lydie's. That familiar feeling of longing, of loss, started to spiral in his middle and spread to every part of his being. To shake it off, he shuddered, rubbed his eyes, then turned to greet a customer.

❦

Hank Lapp did not bring any jars of prickly pear jam to sell at this week's market. He erased the bursting firecrackers that Lydie had made on his sign and wrote in JOKES FOR SALE. 10 CENTS EACH.

Lydie was helping Fern set up her jams on her stand as she heard Hank's booming voice ring out. "I DON'T have ALZHEIMER's. I have SOME-TIMERS. SOMETIMES I remember and SOMETIMES I DON'T!" He held out an empty jar to a young fellow with a bicycle who, curious, had stopped to listen to a joke. The biker took pity on Hank and stuffed a dollar in the jar. But when Hank started to tell him another joke, he got on his bicycle and rode off.

When there was a lull between customers at Fern's stand, Lydie said, "What's happened to Hank's jams?"

"Edith saw that cartoon in the newspaper and was not amused." Fern took a few more jars of jelly out of a box. "She's determined to find out who drew it and give them a piece of her mind."

"Oh?" Lydie busied herself with setting the jars in a straight line.

"After seeing these chalkboards, I'd say she's got a pretty good idea of who's responsible."

"Think so?" Lydie's voice had a wobble to it.

"Edith's gone to find her right now." Fern cracked a rare smile. "Who would've thought Patsy had a little mischief in her?" She pointed down the aisle, to where Edith towered over the tiny blond, giving her a stern lecture.

Oh no. Lydie had one of those terrible feelings, like something bad was about to happen. She hadn't meant to get Patsy in trouble. Just then, a large family came up and asked to sample each flavor of Fern's jams, and after they had bought several jars, Lydie looked up, and Edith and Patsy were gone.

As soon as she finished emptying the last box, she told Fern she'd be right back, ignoring Fern's eye roll in response. She hurried over to find Patsy at her mother's stand. "I heard Edith Lapp was looking for you."

"The nerve of that woman! She accused me of being the one who drew that cartoon about her awful jam."

"What did you tell her?"

Patsy smiled a knowing smile. "That everyone knows the cartoonist is the *Stoney Ridge Times* reporter."

Lydie's eyes went wide. "Everyone thinks he's the one behind the drawings?"

"Of course. He's the one who's always poking around. Taking pictures of us even though he knows we don't like it." She gave Lydie an odd look. Smiling, but not really. "Who else could it be?"

Lydie swallowed a grin. This was a wonderful turn of events! While watching the vendors at the market this morning, another doodle idea had popped into her head. She couldn't wait to find a quiet spot and sketch it before she forgot it. She slipped off to a place where no one could find her—Fern's buggy.

She had no idea how much time had passed when she heard an angry voice. A familiar, angry voice. "Tell your brother to shut his trap about his organic kick."

Sitting in the passenger seat of the buggy, Lydie popped her head up. Through the windshield she saw Owen Miller shouting at Mick Yoder, though Mick wasn't arguing back.

"Oh, come on, Owen," Mick said in that smooth-as-silk voice he used to calm his sheep down whenever they got jittery. "Nathan doesn't have that kind of influence over anybody, especially not farmers."

Lydie, who had been listening with increasing interest, now broke into the conversation. "He does, actually."

The two whirled around to locate her overly loud interruption. She popped her head out of the window, and Owen's eyes narrowed in recognition. "You. You're the girl from Dok Stoltzfus's office."

"She's not a girl," Mick said. "Lydie's my neighbor."

Ignoring him, Lydie said, "People are impressed by Nathan's farming methods. Really, really impressed. And he doesn't consider organic farming to be a *kick*."

"Lydie," Mick said in a warning voice.

"He truly believes that it's better for farmers to stop using pesticides and fertilizers and—"

Owen walked up to the buggy window and stared at her, smiling coldly, with nothing behind it but teeth. "It's not *better* for farmers. He doesn't respect the science. He's hurting innocent people by spreading myths and lies."

"Nathan?" Lydie said. "That doesn't sound at all like him. Nathan doesn't lie."

Owen leaned close to her, still wearing that wild smile. "If his own brother can't shut him up, then maybe you should do it." He looked back at Mick. "Somebody needs to." With that, he sent a thick stream of tobacco juice splatting into the ground and went on his way.

Lydie looked at Mick to say something, do something, to go after Owen Miller and defend his brother. All he said was, "What'd you have to do that for?"

"Do what?"

He walked over to the buggy window. "I mean it, Lydie. You made Owen mad! Why'd you have to jabber on and on about Nathan?"

"Are you kidding?"

"No! Some friend you are."

"What did *I* do?"

"It's what you didn't do. At least for me. I know you haven't said anything to Patsy Glick about me. She looks right through me whenever I try talking to her, like I'm invisible." He braced his hands on his hips. "And then you get Owen all riled up."

And suddenly she saw a bulge in his cheek. Tobacco chew!

Lydie felt like smacking Mick. All her thoughts blurted out, one right after the other, in one long stream of consciousness. "Mick, I don't know what's going on with you lately, but whatever it is, I'm sick of it. Why in the world are you so enamored with Owen Miller? He's turning you into . . . him!" She should've stopped right there, but no, she was on a roll. "And what makes you think I can change Patsy's mind about you? She doesn't even think twice about you, Mick! Hasn't it ever occurred to you that maybe she's interested in someone else?"

Mick's face blanched. "Who?"

For once, Lydie held her tongue. She turned to face the windshield. Mick turned on his heel and left her without another word.

13

On Wednesday afternoon, David was in his office at the Bent N' Dent when Edith Fisher Lapp stormed in and dropped the newspaper on his desk. "You need to do something about this."

"What?"

She pointed a finger at the newspaper. "That."

David picked it up and saw a cartoon of a man who looked remarkably similar to Hank Lapp, standing behind a card table. His sign read JOKES FOR SALE. ~~10 CENTS~~ ~~5 CENTS~~ 1 CENT.

"That newspaper reporter is behind this. He's been poking fun at us for years. It's high time you do something about it."

"Edith, as I recall, in the past you've enjoyed those cartoons. I believe you said that they kept us humble."

"That was when they were about Walt Yoder. That old goat needs a little humbling. But two weeks in a row, they've been aimed at my Hank. These are just downright mean."

"Is that how Hank feels?" David knew, without a doubt, that Hank was loving the attention. He'd been in the Bent N' Dent earlier today, laughing about them, showing off the cartoon to anyone who walked through the door. "Hank has a pretty thick skin." Unlike his thin-skinned wife.

"That's only because Hank doesn't realize when someone's making fun of him."

"I don't think these drawings are meant to be mean-spirited. They're really just little slices of the Plain life."

"Exactly. And should be kept private."

"When Hank was selling his jokes at the market, it was very public. Very loud."

She narrowed her eyes. "You're defending these cartoons because they're good advertising for your farmers' market."

"I'm not!" Though they were.

"Let's just see how you feel when you're the object of one of these vicious satires."

Vicious satires? That was dramatic. He peered at the illustration to find a name in the corner, but there was none. "Edith, are you positive that the newspaper reporter is the one who draws these?"

"Absolutely."

"How do you know?"

"Patsy Glick told me so. She reminded me that he's been taking pictures of the Plain folks for years without permission." She pointed a finger at one of the photographs taken at the farmers' market. "Look. Right there. See Fern's face?"

David had to hold the paper up to his nose to identify Fern. The figure was turned halfway around at her booth.

"I'll speak to the editor. He's a good man." He hoped that might be enough to appease Edith. When she didn't make a motion to leave, he added, "Is there anything else you'd like to say, Edith?"

"This farmers' market is a bad idea. I knew it from the start. We're meant to live in this world but not be of it."

Patience, patience. David cleared his throat. "So you think that selling produce our local farmers have grown is being of this world?"

"You should've kept it to just the Plain farmers, instead of letting everybody and their dogs in."

"Amish-only vendors couldn't support the market. Or Amish-only customers, either."

"I don't mind if the customers are Englisch."

David leaned back in his chair. "Let me get this straight. You don't want to allow our non-Amish neighbors to have an opportunity to sell their produce alongside Amish farmers, but you have no objection to accepting cash from them."

"Exactly."

Could Edith not see the hypocrisy in that? Apparently not.

"You're too soft, David. Too cozy with the Englisch. Everyone says so."

David wasn't a man who offended easily, but those vague "everyone says so" comments got under his skin. How did a man defend himself against a remark like that? "Who's everyone?" he countered, and instantly regretted stooping to Edith's level.

"Your own mother. She told me so, just yesterday. She said she's come to put your household in order. She said you're far too liberal, in every way. As a bishop, as well as a father."

David said nothing. There was a bitter taste in his mouth, slightly metallic, like he'd just had a spoonful of Edith's prickly pear jam.

"She said the household is chaotic. Sheer chaos."

His jaw pulled rigid. "Sounds to me like you're repeating gossip."

One of Edith's thin eyebrows arched. "No, I am not. I'm going right to the source with it." A trace of a smile twisted her mouth. "I thought you should know. This is how everyone thinks about your leadership, even your very own mother." And with that, she finally left.

David let out a puff of air. Talk about humility. He'd just

been served a large dose of it. After a few moments, he picked up the office phone and called Birdy. As expected, the machine picked up, so he left a brief message. "Birdy. It's David. Call me as soon as you can."

Birdy's first piece of advice was to speak to the editor of the *Stoney Ridge Times* and see if he could confirm that the reporter was actually the one behind the cartoons. Her second piece of advice was to ignore Edith's criticism, even if she was just repeating what his mother had told her. "Edith has never quite gotten over having to bend at the knee to make a confession last year. I suspect that she amplified anything your mother might have said to her and sharpened its point."

When David asked again when Birdy thought she might return home, she hedged.

"Have you found a solution for your mother's living situation yet?"

No, not quite. "I'm working on it," he said. Working on thinking about it, anyway. *Especially today*, he thought after Birdy ended their call. His mother had a way of sending off arrows that hit him like a bull's-eye, right to his most insecure spots. Like Edith's dig that David was too soft, too liberal, interacted too much with their Englisch neighbors. Ever since he had drawn the lot to become bishop, it had been a constant refrain from some of the older church members. Whenever such criticism reached his ears, it stung. It lingered. Doubts grew.

He'd had enough experience in this leadership role to immediately take those moments to the Lord, to ask him to search his heart and shed light on areas that needed attention. And to release the offense to the Lord. To ask for healing from the offense before bitterness set in. It was an effective strategy . . . except when it came to his mother.

Maybe everyone had that one person in their life who was

hard to accept, hard to forgive. Like Paul's thorn in his flesh—a continual source of aggravation. How had Paul handled this hardship? Through thanksgiving. Through an awareness for the gifts that this thorn-in-the-side brought to him. Empathy, humility, utter dependence on the Lord.

David dropped his chin, ashamed. He'd never thought to thank the Lord for all he'd been given *because* of his mother's difficult personality. Like his desire to build bridges between people. Over the years, he'd had to do so much apologizing for his mother's harsh words, he'd become very comfortable in the role of mediation. Maybe that's why he felt more inclined to work with the non-Amish to help the larger community.

What else?

Hmm. He was the only family member who had a close relationship with his sister who'd left before she'd been baptized. There was no cause from the Ordnung to keep her at a distance, but his mother did, and his brother Simon followed her lead. David had always been able to see the situation from Dok's point of view. He remembered how their mother would make his sister acutely aware of all the things she didn't do well. All of her weaknesses, none of her strengths. Finally, she had to flee to find a life in which she had some purpose.

He gasped. *That's exactly what's been happening to Lydie.* The awareness struck him painfully, as sharp as a cinder to the eye.

His mother had spent the better part of breakfast criticizing Lydie. Last night, she had gotten some ice out of the freezer and forgotten to shut the freezer door all the way to seal it. In the morning, there was water dripping on the kitchen floor. The food in the freezer had thawed out and spoiled. It was thoughtless behavior, it was wasteful. And it was not an unusual thing for Lydie to do.

But his mother! She wouldn't let up. Pounding the table with her palm, she said, "Why don't you ever *think*?"

It was too much for Lydie. David could see it coming. At first she looked stricken, then like she was trying not to cry.

"Do you think I want to be like this? I don't! You make it sound like I don't even try! I wish you could be me for just one day so you'd get an idea of how hard I work to keep everything from turning out even worse." Fists clenched, she jumped from her seat. "I wish you could understand how it feels to always have everything turn out all wrong when I try so hard to do it right!" With that final remark, she grabbed her lunch bag and hurried out the door to head to work.

For one startling moment, David felt as if he were suddenly fifteen years old, sitting at the kitchen table, listening to the same argument between his sister, Ruth, and their mother.

The rest of the meal was eaten in cold silence. David knew if he started to say anything, it would be words he'd soon regret.

As soon as he arrived at the Bent N' Dent, he went to his office, picked up the phone, and dialed Dok's number. When it clicked over to voicemail, he almost hung up. But then he just said it. "David here. I've been giving a lot of thought to what you had to say about Lydie the other day, and . . . I'd like to hear more." He paused, swallowed past a lump in his throat. "And, Ruth, thank you for caring about my daughter."

❦

When Lydie arrived home that afternoon, she just couldn't bring herself to go inside and face Mammi. She felt terrible about leaving the freezer door open, wasting all that food. Such a *stupid* thing to do!

But Mammi made her feel like God had made a mistake when he made Lydie. As if she didn't think so herself!

Out of habit, she wandered over to the hole in the hedge to look down over Black Gold Farm.

She saw Sarah out in front of the house, holding on to the porch railing. For some reason, she turned, and noticed Lydie

161

up on the hill. Sarah waved to her, beckoning her to come down, but Lydie paused, craning her neck to see if Walt Yoder's buggy was in its usual spot. Happily, there was no sign of him, so she hurried down the path. About ten feet away, she realized something was wrong. Her gaze moved over the woman's pale face. "Are you all right?"

"Oh Lydie, I'm so glad you saw me waving. I'm having trouble catching my breath."

"Let's get you inside." Lydie helped Sarah lean against her to hobble toward the front door. As she held open the door, the cool of the house reached out to them. "It'll be good for you to get out of the heat." It was the first summer-like day, warm even for June. Hot and humid, a drippy day.

Lydie helped Sarah onto the sofa, then crouched beside her. There was an odd whistling sound to her breathing. "Sarah, has Dok ever said you might have something called asthma?" Lydie only wondered because just yesterday a mother had brought a little boy who suffered from asthma into Dok's office, and he had sounded wheezy and whistling like Sarah.

Sarah's labored breathing made her words come out as a gasp. "I don't know." She was growing worse, with breaths coming short and shallow. Just getting to the sofa seemed to drain all the energy from her body.

"Is anyone else home?"

Sarah shook her head.

What to do? What to do? Yesterday, while the little boy with asthma and his mother were in the exam room with Dok, Lydie had taken mail back to Dok's desk and noticed a magazine about herbal remedies in the stack of mail. She slipped into Dok's chair and read an article about asthma, losing track of time until Hank Lapp shouted down the hallway, "Where'd everybody go?" Dok burst out of the exam room and glared at Lydie, who was still reading the magazine at Dok's desk. She pointed to the waiting room and Lydie hustled.

Something blue outside the door caught Lydie's eye. A flow-erpot on the porch, full of newly planted blue lobelia. Lobelia! She stood up. "Sarah, I've got an idea to help."

Sarah grabbed hold of Lydie's arm and held it so hard it hurt. "Don't . . . leave . . . me."

Lydie pried her hand off her arm. "I'll be right here, the whole time." She grabbed a handful of lobelia. In grabbing it, the flowerpot knocked over and broke, but she'd clean it up later. In the kitchen, she macerated the lobelia on a cutting board. "Hold on, Sarah! I'm almost done." She looked through the spice cupboard and grabbed the cayenne pepper. Squeezing her eyes shut, she tried to pull from her mental files the image of the article from Dok's magazine. *What was it? What was it?* Three parts tincture lobelia with one part tincture cayenne pepper, added to water. She mixed it all together in an empty coffee cup she found in the sink, grabbed a spoon, and hurried over to Sarah.

By now Sarah was gasping for air. "Call . . . Dok."

"I will. But first, try a few drops of this." Lydie tried to spoon it into Sarah's mouth, but she batted her hand away. "Sarah, try to swallow a little. Please try. I think this will help."

Sarah shook her head, pinching her lips together like a child.

Lydie held another spoonful up to Sarah's face, hoping it added up to about twenty drops of potion. "Please trust me." No one had ever died from ingesting lobelia—that fact she distinctly remembered from the magazine article.

Sarah looked terrified, but she was desperate. She swallowed the spoonful, gagging, and within seconds—literally within seconds—the spasms subsided. Her airway started to open up. After a few minutes, she said, "I'm . . . feeling better." She seemed shocked. Lydie was equally shocked. It was like watch-ing a miracle unfold.

As soon as Lydie felt confident Sarah continued to improve, she ran down to the phone shanty to call Dok. She didn't pick up, so Lydie left a message to have her drop by as soon as she could, ran back to the house, checked on Sarah. By now, color had returned to her face and her breathing was normal. The crisis seemed to be over, but Lydie felt relieved when she saw Dok's car pull into the driveway. Oh good! Right behind Dok's car came a buggy with Walt Yoder inside. Oh no.

Lydie's stomach twisted in a tight knot.

Walt hurried out of the buggy and bolted to Dok's car. Dok must have filled him in on Lydie's voicemail because he kept glancing at the house with a worried look. It was sweet, Lydie thought, to see Walt's concern for his wife. He was such a cur-mudgeon, such a crotchety man. It made her heart soften for him, ever so slightly.

Then Dok must have mentioned Lydie's name, because his big bushy eyebrows rose and his mouth fell open. He stormed up the porch steps and burst into the house, pointing a long accusing finger at Lydie. His mouth tightened, then fierce words burst out of him. "What did you do to her?"

Lydie's eyes went wide. "I didn't do anything!"

Sarah reached out a hand to him. "I don't know what I'd have done if Lydie hadn't come when she did."

Doubtful, Walt frowned, but backed off. He pulled out a chair for Dok to sit next to Sarah. She took Sarah's blood pres-sure and listened to her breathing, while Walt squatted beside the couch.

"Whatever concoction Lydie whipped up, it worked," Sarah said.

"Concoction?" Walt's head jerked up and around as if he was pointing with his beard.

Even Dok looked concerned. "Lydie, what did you give her?"

"I ground up lobelia and added a dash of cayenne pepper. I gave her a teaspoon." Lydie handed the cup to Dok, who smelled the mixture, then tasted it.

"Hmm."

Walt pointed at Lydie. "Did she poison her?"

"Not at all. She made a good decision. There are ingredients in lobelia that can instantly help open the airways that asthma closes up. In fact, Sarah should take another teaspoonful every thirty minutes, as much as three to four times." Dok's eyes narrowed at Walt's pointed finger. "Your hand is trembling."

He yanked his hand out of the air and stuffed it in his coat pocket. "No it ain't."

"Have you noticed that before?"

"Stop fussing over me. It's Sarah you should be fretting over."

Dok rose from crouching next to Sarah. "I want to find out what could be causing Sarah to have full-blown asthma."

"I wonder if the cause could be found in our fields."

Everyone turned to see Nathan by the door, leaning against the jamb. Lydie hadn't even heard him come in.

"That's a lot of nonsense," Walt said. "There's not a farm in Stoney Ridge that doesn't farm in the same way as us."

"We use more chemicals than other farmers. A lot more. And Mick's trying that GMO corn this year."

Dok folded her stethoscope and put it in her bag. "Tell me more, Nathan."

He pushed off from the doorjamb. "Mom's coughing has been getting worse. The more I read about effects of chemicals and pesticides, the more it makes me think she might be getting sick from them."

Walt hooked his hands on his hips. "Is that so? Then why aren't you sick? Or Mick?" He patted his chest. "Or me?"

Dok intervened. "Sarah has a weakness with her respiratory system. She's always been more prone to winter colds that settle in her chest. It's possible that she's just more sensitive to whatever chemicals could be in the air." She closed her medical bag. "Walt, it's just something to consider. That's all Nathan's trying to say."

Walt huffed.

"I need to get going," Dok said. "Sarah needs rest. Walt, why don't you help your wife up to bed. And I want you to come into the office soon for a checkup." Walt frowned at her, but Dok paid him no mind. She put a hand on Lydie's shoulder. "Quick thinking, Lydie. Good work." She left for her car as Walt helped Sarah up the stairs.

Lydie and Nathan were alone. He was looking at her with a mystified expression. "How did you know what to do?"

"I read about it in a magazine at Dok's. The Native Americans used to smoke lobelia as a treatment for asthma."

He smiled that old Nathan smile, which always made her want to smile too. So she did.

"You're always doing things no one else would ever think of."

It was true that Nathan had never once complained about her the way others did. All the time she'd known him, he'd never given her an odd look and said, "What were you thinking?" or shaken his head over some dumb thing she'd done . . . or tried not to do. "You must be the only one who thinks that about me."

He squinted at her. "What makes you say such a thing?"

"Because . . ." *It's true. That's why.* Couldn't he see that? She stood before him with her hands linked behind her back, and she almost lost herself in those beautiful blue eyes, looking at her with such concern. His face was so dearly familiar to her. A bittersweet ache began in her chest, and she made herself avert her eyes.

She started to turn away, but he stayed her with a hand on her arm. "Lydie, why can't we go back to the way we used to be?"

"Because . . ." Because he deserved better. Because she would only disappoint him, the way she disappointed everyone. "Nathan, please stop thinking about me. You should only be thinking about Patsy Glick."

He shook his head at her like he'd never considered the question before. "Patsy? Why should I only be thinking about her?"

"Because . . . she's so right for you."

"Lydie, wait!"

She was already slipping out of his hand, moving away from him, out the door to head up the path.

14

David opened the door of the Bent N' Dent the next morning and held up the full coffeepot. Bingo. His sister saw him and made a beeline to the store. He poured a mug for her, and half of one for him, and they sat down on the rocking chairs.

Dok took a sip of the coffee. "Not bad for an old bishop."

"Thanks."

She eyed him. "Is Birdy coming home soon?"

"I hope so. Katrina's getting close to being full-term."

"So that's the reason Birdy's stayed so long? Seems like she should've been able to find a mother's helper."

David took a long sip of coffee, stalling. "It makes her happy that Katrina wants her to stay." That was true.

"No doubt Birdy's happy to have a little breathing room from her mother-in-law."

That was also true.

From the look on his face, Dok must have known she shouldn't have made that remark out loud. "Sorry! Sometimes I lack a filter."

Like Lydie.

"So, what's up?"

Where to start? David knew Dok didn't have much time, so he cut right to the chase. "Mom's been working on a plan for Lydie."

Dok cringed. "What's she doing?"

"Giving her specific things to work on. Like . . . slowing down. Finishing what she starts."

Dok pondered that for a while. "I can't say that there's anything wrong with those directives. The only thing is . . . I have a feeling Mom is making her feel as if there's something wrong with her. That's Mom's parenting strategy—a lot of blame. Lydie would be receptive to self-incrimination. The way Lydie is . . . the way she thinks and acts . . . I know it can be challenging. But it's not her fault, David."

"I agree. It's not Lydie's fault." He let out a deep sigh. "It's my fault."

"Your fault? What makes you think that?"

"She's grown up under the floodlight of being a bishop's daughter. Everything we do gets noticed . . . and commented on. We're either criticized or we're put on a pedestal. Neither is right. Having a bishop for a father hasn't been easy for any of my children, but I think it's been especially hard for Lydie. When she makes mistakes, everyone knows. Everyone talks."

"And somehow you think that because she's a bishop's daughter, it's influenced her to have ADHD?"

He wouldn't put it that way, not exactly. "I've wondered if she didn't get the kind of attention she needed at times when she needed it."

"So, if you were a better parent, she'd have an easier time managing her life?"

Slowly, David nodded.

"David, you are a wonderful father. Sure, you're flawed. But you've always done your best. Lydie is the way she is because God made her that way, not because of your shortcomings."

"I believe that too. That's why I don't like the idea of labeling her with a disorder. As if the rest of us live in order and stability. We don't. We all have our own kind of disorders. Hers is just . . . a problem of paying attention."

"ADHD is far more than a disorder of attention. It influences every part of Lydie's life. Her friendships, her routines, her communication—anything requiring planning or foresight or coordination of skills. How many times has she lost a job?"

Too many to count.

"You have to admit that her behavior has an effect on the entire family."

It did. Everyone felt frustrated with living with Lydie. He remembered one of many incidents—the time Emily asked if she could move into Molly's room rather than continue to share a room with her twin. It was rare for Emily to get upset, but that time, she was fed up. Lydie had borrowed a library book that Emily had checked out and lost it. Emily, an avid, dedicated reader, had been put on the library's do-not-loan list until it was returned or paid for. Emily was mortified.

He sighed. "Okay. I admit that Lydie's issues are, well, significant."

"And don't you agree that she needs help to figure out how to manage those issues?"

"Yes. And Mom's trying to give her that help."

"No," she said. "Mom is ordering her around. She's not helping Lydie develop internal skills. You'll see what I mean when Mom leaves for Ohio. If she ever leaves . . ."

David jerked his head up. "What does that mean?"

"Lydie mentioned that Mom plans to stay in Stoney Ridge."

"That hasn't been decided yet."

Dok snorted. "By her or by you?"

David frowned. This conversation was veering off in the wrong direction. He needed to rein it in and get it back on track. "But aren't you trying to fix Lydie too?"

"No. First of all, I don't believe she needs fixing. The way her brain is wired could be, should be, a gift. Now, that said, I realize it comes with some difficulties. I think she needs support so she can learn to better manage her own life. The goal is to internalize those skills, so she has the ability to live the life she wants to live. Skills like . . . time management. Or staying on task. Or planning for the future."

He wanted those things for Lydie. He really did.

"There's so much hope, David. So . . . can I get her tested for ADHD?"

"No."

Dok put her fingers on her temples, like she had a sudden headache. "I just do not understand why you're so resistant to it."

"I can't explain it. It's just a feeling I have."

"But, David, I've seen how open-minded you've been in other circumstances. One example is Luke Schrock. You were the one who got him into rehab. And look at him now. He's your deacon. And he's really good at it."

"This is hardly the same thing."

"Maybe not, but I don't see why you'd be willing for Luke to get help and not Lydie."

"Luke was self-destructive. He had an addiction. But he wasn't born that way. Lydie is the way she is. She's the way God made her."

"But don't you see how a diagnosis could help her?"

"I don't like labels. Labels are for cans and jars."

She stared at him with a stunned look on her face. "You sounded just like Mom right then."

That hit David hard, like a sucker punch to the gut. Dok was right. It *was* something his mother would say. "Ruth, do you take medication?"

"I do."

That's exactly what worried him. Maybe it wasn't fair, but he believed the Englisch overmedicated, using pills to solve problems. Pills were easier than changing behavior. Maybe that was the core of his reluctance to have Lydie assessed. If she was diagnosed with ADHD, she would be pressured to take medication.

Dok seemed to read his thoughts. "But that's not all I do. I've learned a lot since I was diagnosed, personally and professionally. Things like adjusting my diet, getting lots of exercise, cognitive behavior therapy, breathing exercises. And then there's practicing mindfulness."

David's head snapped up. "What?"

"Practicing mindfulness."

"That's what I thought you said. It sounds . . . like something outside of our faith." Something New Age. Mystical. Hokeypokey.

"Slow down a minute." She waved a hand in the air. "Let me use vocabulary that you understand. Mindfulness is about helping the mind to slow down, to stop racing. It helps the body relax. Ideally, it helps the soul regain an awareness of God. 'Be still and know that I am God.' *That* is mindfulness."

Despite his reluctance, David found himself intrigued. There had been a time when he had encouraged his church members to meditate on God's Word and a number of them had complained. It was only when he showed them the Scriptures that said the very same thing that they were willing to open their minds. It had troubled David then to see how assumptions closed off minds from the very Word of God. And yet here he was, doing the exact same thing. Just like his mother. Inwardly, he shuddered.

"If you still feel skeptical, I just read a study that found in less than eight weeks of training in mindfulness practice, people with ADHD experienced an improved ability to focus and shift attention." She held out her arm and bent it. "Think of it like a muscle. The brain responds to repetition the same way as the body responds to physical exercise."

It was starting to make sense to him.

"David, Lydie has such a malleable heart, she's so humble—I'd like to see what happens if she gets specific guidance. Not her grandmother's version of guidance. I'm talking about someone who understands ADHD and who also loves her." Dok leaned forward. "If you aren't open to testing, or medication, how would you feel . . . what if I just worked with her?"

David glanced at her. "How?"

"Mostly with mindfulness exercises. I think mindfulness can help her better understand herself and then make better choices about managing her life." She tilted her head. "David, I understand how Lydie is feeling. She doesn't fit into a culture that values conformity. She's like a square peg in a round hole. Everyone needs love and acceptance. She'll look for it in other places. It's just too . . . frustrating . . . to stay. Trust me on that." She looked at him, almost pleading. "Maybe if someone could have helped me when I was Lydie's age . . ." She glanced at her watch, as if she feared she might be running late. But then the crack in her voice betrayed her thoughts. "Maybe if things had been different . . ."

If Mom had been different. That's what she meant. If Mom could have let go of expecting her version of perfection from her daughter, Dok could have found a way to stay Plain. David felt a sweep of loving tenderness for his sister. Her entire life was focused on caring for others. Their mother had yet to understand what kind of a blessing her daughter was, to so many people.

"Mom is determined to make a difference with Lydie. Sounds like you are too. Would you consider talking to Mom about some of your ideas?"

"WHOA!" Dok's eyes went wide. "Hold it. I was never able to make a dent in her thinking."

"I don't disagree that Mom doesn't change her mind easily, but what is there to lose by trying? And there might be much to gain."

A pause settled between them. Dok eyed him suspiciously. "Is this your way of trying to bring about a reconciliation between us?"

He smiled. "Mom's methods might be hard to take, but she does love Lydie. And you love Lydie. You're both trying to help her. If that happens to bring the two of you to a better place, then the glory goes to God."

Dok took some time before she answered. "I'll talk to her. But only if you are present to act as referee."

"Thank you, sister."

Dok lifted her chin. "No promises."

"Understood."

Her phone beeped and she glanced at the incoming text. "Sorry. Trying to get some tests scheduled for a patient. I'd better go." She handed him the mug and left.

<hr>

It was still dark but for the yellow glow of a kerosene lamp hanging in the middle of the ceiling and another one sitting on the table. David watched his mother move across the kitchen. It was such a familiar sight to him; she was always in motion, rarely at rest. His eyes were drawn to those hands, such nimble hands, always absorbed in a task.

"Mom, Lydie's been working at the doctor's office for two months now."

His mother remained at the kitchen sink, swishing the dish soap around in the water.

"Ruth has had a chance to get to know Lydie. She's observed how she's handled different situations that have occurred at the office."

"Is this your way of saying Lydie's about to get fired?"

"No, not at all. She's been very impressed with how Lydie has reacted under pressure, like she did with Sarah when she had that asthma attack. And there's been a couple of things that she's noticed that have concerned her too. Same concerns that you have. Like how Lydie starts things and doesn't finish them. She thinks Lydie might have something called Attention Deficit Hyperactivity Disorder."

His mother's mouth tightened. "Well, she's the doctor, after all."

"Indeed, she is. She's a very good doctor. She's had a lot of schooling, a lot of experience in her practice. She's also been studying this ADHD." He had no intention of telling his mother about his sister's diagnosis. "She has some ideas to help Lydie. Very good ideas, ones that I think could be quite beneficial."

She stilled but kept her eyes on the dishwater.

"Mom, have you heard about this ADHD?"

"Amish children don't have it. I know that much."

"Now, that's not true. Amish children just aren't diagnosed with it. We have just as many problems as the Englisch."

"We have problems, but not the same ones."

David sighed. This wasn't going in the right direction. "The thing is, you both have opened my eyes to some concerns about Lydie. So I'd like you and Ruth to have a conversation about how best to help Lydie."

She turned so abruptly that water from her hands dripped on the floor. "You don't think I'm helping Lydie?"

"That's not what I said. All I'm saying is that you and Ruth could learn a lot from each other." He rose, grabbed a rag, and wiped up the soapy water on the floor. He laid the rag on the counter next to the sink, leaning his back against it, folding his arms over his chest. Softly, he said, "Mom, this is about Lydie. Can you do this for her?"

"Ruth won't speak to me."

"She will. I've already asked. She would like to have this conversation with you, Mom. So are you willing?"

Tillie slowed her angry scrubbing of the dishes. "Are you asking as my son or as my bishop?"

"Both."

"For Lydie, I'll do it." She gave David a hard look, then her face softened, just a tidge. "It's hard to say no to a bishop."

"Isn't it though," David said, then bent over and gave his mother a kiss on the cheek.

15

David gave careful thought as to where the meeting between his mother and Dok should take place. It would be the first time they would have a conversation in years and years. After Ruth had left home as a teenager, Mom treated her as if she were put under the church ban, even though she wasn't. David was convinced that it was the hurt his mother felt by Dok's leaving that caused her to harden. Dok didn't see it that way. She attributed the coldness to the fact that her mother couldn't control her daughter. Maybe they were both right. Whatever the reason, the two had rarely seen each other in thirty years.

Thirty years!

But the Lord was always at work, even in the silent times.

After all God's repair work that David had observed over the years, it shouldn't have surprised him that the Lord would use his daughter Lydie as the reason his mother and sister came together. It shouldn't have, but it did. Their love and concern for Lydie was something they had in common.

Just think of the Lord's perfect timing in this situation: Lydie happened to be filling in for Dok's receptionist at the very same time that Mom had come to live with them. Dok started to get to know Lydie, really know her. She raised the alarm of ADHD to David.

Even Birdy's absence played a role in it. Without Birdy and the little boys here, his mother had time to focus her attention entirely on Lydie. Once Dok had been made aware of the Tillie Stoltzfus Improvement Program for Lydie, she had dropped her own defenses and been willing to meet with Mom.

After much mulling, and a long phone conversation with Birdy, David decided to hold the meeting at Dok's office. He doubted his mother had ever observed her doctor-daughter at work. It would be good for his mother to be out of her element, and for Dok to be in hers. He set up the meeting for Saturday morning, when the office was closed and Lydie would be at the farmers' market, but he waited until Friday night to tell his mother what he had planned.

His mother's thin lips drew even thinner. "Why can't Ruth come here?"

David had expected a backlash. "She needs to stick close to the office."

"Your office at the Bent N' Dent would work."

"Saturday mornings is when the old men arrive to play checkers. You can't hear yourself think."

That, Tillie couldn't object to. But she wasn't happy about it. As she moved around the kitchen, she reminded David of a wet hen, flustered and irritated.

By Saturday morning, her mood had gone from bad to worse. On the buggy ride to Dok's office, she took the opportunity to point out every single thing David had been doing wrong lately, from stacking cans incorrectly at the Bent N' Dent to an overabundance of "uh's" in his sermons. The difficult thing was that her appraisals were correct. Her critiques were valid. They always were. But instead of constructive feedback, this advice made David feel deflated, discouraged, depressed. Overly aware of his flaws and shortcomings.

David tried to let his mother's words flow through him while he drifted on his thoughts, noticing the beauty that surrounded him. The blue sky, the singing birds, the green leaves that canopied the tree-lined country lane. It was a strategy he had learned as a teenager, taught by the apostle Paul. "Whatsoever things are true, whatsoever things are honest, whatsoever things are just, whatsoever things are pure, whatsoever things are lovely, whatsoever things are of good report; if there be any virtue, and if there be any praise, think on these things."

Lord, he prayed, *this beautiful Saturday morning is a gift from you. And this meeting between Mom and Dok—that, too, is a gift from you. Bless this coming hour. May it result in continued blessings—for Lydie, but also for Mom and Dok. Amen.*

David felt his soul settle, as it always did when he regained his awareness of God's presence. A healthy detachment filled his mind, and he was able to separate himself from his mother's henpecking and realize she was just scared. "You can do this for Lydie, Mom."

She turned her head to look out the window, but she said nothing more. He turned into the parking lot at the small medical office building and pulled the horse to a stop beside Dok's car. As he helped his mother out of the buggy, he noticed her eyes were on the car. "Rather flashy, don't you think?"

Not really. It was a charcoal gray SUV. "Looks a little like a buggy."

His mother let out a clucking sound of disapproval. The door opened and there was Dok, wearing her white coat. Smart move, David thought, as he saw the startled look on his mother's face. In her mind's eye, her daughter had remained a rebellious teenager. The woman who stood at the threshold of the door was a middle-aged professional doctor.

After a moment of awkward hellos at the door, they moved into the waiting room. Mom's attention went immediately to the receptionist's desk. Folders were stacked in a haphazard way, pens and pencils and stray papers covered most of the large daily planner, and yellow Post-it notes were stuck in any remaining open space, including the top of the telephone.

"Yes, that is Lydie's workplace."

Mom huffed. "A complete mess."

Dok nodded. "I wanted you to see it."

Mom frowned. "You should expect more from your employee."

David found himself cringing whenever a sentence started with "You should." There was something about it that felt like a scolding finger. He gave his sister a side-eye, wondering if she was already regretting this meeting.

But Dok seemed unperturbed. She motioned to the chairs. "Let's have a seat." She remained where she was, leaning her back against Lydie's messy desk, and David thought that, too, was a smart move, as she remained slightly above them. "David has said that you've expressed concern about Lydie."

Mom lifted her chin. "I am concerned about her."

"Can you describe what you've observed that troubles you?"

Another smart move on Dok's part, David thought. Asking Mom for her opinion was a good move.

"Forgetful, easily distracted, fidgety. She never looks behind her to see what she's left. She starts things and never finishes them. I have to tell her things over and over and over."

"And is that helping?"

"I believe it is. Just tell her what you expect. And keep telling her."

Yes, that pretty much summed up his mother's parenting strategy. David kept his eyes on the tops of his boots.

"So what happens if you're not there?"

His mother lifted a palm toward Lydie's messy desk. "That's what happens. That's why it's good I arrived at David's home when I did. Frankly, I don't know what she'd do without me.

I don't know how she'll ever . . ." She caught herself, clapping her lips shut.

When she didn't finish her sentence, Dok prompted her. "What don't you know?"

Mom's eyes were on her hands, clenched together in her lap. She took so long to answer that David wondered if she might not. But then she spoke, so quietly that David had to lean in to hear her. "I don't know how she'll ever manage to have a life without someone telling her what to do and how to do it. I don't know if she'll ever have a normal life. She needs a . . . full-time minder."

David's eyes filled with tears. So *this* was at the heart of his mother's obsessive worry about Lydie. It dawned on him that what kept him up at night was a fear that Lydie might leave the church. His mother's worry for Lydie—that she may not ever be able to live without help—that was a far more accurate concern. That apprehension covered whether she stayed or whether she left.

He glanced up at Dok. There was tenderness in her eyes as they fixed on Mom's white-capped head.

Then Dok snapped into action. "Actually, I think that's a great place to start. We all want Lydie to have a normal, happy life. And I think she can, but she's going to need some specific strategies. David might have told you that I suspect Lydie has undiagnosed Attention Deficit Hyperactivity Disorder."

"He told me," Mom said, stiffening. "Personally, I think if she just tries harder—"

Dok cut her off. "It's not just a matter of expecting her to try harder. In fact, Lydie actually has to work much harder than others, just to achieve similar results. Her mind simply doesn't know how to break down a task so that it's manageable."

Mom's spine straightened. "She does just fine when I tell her what to do. As long as I stay right there to make sure things get done."

David couldn't bring himself to look at his sister's face. He knew what she was thinking: ARE YOU KIDDING ME?

"Well," Dok said, her voice calm and controlled, "that would place the burden of changed behavior on someone other than Lydie. But Lydie isn't directly contributing to those new habits. When that external pressure goes away, so does the behavior. But I think we can do something for Lydie to help her overcome ADHD. Together, we can help Lydie learn some new habits so she can sustain them without needing external pressure." Dok shifted to pick up the planner on Lydie's desk. "Starting with this. I gave this to Lydie when she first began working for me." She opened it and there was nothing written inside. Nothing.

Mom snorted. "Well, doesn't that just say it all."

Dok's eyebrows rose. "What does it say to you?"

"That your system won't work."

"What it says to me is that Lydie feels overwhelmed by these blank pages. When someone feels overwhelmed, their brain goes to fight or flight. Lydie flees. She doesn't even try. She thinks she would fail, so she shuts down."

"She shuts down," David echoed. Dodging. A quality he recognized in himself and didn't like.

"The fact that Lydie hasn't used the planner," Dok continued, "was one of the tip-offs to me that she has trouble prioritizing what's important from what's nonurgent. Starting next Monday morning, everything she does goes in her planner. I will ask her to schedule everything, and I mean everything. This will help her break down tasks into manageable steps. She will have it with her at all times, and check it regularly. If something isn't in the planner, then it doesn't exist. This way, you can let the planner do your job."

Slightly intrigued, Mom leaned forward in her chair. "How?"

"Instead of telling Lydie to make her bed and stand over her until she does it, you just need to ask if she's checked her planner."

"I don't see how a planner will help a grown woman remember something as simple as finish making her bed."

"It will help Lydie create routines that work for her."

David could see, from the skeptical look on Mom's face, that she remained unconvinced.

Dok must have realized the same thing, because she tried another tack. "The planner will help Lydie break larger tasks into smaller parts, with due dates and timelines. For example, more often than not, Lydie arrives late to work. I want her to arrive early. There's much less stress in arriving early. So in the planner she will mark down exactly when she needs to leave the house."

Mom leaned back. "She needs to get up earlier, that's what."

"Right! So that goes in the planner too. Even setting the alarm the night before. Everything goes in the planner."

"She'll have to carry her alarm clock with her everywhere."

Dok smiled. She reached into her coat pocket and pulled out a woman's wristwatch. "This will help Lydie stay on top of time. Out of sight, out of mind. In sight, in mind."

Brilliant! David thought.

"All wrong," Mom said. "This is no way to handle Lydie."

Dok exchanged a look with David. "Okay, then what would you do for her?"

"Minimize distractions. Increase organization. Goodness, that's what I try to do each time I've come to Stoney Ridge. David's house and store are kept in absolute disorder. I do my best to bring order out of the chaos, but the next time I return, it's back to bedlam."

David's mouth dropped open. Bedlam? Chaos? Hardly that.

Before he could object, Dok stepped in. "You bring up a couple of good points. Clearly, you've found that staying highly, highly organized has helped you manage your own life."

Oh, bad move. It was that second "highly" that ratcheted things up.

"Don't tell me that you think I have this . . . alphabet disorder?" His mother did not appreciate receiving such a diagnosis.

"It can present in many different ways. Not everyone has the same ADHD issues."

As Mom started to rise in her seat to leave, David stayed her with his hand. "Ruth isn't trying to diagnose you." He gave Dok a sharp glance as she had opened her mouth to say something, and he was pretty sure she was going to say something that would rile Mom up even more. "Ruth is talking about helping Lydie. That's why we're here this morning."

Dok snapped her mouth shut and gave a nod. Slowly, Mom settled back in her chair. "David's right. This is all about helping Lydie. All I was going to say was that you're already doing something right through modeling. It's so much better to demonstrate in your own life how you manage your life, rather than telling Lydie how to do it. Showing is so much more effective than telling."

"In other words," Mom said in that tight-lipped way, "you're suggesting that I stop managing Lydie."

"Hold on. What I'm trying to say is that you will have more impact on her by modeling the changes you'd like to see in Lydie. For one thing, try to devote your complete attention to one given activity at a time."

David let out a surprised sound. "What? But Mom's always doing three things at once."

"Right!" Dok said. "That's just the kind of thing that provides no help at all for Lydie. But if you were to put your needlework down as you talk to her, or stop stirring the pot of soup and give her your full attention . . . now that would be a wonderful example for her. Everything changes when you start paying attention."

Mom frowned. "It seems to me that I'm the one who has to do the changing."

Dok let out a sigh of exasperation. "I know you love Lydie. Your role needs to be one of support and encouragement."

David couldn't help but chime in. "And please stop making dismal predictions about Lydie's future."

His mother's mouth dropped open. "Like what?"

"Yesterday, at breakfast, you said that if she ever had children, she should never leave the house because she would forget all about them and lose them at the market."

Mom lifted her chin. "I only said that after she mentioned she lost her winter coat."

"And then last night, you said you were going to have to help her with every little thing for the rest of her life."

Dok rolled her eyes. Mom frowned. David felt relieved to have those kinds of remarks out in the open, and a little guilty that he hadn't addressed them when they occurred. He should have. How was it possible for him to deliver hard news to his church members, to step into the minister's role as a strong leader, to tell an outsider like Chatty Kathy that she couldn't sell her imported produce at the farmers' market . . . yet be so passive at home, with those he loved so dearly? It shamed him.

"What David is trying to say is to let go of assumptions. And let go of perfectionism too. Whenever you see Lydie make a stride in the right direction, acknowledge it. Appreciate the effort." Dok seemed to know this was a good place to end. "I think you can make quite a difference, Mom. Change is always possible."

Wasn't it though? It was the first time in thirty years that David had heard his sister address their mother, right to her face, as Mom. He wondered if she knew she'd done it.

∾

Great, just great.

The toilet wasn't working at Dok's office on Monday morning and Lydie had to run across to the Bent N' Dent to use that one, and she'd thought—for sure!—she'd locked the office door behind her, but there was Mick, coming out of the office just as Dok's car pulled up. Even worse, he went over to open the car door for her.

Lydie made her way slowly through the parking lot, cringing. As usual, Mick did all the talking. Dok was listening to him. That warm, rather maternal look in her eyes had sharpened with suspicion.

Lydie sidled far around them to not interrupt their conversation, though she knew they saw her, and she went into the office. Surely, she was going to be fired. She went inside to her desk and sat there, hands folded together, bracing herself for Dok to come in and say, "Lydie, I'm sorry but this isn't working out . . ." How many of those conversations had Lydie been given? Way too many.

When the door opened, Dok set her medical bag on Lydie's desk, pulled up a chair from the waiting area, and faced her. "Lydie, we need to have a talk."

Lydie started to get her sweater on. Getting fired was so . . . awkward. Everyone felt bad. Mostly Lydie. "Dok, please don't feel concerned. It happens a lot."

"What does?"

"Me getting fired. I'm used to it. You don't have to explain anything."

Dok blinked. "I'm not firing you."

"Not yet, but you're thinking about it."

"You're wrong. In fact, firing you is the farthest thing from my mind."

Lydie froze, one arm halfway through a sweater sleeve. "Then what are you thinking?"

Dok smiled. "If you might be willing, I'd like us to work together on a few things."

To Lydie, that sounded a little like probation, and she knew, from experience, it would only be a matter of time until it ended in the same place. She was just about to say so when Dok's phone beeped.

Dok pulled out her phone to listen to the voicemail. She slipped her phone back into her pocket. "I need to return this call." Out of her medical bag, she pulled a book with the title *Living with Adult ADHD*. "Lydie, there's a book I'd like you to read, and then we can talk about it."

"That's it?"

"For now, that's all."

"But . . . what about Mick? I thought I'd locked the door when I ran over to the Bent N' Dent . . . but I must have forgotten. He shouldn't have even been here this morning."

"He told me that he wanted to apologize to me and to thank me for not pressing charges." Dok put the chair back. "I told him the only reason I didn't press charges was because all he stole was baking soda."

"You're really not going to fire me?"

"No. But you do need some guidance to help you stop spending so much time putting out fires, and help you to think ahead to prevent those fires." The phone rang and Lydie answered, while Dok went back to her office.

All day, whenever the waiting room was quiet, Lydie read the book Dok had given her. She sat at her desk through lunch, reading. By five o'clock, she had finished. She looked at the book's title. This explained *so* much. Whatever it was that was wrong with her . . . it had a name. It was a real thing!

So many things in the book described her to a T, almost as if the author had been following her around for years, taking notes. She was perpetually late because of time mismanagement, she procrastinated, she had absolutely no idea of how to prioritize things, she had trouble staying focused on a task, she was forgetful, she lost things, she was disorganized, and the worst of all . . . she constantly disappointed others. Her sisters accused her of not listening to them. Most illuminating of all, how a person with ADHD *felt*. Lydie felt terrible about herself, her abilities, her future. Sometimes it seemed as if she couldn't escape a dark cloud that kept following her. She did her best to hide it, to ignore it, to pretend it didn't matter, but it was always there. She went back to Dok's office and handed the book to her. "This is me."

Dok nodded. "This is you."

16

D ok made two cups of hot tea and handed one to Lydie. They were in Dok's office, but instead of sitting behind her desk, Dok chose to sit in the seat beside her. "Lydie, I gave you that book to help you understand Attention Deficit Hyperactivity Disorder. For you, for most women, the hyperactivity piece of it doesn't fit, but the Attention Deficit Disorder does."

In a way, it was comforting to Lydie to hear the reason she acted the way she did. "Is there a cure for it?"

"ADHD isn't curable because it's not a disease. The challenges are real, and they can affect others around you, especially family and close friends."

"I always knew there was something wrong with me." She'd even wondered if she might've been dropped on her head as a baby and no one wanted to tell her that awful truth.

"You think there's something wrong with you? No! I don't even want you to think that. Instead, I want you to realize that there's a lot right with you. Quite a lot. You're creative and compassionate and such a good problem solver. You're great in a crisis, and you have such a humble heart."

All those compliments were nice to hear, but they weren't the reason Lydie was here today, after closing time, with such a serious look on Dok's face.

"Without getting properly evaluated, there's no way of knowing if you have ADHD. I've spoken to your dad and he is dead set against the evaluation. He doesn't like labels, and he's convinced that if you're formally diagnosed that you'll be pressured to be put on medication—"

"Will I? Could medication fix me?"

Dok paused. "Once again, you don't need *fixing*. Lydie, you have many wonderful qualities. Don't discount the gifts God has given you. I'd like to help you learn to feel comfortable being you, while also accepting areas that need improvement." She leaned back in the chair and clasped her hands together in her lap. "I need to respect your dad's concerns about testing and medication, as archaic as I might find them to be. But he did agree to letting me coach you. To teach you some helpful behavior modifications."

"Behavior modifications," Lydie echoed. Those sounded weird.

"I can explain more tomorrow. I promised Matt I'd get home by six to help tear up the bathroom linoleum. The floor guy is coming in the morning to lay tile." She set the teacup on the desk, then paused. "So what do you think? Are you willing to work with me? I really think I can help you."

"You mean, I don't have to be this way all the time?"

Dok smiled. "Just watch."

Lydie could hardly believe it.

"Tomorrow, then, we'll get started on some behavior modifications. I think you'll find them to be life changing."

An image of Nathan popped into Lydie's mind. Imagine if she could be normal, so normal that she wouldn't have to feel ashamed anymore, or embarrassed, or keep disappointing the people she loved. Imagine if she didn't have to worry that

Nathan would stop loving her once he realized what she was truly like. Her relief was so great she felt nearly dizzy with it.

She lifted her chin and looked Dok right in the eyes. "I'm all in."

∞

It happened overnight. One day Nathan was replacing some young tomato plants that had fallen victim to a mole, the next day he could barely make out the narrow dirt path between rows of flourishing, sprawling vegetables. His fields were no longer dark soil laced with thin ribbons of green but a thick tapestry made up of varying shades of green. Harvesting was constant, keeping him in the fields from dawn to dusk. If he wasn't picking produce for Saturday's farmers' market, he was weeding, pruning, or in the greenhouse, sowing seeds to keep the baby plants coming.

Slowly, he walked along the rows of bushy tomatoes, examining branches for any leaves chewed to the stem, evidence of the tomato hornworm. Lydie once called it a prehistoric caterpillar. Nathan called it a major pest. Hornworms were hard to spot because they were the same color as leaves. They could defoliate a plant in a day.

He was particularly protective of his varied tomato crops, soon to ripen. He had high hopes to sell tomatoes as his main crop, come midsummer. The lady with gray braids had told him that vine-ripened tomatoes were the bread-and-butter crop of farmers' markets. Folks would wait in long lines to buy tomatoes, she said, especially heirloom.

Nathan had never known heirloom tomatoes existed until last summer. It was Lydie who had introduced him to these curiously named varieties. Box Car Willie, Radiator Charlie's Mortgage Lifter, Pruden's Purple, Stupice, Black Plum, Sun Gold, Striped German, Cherokee Purple, Sungella. She'd gone to the Lancaster Central Market with her sisters and brought home a basket full of unusual-looking tomatoes for him. Their looks were questionable—nothing like the uniform, easy to grow, thick-skinned Roma that his mother preferred to grow for canning. These odd-looking tomatoes were irregular shapes and sizes, and strangely colored. Some striped, some almost tie-dyed. Their soft skins made them highly perishable and difficult to pack—the very reason that most farmers refused to grow them.

But the taste, the texture. *Amazing.* They held a perfect balance of sweetness and acidity.

As he stooped to prune suckers off some bushy tomato plants, he thought of a conversation he'd had with Hank Lapp at last Saturday's market. Most of Hank's customers were ten-year-old boys who appreciated his lame jokes. During slow times at his card table—of which there were many—Hank would wander over to Black Gold Farm's booth and sidle in behind it, as if he were Nathan's partner. "Did you KNOW that folks ONCE thought tomatoes were POISON?"

Nathan ignored Hank until he had finished with a customer who wanted delicate squash blossoms. He handed her the bag, took her money, gave her change, and then said, "Yes, Hank. I knew that." He hoped that might be the end of Hank's news flash. But no.

"Did you HEAR about the FAMILY in TENNESSEE?"

"No."

"They sat down for the season's first sliced tomato. And suddenly they were all SEEING THINGS." He staggered a few steps, swatting imaginary things in the air. "Turns out they were POISONED."

Standing in line at Nathan's booth, a small woman wearing a printed Mennonite dress had made the mistake of listening to Hank. "So what happened?"

"The son had . . . whatdoyacallit . . . STUCK a vine . . . onto another thingy . . ."

Nathan wished Hank would just go back to his card table and try to sell jokes. He handed the Mennonite woman a bag of beans. "He means grafted."

"THAT'S IT! Grafted. He grafted a TOMATO VINE onto a POISONOUS PLANT."

The Mennonite woman seemed truly concerned. "Which one?"

Hank frowned. He didn't like having his stories dissected. "Does it MATTER? The point is DON'T DO IT."

The Mennonite woman gave him an odd look. "Do what?"

"Graft a TOMATO onto POISON PLANTS."

Nathan had wondered if he should point out that a tomato's leaves were, in fact, toxic if ingested, but tomatoes didn't produce toxins that were carried up to and concentrated within the fruit. On second thought, he decided not to bother. Hank would probably get it all mixed up and start a rumor around town that tomatoes cause hallucinations. The Mennonite lady paid for her beans and walked away. Nathan doubted she'd ever return to his booth.

Ah, well, he thought, standing tall, stretching his back after being stooped over while pruning his plants. Hopefully, there would be a lot more customers in the next few weeks.

Nathan made one more pass along the rows of tomatoes. He took in a deep breath of the unique tomato plant scent. It pleased him to see green orbs hanging off branches. He bent over to see something dark moving on a yellow flower. A bee. Wait. His lifted his head to gaze around the tomato plants. Two, three, four.

He laughed. Then he let out a whoop. The bees were back!

Lydie hardly slept that night. She arrived at Dok's office thirty minutes early, eager to start the life changers . . . whatever they were. When Dok's car finally pulled into the parking lot, Lydie opened the door to greet her. "I'm ready."

Dok closed her car door and whirled around. "You're already here?"

"I've been waiting."

"Okay." Dok smiled. "Let me just get inside and put my things down."

Lydie had pulled a chair for Dok next to the receptionist's desk and had a mug of hot coffee waiting.

Dok handed Lydie her coat and bag, sat down, took a sip of coffee, and settled back. "Lydie, what's one thing you'd like to change about the way your mind works?"

Oh, so many things! "I suppose . . . if I had to pick just one thing, it's that my mind tends to wander." Quite a lot. Like right now, she was thinking about Dok's shoes and if they were new.

Dok smiled. "I can help you with that. It starts with being mindful."

"Mindful." Lydie had no idea what that meant.

"Being mindful is another way of saying that you give whatever you're doing, anything at all—that one thing—your full attention."

Like how she felt as she made her bed under Mammi's beady-eyed gaze. "To get it done faster?"

"No, not really. Speed isn't the goal. Just the opposite. It's a way to slow your busy mind down. An ADHD mind has a wider-than-wide lens of attention. A mind that races like wildfire through a forest. I want to give you some exercises to help fully engage your mind, so that you're training yourself to focus on one thing at a time."

That sounded . . . wonderful. "I'm ready."

"As you're doing a task, pay close attention to what you're actually doing. Notice one thing to see, one thing to hear, one thing to smell, one thing to taste, one thing to touch."

"Hmm. That sounds extremely distracting."

"It's not. Start with something simple, like peeling a carrot.

Focus on the carrot rather than ruminating about your day or thinking about what needs to be done tomorrow."

Odd! That's just what happened last night. Exactly that. Except it wasn't a carrot she was peeling but a . . . what was it? A cucumber? An apple? She couldn't remember . . . because she wasn't paying attention to it. No. Scratch that. She wasn't being mindful.

A butternut squash! That's what it was. And the reason she wasn't paying attention to it was because she didn't particularly like squash. Mammi did, and served squash at least once a week. Terrible.

"Uh, Lydie? Are you listening?"

Lydie startled. "Yes! So . . . you want me to be mindful about peeling a carrot."

"Yes. To practice cultivating more focused attention. You see the orange color of the carrot. You hear the scraping sound that the peeler makes, or maybe the snap as you cut off the carrot tops. You can smell the carrot, you can taste a peel, or a slice. And touch is obvious, as it's in your hands as you peel."

"And why? I mean . . . it sounds very nice . . . but why? What does that do?"

"There are so many benefits to mindfulness! Trust me on that. You'll remember more things. You'll make fewer mistakes." Dok paused to sip the coffee "With practice, I think you'll find yourself able to guide your attention out of distracting thoughts or feelings and steer them back to the present. Back to the task at hand, or the person in front of you."

Lydie gave her a sharp look. Sometimes it felt as if Dok could read her mind. Softly Lydie said, "Alles had sei Zeit." *There is a time for everything.*

Dok lifted her head. "Yes! Alles had sei Zeit." She clapped her hands together, and for just a moment, she reminded Lydie so very much of Mammi. *That* was a first. "Yes, Lydie, exactly that. There's a time for everything."

"That reminds me! A patient asked if she could buy that painting." It was a sunset, or maybe a sunrise? Underneath were words in calligraphy: *A Time for Everything*.

Dok looked to see where Lydie was pointing. "My painting?"

"You painted it?"

"I've done all of the paintings in the office. I think it's important to have an outlet of creativity. I don't have much time for it, but I love it."

"I . . . doodle a little."

"A little?" Dok laughed. "Lydie, you doodle a lot. All over your notepad, all over the telephone messages. You have a wonderful sense of capturing images, and spatial awareness, and likenesses. Don't ever stop doodling."

Lydie was just about to confess to her about the drawings she submitted in the *Stoney Ridge Times* . . . it was on the tip of her tongue. But Dok's phone buzzed and her attention turned to it and the moment was gone.

As Dok rose from the chair to make her way to her back office, it dawned on Lydie how it felt to have someone's attention drift away, right in the middle of a conversation. How many times had she done that to others? More often than not. A cell phone might not have been the source of the interruption, but her mind had left the room.

∿

Nathan walked past the small flock of sheep to head to the greenhouse but stopped short when he saw his brother, Mick, bent over a lamb. "Everything okay?"

Mick's straw hat barely lifted in acknowledgment. "Everything's fine." His voice had an edge to it.

If it wasn't about the farm, they hardly talked much these days, not like they used to. Not like in the pre–Owen Miller days.

Mick scooped the lamb up in his arms and strode to the gate. Nathan unhitched the gate lock and swung the door open for him. He could see some blood on the lamb's wool.

"How'd she get hurt?"

"Not sure. Just a gash on her leg. I'm gonna clean it up and keep her in the barn tonight. Then I'm heading over to Lydie's. Working on the shed." He emphasized the word *shed*, as if to indicate he had little interest in the shed but plenty of interest in Lydie.

Mick liked to remind Nathan of how close he and Lydie were. And to remind him that he was out of their tight circle of friendship. Way out.

Maybe it never was a circle. He remembered Emily, Lydie's twin sister, once saying that all Mick and Nathan shared in common was a love for Lydie. It was true Mick had always been fond of Lydie and he was even more fond of beating out Nathan. Nathan was confident that Lydie had never told Mick about that ice-skating day on Blue Lake Pond, but his brother was no fool. He knew something had happened to create a gulf between Nathan and Lydie, and he had swept in to fill the void.

The sound of buggy wheels made them both turn toward the driveway, wondering who had arrived. Mick squinted. "Well, I'll be. Patsy Glick has come calling."

Patsy pulled her buggy to a stop and hopped out. She was wearing a light blue dress and a black apron, and as she came toward them, Nathan noticed Mick's face went all goofy and soft.

"Fetching," Mick said, under his breath, and Nathan wondered if he realized he'd said it aloud. He thrust the lamb into Nathan's arms and met her halfway. He said something to her, but she didn't stop, she just walked right around him and kept coming until she was right in front of Nathan, smiling sweetly.

"I came to get this week's list for the chalkboard signs," she said. "When you didn't drop it by, I knew you must be busy with your fields, and since I happened to be driving past . . ." She noticed the lamb in Nathan's arms. "Oh, such a sweet baby."

She drew closer to Nathan to pet the lamb, so close he could smell a familiar scent of lavender. Lydie's shampoo. Nathan suddenly realized that if Patsy was standing close enough that he could catch the scent of her hair, she could probably smell him too. The sun beat down fiercely, and he could feel sweat running off him. He'd been working in the fields all day and knew he smelled pretty ripe. He backed up a step.

She took a step closer. "I love animals, especially sheep. They're so . . . docile."

Docile was exactly why he didn't like sheep. Too dull, too predictable, too meek. "Careful. This one has a gash on its leg. It's bleeding."

A funny look covered her face. "Don't tell me that you take care of the animals too. All those beautiful fields, everyone at the farmers' market, and a baby lamb too? My goodness, Nathan, is there anything you can't do?"

By now Mick had joined them and grabbed the lamb out of Nathan's arms. "Plenty. You should watch him try to ride a horse. He can't stay on. Falls off like a sack of potatoes, every time."

That was true. Nathan had fallen off horses more times than he could count. Patsy was looking at him as if she couldn't imagine him falling off anything, and it felt kind of nice to be admired by such a pretty girl. Mick was right. She *was* fetching. Suddenly he realized he'd been staring and became self-conscious. "I have the list in the greenhouse. I'll go get it."

"You go do that. Me and this baby lamb will keep Patsy company. Take your time, little brother."

Nathan crossed the yard to the greenhouse, both amused and puzzled. He was amused by Mick's evident crush on Patsy and puzzled by it. Why would he risk losing Lydie? He just didn't understand his brother at all. Or maybe it was Lydie he no longer understood.

He opened the door to the greenhouse and paused, turning back. Mick was yakking away to Patsy, but she seemed only mildly engaged. When her eyes locked with Nathan's, she smiled that enigmatic smile of hers and gave him a little wave. With the late-afternoon sun streaming down on her, she almost looked like an angel. Nathan lifted his hand in a wave. Mick turned and scowled at him.

Now *that*, he had to admit, felt pretty good.

17

The next morning, Lydie was so late to work that she was in a total panic, especially as she faced the sloping hill that ran alongside Black Gold Farm. Nathan was just pulling out of his driveway and had started down the road, so she grabbed on to the side of his buggy and scootered alongside it. When the turnoff came to the lane that led to the Bent N' Dent and Dok's office, she let go and zoomed away. She doubted Nathan had even realized the help he'd provided to her. So like Nathan. He was always helping everyone.

Dok was at Lydie's desk, waiting for her with a solemn look on her face. As Lydie closed the door behind her, Dok pointed to the clock on the wall.

"I'm sorry. I overslept, and then I couldn't find my kapp, and then—"

Dok held up a hand to stop her. "Lydie, it's okay. The first patient had to cancel, so there's a little time. And this is a perfect opportunity to address a few things."

Oh no. "What kinds of things?"

"First, have you ever asked yourself why you're always in such a hurry?"

"Because I'm usually running late."

"If that's true, and from what I've observed, I'd say that is a very accurate self-assessment, then what can you do to eliminate the distractions or unnecessary responsibilities that make you run habitually late?"

"I . . . don't know. I've never really thought about it."

"It's worth thinking about. It's good to know where your spare time is going."

Probably to doodling.

"Here's a strategy. Plan to arrive ten minutes early. Anywhere you have to go, be ten minutes early."

That sounded logical. Okay. Lydie would try it. Starting tomorrow!

"It's all part of finding doable routines and keeping up with them."

"Wait, is this another strategy?"

"Well, sort of. It kind of blurs together with knowing where your time is going. Eating meals at regular times. Going to bed at the same time each night. Routines make a big difference."

Oh wow. Lydie's eating habits were completely erratic, thanks to Patsy Glick's chalkboard-sign kidnapping. And she never went to sleep at the same time. Last night she was reading a book and didn't turn off her flashlight until way past midnight.

"Am I throwing too much at you?"

"No, I don't think so." *Arrive ten minutes early. Eat at regular times. Go to bed at the same time. Create doable routines and keep up with them.* Those sounded very reasonable.

"Good. Because there's something else I've noticed about you."

Lydie stilled. There was more?

"How easily overwhelmed you get."

Oh. *That.* Like now. This was a lot to take in.

"There's a tip that can help you manage overwhelmed feelings."

"I'm listening!"

"The answer comes with breathing."

"Breathing," Lydie echoed.

Dok smiled. "When you're feeling overwhelmed, slow down each breath and extend your exhalation."

"Right." She scrunched up her face. "And . . . what does that actually do?"

"You'll find yourself far less overwhelmed when your mind can be calmed down. Let's start with what's happening when your mind feels overwhelmed. Say, for example, if you know you're running late to work."

Like this morning.

"That stress can trigger a chain of events to start happening inside your body. It's called 'fight or flight.' Breathing becomes shallow, your heart starts racing, your muscles tighten up—ready for action. And your mind probably feels like—"

"A Ping-Pong ball."

"Exactly." Dok chuckled. "Thoughts in your brain keep bouncing and bouncing. But when you pay attention to each breath, your whole body starts to relax."

"Right. But how?"

"When you're feeling overwhelmed, anchor your thought in the sensations of breathing. In and out. Filling your chest with air, then releasing it."

"Anchoring," Lydie echoed.

"Anchoring is just the word for it too. It doesn't mean your attention won't drift back to feeling overwhelmed, the way a boat might drift from its anchor. But if you keep returning your thoughts to your breath, it's like the pull of the anchor. Your body and your mind will start to calm down."

Lydie liked the sound of that. She let her mind roll over that imagery. She'd never thought consciously of breathing. Not ever. But then again, it almost seemed a little too . . . simple.

Dok was studying her. "Your reaction is just like your dad's. Full of skepticism. I'm going to tell you just what I told him. We need to pay attention to breathing because God taught us to. Its importance is scattered all through the Bible. God breathed life into Adam. Jesus breathed the Holy Spirit onto his disciples. In fact, the Greek word for Holy Spirit is *pneuma*, which means breath."

"As in, pneumonia?"

"Yes. *Pneuma* is the root word. Breathing might be an automatic reflex, but it's something we need to pay attention to, because God did. He pointed out how relevant breath is to us, over and over." Dok crossed her arms and leaned back in Lydie's chair. "I practice this all the time. Every day." She paused. "I focus on my breathing."

"That's it?"

"That's all there is. It might seem simple, but it's not. Worth it, though." Dok's watch beeped and she rose. "I'd better get ready for the day."

"Breathe," Lydie said quietly to herself, but Dok must have heard her.

At the doorjamb Dok turned back. "'The spirit of God hath made me, and the breath of the Almighty hath given me life.'" She smiled. "Stick with me on this, Lydie. You'll be amazed to see what the Lord can do in a single breath."

Lydie put a hand on her abdomen, the way Dok had showed her, and breathed in, held her breath, then slowly exhaled through her mouth. She did it four times, slowing down each time. And to her surprise, a sense of calm returned. Or maybe . . . returned wasn't the right word, because Lydie had rarely experienced a sense of calm. Maybe . . . calm had arrived.

❦

David was late in writing this week's sermon, but not late in thinking about it. The more he considered mindfulness, the more he felt Dok was onto something. This world tugged and pulled to keep a person's mind distracted from the Lord. It took effort to keep returning one's mind back to an awareness of God's presence.

When David was a boy growing up in Ohio, he had a Mennonite schoolteacher who loved baseball as much as David's older brother, Simon, did. One October, during the World Series, this teacher allowed David and Simon to sit in his car during lunchtime and listen to the radio. David remembered how the teacher would turn the dial to find the right frequency, and how the static would finally ease away until the sports announcer's voice came through loud and clear.

If David were to try and describe what prayerful mindfulness was, that memory nailed it. Tuning out the noisy, distracting static until the Lord's voice came through loud and clear. He even remembered how the teacher had to keep adjusting the dial because, for some reason David couldn't understand then and still couldn't understand, the frequency could get lost. It took constant adjusting to stay dialed to the right airwaves. A verse from the book of Isaiah came to mind: *He wakeneth morning by morning, he wakeneth mine ear to hear as the learned.*

Wasn't that an image of how the believer should live his life? Brief morning and evening devotions were a fine habit for his church members, but for too many, those brief devotions sufficed for all the thought and attention in a day given to the Lord.

It wasn't enough. But how could he convince his church of that? He needed a reason, an example. He couldn't mention the radio analogy without ruffling the feathers of some of his church members. They'd hear only the part about a Mennonite teacher letting pupils listen to a car radio and miss the whole point.

All these thoughts rumbled through his mind as he drove home from the store one evening. He turned the horse onto the lane that led past Black Gold Farm. Far in the distance, David slowed his horse to a stop when he caught sight of Nathan in his fields, bent over, examining a plant. Walking the beans, an old-fashioned term used for hand weeding, but Nathan meant more by it than just pulling weeds. As he walked the beans, he was examining his varied plants, on the lookout for pests or disease—and if found, could be dealt with promptly. He was evaluating a plant's growth, deciding if its needs were being met. When Nathan walked the beans, he was paying attention to his crops. David knew all this because Nathan had told him so.

The phrase "walking the beans" kept rolling over in his mind. Farmers would certainly relate to the notion of caring for one's crops, but what about using the old-fashioned phrase as a metaphor? Walking the beans wasn't just meant for the fields. It was a way of saying that a man, or a woman, should pay close attention to all that the Lord had given them. Their family, their children. The work of their hands.

David saw Nathan straighten, stretch his back, take a few steps, then bend over again . . . and a thought dawned. Those fields! Walking the beans. This young man had given him a perfect illustration from nature of what could happen when one attuned himself to the voice of the Lord. Walking the beans meant catching problems before they became insurmountable.

His horse shifted its weight, as if to remind David that dinner lay waiting at home. He picked up the reins and the horse lunged forward, eager to get to the barn.

As the buggy rolled down the shaded lane, David realized why he'd been so struck by Nathan's farming phrase. He was the one who needed to walk the beans. David had yet to look for a suitable, sustainable living situation for his mother. He spent most of his time away from home hiding at the Bent N' Dent. He'd started the *Living with Adult ADHD* book that Dok had given to him but hadn't taken the time to finish. He was the one who needed this sermon.

On Friday morning, Lydie arrived at work—ten minutes early, three days in a row!—and cringed when she saw Dok's car in the parking lot. She hurried inside the office and held her breath when she saw Dok seated at her desk. Her messy desk. "I meant to tidy up yesterday," she said, "but—"

Dok held up a hand to stop her in midsentence. "I came early for a reason. I wanted to ask you, Lydie, how are the mindfulness exercises going?"

She set her lunch bag on her desk. "Good, I think."

"Have you noticed any changes?"

Lydie glanced at the wristwatch Dok had given her. "Well, I'm not late today." Now that she thought about it, she hadn't been late all week. "Mammi noticed that I'd made my bed three days in a row." She'd been getting to bed earlier, which helped to wake up earlier. A small thing, but it made a difference.

"Anything else?"

Hmm. She had been trying to be mindful, but she hadn't thought about being mindful of being mindful.

"Never mind. Just keep practicing mindfulness and I think you'll start noticing more. As for today, I have another behavior modification exercise for you." Dok reached over to pick up the planner she'd given to Lydie on her first day and opened it up. It was empty. "Starting this very morning, I want you to fill in the planner with everything you need to do today."

Lydie cringed. "Did I mess up another patient appointment?" Or, like she did on Monday, more than one.

"This isn't for patient scheduling. This is for you. Mark down every single task that needs to be accomplished. Break down each task into small steps. Think of it like cutting down a tree, and now you need to chop the wood and then you need to stack it. Or think of cooking a meal. It's usually done in steps. Planning, preparing, cooking. See what I mean? Break it all down, sequentially. Nothing's too small for this planner."

"Right. Got it. But, um, what's the purpose of such . . . detail?"

"It will help keep your mind on your task, and it'll help you see a task all the way to the end. Each time you finish a step in a task, check it off."

"Okay." That, she'd enjoy.

"From now on, if something's not in the planner, it doesn't exist. This planner stays with you at all times. It'll become your best friend. Trust me on this. Keeping a planner changed my life."

Dok headed back to her office, and Lydie picked up the planner and held it in her hand. Wow. This little book was going to change her life? Hard to believe.

David had worked hard on his sermon and practiced it twice. But after he delivered it on Sunday morning, the church grew oddly silent. Afterward, fellowship was lacking the usual conviviality. On the Sunday evening phone call with Birdy, he tried to explain about the morning. "I'm not quite sure what fell flat. It's not that all of my sermons are well received, but this one, I felt, had a lot of substance to it. I felt as if the Lord had given me some unique insights this week as I prepared it."

"David," Birdy said in her kind way, "did you happen to mention, specifically, that the fields were being farmed by Nathan Yoder?"

"Of course. Because it's so apparent to all. Anyone who drives past Black Gold Farm can see the difference from last year to this year. It's such an ideal, timely image from nature. Nathan is doing something remarkable with his fields. Something astonishing. And it's because he's walking the beans. Birdy, I can't wait until you come home and see those fields for yourself. You'll know exactly what I mean. Why I used those fields as an illustration for my sermon."

There was a long pause on the other end. A meaningful

pause. So long that David knew Birdy was trying to get him to think and reflect. Then it hit him.

"Oh no. I shouldn't have made it so personal, should I?" Oh no. No, no, no, no. He should have known better than to shine the light on one church member above others. He did know better. His stomach tightened up.

"I just wonder if there might be some offended feelings."

David felt a little queasy. "I should have run this by you first. I just didn't . . . think." Ironic, considering the sermon was about being mindful of one's task. "I said it looked like the garden of Eden."

Birdy gasped. "You didn't."

"I did."

Another long, long pause. "Well, David, let's pray that the Lord will use this for good."

They finished chatting, and David hung up the phone feeling a little better. Until he left the phone shanty and noticed a long line of gray-topped buggies heading down the road toward Black Gold Farm. He didn't have to wonder for long as to the reason. Hank Lapp stuck his head out of his buggy to yell, "GOING to have a LOOK at NATHAN's GARDEN of EDEN for myself!"

Apparently, no one in Stoney Ridge had noticed Nathan's fields except for David, not until this morning's sermons.

⸺⸺∞⸺⸺

On Monday afternoon, as Lydie scootered home from Dok's office, she nearly scooted right into a tree when she turned the corner and saw buggies stacked up, slowly inching their way along. It was so quiet. At first she thought there'd been a funeral and she might have missed listening to the death message when it was announced in church. Then she realized that people in the buggies had slowed to a crawl to get a long look at Nathan's beautiful swirling fields of growing fruits and vegetables.

The sight gave her a smile. Nathan deserved this. He cared

about Black Gold Farm, but he also wanted to help other farmers improve their yields by nourishing their land. To use her dad's favorite phrase, Nathan's intent was for the common good.

She let the scooter come to a stop and leaned against a tree, watching. Noticing. Thinking. Mentally doodling.

18

Lydie had lost count of how many patients in Dok's waiting room talked about her doodle in this Wednesday's edition of the *Stoney Ridge Times*. She kept her chin tucked low whenever it was brought up, or when the newspaper was shared with another patient. She'd taken a lot of time with this doodle before dropping it into the mailbox, but she probably should have taken even more time. She shouldn't have made the location quite so obvious. In place of the sign that read *Black Gold Farm*, she inserted *Amish Garden of Eden*. And the caption below all the buggies read "Amish traffic jam."

So, everyone in Stoney Ridge, Plain *and* Englisch, seemed to know these were Nathan Yoder's fields. Everyone, including Owen Miller.

On Thursday morning, he came to Dok's office for his weekly allergy shot and overheard two women talking about the doodle in the newspaper. Seated at her receptionist's desk, Lydie watched him from the corner of her eye. His leg couldn't stop fidgeting, but his narrowed focus was on those women. She could see his temper rising as they laughed and laughed, pointing at the paper.

"There's nothing funny about *that*," he said.

The two women stopped laughing and looked over at Owen, noticing him for the first time. "Have you been down that road lately?" one said. "It's blocked with gawkers. Nathan Yoder's worked a miracle in those fields."

Owen rose to his feet. "You want to see a real garden of Eden? Go take a look at his brother Mick's corn crop. That's the real deal." He left the office in a huff.

As soon as Lydie got home that evening, she went to the hole in the hedge that bordered Black Gold Farm. She could hear the rustling of corn leaves in the wind even before she could see Mick's acreage. As far as the eye could see was a sea of dark green cornstalks. Healthy, thriving, as much as she could tell. Mick's corn crop looked incredible.

The night was sticky warm and Nathan had trouble sleeping. His hands and arms were covered with a red rash. All day long he'd been harvesting produce to sell at tomorrow's market—the last of the mature lettuce crop due to such hot weather, the first of the ripening heirloom tomatoes for the same reason. He'd filled bins with Kentucky Wonder beans, cucumbers, dark Romanesco zucchinis, and Pattypan squash. Those he blamed for his rash. Their thick stalks, massive leaves, and sprawling vines were swathed with tiny thorns. Just sharp enough to leave him scratching and itching all night.

He was especially pleased about how many zucchini squash blossoms he'd been able to harvest. Last week, a foodie crowd customer had told him she would buy every blossom he could deliver this Saturday. She was having a dinner party tomorrow night and planned to dip the blossoms in a tempura mix and fry them for her guests. While he had no desire to eat a flower, he felt a joy that the food he grew was providing sustenance for others.

He'd learned a lot from the foodie crowd, things he wanted to remember for next summer's harvest. They were dedicated, loyal customers, with a passion for good food. They were unconcerned about the price of produce, only interested in the varieties. He'd had fascinating conversations with foodies at the market and felt as if he was able to identify true foodies by the questions they asked. He smiled, thinking of a market moment last Saturday morning. Patsy Glick had come by his stand and noticed the long line of customers, so she had offered to help him. A foodie handed Patsy a bag of green beans to weigh on the scale and asked her the variety. Patsy answered with a shrug. "A bean is a bean."

Nathan and the foodie crowd customer gasped out loud. "Blue Lake," Nathan quickly said, handing the foodie her bag of beans.

After the customer had left, he must have given Patsy a patronizing look because she lifted her palms in the air. "What?"

"It's like saying your brothers are all boys. Like they don't have a name."

Confusion covered her face. "Are you trying to say that your plants are like babies?"

Well, sort of. Each plant was a living thing to him, something he spent time fussing over. Kinda like his babies.

A customer interrupted them and the conversation was forgotten. He hadn't even thought of it until now. He scratched his arms and rolled over to face the window, hoping for a breeze. The air was still, the heat wave had yet to break. Tomorrow would be just as hot as today.

At least his plants loved July's heat and humidity. The harvest was constant, and he dared not let up. Come August, he'd start spinach, lettuce, and kale seedlings in the greenhouse, as well as onions and garlic. Carrots and radishes too. He wouldn't set the seedlings out in the fields until September, when the other crops were winding down. All but the pumpkin patch. He planned to let the pumpkins stay in the field until a frost or two hardened them off. In October, he would sow fava beans directly into the soil and let them grow. After the first snowfall or two, he'd till them under, start fava bean seedlings in the greenhouse for a February sowing, and the process would begin all over again. Assuming he'd have a chance to do it again. Mick's GMO corn, by all appearances, was living up to its promise of being a Wunderseed. It seemed to be impervious to problems.

He hadn't been quite so lucky, especially with the moles. Such well-tilled soil only made moles' digging work easier. Still, despite a few other pest outbreaks this summer, he'd been able to head them off before there was much damage. It took steady vigilance. Something was always threatening the crops. With each problem came an opportunity. When snails and slugs became prevalent among his strawberries, he went straight over to Penny Weaver's, known in Stoney Ridge for her fondness for fowl, and bought a dozen ducks. When the ducks had reduced the snail population and started nipping greedily at his strawberries, he borrowed Hank Lapp's dogs and let them loose in the fields. The ducks quickly took to the skies. The moles disappeared into their holes. It was all about balance.

This was the farmer's life and Nathan loved every minute of it. This, he knew, was what he was meant for. Caring for the earth in the way it *should* be cared for.

He flopped on his back. Maybe it wasn't just the itchy rash that was keeping him awake. After seeing the height of Mick's cornstalks in mid-July, he was pretty sure that, come fall, he would be faced with a hard decision. The deeper he dove into organic farming, the greater his commitment grew. He now knew he could never go back.

~

The last patient of the day was Walt Yoder. He came into the office, growled "I'm here to see Dok" at Lydie, and she sent him right back to wait in an exam room. She'd already thought it through, long before Walt arrived. She couldn't stand having him sit and glare at her in the waiting room. His visit took a long time, so long that Lydie went outside and told Patsy Glick that she couldn't leave until Dok left. "You can go on home. I'll scooter over to your barn after Dok leaves."

Patsy hesitated. "I don't know . . ."

"It doesn't get dark until after nine o'clock. I'll get the boards done."

Still, Patsy waited.

"What?"

"I just don't get the feeling that you're doing anything to help me with Nathan."

"I've tried! I really have. But I work full-time. You've got me doing boards each evening. I have no free time to do much of anything else." Especially when she needed to keep up with Dok's strategies. That planner took a huge amount of time each night. Hard work, but it was helping. She was feeling encouraged by her progress.

Patsy frowned. "Tomorrow morning, then, at the market. Nathan always needs an extra hand behind his booth."

"So does Fern."

"I'll get one of my brothers to help Fern. You be sure to help Nathan. Tell him all the things you like about me." She smiled. "Easy peasy."

Dok's office door opened and Walt Yoder came out, scowling at Lydie. Patsy's voice lifted sweetly. "Hello, Walt. How are you today?"

He shifted his scowl to Patsy and then his face brightened. "Hello, Patsy. Say hello to your folks for me." He unhooked his horse's reins from the hitching post and climbed into his buggy, then drove off.

Lydie started walking backward toward Dok's office. "I'll come over soon." She turned and went into the office.

Dok was seated at Lydie's desk, head down, writing on a message pad. "Walt's going to need a few tests, so I'm making a note to myself to get things set up for him." She finished and folded the note, tucking it in her pocket, then leaned back in the chair. "Lydie, how's it going with the planner?"

"Good, I think. I'm starting to do better at breaking a task down into steps. It helps me not feel so overwhelmed." A few days ago, Lydie had a huge insight about herself. Whenever she felt overwhelmed by how big a job was, she would stop what she was doing and move on to something easier. Breaking things down helped her to focus on one step at a time instead of tackling an entire task, which overwhelmed her.

Dok smiled. "I've noticed a lot of improvements. Even small things, like closing cupboard doors in the exam rooms."

Oh, *that*. A bad habit. Lydie's sisters were always complaining that she left doors and drawers open.

"So then, it's time to add another strategy. Pull up a chair."

Lydie dragged a waiting-room chair over to her receptionist's desk and sat across from Dok.

"This strategy is a game changer." She clapped her hands on her knees. "Prioritizing."

"Isn't that what the planner is for?"

"Yes. But now we're going to turn up the heat and take it up a notch. You're already doing it."

"How so?"

"Yesterday, when Billy Zook fell off a swing and broke his arm, you went right into action to cancel the afternoon appointments."

"But I knew you had to leave to take Billy to get an x-ray."

"True. So you're understanding *my* need to prioritize. Now I want you to start looking at *your* own life. When new ideas or tasks or opportunities fall your way, you have to evaluate their importance. If it's a high priority, schedule it in. If it's a low priority, schedule it for later on. Kind of like Billy's broken arm. Obviously, it's high priority. But it doesn't mean I won't be seeing patients at other appointment times."

Lydie glanced at her own planner. This new priority strategy would require flexibility. She decided she would start using a pencil instead of a pen.

"Here's a tip I learned the hard way so you don't have to. Check your daily priorities first thing in the morning . . . *before* you start responding to the priorities of other people." She leaned forward. "Lydie, you're a very nice person. And I've noticed that you have a hard time saying no. You've got to start practicing."

"Practicing nos."

"Exactly. Work on the easy things first. Say no to the things you really don't want to do."

As Dok left to head back to her office, Lydie thought about the party this Saturday night that horrible Owen Miller was throwing. She'd finally caved in and said she'd go because Mick had kept badgering her. She wished Dok had given her this talk a few days ago.

19

It was Saturday morning. Patsy met Lydie and Fern's buggy as they pulled into the parking lot of the high school.

"I'm glad you're early," Patsy said, smiling, as she took the reins from Lydie to tie the horse to the post. When Lydie had climbed out of the buggy, Patsy whispered, "Thanks."

"For what?"

"Nathan's driving me home today. Whatever you said to him, it's working. I can tell . . . he's started to notice me. In fact, I think he's smitten. I'm sure of it."

Smitten?

"I gave Nathan an idea that he thought was brilliant. Just brilliant. He said so himself."

"What idea?"

"A basket of seconds." Patsy flashed her most innocent look.

Hold it just one minute. That had been Lydie's idea! During one of the kidnapped-by-Patsy chalkboard sessions, she had brought along a bag of cherry tomatoes because she was hungry from missing supper and Patsy never brought her much of anything to eat. She had casually mentioned that the cherry tomatoes were from Nathan. He had shared with Mammi some of his produce that didn't look quite good enough to sell at the farmers' market—split tomatoes, scarred zucchini, sunburned peppers—and they tasted every bit as delicious as the produce he displayed each week. "He should just sell the second-best vegetables at a discount," Lydie had said to Patsy.

And apparently, Patsy had shared the idea with Nathan.

"Fern! I'm glad you're here," Patsy said. "Nathan brought so much produce that he needs an extra hand today. I'd help, but my mother needs me. So I told him I'd send Lydie over."

As Fern climbed out of the buggy to join them, she gave Patsy a suspicious look. "Since when does Nathan Yoder need someone to do his bidding for him?"

Patsy pursed her lips, reminding Lydie quite a bit of her mother. "I'm just trying to be neighborly. You don't mind, do you, Lydie?"

Yes, she did. The only way to keep her feelings in check about Nathan was to stay far away from him. "Okay with you, Fern?" Her voice sounded feeble, even to her own ears.

"As long as one of you carries these heavy boxes to my stand, I don't mind who helps."

Patsy picked up a box of jam jars. "You heard her. Go!"

Lydie hurried over to Nathan's stand. For once, Patsy was right. It was a *mess*. Pure chaos. Baskets of produce were everywhere. Large wicker baskets brimmed with beans, overfull, heaped high, but they were all mixed up. Nathan's back was to her. He was scribbling things down on paper. "What happened?"

At the sound of her voice, Nathan spun around, a look of panic in his eyes. "I was turning into the school parking lot when a motorcycle ran through a stop sign and I had to veer off the road. All the baskets tipped over in my cart."

"Right. But what are you *doing*?"

He held up a paper and pencil. "I can't find my sidewalk sign anywhere, so I thought I'd just tape a bunch of paper signs up so customers know the prices." He looked around. "But I can't find my scale, so price per pound seems rather irrelevant."

Lydie's gaze swept the mixed-up baskets and boxes and she had no idea what to do next. Or first. It was overwhelming. "Billy Zook's broken arm!"

Nathan's head jerked up. "What? Someone has a broken arm?"

Did she really say that out loud? "Nathan . . . this is the time to prioritize. First, beans belong in their rightful places." She sank to her knees and started with the mixed-up beans: one basket filled with green Kentucky Wonders, one basket with Blue Lakes, and in the third basket, she did a color split, half with Royal Burgundies and half yellow wax beans. "Do you have another basket for the Dow Purple Pod beans?"

Nathan was in the middle of dumping a box of zucchini out on the stand and stopped. "You know the varieties?"

"Of course."

He got a pleased look on his face, then finished dumping the rest of the zucchini out. "Those small baby beans can go in a small basket. They're for the—"

"Foodie crowd." She smiled. "See? I listen when you tell me something." So many people didn't think she did. She did listen! She just didn't always remember what she had listened to. Her smile faded. "What are you doing?"

He glanced at his pile of zucchini. "Stacking zucchini."

She jumped up. "I just read an article in one of Dok's magazines about how to display produce at a farmers' market." She had only read it because of Nathan. "The goal is to create an appearance of abundance. People gravitate to abundance." She piled the zucchini in a pyramid. On the other side of the pyramid of zucchini she stacked yellow zucchini, also neat and tidy. And then the scalloped-edged Patty. On the other side, she set out baskets of clusters of bright red Husky tomatoes. "There."

He watched her, amazed. "Pile it high, watch it fly."

She laughed, and he grinned, and they stood there, locked eyes, for way too long. She felt heat start to flood her cheeks.

Think, think, think. "Patsy!" It burst out of her in an overly loud voice.

"Patsy?"

"Doesn't she always look like she just stepped out of a shower?" Such a *stupid* thing to say! But she had told Patsy she'd say something nice about her and that was the first thing that came to mind. The only thing.

Nathan looked a little baffled. "Well, yes. I suppose she does look . . . put together."

Unlike Lydie, whose hair was constantly escaping its pins, and whose apron could've used ironing—she had yanked it off the clothesline as she rushed to get ready for the market this morning. She saw Nathan's gaze turn toward Patsy, over at her family's stand. Patsy noticed, and gave Nathan a little feminine five-finger wave, and he lifted a hand in response and smiled.

Lydie wanted to gag. "So, what next?" That, too, sounded way too loud.

He glanced around. "Bunch the greens. Start with basil." He brought out pails of greens—basil, spinach, kale, Swiss chard.

"On it." She snapped rubber bands around bright green bunches of basil and turned to the spinach.

Nathan had set out a jumbled basket of produce and taped a sign to them: SECONDS. CHEAP. "What time is it?"

She glanced at her wristwatch and gasped. "Ten minutes to nine!"

The last few minutes before the market opened passed like seconds. Nathan rushed around taping up more price signs.

"Nathan, you need to go ring the bell."

"Right." He looked around his stand. "Better, but not ready yet. I've just never had this much produce to display before." He picked up a box and stacked it on another box. "And I still haven't found the scale."

Lydie grabbed the papers and tape out of his hand. "Go! I'll take care of everything."

Nathan hesitated, then gave her a nod and headed down the long aisle to ring the opening bell. Lydie stopped rearranging produce to tidy up the area. She found the scale (phew!) and set it up on Nathan's stand—his door-on-top-of-sawhorses. Under a large box she found his chalkboard, facedown, most of the writing she had done at Patsy's barn was smudged. She dashed back to Fern's table, grabbed a piece of chalk, and dashed back to crouch in front of the chalkboard. She wiped the entire board off with a corner of her apron, then rewrote everything she could remember. Quickly, she yanked Nathan's paper price signs off his door-stand. She rewrote one sign and taped it on: NEARLY PERFECT PRODUCE. $1 PER POUND. From a few yards away, she looked at the stand, seeing what else needed to be done. She moved the bean baskets closer together, and balanced a pile of small paper lunch bags in the middle. An invitation to customers to fill their own bags.

There. *Transformed*. Black Gold Farm's stand looked better than it ever had. Tidy, almost overflowing with colorful produce, ready for customers.

Too soon, the opening market bell rang and people poured down the aisle. In a matter of minutes, Lydie was weighing produce, taking cash, making change, and talking to customers. That part, she liked best. One woman asked her if she had a recipe to recommend for the Husky cherry tomatoes, and Lydie said, "Roast them, add them to spaghetti noodles, olive oil, salt, and pepper. Just before serving, toss in minced basil. Lots of basil." Mammi had given Lydie a bowlful of that very dish last night, after she got home from Patsy's chalkboard writing session. She handed the woman a bundle of basil.

"I'll take two," the lady said, and Lydie handed her another bunch.

Nathan sidled behind the stand and helped with the next customer. The two of them worked side by side, handling the first wave of customers. That was something Lydie had learned these last few Saturdays. Customers arrived in waves. When there was a pause, regroup and clean up and get ready for the next wave.

"Lydie, you're a natural at this."

The compliment took her so by surprise that she had to stop and stare at Nathan. When his eyes caught hers, there was a fiery sparkle in them that made her remember kissing him at Blue Lake Pond. Her mind went blank and she felt herself blushing. "I'm what?"

"You're a natural. Selling. No . . . more than that. Connecting with people."

"No, not really."

"Yes. *Really*. You have a way with people. No wonder Dok likes having you work at her office. I bet you're really good at that job."

Impossible. She wasn't good at her job. She made mistakes every single day.

"You have this bottomless energy thing about you."

Now that, she couldn't deny. She did have a lot of energy. Way too much, Mammi said.

Nathan was picking up beans that had dropped on the ground in front of the stand. He glanced around, then did a second look. "The chalkboard. You found it."

"I did. It was under a box."

He kept staring at it, an odd look on his face.

"What's wrong?"

"It's just that . . . it's different than it was this morning, when I picked it up at Patsy's."

"Oh, that. The chalk had smudged so I redid it. I mean . . . I rewrote the prices. I mean . . . I wrote the prices."

"But how'd you know what to write? How'd you know the prices?" He turned to the NEARLY PERFECT sign on the now empty basket of seconds. "And how'd you know—"

"Look!" She pointed behind him. "Another wave's coming."

It was like a bus just pulled up to dump more customers at the opening. A crowd was making their way up the aisle. "Watch out. These are the nine-thirty people. They're fussier than the nine o'clock ones."

Nathan grinned. "Good observation! The nine o'clock people are the ones that want to get in and get out. The nine-thirty people are the foodie crowd. The fussies. They have to squeeze and sniff everything." He peered over the stand at the cashbox. "I'd better go see if someone can swap a twenty for one-dollar bills."

"I think Fern brought extra singles."

As soon as Nathan disappeared, Lydie found herself scrambling to weigh beans and zucchinis, and replenish the basil bunches.

An elderly gentleman squeezed a zucchini. "Is this a cucumber?"

"No, it's a Romanesco zucchini," Lydie said. "It's an old Italian variety."

He peered at the squash, clearly not helped. "My wife sent me to get cucumbers."

Cucumbers! Where were the cucumbers? "Hold on!" Lydie looked under another box and found a box of dark green cucumbers. She held one out to the gentleman.

"My wife said to get three."

A middle-aged woman waved a bunch of basil in her face as she bent down to grab more cucumbers. "Do you have more?"

"Yes, one second. I'm just finishing up with another customer." She handed three cucumbers in a paper bag to the gentleman. "That'll be two dollars," she said, hoping he'd give her exact change. But no! He handed her a five-dollar bill and walked away with her last three singles. She looked over the woman's head to see if Nathan was on his way back with dollar bills. No sign of him.

"I want four more bunches. I'm making pesto." The woman sounded annoyed.

"Coming right up." Lydie bent down and grabbed an enormous amount of basil, snapping a single rubber band around the entire bouquet. "Here you go. A dollar a bunch."

The woman sniffed the bouquet, eyeing it warily. "Are there really five bunches in this?"

"More than five." Good grief! There was a long line of customers behind this woman. But then she handed over five single dollar bills, so Lydie added one more bunch of basil to her bouquet. Just in case.

∞

All morning long, until he rang the closing bell for the market, Nathan had to keep himself in check. Whenever there was a lull in customers and he'd realize Lydie was by his side, just like in his imagination, he wanted to pull her into his arms and say, *It's finally happened! We're back on track. Working like a team together, the way we always did.*

He wanted to say to her, *I have missed you so much. I've missed your out-of-the-blue remarks. I've missed your spunk, your candor. I've missed your quirky humor. I've missed everything, Lydie. Everything.*

He wanted to say all that and more, but he held back. He was worried he would scare her off, that any progress made toward repairing their friendship would disappear. And so his heart wasn't able to say what it wanted to say. But it was the best morning he'd had in a very long time.

And the afternoon wasn't bad, either.

Nathan had offered to drive Patsy home because she'd said her mom was heading to Edith Lapp's after the market closed and she was going to have to walk home. How could he not offer to help her out when she'd done so much for him? He was pleased to learn that she was planning to be baptized this fall, and hoped she wasn't the only reason his brother, Mick, had a sudden change of heart and raised his hand to start the classes.

Ah, Mick. It probably was the only reason he was getting baptized. The more Patsy ignored Mick, the harder he chased her.

Nathan tried not to think of how much he would enjoy the look on his brother's face when he casually dropped the news at dinner tonight that he'd driven Patsy home from the market. He might even mention that he stayed for a while, and played ball with her brothers, and helped her dad saw a dead branch off a tree. He might even mention that Patsy's dad clapped him on the back and told him to come back anytime. Nathan thought he might just do that, because he'd enjoyed the afternoon with the Glicks. And all of that was the truth.

But no. If he were to tell Mick about his afternoon with Patsy, it would be for all the wrong reasons. He sent up a quick prayer for forgiveness. He'd learned long ago not to compete with Mick. It didn't stop his brother from turning everything into a contest between them, but Nathan knew that joining in felt . . . wrong.

If Mick wanted to cheat on Lydie, that was his business. She was his to lose.

⁓

Lydie should never have let Mick talk her into coming to this party. As they arrived, music was blasting out of the house. She wasn't even sure whose house it was. At the front door, she said, "I don't think I should go in there."

"Relax," Mick said. He pushed her through the door into a cloud of cigarette smoke.

Or was it cigarette smoke? A sickly sweet odor pinched her nose. "What's that smell?" It reminded her of burning alfalfa.

Mick wasn't listening. He had spotted someone across the room. "Well, well. Look who's rocking out. I didn't believe Owen, but he was right. She *is* a party girl."

Lydie followed his gaze to a girl with hair color that was not seen in nature—kind of a shimmering, glittery pink. At first she thought it was the girl's hair that caught Mick's attention, but then she realized the girl was wearing a halter top, with her bare back entirely exposed. Then the girl swung around. Wow. Her facial features . . . she was a dead ringer for Patsy Glick. Lydie squinted through the haze. Hold on! She *was* Patsy Glick.

Mick started over toward her, but Lydie grabbed his arm. "Wait. Just wait right here. Let me go talk to her first."

He frowned, then his face relaxed into a knowing smile. "Gotcha. Grease the wheels. Talk me up."

Fat chance. She had more on her mind to discuss with Perfect Patsy than Mick. Slowly, she wormed her way through the knots of strangers. "What are you doing here?"

Patsy's eyes went wide when she saw Lydie. "What are *you* doing here?"

Disgusted, Lydie pulled Patsy by the elbow over to a corner where they could hear each other without shouting. "Why are you dressed like . . . that?"

"Me? Look at you. You're in street clothes."

"But at least I'm covered up! You . . . you're practically naked."

Patsy rolled her eyes. "I'm just having a little excitement before I get baptized this fall. It's all in good fun."

"I don't even know what to say to you. What would your mother think?"

Patsy scoffed. "That's the pot calling the kettle black! You know all about a good time. Mick told me you're jumping the fence."

"What? Mick told you that?" He had promised Lydie he'd never say a word to anyone. Not to another soul!

"But . . . what about Nathan?"

Patsy frowned. "What about him?"

"I thought you liked him. I thought you were serious about him." That was the only reason Lydie had agreed to play matchmaker for them.

"I do. I am. Very serious. Very, very serious." She leaned in. "I've decided he's the *one*."

"But does he know you're a . . ." She waved her hands at Patsy's outfit.

Patsy narrowed her eyes. "I'm a . . . what?"

The music stopped, but Lydie's voice stayed loud. "A party girl?" Everyone stopped and turned toward them.

"I'm not," Patsy hissed. "I'm only having a little fun." She poked Lydie's arm. "You'd better not tell Nathan you saw me or . . ." She leaned in close. "Or . . . I might have to tell your dad that you're the one who submits those drawings to the newspaper."

Lydie swallowed. "You told Edith it was the reporter for the *Stoney Ridge Times*."

"I thought it was him until I saw you sitting in a corner at the Sweet Tooth Bakery, doodling away, just like you used to do in school." She gave a smug smile, with just a hint of meanness. "Personally, I think the doodles are amusing, but my parents think someone is out there watching them, looking for ways to mock them. That's how most *everyone* in Stoney Ridge feels about them. Your grandmother, for one." Satisfied, Patsy disappeared into the crowd.

Someone turned on music again and then everyone went back to drinking and talking and laughing and dancing and smoking.

Mocking? Lydie wasn't trying to mock anyone. Not really. They were just lighthearted moments in the Plain life. And good grief . . . didn't everyone need lighter hearts? She thought so.

Hot. It was so stifling hot in here. She couldn't stand it and didn't know how anyone could. Inching past dancers, slipping between them, she finally made it to the door. Just as she stepped out into the fresh air, hard fingers dug into her arm and she was spun around, abruptly.

Owen Miller. *Ugh*.

"Nice to see you out of your old-fangled garb." He had to talk around a wad of chewing tobacco in his mouth. He reeked of it.

She yanked her arm out of his viselike grip. "I came out here for fresh air."

"I came out here to remind you to shut Nathan Yoder up. He's ruining my business."

"Nathan's not trying to ruin you. He's just doing what he thinks is best. He can't help it if other farmers see that his ideas about organic farming are good."

"Get him to shut his trap. Or else."

"Or else what?"

He ran the back of his hand lightly, lightly down her throat. The hairs at the back of her neck stood on end, but she held his stare. "You really don't want to find out." He smiled, but his eyes remained cold, and he went back inside to the party.

When the door shut behind him, she leaned against the porch railing, and her breath gusted out of her with such force, it left her feeling dizzy.

Two *or elses* in less than five minutes! She was done with parties. She had to get out of here. She felt . . . overwhelmed.

Think, think, think. What did Dok say to do in moments like these?

Breathe in, breathe out. She put her hands on her abdomen and felt the fresh air fill her lungs, then empty. In and out. She thought of the Lord filling Adam's lungs with air for the very first time. Breathe in, breathe out. She thought of Jesus breathing the Holy Spirit onto the disciples. Breathe in, breathe out. She felt herself calming, and each time her mind bounced back to Patsy and Owen, she reined it in. Breathe in, breathe out.

"Lydie?" Mick's call floated toward her from inside the door. He must have been looking for her. He pushed the door open. "There you are! Come back inside."

"Mick, I want to go home."

"Home? Why? We just got here."

"I'm just . . . not feeling well. The heat. That smoke." She shuddered.

He frowned, then his face brightened. "Take my buggy. I'll hitch a ride home with Pink-Wigged Patsy." He wiggled his eyebrows.

"Mick . . . did you know she was here tonight?"

"Why do you think I've been trying so hard to get Owen to invite me?"

"Seriously?" Lydie shook her head. "You consider him a friend and he's never invited you to his parties?"

"Do you always need to point out the obvious?" Mick looked offended. "He's selective about who comes to his parties."

"Hold on. Has *Patsy* been coming to these? Regularly?"

"Bingo."

Lydie put her hands on her cheeks. "I thought I knew her, but I don't." Nobody did. Patsy had everybody fooled. Everyone except, it seemed, Mick. And creepy Owen Miller.

"Let's just say, there's more to Patsy than meets the eye." He bounced his bushy eyebrows in that knowing way. "And what meets the eye is pretty sweet."

Fine. She was done trying to protect Mick from getting his heart broken. She had Nathan to worry about. Owen Miller meant business.

So did Patsy Glick. And now she realized that Nathan and Patsy couldn't be more mismatched. She couldn't leave Stoney Ridge, not yet. Not until she had untangled this big mess.

20

The next day was an off-Sunday. In the late afternoon, Lydie was flopped on her bed, writing in her planner, concentrating so intently that she hadn't realized Mammi had come into her room and was standing right beside the bed. Not until Mammi cleared her throat.

Startled, she dropped her pencil. "Mammi!"

"Lydie, stop what you're doing and take this loaf of zucchini bread over to Fern Lapp's." With two hands, she held out a package wrapped in aluminum foil.

Take time in making a decision. Dok's voice echoed through Lydie's head. *Take two deep breaths, pause,* then *respond.* She inhaled in and out, in and out. That only took seconds, but it felt like minutes had passed. "I'm sorry, Mammi. But as you can see, I'm in the middle of something."

Mammi didn't miss a beat. "She gave me the zucchinis and I promised her I'd bring her a loaf of zucchini bread. I completely forgot to take it to her yesterday." She kept holding out the loaf of bread, waiting for Lydie to jump up and do her bidding, like she always did.

Don't say yes just to be nice. Don't say yes just to make up for all the mistakes you've made before. It's okay to say no.

But, Dok, Lydie thought, *this is Mammi! The hardest person in the world to say no to.*

Then she remembered that Dok already knew all that. After all, she had been raised by Mammi. "If it's that important, you're going to have to take it to Windmill Farm yourself. If it can wait, when I'm done with my project, I'll take it over to Fern's." She swallowed. "Mammi, I'm trying to finish what I start. It's important for me to stay focused on what's in my planner."

Mammi stared at Lydie for the longest time. "Fine," she said, huffy. "Fine. I'll take it over myself." Her lips held a tiny twitch of a smile.

❧

David drove past Black Gold Farm and let Old Jim slow to a stop. Each time he came by, he saw something new. Today, he noticed bright red tomatoes on thick green bushes. Rows and rows of them. A heat wave had settled over Stoney Ridge, and it looked like Nathan's tomatoes were benefiting from it. He took off his straw hat and wiped his forehead with the back of his sleeve, glad something was benefiting from this heat.

He wished Birdy were here to see the transformation of Black Gold Farm under Nathan's management. She would be cheering him on.

When Frank Miller's son had first started aerial spraying, Birdy had wanted David to put an end to it. It had caused some friction between them because David, not being a farmer, had a policy of letting the farmers make their own decisions about how to manage the problems on their farms. As long as the Plain farmers weren't up in the air with the pilot, he just didn't feel right about objecting. Farmers like Walt Yoder were doing all they could to make a living.

Birdy had grown exasperated with David. "Just because it's not wrong doesn't make it right."

In the end, he did tell Walt Yoder that he had to notify his neighbors when he planned to have the spraying done. And that Walt should wait for windless days, preferably cool. David thought it was a fine compromise. Birdy felt otherwise. She kept the windows closed whenever the Yoders were spraying their fields, even when they had a heat wave like this one. Worse than this one. He had to smile. Birdy had a way of getting her point across.

His smile faded. A week ago, he'd called his brother, Simon, to see if he might be ready for Mom to return to Ohio. Simon had yet to return David's call.

∽

July was almost over. So far, the produce that was coming out of Nathan's fields surpassed his expectations. Now and then, there'd been a few problems, but they were manageable. Come August, Nathan expected to be astonished. He'd always thought of it as the month of miracles.

A summer storm blew into Stoney Ridge on Thursday, breaking the heat wave that had gripped the area the last few days. It had rained all day yesterday, and today was cool, the soil moist but not muddy. A good day to harvest carrots, radishes, and beets. As he made his way down the long rows, he bypassed the smaller specimens, letting them enjoy another week to grow. It was a good day to be a farmer, a great day, and Nathan finished up with a deep sense of satisfaction.

That feeling lasted until supper. His father asked him about what he was bringing in from the fields today. "Seemed like you spent all day in the same place."

"No, not at all," Nathan said. "I was just moving slowly over the rows. Harvesting for tomorrow's market."

His father jabbed his meatloaf with his fork. "You'll not make much progress going at that pace."

His dad was always trying to tell him how to farm. Why couldn't he just let him do things his way?

"Walt, he's doing just fine," his mom said. "Just think of how people talk about those fields of his."

Nathan gave his mom a slight smile. Contradicting Dad wasn't something she did often. She seemed pleased by what Nathan was trying to do. As if she understood that he was reaching back to her father's ways, to setting the farm right.

Mick might have sensed it too. He glanced at Mom with a scowl on his face. He hadn't had much to say tonight until now. "It doesn't matter how long Nathan takes to bring in a carrot. Have you seen my corn? There's not enough carrots in his fields to match what this year's corn crop will yield." He'd started by talking to Mom, but finished by looking to Dad. For approval, for a blessing. But none came.

His dad shook his fork at Mick. "Looks to me like the mosaic virus has a hold on your corn."

Mick dropped his eyes. "I've got it handled."

What would it take? Nathan thought. Would he and his brother always look to their father for something he'd never give them? Maybe he just didn't have it to give. His mother had once said that his father's upbringing had been a harsh one. Was that why he couldn't show any love to his sons? If Nathan were to have children of his own one day, and he hoped he would, he was determined to be a different kind of father. One like David Stoltzfus.

Nathan knew that he was unlikely to come out a winner this summer, at least by his father's and Mick's standards. But he still wouldn't change a thing. The wide variety of crops, the farmers' market, the connection he'd been making with other farmers. As far as he was concerned, even with a miracle month ahead, he'd already been given some miracles.

On Saturday morning, Lydie was behind Fern's booth at the farmers' market when Owen Miller appeared out of the crowd. "I'll take some of that jam," he said with an oddly cold smile. As Lydie handed him a jar, he leaned over to whisper, "Don't forget our little chat at my party."

As if she could forget!

Owen walked off without paying for the jam. She shivered, feeling the beating of her heart as loud as a drum. "Such nerve," she muttered.

Fern appeared out of nowhere. "What was that all about?"

"I thought you were taking a break."

"I was. Now I'm back. Why do you look like you've seen a ghost? What did he want?"

"Your jam." Lydie shrugged, like it was no big deal, but it was. She felt jittery by Owen's visit, distracted, and she tried to keep an eye on Nathan. The line for his booth went all the way down one aisle, all because of his colorful, odd-shaped heirloom tomatoes. They were like a magnet at the farmers' market.

And suddenly, there was Patsy, standing right in front of Fern's booth, with a cat-that-swallowed-a-canary smile. "Doesn't Nathan's stand look particularly inviting? I brought him those baskets to use. I think those display baskets are the reason he's selling so well this morning, don't you think?"

Fern scoffed. "I think what's in those baskets is what's selling so well."

Lydie glanced at Fern, a little surprised by the sharpness in her tone.

It sailed right past Patsy. "You'll have to try to get over to my mother's booth, Fern. She's giving away free samples of her strawberry jam." She moved right along, straight toward Nathan's stand.

"Martha'd better give it away before it goes bad."

Lydie turned to Fern. "Are you feeling okay? You seem a little . . . um . . . testy."

"Martha Glick's strawberry jam jars didn't seal right so she's telling everyone it's a special kind of refrigerator jam."

Fern was selling strawberry jam today too. A little more expensive than Martha Glick's, but then again, the lid had sealed so it wouldn't go bad in a week. Still, there weren't many customers lining up for Fern's jams. Martha Glick seemed to have cornered the market on strawberry jam sales today. After a long stretch without a single customer, Lydie asked Fern if she'd mind if she took a break. She wanted to see for herself if Nathan really was causing Owen Miller to lose customers. She sidled along the edge of the booth, listening to Nathan's conversation with a middle-aged man wearing a large-brimmed hat.

"My wife says she can't go back to a store-bought tomato after tasting yours."

Nathan weighed the man's tomatoes on his scale. "These heirlooms are pretty special."

"So why don't more farmers grow them?"

Lydie knew that scratchy voice. She craned her neck to see the Stoney Ridge reporter, jotting down notes. He'd been standing on the other side of the middle-aged man in the big hat, and it looked like he was trying to interview Nathan.

"They're hard to grow," Nathan said. "Sensitive to disease. Thin-skinned, which makes them hard to pack. Plus, as you can see, their shapes are kind of odd."

"But so sweet." The man in the big hat took his bag of tomatoes from Nathan and handed him a few dollars.

"They're so sweet," Nathan said, "because they're vine-ripened. You'll never get that flavor in a store-bought tomato. That's why people shop at farmers' markets."

None of that sounded terribly threatening to Lydie. Maybe Owen Miller was just paranoid. Probably so. He seemed the twitchy paranoid type.

But Nathan, being Nathan, couldn't leave it at that. "Besides the taste, you can't beat the health benefit of these tomatoes, farmed without any pesticides or man-made fertilizers."

"Organic?" The photographer jotted down notes.

"I'm in year one of the certification process," Nathan said. "So these tomatoes are just the start. Come back next week and my eggplants will be coming in. Peppers too."

"I'll be back," the man said. "And I'll bring my wife. She keeps talking about this organic trend."

"No trend," Nathan said. "It's here to stay."

The reporter wrote it all down, then closed his notepad and went on his way. Lydie's stomach tightened.

Lydie slipped behind Nathan's door on sawhorses and whispered, "Nathan, I wonder if you shouldn't talk up your organic farming quite so often."

He gave Lydie a second look, as if he hadn't realized she was standing there. "What? Why?"

"Well, isn't it possible that other farmers might feel like you're running down their methods?"

He scrunched up his face in confusion. "Aren't you the one who encouraged me to find a way to make my produce stand out?"

That's right. She did. She even wrote it on his sign each week—Nearly Organic Produce—though he thought it was Patsy's doing.

"Is it possible that Owen Miller's business might be suffering because you're getting so much attention as an organic farmer?"

He gave her a funny look. "Why should I worry if Owen Miller's business suffers?"

Because he thinks it's suffering, she thought. *And he blames you for it.*

"I thought you supported organic farming."

"I do! I really do. It's just . . ." It was just that Owen Miller didn't, and Lydie wanted to make sure Nathan wasn't going to be a target for trouble. She hesitated so long that another customer interrupted and asked Nathan how he grew such fla-vorful carrots. Nathan responded by enthusing on the wonders of natural soil amendments and the moment was gone.

This was exactly the kind of thing that Owen Miller meant when he said to get Nathan to shut his trap. Or else.

Lydie took in a deep breath. *This is fine. It's all going to be fine.*

But just the same, she spent the afternoon tucked in a corner at the public library, doodling. She drew an Amish man behind a booth at a farmers' market. He handed a jar of jam to an Englisch woman. Underneath was the caption: "All fresh. Made organically. Better eat it in the next two hours."

She'd learned her lesson. This time, Lydie didn't make any identifiable features on the characters.

It rained all day Sunday. Church had been held in the barn at Beacon Hill. Afterward, space was cleared and the benches were readjusted for the fellowship meal. Around noon, most families had headed home, but Nathan and Mick and Micah Weaver and a few others stayed to help load the benches from the barn back into the bench wagon. Nathan was heading to the barn to get the last bench when Patsy Glick stopped him, right inside the door. "One of my brothers wasn't feeling well so my folks went on home. I was hoping you might be able to give me a ride."

Nathan hesitated. Patsy lived out of the way and the rain would only lengthen the drive. But how could he say no? "Sure, if you need a ride."

She beamed and he smiled in return, hoping it didn't look as insincere as it felt. The *Organic Farm Journal* had arrived in yesterday's mail and he'd been looking forward to reading it this afternoon. He went to find Mick to tell him he'd need to hitch a ride home with someone else, unless he wanted to take the long way home via the Glick house, but when he saw Hank Lapp standing inside the bench wagon with Mick, Nathan decided to shorten his message by just telling his brother to find a ride home.

Hank, being Hank, had to get involved. "Taking HOME a SWEETHEART?"

Intrigued, Mick cocked an eyebrow, and Nathan spun on his heels, ignoring their laughter. He crossed the yard to the barn where Patsy was waiting with an umbrella to share. Together, they hurried out to where the remaining buggies were lined up. Patsy climbed inside while Nathan ran out to the pasture to bring in his horse and hook him to the buggy traces. Leaving the driveway, they passed by Mick. Patsy waved that little-girly wave she did, and Nathan lifted a hand in the air but quickly dropped it. His brother had a strange look on his face, all pasty white, as if he'd just been kicked in the gut.

21

The rain continued off and on for three straight days, but Wednesday brought a blue sky with just enough wind to dry things out quickly. A perfect summer day, Lydie thought as she scooted home from Dok's office, for three reasons. It was warm but not hot, the air soft but not humid. The last two patients for the day had canceled, so Dok closed the office early to go help her husband with some remodeling project. And Patsy's family had company visiting, so Lydie had time off from chalkboard writing. She was even looking forward to having supper with Mammi.

There'd been less lecturing from her grandmother lately, less pointing out Lydie's flaws. She wasn't sure if that was because she'd been working so hard on Dok's strategies and Mammi had noticed the improvements . . . or if not being home much because of Patsy's chalkboard kidnap sessions gave Mammi more patience for Lydie. Either way, life was good at home.

Life was good at work too. Just today, Dok had congratulated Lydie on making significant strides. She wasn't making the kinds of blunders that she normally did. She hadn't been late, she hadn't messed up any patient appointments. She even noticed less ups and downs, which Dok said had to do with regular sleep and regular meals. Dok's strategies were making a difference. They probably seemed so simple, but they weren't easy for Lydie. They took effort. Worth it, though. Worth everything.

She slowed the roll to a stop when she saw Nathan working at the edge of his fields at Black Gold Farm. He turned, as if he sensed she was there. She lifted a palm, and he tossed his trowel into a bucket and walked over to her.

"Looks like it's been quite a bountiful summer, Nathan."

Pleased, he dipped his chin in a nod. Pushing back his hat with the back of one hand, he pointed to a basket with the other. "I just picked a bushel of heirloom tomatoes, if you might like to take some home."

She dropped the scooter and slipped in between the rails. "Mammi would love a few." She held out the corners of her apron for Nathan to drop some tomatoes into. Big, oddly shaped, varied-colored tomatoes that practically oozed delicious flavor. The corners of her lips turned up. "These should make Mammi as happy as she is for a cinnamon roll from the Sweet Tooth Bakery."

He smiled at her a flicker of a second too long, and something fluttered in her stomach. *Just friends, just friends, just friends.*

A small plane crested the hill from Lydie's house and swooped down toward Mick's cornfields. Nathan glanced at it, frowning. "Owen Miller is spraying the corn today."

"Couldn't the spray reach your acres?"

"It would if there weren't a buffer with the house and the greenhouse. Plus Mick's acres are down low, so there's no run-off in my fields. That was part of our deal." He took off his hat and wiped his forehead. "Still, I wish he wouldn't do it. The farm, all of the land, it's all one thing. All interconnected. I can't get Mick or Dad to see that."

"I thought Mick had a miracle seed growing."

"That GMO seed eliminated the problem of cornworm, but it's done nothing for mosaic virus. The entire corn crop is infected. There's no cure for it, though that doesn't stop Mick from thinking that more chems will knock it out."

The barn door opened and Mick came out. He took a few strides, stopped, and lifted his arm in a wave to the pilot. Walt and Sarah came out of the house to stare at the sky, watching the little plane release a cloud of spray over the cornfields, then circle and spray again.

Lydie's gaze shifted past Nathan to his lush, massive fields. Such a contrast to Mick's acreage of solid corn. Nathan's fields had long, winding rows of varied, colorful plants in different stages of growth. The entire appearance looked inviting, appealing, like it was beckoning people to come over. Come see the garden.

She turned to him. "Nathan, there's something I need to tell you. About Patsy Glick. Something you should know."

"Patsy? What about her?" He had a curious look on his face, waiting for her to explain.

Over the last week, Lydie had wrestled with herself about whether she should let Nathan know that Perfect Patsy should be called Party Patsy . . . or whether she should leave it alone, let him figure it out for himself. Patsy had warned her not to tell Nathan, even threatening to tell others that Lydie was the *Stoney Ridge Times* doodler.

Even with that threat in mind, it wasn't easy for Lydie to ignore what she'd seen at Owen Miller's house party. Lydie felt responsible for Nathan. After all, she was the one who had kept encouraging him to notice Patsy. So in the end, she decided he deserved to know.

She lifted her head to tell Nathan so, but as she did, she saw his face change, contorting with alarm as his eyes focused beyond her. She spun around to see the plane sweep low over Nathan's fields. Too low.

Hands on his hips, Nathan took a step. "Vas in die velt?" *What in the world?*

Suddenly it dawned on Lydie what was just about to happen, and it shocked a cry out of her. "No!" She dropped her apron and ran toward the plane, waving her arms, but it was too late. The plane released a white spray over Nathan's fields. His beautiful garden. "Stop! No!!!" Screams tore out of her throat. She would have run right into the fields if Nathan hadn't caught up with her. He wrapped his arm around her waist, holding her fast while she flailed and clawed at the sky. "Don't let him do this!"

And then there was silence. The pilot cut off its spray as the plane ascended up, up, up. She watched the plane disappear over the hills. "Oh, Nathan," she said, her throat burned raw. Her legs were shaking so hard she had difficulty standing up and could feel herself swaying, but he kept his hold on her tight. She turned to him. "Owen Miller. He did this to you. He did it on purpose, just to spite you! He's . . . just awful! I hate that man."

His eyes were sad, shiny, but his countenance was completely calm. "No. Don't hate Owen. Don't even think it."

How could he just accept this? "Nathan, don't you see? You haven't just lost a year of getting certified as an organic farm. You've probably lost the farm. To your brother! Mick hates farming! You love it. You'll have to leave Stoney Ridge to find another place to farm." Young farmers were leaving all the time, heading to different states to buy cheaper land.

Nathan turned to her with a solemn look. "Would that matter to you if I lost the farm to Mick?"

Would it matter? Of course it would matter! Nathan deserved to run Black Gold Farm. Not Mick! He would farm just the way his father farmed. Before she could say as much, his parents joined them out in the field, their faces ashen. Mick followed behind, not quite so ashen-faced.

Sarah, her face etched with worry, went straight to Nathan to put her arms around him.

"It'll be all right, Mom," Nathan said.

Walt ran a hand over his beard, then crossed his arms over his chest. "I'm sure it's just a mistake. No harm done."

"Probably just a mistake," Mick echoed.

"No harm done?" Lydie couldn't hold back. "This was no mistake! Owen Miller blames Nathan because he's lost customers this summer. He sprayed those fields on purpose!"

Walt turned to her with a frown. His bushy brows sank toward his nose. "I suppose we're going to be seeing this scene in one of them drawings in the newspaper this week."

"Walt, what are you talking about?" Sarah looked at him, confused.

Walt pointed a finger at Lydie. "She's the one who's been poking fun at us."

"Lydie?" Eyes wide, Sarah clapped her hands to her cheeks. "No. Not you! You'd never mock your own people."

"Sure, it's her," Walt said. "It's been her all along."

Mick let out a snort. "No way, Dad. Lydie never spends any time thinking about being Plain. Why, she's just about ready to jump the fence."

There was a moment of stunned silence. Lydie felt her heart pounding. She tucked her chin. She couldn't even look at Nathan.

"Well, I can't say that surprises me," Walt said. "I never did think she acted like one of us."

Nathan took a step toward her. He put his hands on her shoulders to make her turn toward him, to face him. "Lydie, could that be true? Are you planning to leave?"

She lifted her head. It hurt to look into his eyes. It felt like a hot wind was blowing through her, right through her. "I need to get home." She backed up a few steps, turned, and had to skirt around the splattered tomatoes. She could feel three pairs of eyes drill into her back as she slipped through the two rails and picked up her scooter, getting ready to head down the road.

And then shouts of alarm filled the air.

Lydie spun around to see Sarah doubled over with her hands on her knees, gasping for air. Walt crouched next to her, Mick stood over her, and Nathan cried out, "Mom, was ist los?" *What's wrong?*

Lydie bolted over the fence and knelt in front of Sarah, who blinked at her through labored, wheezing breaths. This was worse than the day Lydie had given her lobelia. "Mick and Walt, get Sarah in the house and have her lie flat on her back. Nathan, go call Dok. Tell her it's an emergency. If she doesn't pick up the phone, call for an ambulance."

Nathan didn't hesitate. He took off for the phone shanty. But Walt stared at her like she'd gone mad. "An ambulance?"

"She's having a full-blown asthma attack. Her airways are closing so she can't breathe." Lydie's heart was thrumming in her ears.

He shook his head in disbelief. "Can't you just use that potion you made last time?"

Lydie looked right at Walt. "She needs medical help. *Now.*"

At that, Mick picked his mother up in his arms like she was a rag doll and hurried to the house. Lydie followed. Once in the house, Mick set her gently down on the sofa. Each tiny gasp Sarah made sounded like it caused her sharp pain.

Lydie knelt beside her and loosened the top pins of her dress. "Sarah, help is coming. Try to slow down your breathing. Breathe through your nose. In through your nose, out through pursed lips." She reached out and held Sarah's hand, shocked by how cold it was.

Walt came inside and pulled up a chair to sit near the couch. "What could have caused this?" Mick asked.

Lydie gave him a look. "Those toxic chemicals."

"The plane?" Mick looked like he was going to be sick.

"No," Walt said. "That's nonsense. Sarah's just got weak lungs. Dok said as much."

The door hinges squeaked open and Nathan came in. "It's not nonsense. Mom has these attacks whenever there's been spraying." He came in and crouched beside his mom. "Ambulance is on its way, Mom. Help is coming." Were it not for Sarah's shallow breaths, she almost appeared like she had passed. Her face was ghostly white, her eyes closed, her lips had turned a husky blue.

Nathan's anguished eyes searched Lydie's. "Is she going to be all right?"

She wanted to tell him that everything would be okay. But she couldn't. She didn't know.

22

They'd been in the waiting room at the hospital's emergency room for over an hour. Walt had been allowed to go in with Sarah. Restless and anxious, Mick couldn't sit still. He walked outside the hospital, back inside, then outside again for fresh air. Nathan sat silently next to Lydie, fingering the brim of his hat.

She didn't even know where to begin, how to explain all that his father and brother had blurted out about her, so she said nothing. Instead, she concentrated on her breathing, in and out, in and out, to settle down her racing, panicky mind.

It wasn't working.

She knew her drawings in the newspaper had contributed to what Owen Miller had done. It had helped push him over the edge. And now Nathan's fields, his hard work! It was ruined. It was her fault.

She squeezed her eyes shut. No matter how hard she tried, she ended up making a mess of things. Maybe she could never be the person she wanted to be. The person everyone wanted her to be. Maybe this was as good as it would get.

Finally, Nathan broke the quiet with the one question she didn't want him to ask. "Is what Mick said true? You're planning to leave?"

She lifted her head. "It's true. I've been planning it for a while now. I just haven't found the right time to go."

"How long have you been planning it?"

She swallowed and looked down at her hands. She couldn't bear to look at him, so she kept her chin tucked.

"How long, Lydie? Is it because I told you I loved you? Is that why you've acted so distant these last few months?"

This was so painful. She had to do what was best for him. "I just haven't wanted you to think there's anything between us," she said, sparing him with a lie. It made her sick to not tell him the truth, but she had to do what was best for him. "There's not." There shouldn't be. He should forget her. Move on from her. Move on to someone else.

He didn't respond for a long time. Then he finally stood up, put his hat back on, and said, "Okay. Okay, then." His voice was flat, quiet, as if a matter had been decided.

Her head shot up. Nathan stood in front of her with his hands loose at his sides, his head a little bent. She could see by the bleakness in his face that he understood now. She could see it in his eyes—a hurt that cut deep. He had stopped questioning her.

He walked away and she could feel her heart breaking in two. Literally ripping. Even her breath struggled to make it in and out of her throat. Shivering, she gripped her elbows, trying to contain herself, as if she might shatter into pieces if she let go.

The doors that led to the patient area opened, and Walt came out, relief covering his face as his sons approached him. "She's going to be fine, just fine. It was only another attack of asthma."

"Did they say what caused it?" Mick said.

"They said asthma can be caused by all kinds of things." Walt glanced over at Lydie, still sitting in the chair against the wall. "Including getting upset."

Mick's face relaxed with relief. "Can we go see her?"

"Ja, ja. She wants to see her sons." Walt and Mick went back through the door that led to the patient area.

Nathan waited. He turned to look at Lydie with an odd gravity. He dragged a hand through his hair, then walked out to join his brother and father.

Lydie was left alone in the waiting room, alone with her thoughts. Reviewing all that had transpired in the last few hours, all the light that had been shed on people's inner thought life.

"Don't hate Owen Miller. Don't even think it." How could Nathan be so forgiving?

"Lydie would never mock her own people." Actually, Sarah, she would. She did. Not everyone, but certain ones . . . like Walt Yoder.

"Lydie never spends any time thinking about being Plain." Mick was wrong about that. Lydie thought about it all the time.

"I never did think she acted like one of us." Walt Yoder was right about that. She had tried and tried, but she really didn't fit in . . . and she probably never would.

Tears started to slip down her cheeks.

A wave of despair swept up from the pit of her stomach and rolled right over the top of her head. She covered her face with her hands. She shouldn't be here. She'd leave today, right now, only she couldn't leave Dok without a receptionist. And then there was Mick. She had something important she had to ask him.

But after that, she would go. Her mind, which had been waffling the last few weeks, was made up.

Supper was unusually quiet, even for the Yoders. After they returned from the hospital, Mom went upstairs to rest while Nathan heated up some leftover soup. He felt shaken by the events of the afternoon. His pristine fields . . . they were ruined. His mother . . . she'd been rushed to the emergency room with the worst attack of asthma she'd ever experienced. And Lydie. She wanted to leave.

248

Dad sat at the kitchen table, lost in his own thoughts. Nathan took a bowl of soup upstairs to his mom, then came back down and slipped into his chair at the table. Mick, who sat between the two men, had turned pale.

"Mick," Nathan said, "you feeling okay?"

"I'm fine," he said, a sharp edge to his voice. He didn't look fine to Nathan.

Suddenly Dad lifted his head. "So then, Lydie Stoltzfus is planning to leave." He jutted his fork at Nathan. "Didn't I always say that girl was headed for trouble?"

Dad seemed almost pleased. "Lydie wouldn't leave," Nathan said. He hoped.

"You just watch and see. She's a fence jumper." Dad took a spoonful of soup and Nathan noted how the spoon trembled in his hand. "Your own brother said so." His gaze swept toward Mick, as if waiting for him to chime in.

Mick was carefully wiping the bottom of his soup bowl with a piece of bread.

Nathan leaned back in his chair. "Dad, what have you got against Lydie?"

His dad tried to spoon up the vegetables in his soup bowl, and gave up. He picked up the bowl and held it to his lips, sipping the soup like a cup of coffee. He set it down, swallowed, before answering. "I just don't want her tempting you boys to go with her."

Nathan pushed away from the table. "Whatever it is you have against Lydie has more to do with you than her."

His father gave him a hard look. "What'd she say to you?"

"Nothing."

"Then why'd you say such a thing?"

"Because it's what I think." Tension filled the air.

Mick cleared his throat. "Couldn't we just . . . eat our supper in peace? It's been a long day."

Dad dropped his eyes to his bowl and returned to eating, and the tension dropped. It dropped, but it didn't disappear.

Lydie waited at the hole in the hedge until she saw Mick cross the yard from the house. She knew he would be checking on the animals before day's end. As soon as he disappeared into the barn, she sprinted down the hill to Black Gold Farm and into the barn, hoping Walt Yoder hadn't seen her. Nathan, either.

Mick was walking up the aisle of the barn and stopped abruptly when he saw her.

"Mick, did you have something to do with Owen spraying Nathan's fields?"

"That's crazy talk." He brushed past her and walked to a horse stall. He grabbed the latch and jerked it open with such force the hinges screeched. He went straight to the horse, bent over, took a hoof between his knees, and started cleaning out the frog.

"I want you to look me in the eyes and tell me you didn't give him that idea."

Mick dropped the horse's foot and straightened, turning toward her. "What makes you say such a foolish thing?"

"I saw you wave to him, right before he banked his plane. Like you were giving him a signal."

Mick flinched a little, but he kept his head up. "And why would I do such a thing to my own brother?"

"Jealousy. My guess it has something to do with Patsy Glick."

They stood there in a standoff of silence, staring at each other. Mick lost.

"That's what I thought." She shook her head.

"You know me, Lydie." He lifted his hands, palms out, and took a single stumbling step toward her. "You know me better than anyone."

"You're right. I do. And I think you're a better man than this." Lydie turned and left him.

The next morning, Nathan woke early and walked his fields. The strange thing was that everything looked just like it did yesterday. Nothing had changed. And yet everything had changed. The toxic smell lingering in the air took him right back to last summer, standing in his father's cornfields. He kicked a cucumber and it splattered apart. He didn't even know what chemical Owen Miller had sprayed on his fields, but he knew he couldn't sell this produce. He *wouldn't* sell it. He turned in a circle. No birds. No bees. Even the moles were probably gone.

Like Lydie. She, too, was leaving. He didn't know which made him feel more despondent—seeing his ruined crops or hearing from Lydie that he meant nothing to her. In one afternoon, every hope and dream he'd had was shattered.

He just couldn't handle being here, not this morning. Instead, he spent the morning in the greenhouse, doing tasks to take his mind off his poisoned fields. When he heard the dinner bell ring, he was surprised how much time had passed.

After another quiet meal, Dad said, "Boys, let's go have a chat on the porch."

Dad went out to sit on the bench. Mick sat on the step, facing his dad. He'd hardly said a word at breakfast and went off to town for a few hours. Nathan had a pretty good idea where this chat was going, so he didn't sit, he just leaned against the porch railing.

"Frank Miller called this morning," Dad said. "He wanted to apologize. He said Owen's plane had a malfunction yesterday."

Nathan crossed his arms over his chest. "And you believed him?"

"No reason not to. I've known Frank Miller for a long time. He's been real good to us."

"Of course he has," Nathan said, somewhat distantly. "You bought every chemical he had to offer."

His father gave him a warning look. "So, then, after all that's happened, it's become clear that Mick's got the upper hand running the farm."

Nathan glanced at Mick. Something he couldn't read moved across his brother's face.

Mick cleared his throat. "Dad, it wasn't Nathan's fault that Owen sprayed his fields."

Nathan glanced at Mick.

"No," Dad said. "Not his fault. But it goes to show how fragile Nathan's kind of farming is. It can't handle a little setback."

A little setback? Aphids and cucumber beetles were a little setback. Lack of rain was a little setback. But drenching his fields with pesticides? That was no setback. That was catastrophic. All the work he'd done the last few months was destroyed in a matter of minutes. Nathan rubbed his forehead. Why bother to defend organic farming to a man whose mind was closed? This outcome, handing over the farm to Mick, *that* he had expected. He just hadn't expected it to end the way it did.

"So from now on, Mick manages Black Gold Farm. Nathan, you'll be working for your brother."

Nathan pushed himself off the porch railing. "So that's that."

"That's that."

Mick stood up. "No," he said. Then, more firmly, "No. I don't want it. Not like this. Besides, I'm no farmer. Nothing like Nathan. So either the two of us run Black Gold together or neither of us do." With that, Mick walked off to the barn.

Nathan leaned back against the railing, shocked silent. So was his father.

Later that afternoon, Nathan was in the greenhouse, patiently misting rows of delicate seedlings with a special tool attached to the hose. Mick sauntered in, looking over the shelves of baby greens like he had planted them himself.

Nathan turned off the hose. "Why'd you say that? You won the farm, fair and square."

Mick stood awkwardly, rocking from foot to foot. He had

his hands clasped behind his back. "Not so fair and square. That was no way to beat you."

"So if Owen hadn't sprayed my crops, you're saying that you'd accept the win?"

Mick dragged a hand down his mouth. "I told him to do it."

"Who?"

Mick let out a sigh. "Owen. It was a plan he cooked up. He was waiting for me to give him the signal."

"Why?"

"Owen blames you for the drop in orders he's had this summer."

"Me?"

"All your talk about organic farming. It's made a difference to the Millers' business. A while ago, he came up with this idea of spraying your fields. At first I said no . . . but then I changed my mind. We had it worked out. When he was spraying yesterday, if I gave him the go-ahead signal, he'd spray your fields."

"Why would you do that to me?"

Mick looked him right in the eye. "You've been courting my girl behind my back."

"Lydie?"

"No, not Lydie. Patsy Glick."

Nathan's eyes went wide. "Seriously? Hold it. I don't get it. What about Lydie?"

"I just let you think Lydie and me were together, just to get under your skin."

"Every time I see you, you're together."

"Lydie's supposed to be helping me get together with Patsy, but she's done a lousy job at it." He pointed his finger at Nathan like a gun. "'Course, you haven't helped, either."

"Mick, I have absolutely no interest in Patsy Glick."

"She said you've been taking her home from the farmers' market."

"She's asked me to."

"You took her home from church on Sunday."

"Again, because she asked me to. I didn't want to! Her farm is way out of the way."

Mick frowned. "Sure seems like you fancy her."

"I suppose I . . . let you think it. Just to get under your skin," he admitted. "Lydie's always been the one I've wanted. Always." He leaned against a wooden shelf. "So that's why you told Dad you didn't want the farm? Out of guilt?"

"Partly. I mean, I shouldn't have let Owen do what he did. I'm sorry for it. I really am. But the truth is, I really don't want to manage the farm. I don't care about farming."

Nathan fixed his brother with an intense gaze. "Then what *do* you care about?" Besides Patsy Glick.

"Livestock, animal husbandry. I've got some ideas to expand Black Gold."

"I'm listening. What do you have in mind?"

"Alpacas. Grown for their wool. Big bucks in it."

"Why don't you get one and try it out?"

"One?" Mick scoffed. "Alpacas are herd animals. It would die of loneliness if I only got one."

Nathan glanced at him. Here was the side of Mick that he hadn't seen in a very long time, not since he had become friendly with Owen Miller. This was the real Mick, the best Mick. It was good to have him back. "I have some ideas too."

"Like what?"

"Like opening up the farm to teach folks about organic farming."

Mick scoffed. "Why would anyone come?"

Nathan smiled. "A few might be interested." More than a few. At the farmers' market, so many had asked for a private tour of his fields that he had started a long list of names, thinking he'd have time in September or October for tours.

A spark lit Mick's eyes. "So then . . . you handle the fields and I'll take care of the livestock. Do we have a deal, brother?"

Nathan's head jerked up. "Don't you want to check this out with Dad?"

"He's hardly lifted a finger this year. Haven't you noticed? My guess is that this whole contest got started because the old man wants to retire."

Interesting. Maybe Mick was more insightful than Nathan gave him credit for.

Mick started toward the door. "You can farm any way you want. But I want the lower paddock with the mud ponds." He wiggled his eyebrows. "Thinking about adding koi."

"Koi fish?"

"Imported from Japan. Big money there too."

Nathan laughed. "Good luck with that."

Mick grinned, headed out the door, then poked his head back in. "Hey. I really am sorry about Owen Miller. He's a jerk."

Yeah. Yeah, he was.

As the door clicked shut, Nathan went back to watering, but his mind was on Lydie. He felt sheer relief to learn that Mick's attention was on Patsy Glick and not on Lydie. But why would she want to leave? He just couldn't figure that out.

Maybe the better question . . . what would it take to make her stay?

As bishop, David was accustomed to getting visits from well-meaning church members who had advice or information to pass on to him. So used to it that the visits didn't bother him. But while he was paying bills in his office at the Bent N' Dent when Walt Yoder walked in and sat down, a grim look on his face, David felt his stomach clench in a tight knot. "Hello, Walt. What's on your mind?"

"Your daughter Lydie. She's been up to no good." He slapped a *Stoney Ridge Times* newspaper in front of David. "She's the one who's been making fun of us Amish."

"What are you talking about?"

"Them drawings." He pointed a finger at David. "That's your girl who's been sending in those pictures."

Oh no. David picked up the newspaper. He glanced at Walt's accusing finger, then took a second look. "Your hand is shaking."

Walt's brow furrowed.

"Can you control it?"

Walt stood and jammed his hand into his pants pocket. "Never mind about me. You just think about stopping your girl from telling tales and spreading rumors. You work on controlling your daughter."

"Interesting choice of words, Walt. As a parent, we do have control over our children, but we aren't in control."

As Walt started to pivot, David quickly added, "Hold on. There's something I want you to think about."

"What's that?"

"It's hard for most of us to admit wrongdoing."

Walt drew close to David's desk with narrowed eyes. "Whatever you heard, it's a lie." He stomped out without shutting the door behind him.

David leaned back in his chair, baffled. He had absolutely no idea what Walt was talking about. He was going to tell him that Mick had come to the Bent N' Dent this morning and told him what had happened at Black Gold Farm yesterday, how he'd played a part in ruining Nathan's fields. He wanted to confess his sin, knowing it would mean he'd be sitting on the sinner's bench next church Sunday. Mick was ready. He said he wanted to admit what he'd done and wipe the slate clean.

That's all David was trying to tell Walt. That it was hard to admit one's wrongdoing.

He wondered what Walt had meant.

23

Nathan had lost count of how many times this week he had thought about giving up. The last thing he wanted to do was to face his loyal customers at the farmers' market on Saturday morning and tell them his fields had been sprayed. He didn't want anyone to know that he had failed to protect his crops.

But something deep within him welled up and choked out the doubts. A true farmer never quit. Plagued by drought, farmers order seed. Recovering from a crop failure, they replant. In the face of floundering produce prices, they expand.

He couldn't quit. There was a bone-deep sense of satisfaction he got from simply growing food and providing it to people to nourish and sustain them. He just could not quit.

Exhaling, he felt a tiny spike of optimism return when he thought about the greenhouse. Inside were rows of trays of baby greens ready for harvest.

It wasn't anything like the bounty he'd hauled to the farmers' market the last few Saturdays of July . . . never mind what he had hoped to sell at his stand throughout the month of August. Bags of baby greens were the best he could do for now. Maybe

Black Gold Farm's stand could make it through the summer. Limping, but alive.

All week long, Nathan doted on those baby greens. He watered them twice a day. With the weather so hot but no rain in the forecast, he misted their tender leaves three times a day to keep the soil moist.

All week long, he also did his best to forget about Lydie. Could he forget her? He wasn't really the forgetting type. Finally, he decided that "getting over her" might be a more realistic goal than forgetting her. He even thought he might invite Patsy to a picnic at Blue Lake Pond on Sunday, but then he realized what a stupid idea *that* was. Taking Patsy on a date would rile Mick. More importantly, Blue Lake Pond would only remind him of Lydie. Of losing her.

So much for trying to forget.

On Saturday morning, Nathan pulled into the parking lot of the junior high school and was tying his horse to the hitching post when he heard a familiar voice.

"I wasn't sure you'd be here today."

He whirled around. There she was. At the unexpected sight of her, he felt his heartbeat give a hitch. "No?" He pulled a bin of bagged greens out of his wagon bed. "Why not?"

"I guess I assumed you wouldn't want to sell your produce . . . after it had been sprayed."

"Poisoned, you mean." He kept on stacking bins of bagged greens. "You guessed right. I tilled it all under." It had nearly broken him, tilling those forty acres under, letting his promising crops decompose in the soil.

She pointed to the bins. "So what's in those?"

"I still have my greenhouse. Those are full of baby greens."

"Most people would give up."

He stopped for a moment to look at her. "A true farmer is always looking forward. Always anticipating another harvest."

"Even a harvest destroyed by Owen Miller?"

"Nothing can stop me, not even Owen Miller. I'll replant and try again. That's what I love about farming. Winter might seem like it will never end, but then spring always comes." He took a step closer to her. "A true farmer doesn't just give up when things get hard. He begins again."

So softly he could barely hear her, she whispered, "It's my fault."

The second her eyes met his, he realized she was about to cry. Lydie never cried, even when she *should*. "What's your fault? Tell me."

"I'm so sorry. So sorry about those beautiful fields. So sorry that I made things worse."

Her words took him so by surprise he didn't know what to say. "You? What could you have done to make things worse?"

She didn't respond. He couldn't help himself. He leaned forward and wrapped his arms around her, and she let him hold her for a long moment. Then she pulled away, sniffed, and brushed the tears from her cheeks. He saw the switch coming. She forced a smile at him and slipped away. He watched her go until she disappeared behind a parked pickup truck. Frustrated, he lifted the rest of his bins out of the wagon and made his way to set up his stand with his bags of baby greens.

An hour later, miraculously, a line formed in front of Nathan's stand. The word had spread about his fields and many stopped by to express sympathy. To his astonishment, he sold out within the hour. It couldn't all be pity. Baby greens were still in short supply at the market. He owed a big thank-you to the lady in gray braids from the Lancaster Central Market. She had given him solid advice. He spent the rest of the morning helping other vendors, trying not to think about Lydie.

Lydie leaned on her elbows at Dok's receptionist's desk, chin in her palms, staring at the door without really seeing it.

"Lydie? Yoo-hoo, Lydie?"

She turned around to realize Dok was standing a few feet behind her.

"I've been trying to get your attention. Didn't you hear me?"

"I'm sorry. I didn't. My mind is a million miles away."

Dok pulled up a chair. "I thought you've seemed a little off the last few days." She lifted a palm toward the top of Lydie's desk. "That was my first clue." It was a cluttered mess. "You've been making so much progress. What's happened?"

Lydie blew out a puff of air. "It's always going to be like this, isn't it? Battling ADHD, I mean. Every day will always be a struggle."

"I wouldn't put it like that. Yes, you'll always have to manage ADHD tendencies, but the more practice you get at it, the easier it will get. You have to give yourself a break on days when you forget to check your planner—"

Lydie glanced down at her desk. She hadn't looked at her planner since that disaster happened to Nathan's fields. In fact, she wasn't sure where her planner was.

"—or days when you lose it." Dok lifted an opened, face-down magazine on the desk.

Why, there was the planner!

"It's part of accepting yourself, Lydie. You're still going to have days when you lose your planner. There will be good days and bad days. It's human nature to focus more on our failings than on our successes. But even if you can't see the changes you're making, I can see them. Your dad is seeing them. Even Mammi is noticing. Yes, it takes work. But most things do. And yes, managing ADHD can be exhausting, but it's so worth the effort."

Lydie looked at her aunt. "You can't imagine what it's like to be me."

"I can, actually. Lydie, I know this because I've lived this too."

"You?" Lydie's jaw dropped open. No way. No possible way. "You have ADHD?"

"Me." Dok smiled. "Like you, it was a relief to have a name for all the frustration I'd been living with for as long as I can remember. My ADHD looks a little different than yours. We each have our own profile, our own proclivities. Mine is to hyperfocus. Whatever I'm doing gets my full attention, to the point where I forget about anything or anyone else. It was a great skill to get through medical school." She seesawed her hand in the air. "Not so great when dealing with people."

"But . . . it seems like you pay attention to everything. And everybody." *Like me. Dok paid attention to me.*

"When something interests me, like medicine, I can pay incredible attention. But there's a lot of things I don't pay attention to. It's never been easy for me to live in a world of efficiency and productivity. I have to rely on people who have skills that I lack. Like my husband, Matt. He balances me out in wonderful ways."

Lydie was still trying to absorb Dok's revelation. "So then, were you like me at my age?"

"In many ways. I felt like I didn't fit in anywhere. Not with my friends, or church . . . especially not with my family." She tilted her head, looking at Lydie with sympathetic eyes. "Is that how you feel?"

Slowly, Lydie nodded. "I don't know where I belong." She wasn't sure she would ever belong anywhere.

"None of us do, until we find it."

But Lydie wondered. "Dok, I'm just not sure God has a place for someone like me."

Dok reached out and squeezed Lydie's hand. "You're wrong about that. God uses flawed people. He recruits the unlikely. You know that as well as I do. It's a theme scattered all through the Bible." She rose from the chair to head to her office but stopped at the doorjamb to turn back. "Your dad told me something a long time ago. Something I've never forgotten. God does not see you for what you are. God sees you for what you can be."

David sat behind his desk at the Bent N' Dent, going through old stacks of the *Stoney Ridge Times* to look for illustrations that Walt Yoder had insisted had been drawn by Lydie. He tore them out, one by one, and looked them over. Some were downright amusing. The red stop sign that said WHOA, in place of STOP. The candle holder with the caption "Amish flashlight."

And then there were some sharp-edged ones. Funny, but with a bite. Now that he looked closely at them, he recognized the church members. Edith Fisher Lapp holding her dog in her arms. Hank Lapp's wild hair sticking up under his black hat. Walt Yoder and his thick bushy eyebrows.

Walt said this had been going on all the way back to the Yoder Toter cartoon. When was that? Two years ago. All this time, Lydie had been sending in these drawings. Right under his nose! He rubbed his face. It was alarming how much he missed in his own household.

That night, after David waited until his mother had gone to bed, he allowed an extra hour for her to be sound asleep, snoring loudly, before he asked Lydie to join him in the kitchen for a cup of hot cocoa. She sat at the table and eyed the folder he had set out. She looked nervous. He passed the folder over to her. She opened it, and she dropped her forehead on the table with a clunk.

"Lydie, why did you send those in without adding your name?"

She lifted her head with a sigh. "That very first one, the Yoder Toter drawing, I forgot to add my name when I sent it in. I didn't really expect it to get printed. And then it was fun to hear people talk about it without knowing I was the one who had drawn it. After that, it just seemed . . . easier to not sign my name. Safer."

"Safer?"

"Yes, I suppose. I could just . . . doodle whatever I wanted to."

"And add whatever caption you wanted."

Slowly, Lydie nodded.

"Do you remember that Thanksgiving when Mammi found those drawings you made of the family? Many of them were hurtful. The ones of Mammi, in particular. As I recall, she was always scolding someone." The sticky part was that Lydie's renditions were amusing. He remembered watching Birdy laugh over them until tears spilled down her cheeks. He sighed. "Lydie, do you understand what this means?"

"Yes, of course. I always make a mess of things."

Actually, that was often true. But that wasn't the point he was trying to get at. "I'm talking about the drawings, Lydie. About the humor in them."

"Right. Humor is a sin."

"No! That's not what I meant at all." David rubbed his forehead. "Hold on. God does have a sense of humor." Look at an ostrich. Look at a hippopotamus. Or a strutting camel. There were so many moments of humor in the Bible—ones David had preached sermons on. Just last week, he had preached on the Israelites in the desert, who complained that they wanted meat over manna, so God sent a wind full of quail. The Israelites ate so much quail it came out of their nostrils. If that wasn't a touch of humor to drive home a point, what was it?

Or closer to home . . . what about the incident that happened just a few days ago, when David—in a hurry—came rushing out of the hardware store to find that someone had parked a car right behind his buggy. He couldn't go anywhere. When the owner of the car finally returned, David gave him a piece of his mind. It wasn't typical of David to lose his temper, but, boy, did he ever let it fly. He was already on edge because he was running late and his mother was waiting for him at the store—and that made him worried because she always rearranged things when left unsupervised.

No sooner had he finished his tirade directed at the owner of the car when out of the hardware store sauntered Hank Lapp, shouting in his regular voice, "HELLO there, BISHOP! SURE enjoyed your SERMON last Sunday."

The owner of the car gave David a *look*—and drove off.

Was that not another moment of the Lord's sense of humor? A reminder to keep a man's temper in check. A man's pride.

"So, then, it's the Amish who have no sense of humor."

Ah, there was the rub. David released another sigh. Many of those illustrations Lydie had sent into the *Stoney Ridge Times* were elbow jabs in the sides of the Plain People. Was that really such a bad thing? So many of the problems in the church came from members who took themselves too seriously. And then they would take others too seriously. Soon, everyone was judging each other. Humor helped to warn the church not to dwell on their petty grievances. "Lydie, gentle humor is a good thing. Sarcasm is not. When your drawings and captions lean toward sarcasm, you're crossing the line."

"But I don't always know when I've crossed the line until it's too late."

"Sign your name to each drawing. If you know you will be held responsible for the drawing and the caption, you'll know where that line is."

She blinked. "I thought you'd want me to stop sending in doodles."

"No, I don't want you to stop." He knew she needed to doodle. "But I have an idea." He reached out to pick up an old, weathered book and held it out to her. "This is a book of Penn Dutch proverbs. In it, I think you'll find plenty of material for your illustrations." He opened the book and skimmed down the page. "Here's one for you. 'En grossi Fraa un en grossi Scheier sin kem Mann ken Schaade.'" *A plump wife and a big barn never did a man a bit of harm.* He handed her the book. "Just be sure the plump wife has no recognizable features."

Lydie took the book and flipped through it, reading here and there. She closed it and looked up at him. "So let's be clear. Am I to understand that you are giving me your blessing to continue to doodle?"

David smiled. "Honey, you have my blessing all the time." He leaned back in his chair. "There's something else I'd like to talk to you about. The signs at the farmers' market."

She looked down at her hands. "What about them?"

"I know you're the one who's been doing them."

The shock on her face said it all. "How did you find out?"

"Fern seemed to have overheard a conversation between you and Patsy Glick."

"Fern! Of course. She hears everything, unless you're talking right to her." Lydie frowned. "I did one for Nathan on the day the farmers' market opened because I knew he wouldn't have time to think about it. And then he thought Patsy had done it and she didn't correct him, because she's trying to get him to notice her and it hasn't been working . . . but he did like the sign and so did other vendors and one sign turned into . . . tons of them. That's why I'm never home for dinner."

Lydie wasn't home for dinners? David wasn't either. He'd been staying late at the Bent N' Dent each evening. Later and later, with each passing week. He felt a little sting of guilt about his mother, realizing she'd been left alone so much. "The vendors have not only appreciated those chalkboard signs, but they'd like to have permanent signs made. Painted ones that could be attached to their stands. They're willing to pay for them. I thought it seemed like something you could do pretty easily." He handed her a typewritten list of the stand owners. These kinds of projects were perfect for Lydie. Short, specific, limited in time. He wished he'd had the insight to see that sooner, instead of trying to fit Lydie into a mold of long-term employment.

This kind of thing—using Lydie's natural ability—was just the right work. He owed his sister an enormous thank-you. She'd helped him understand his own daughter.

Lydie read down the list, biting her lower lip. "You think I could really do this?"

"I have no doubt you can do this. Just start small. Build from there."

She tucked the list into the old book of proverbs. "Well, then . . . I guess I have some work to do."

"Lydie, one more thing. Something I learned long ago." He reached over and put his hand on hers. "The Lord God did not make a mistake when he made you. Everything about you was ordained from the beginning. You have to start believing that."

David watched her go, thinking that she'd left the room holding herself a little differently. Filled with purpose, that's what it was. He leaned back in his chair, clasped his hands behind his neck, and smiled.

In the morning, Lydie's mind was brimming with ideas for doodling those old proverbs, bringing them to life, as she scooted down tree-shaded lanes on her way to work. She was skimming past Nathan's tilled fields and slowed at the sorry sight. Wilted green and brown leaves, stems sticking up haphazardly, a red tomato here and there. Everything had been buried prematurely under the brown soil, tilled under to decompose. Running through her mind was a saying she'd come across in her dad's book: Es is net alle Daag Aern. *Harvest comes not every day.* And not every year, either. Not this year, not for Nathan.

He amazed her. Such diligence, such persistence, despite what she knew was crushing disappointment. If she'd been in Nathan's shoes, she would've given up trying to farm after the Owen Miller disaster. If she had been the one to lose Black Gold Farm, she would've left town. She would've left her family.

266

Not Nathan. A true farmer never quits, he'd told her at the farmers' market. So he tilled the crops under and started again. He refused to give up on Black Gold Farm, on his dream to convert it into an organic farm. Nathan never quit.

Then it dawned on her *that* was the very reason he had never quit on her, either. He just did not quit. Not on his farm, not on Lydie.

She did, though. When anything got too hard, she quit. Or let herself get fired. She was a quitter! She had quit on people. She had quit on church. In a strange way, she realized she had quit on the Lord, or maybe she had assumed he had quit on her. But that *wasn't* true. She knew that, from Scripture, from a lifetime in church, from her dad's teachings. She knew that, from Dok. It was a startling discovery, like someone was holding a mirror up to her and she was seeing herself for the first time.

This awareness was so great, the understanding so profound, she felt dizzy with it. This *had* to change! She had to change.

And suddenly there was Walt Yoder standing in the middle of the road, hands on his hips. Lydie came to such an abrupt stop that she nearly fell off the scooter.

He jabbed a finger in her direction. "You told your father lies about me."

"I didn't," she said, shaking her head. "I've never told anyone about those *National Geographic* magazines. And I never will. That's between you and the Lord." She bit her lip. "But I know you told Dad I drew the doodles in the *Stoney Ridge Times*." It was weird, she thought, how his face never changed expression. Had he always been that way? So crotchety. She couldn't even remember the last time she had seen him smile. There was just no way to get through to him. Why bother to try?

She got back on her scooter to leave, then changed her mind. "Actually, it's fine that you told my dad about the doodles. It's good, in fact. It wasn't right of me to hide behind them. I truly didn't mean to hurt anyone with them, I really didn't. But as my dad said, by not signing my name to the doodles, it became too easy to cross the line. It's better when things are out in the open. I'm . . . better for it." Then she went on her way.

As she veered down the road that went past Black Gold Farm, she laughed, feeling light-headed all of a sudden. Feeling lighthearted. She felt as free as a bird.

David had completely forgotten about Mick's rebuilding of the shed until Birdy asked about it during last night's phone call. After breakfast, before he left for the Bent N' Dent, he refilled his coffee mug and went to see what progress had been made. Halfway down, he stopped, shocked. The concrete block foundation that Mick had laid was enormous. It wasn't the size of a shed, it was the size of a small barn. The amount of stacked lumber was absurd. What had that boy started? Started and stopped. So typical of Mick Yoder—the bigger, the better. He had absolutely no common sense.

Then David caught himself. Who was he to point blame at Mick? David had never once thought to check on the shed. To follow up with Mick. He'd completely forgotten about it.

He exhaled a sigh of discouragement. Wasn't this the message the Lord had been trying to drill into him all summer long? *Pay attention, David! Walk the beans.*

Down near the building site, he walked around the full foundation. An idea started to take shape in his mind. A brilliant idea. This . . . this could be a Grossdawdi Haus. The perfect living situation for his mother. Separate, but within shouting distance if she needed anything. It couldn't be more ideal—for his mother *and* for his wife. For him. The answer had been here, all summer long, waiting for him to notice.

He looked up at the sky. "Thank you, Lord."

A big grin spread over his face. Birdy and the boys would finally come home!

24

Another summer storm blew through Stoney Ridge
later that week. Dodging raindrops, David ran from
the little barn to the house. He was late again and
braced himself for his mother's sharp reprimand. But when he
came into the kitchen, she was seated calmly at the table, working on some mending. Outside were lead gray skies, darkening
the summer evening. The only light was the yellow glow of a
kerosene lamp hanging in the middle of the ceiling and another
one on the table, shedding light on her handiwork.

She glanced up and smiled when she saw him. "Lydie's upstairs, working on her planner. We've already eaten, but I can
heat supper for you."

"No, thank you. I'm not hungry." He was, actually, but he
hadn't expected a warm welcome, a peaceful setting, and he
didn't want to jeopardize the tranquility of the moment. He
wanted his mother to stay right where she was, to remain in the
same mood. There was much to discuss tonight.

She glanced at him over her bifocals. "I haven't seen much
of you lately."

"There's been a few problems to deal with."

"There always will be, David. A church is made up of flawed people."

Wasn't *that* the truth. Led by flawed people too. He pulled out a chair and sat down. "Mom, there's something I'd like to talk to you about."

"As would I." She set down her mending. "I've been pleased to see some changes in Lydie recently. She isn't running around like her hair is on fire quite so often." A slight smile tugged at the corners of her lips. "Perhaps there's hope for that girl yet."

"I think you're right. Working at Dok's office has been an answer to prayer. Ruth has been just the right person for Lydie at just the right time."

His mother peered at him with a quirked brow. "And I'm not?"

"Certainly. Of course you've been a blessing."

"You're very fortunate that I came when I did. Birdy up and left you, high and dry. We have the Lord to thank for my timely arrival." She took off her eyeglasses and polished them with her apron.

How was it possible for her to not realize that Birdy fled at the first opportunity? That he and Lydie avoided being at home? How could his mother's self-awareness be so myopic?

She slipped her glasses back on and knotted her hands together on the tabletop. "Well, that's all I wanted to tell you, that I've been delighted to see the progress in Lydie. So what's on your own mind?"

"Mom, you never did say how long you planned to stay."

Her shoulders stiffened and a wary look filled her eyes. "Considering Birdy's away, I can't imagine why you'd even ask such a thing."

"Actually, Birdy's coming home with the boys."

His mother cocked an eyebrow. "It's about time. People have been talking."

"Not really. Everyone understands."

"You're too forgiving, David."

"That, I believe, would be an impossibility. Anyway, with Birdy coming back, I wondered what your plans were."

She stared at David, her face settling into deep lines, and he stared back. A silence drew out between them, underscored by the steady sound of rain on the roof above their heads.

He reached out to cover her hand with his. "Mom," he said softly, "why did you leave Simon's house?"

She yanked her hand away. "I told you."

"No, actually. You didn't. You just said you thought it was time to come to Stoney Ridge to live."

Tears welled in her eyes. Now he'd done it. She was starting to cry. "Simon . . . ," she said, then sighed. Her sigh seemed to drain all the energy from her body, and David was struck by how drawn and tired she looked. Old. She looked old. "Simon," she started again, "told me I had to leave his home. That I wasn't needed any longer."

She swiped a tear off her cheek, one after the other, but soon there was a steady stream, and she covered her face with her hands.

There was a strong, deep-rooted oak tree in the front yard of David's childhood home. He remembered a fierce summer storm in which a lightning strike had split that tree right down the middle. He would never forget the sound of it, the feeling of fear it evoked, and afterward, the awe at the sight. That's how he felt as he watched his mother sob, her shoulders shaking. He saw her heart breaking.

David should have known something had prompted the move to Stoney Ridge. He should have called Simon right away. Or tried him again and again until he finally returned David's call. He couldn't even remember the last time he'd spoken to his brother. Last Christmas, maybe? Simon suffered from bouts of clinical depression, and talking to him on the phone was awful and painful, for both of them. It had been easier to just stop calling rather than try to coax his brother to talk.

He reached out and covered his mother's hand with his, giving it a gentle squeeze. "Did he say why you wore out your welcome?" His mother had been living with Simon for the last twenty years.

"One day he just got up from his bed and walked into the kitchen. He told me it was time I came to live with you in Stoney Ridge." Her eyes grew shiny. "He said that he couldn't breathe around me. That I suffocated him, the way a candle is suffocated by a lack of oxygen in the air." Her voice took on that tinny sound. "Such a ridiculous thing to say, don't you think? Blaming me for his depression. So ungrateful." She waited for David to agree with her, the way he'd always done, to appease her and make her feel better, but this time, he didn't. She narrowed her eyes. "Don't tell me you agree with Simon!"

"Suffocate is a strong word." He cleared his throat. "Stifle, maybe?"

Behind her polished lenses, her eyes filled with tears. "All I've ever tried to do is to help my children."

"That's true. That's been your intention. But, Mom, there's helping . . . and then there's overhelping."

"And you're accusing me of overhelping?"

David spoke slowly, carefully. They'd seldom talked this way before, and he was afraid of saying the wrong thing, of triggering more of her defensiveness. "I'm not accusing you of anything. And I'm sorry Simon hurt you. But surely you can see what Simon meant in how you tried to help Lydie."

"Lydie? You're saying I suffocated her too?"

"You tried to manage her. It was Ruth who helped us see that method wasn't going to bring lasting change. Your role with Lydie—and mine too—is to support her. Not manage her. Ruth's advice is sound. She's been right about Lydie all along. And, Mom, you must know that, deep down, because you accepted what Ruth said and stepped back. You gave Lydie the room to manage her own life, mistakes and all. Hasn't it been remarkable? She's been making strides."

His mother picked up her mending and started to stitch again. It was her way of saying the conversation was over. But it wasn't.

He cleared his throat. "Mick Yoder started the foundation on that shed, but that's as far as he's gotten."

Mammi scoffed. "I don't doubt it."

"I happened to go look at it the other morning. I don't know what Mick was thinking, but he doubled the size of the original shed. It's rather . . . large."

"That boy has no common—"

David jumped in to cut her off. "There might be a silver lining in Mick's procrastination. It occurred to me that with such a large foundation, the shed could be turned into a Grossdawdi Haus. Or in our case, a Grossmammi Haus."

His mother's hands slowed.

"There's plenty of time to customize it. To make it nice. Livable."

"What exactly are you trying to say?"

"It seems like it could be a fine place for you to live permanently, Mom. Close enough that we're right here if you need us. But far enough away to give you a little breathing room from a busy household with two loud little boys."

"I see." Her voice grew sharper. "Out of your life, you mean."

David felt that familiar knot of meekness lodge in his throat. "You've been very supportive. But we still need a little space from each other." It wasn't easy to be so direct with his mother. As she grew defensive, there was a sharpness to her voice that made David feel as if he were six years old, getting reprimanded.

Say it. Just say it. He braced both hands on his knees, trying to steel himself. His glance lifted. "There's something else."

"What's that?" Her voice sounded impatient with him.

"You're sitting in Birdy's chair."

Her brows flew up her forehead. "Why haven't you said something?"

"I should have. That very first night, I should have pointed it out."

"I didn't raise my sons to be meek. But you and Simon, you both have no backbones. Your sister, now she's the one with the backbone."

True. David and Simon avoided conflict with their mother. Ruth faced it head-on.

"You might not have even realized it, Mom, but Birdy should be the one sitting next to me at our own kitchen table. It's a little bit of a metaphor. You don't always recognize what your role is when you come to visit. There's a place for you at our table, in our lives. But that doesn't mean that Birdy gets pushed out of her place. I think this will be best for all of us, to live close to each other but not under the same roof. Birdy and I, we need to manage our own household. And I'm sure you'll enjoy the boys more when you have shorter doses with them."

His mother took a long look at him. "If I've overhelped . . . or stifled anyone . . . it's only been out of love."

"We know that." David rose to reach out and hug his mother.

His mother wasn't an affectionate woman. She didn't see the hug coming and stiffened like a statue. But he was happy to have hugged her, and for a flicker of a second, all was well again.

She patted the tabletop. "So if I'm the one who's going to live in that Grossmammi Haus, I want to be the one to plan it out. Down to the last nail."

He laughed. "Done." He put his hands on his hips. "There is one person you might want to ask for advice. She and her husband are remodeling their house and I think she'll have a lot of good tips for you. Assuming, that is, that you listen to her. Really listen."

Mammi's eyes narrowed. "Who?"

David smiled. "Your daughter, Ruth."

"You just don't give up on people, do you?"

"I try not to. Thankfully, neither does the Lord." He kissed the top of her prayer kapp and went upstairs to bed, feeling happier than he had in a long time. Months.

Birdy was coming home!

❧

Mick picked Lydie clear up off the ground and swung her around. And then they both laughed and he set her down.

"What's put you in such a good mood?"

"A bunch of things. First off, Owen Miller was caught selling that baking soda to some young punks from the junior high school. Dok's own husband made the arrest."

Lydie's eyes went wide. "Can you get arrested for selling baking soda?"

"You can if you're caught in a sting. Apparently, he's been selling drugs to minors for the last few months."

A smile tugged at the corner of her lips. "I shouldn't be happy that he's been caught . . . but . . . I am." Thrilled, in fact.

Mick lifted his hands. "What goes around, comes around."

"Did you give the baking soda to him?"

"Me? I didn't go through Dok's drugs! Owen did."

"But you let him."

"Actually, I didn't. He said he had to go to the bathroom. I didn't know he was rifling through Dok's office." Seeing the look on her face, he quickly added, "I promise. I truly did not know. It'll probably be good for him to get a little time in the cooler."

"Some friend you are."

He slapped his palm against his chest. "I didn't do anything."

"Exactly." She folded her arms against her chest. "You let Owen Miller turn you into someone you're not."

He tightened his lips. "You're still mad about Nathan's fields."

"Yes. Mad, disappointed, disgusted. You're better than that,

Mick. Nathan deserves better than to have his own brother treat him so badly."

"You're right. Really, I know you're right. I told your dad."

Lydie's mouth dropped open.

"Don't look so shocked. I'm going to sit on the sinner's bench next church Sunday. Your dad told me I needed to come clean to Nathan. I did. I apologized. And he was pretty cool about it. In fact, we're going to share the management of Black Gold Farm. Which means that he will run the farm and I will finally get to expand the livestock." He clapped his hands together. "But there's even better news. Patsy Glick told me I could take her home on Sunday night from the Singing."

A laugh burst out of Lydie. Maybe Patsy was just the right one for Mick, after all. He had to work for her.

But he looked a little hurt by her laugh. "What's so funny?"

"Nothing. I think you and Patsy deserve each other."

His brow furrowed, as if he wasn't quite sure that was meant as a compliment. "Last piece of good news. It's all arranged. My aunt's expecting you in Williamsport by the first of the month. She's willing to give you a job at her Clam Shack and you can rent a room in her house. She's the black sheep in the family, so you don't have to worry too much about breaking her rules."

"Oh. The first of the month," Lydie said, her voice fading uncertainly. "That's . . . not far off."

"I thought you'd be happy. You still want to leave, don't you?"

She wasn't so sure. In fact, she hadn't even thought about it since she talked to her dad about painting vendor signs. "I, um, I should wait until Birdy and the boys return home. They're coming soon, you know. That shed you started and stalled out on, Dad's hiring someone to finish it. Mammi is going to live in it."

He slapped his palm against his head. "Oh, man . . . the shed. I forgot all about it."

"Mick, have you ever thought you might have Attention Deficit Hyperactivity Disorder?"

"Nope. Never heard of it. Sounds contagious."

"It might be. But, my friend"—she socked him on the upper arm—"there is help to be had for it."

∿

It had rained all day, and as the clouds were breaking up, the setting sun was spectacular. The rim of each gray cloud was glowing, with splayed sun rays in every direction. Lydie went outside to watch it for a few minutes, and it made her think of a proverb from the book her dad had given to her. Die Sunn scheint as hinnich de Wolke. *There is sunshine also behind the clouds.* On an impulse, she crossed the yard to head toward the little barn to doodle.

She pulled her sketch pad out from the trunk and sat on top of it, drawing the clouds in the sky. She wasn't sure how much time had passed when she heard someone knock hard on the front door. Quickly, she pushed the pad under the horse blanket before leaving the barn to see Nathan banging on the door like there was a fire.

"Nathan! Nathan!" She waved when he turned to her voice.

He sprinted over to her. "Where's your father?"

"Dad and Mammi went to the bus station to pick up Birdy and the boys. What's wrong?"

"It's my dad. He's . . ." He turned and looked at the hedge that lined the two properties.

"Has something happened to him? Should I call Dok?"

Nathan shook his head. "She's over at Black Gold now." He covered his face for a moment, then dropped his hands, walked into the little barn and sat on the trunk, right on top of the blanket where her doodle pad was hidden. "Dad's test results came back. Dok came to the house to deliver the news. She says he's got something called Parkinson's disease." He glanced up at her. "Did you know?"

"No. I only knew that Dok wanted him to have some tests." A bunch of tests. Lydie sat down beside Nathan. "I'm so sorry, Nathan."

He leaned over, elbows on his knees, hands covering his face. "I should've realized he wasn't well."

"Have you noticed symptoms in your dad?"

He dropped his hands and straightened up. "His hands, those tremors. And the other day, I was watching him walk to the barn and noticed he was sort of shuffling his feet. At night, his speech will get a little slurred. But I thought he was just starting to get old. I thought that was the reason he hasn't shown much interest in the farm, not like he used to. Mick and I both figured he was just tired of it all." A tear slid down his face. "He's not easy, I know that. But he's still . . ."

"He's still your dad." Lydie understood. That's why she never told her father about Walt Yoder and the bare-chested women he ogled in the *National Geographic* magazines. She kept it to herself for Nathan's sake. "Did Dok say how the disease will progress?"

"No. Just that he's in early stages and there's a lot of medications that can delay symptoms. It all makes sense, though, why he split the farm in two. He must've known something wasn't right with him." He lifted his hat and rubbed his forehead. "How's that for irony? Mom's asthma will probably get better now that the fields will stop getting treated by Mr. Chemical and his evil son. But Dad is getting sick." He looked up at the barn rafters with a sigh. "I asked Dok if all those chemicals he's doused on the fields have caused his sickness. She said it can't be proven, but I'm convinced there's a connection."

He went on, Nathan-style, to describe how toxins built up in the body. He lost Lydie in such detailed explanation, but she let him talk until he was all talked out.

And then Nathan shifted on the trunk. "Something keeps stabbing my leg." He stood and lifted the horse blanket up to reveal Lydie's sketch pad. "What's this?" He flipped the cover and happened to land on an early attempt of a doodle of his dad, driving the Yoder Toter. He looked at her, one eyebrow arched.

She sighed. "Your dad was right. It's been me."

"Yeah, I know." He plopped back down on the trunk. "I've known all along."

Her eyes went wide. "How? How did you know?"

"I know the way you draw. I know the way you think."

"Aren't you angry?" He didn't seem at all angry. In fact, she thought she saw the barest hint of a smile in his eyes.

"Why would I be mad? They're funny. They're creative. You have a way of making us all laugh at ourselves and not take life so seriously. It's one of the reasons we need you, Lydie. It would break everyone's heart if you left."

"Not everyone's." Definitely not Walt Yoder's.

He clasped a hand against his chest. "Mine. It would break my heart if you left."

Dear, sweet Nathan. Why couldn't she make him understand? "Don't you see? This is just the kind of thing I do that ends up creating a disaster. That drawing in the newspaper, the one about the Amish garden of Eden . . . I made things even worse. I was trying to help, but I think it pushed Owen Miller right over the edge. I think that's why he sprayed your fields."

"Sounds to me like you think you're to blame for Owen's wrongdoing."

Was she? But it wasn't that simple! "I meant that those are some examples of how I mess things up . . . just by being me." She fumbled for the words to make him understand a moment longer. Then she found them. "Dok thinks I have something called Attention Deficit Hyperactivity Disorder. It has something to do with how the brain works. It's why I'm always late and why I forget things and why things so often go haywire if I'm involved. It's not an excuse. But it is real. I'm working on ways to manage it, but ADHD will always be part of me. Always! I'm just not your . . . normal girl."

His face softened into a smile, and a tenderness came into his eyes. "I know."

She tucked her chin, swallowing hard. *Don't cry, don't cry, don't cry.*

He shifted on the trunk to face her. "What kinds of things do you do to manage it?"

She took a moment to gather her thoughts together, her whole self, together. "Well," she said, lifting her head, "Dok gave me a planner to write everything down that needs to be done. And she's taught me about how to prioritize, and how to say no. I'm trying hard to finish what I start. Oh, and then there's breathing exercises."

"Breathing exercises?"

"Yes. Don't laugh."

His face sobered. "Not laughing."

"Focusing on breathing has been a huge help. Probably the biggest help, next to the planner. That's been really big. But concentrating on breathing helps me to slow down and think and not bounce off to something else like I usually do."

"Are those things helping?"

"Yes." They'd been helping quite a lot. She was hardly ever late for work, and her desk stayed tidy, and she didn't feel quite so frustrated with herself. At least, she hadn't until Owen sprayed Nathan's fields. Then everything went south. She'd fallen off the horse, but she remounted. She was back in the saddle. She wasn't going to give in to ADHD.

"Well, it's good to work on our weak areas. It's like my fields. I need to know what the soil is lacking so I can fix it."

"That's the thing, Nathan. You're a fixer. But you can't fix everything. You can't fix this."

"Remember when you asked me why my dad didn't just accept the crookedness in the slope in the fields?"

"I remember."

"You were right. Once I accepted the crookedness, I planted the entire acreage in contour strips. I made the adjustment and it worked. Better than I could've ever imagined." He leaned forward. "So what if I want to . . . accept the crookedness in you?"

"Why? Why would you want my crookedness?"

"Because it's all part of what makes you . . . you." He brushed a stray lock off her forehead. "Please don't leave."

"I don't want to disappoint you too." She felt her chin begin to tremble. Because that was the worst of it. That's what staying meant. If she stayed, then she'd eventually disappoint him. She'd cause him great regret.

"You could never disappoint me."

Why wouldn't he listen? "Nathan, even with all of Dok's behavior modifications, I'm still me. I still make a mess of things. You deserve to be with someone like Perfect Patsy, who never says the wrong thing or does the wrong thing. Hardly ever. Actually, scratch Patsy. You should be with someone better than Patsy."

"You're the only girl I've ever wanted." He cupped her face in his hands. "You are what matters, Lydie. More than Black Gold Farm, more than the farmers' market, more than anyone else. Without you, my life is empty. With you, it's full."

Her mouth fell open and she couldn't even breathe. "Nathan . . ."

He shook his head. "You don't have to say anything. It's just true. I've been crazy about you since the day you moved to Stoney Ridge and drew a doodle of the teacher, sound asleep at her desk."

He remembered that? She'd been only six years old.

"I love you, Lydie."

She gazed into those beautiful blue eyes. In them she saw

acceptance, understanding, and love. She saw love in those eyes. Somehow, he loved her, just as she was. Her tears broke free and slid down her cheeks. He loved her! He *knew* her and he *loved* her.

Nathan kissed away her tears before he kissed her on the lips, gently at first, and then his arms folded around her and she leaned into him and his kiss deepened and she felt dizzy with happiness. Just the way she had felt when he kissed her at Blue Lake Pond.

She loved him so much. There was no other way to put it. She didn't want to leave, she wanted to stay. She wanted to stay to be with *him*. This realization hit her in a way she had never expected. "Nathan, I love you too!" She flung her arms around his neck, knocking his hat off so that it sailed across the stall. He laughed and she laughed, and they kissed again and again and again. She thought of something else that Dok had said. That no one knew where they belonged until they found it for themselves.

A horse whinnied as it turned up the driveway hill and some familiar shrieks floated through the air. Timmy's and Noah's shrieks.

She pulled back and put her hands on Nathan's chest. "They're here! Birdy and the boys."

He stood and picked up his hat and brushed it against his leg, gave her a hand, and they went out to welcome everyone home.

Discussion Questions

1. Lydie Stoltzfus felt as if she was a square peg in a round hole. She just didn't fit in her close-knit Amish community, not even in her family. How was she correct in her assessment of herself? And where was she mistaken?

2. Working as a temporary receptionist for Dok Stoltzfus kept Lydie grounded in Stoney Ridge, in more ways than one. In what ways did Lydie change as she started to work as Dok's receptionist? What events or persons had the biggest influence on her?

3. Lydie constantly accepted blame for her ADHD-related mistakes. She felt inadequate about everything. Unworthy of Nathan's love. When have you struggled with similar feelings of insecurity as Lydie had?

4. Nathan's conversion of his fields provided some interesting metaphors in this story. David caught one, as he watched Nathan "walk the beans." Lydie stumbled on another when she suggested Nathan "accept the crookedness" of the land. Any others?

5. David Stoltzfus had a knack for making sermon illustrations from everyday experiences. After Nathan described that he wanted to fortify his plants' immune systems to fight off predators, David likened that thinking to how a Christian could fortify his mind, through Scripture and prayer and worship and community, thus creating a defense to ward off attacks from the Evil One. How did those silent monologues of David deepen the story?

6. Another time, David compared Nathan's "walking the beans" to paying attention in life. What areas in your life might benefit if you "walked the beans"?

7. What about Mick? Did you feel any sympathy for him? What kind of effect do you think Walt Yoder, his father, had on him? What about Walt's effect on Nathan?

8. Owen Miller had a strong influence on Mick. Why do you think Mick was so enamored with him? When has there been a time in your life when you've felt drawn to someone who hasn't pulled out the best in you? What lessons have you learned?

9. How would Nathan describe Lydie? How did she describe herself? Is there a difference in the way you view her and the way she viewed herself? Why?

10. Mammi, and even David, thought Lydie's problems could be solved if she would just buckle down and apply herself. Dok understood that Lydie couldn't just work harder. She knew, because she recognized herself in Lydie. How did that revelation change everything . . . for David as well as Lydie?

11. Mindfulness is trendy right now. What were your thoughts as Dok tried to talk David into considering mindfulness exercises for Lydie? Did you freeze up, like David did? Assume it was New Age-y? Dok connected it to a spiritual discipline taken right out of Scripture. ("Be still and know that I am God" [Ps. 46:10 NIV]; "You keep him in perfect peace whose mind is stayed on you" [Isa. 26:3 ESV].) Does knowing that make a difference to you?

12. Dok said that Lydie reminded her of a butterfly, trying to find a place to land. What were your thoughts about Dok's last words (in this book) to Lydie that no one knows where they belong, until they find it for themselves?

13. Do you have any friends or family with ADHD? How has Lydie's story changed your thinking about them? Hopefully, you have another view of the importance of providing patience and understanding to that person, how such tolerance can help that individual reach his or her potential. While there are certainly frustrating aspects of a person with ADHD, there are also gifts. Creativity, spontaneity, passion, out-of-the-box thinking . . . those are just a few. What other gifts do you see in your loved one with ADHD?

14. The heart of Lydie's story circled around self-acceptance—not in a "Just Think Positive!" way, but through receiving love and acceptance from God. How would you connect Nathan's delight in Lydie's "crookedness" to how the Lord loves and accepts us, just as we are? If you struggle with this belief, please think again. It's foundational. Here's a place to begin: "For God so

loved the world that he gave his one and only Son, that whoever believes in him shall not perish but have eternal life. For God did not send his Son into the world to condemn the world, but to save the world through him" (John 3:16–17 NIV). For God so loved the world . . . and that includes *you*.

Author's Note

Diving deep into ADHD has been a fascinating study for me. While I don't have ADHD, there seem to be quite a lot of people in my life, young and old, who do. It's been invaluable to research the topic thoroughly and learn how the ADHD brain is wired and to understand certain behaviors. While ADHD is not an excuse, it does create its own challenges. Through learning more about the disorder, I've gained empathy and understanding.

For example, a very good friend of mine was diagnosed with ADHD as a child. Months will go by in which I don't hear from her. She doesn't respond to texts or emails or phone calls . . . and then suddenly she'll call and "firehose" me with information. In the past, I've felt annoyed with this friend and have tired of the "my terms only" kind of friendship she offered. It felt imbalanced. Since studying ADHD, I have much more sympathy for her. I can see more clearly the parts of her that are so creative and funny, and I'm more understanding of behavior she can't control. I've come to realize that it's just "the price of doing business" with that particular friend. And she's worth it.

So are the people who helped me bring this story to life. My first reader, Lindsey Ross, who gives it to me straight. She let me know the first chapter wasn't working (first chapters are so important!), so I deleted it and started over. I'm grateful for such candor.

A thank-you to my agent, Joyce Hart; my editors, Andrea Doering and Barb Barnes—who always, always polish a story to make it shine. And to the marketing/publicity whiz team: Michele Misiak, Karen Steele, Brianne Dekker, and so many others. And Zac Weikal, a stellar assistant.

To the Lord, my humble gratitude for allowing me to communicate his Word through stories. *Me!* Wonders never cease.

Last note. While I do believe ADHD is a real thing, evidence is mounting that a growing dependence on digital devices could be giving all of us some ADHD-like symptoms. Have you wondered if distractibility is becoming a problem for you? Or has a spouse or child remarked on how often you pick up your phone to check a text message or scroll Instagram? You might remain physically present but your mind has wandered away. For me, the answer is, regrettably, yes.

So I've been working on a few strategies gleaned from Dok: Finishing a task before moving on to the next. Turning my cell phone to silent when I'm spending time with others. Arriving a few minutes early to places, instead of a few minutes late. When I do, life is . . . calmer. More manageable.

It seems that one of the lessons of this book is to "walk the beans" of technology's role in my life. In other words, to pull the weeds before they take root.

Recommended Resources for Understanding ADHD

ADDitudemag.com—Excellent online magazine, with helpful webinars by noted professionals.

Barkley, Russell A., *Taking Charge of ADHD: The Complete, Authoritative lexia, Dysgraphia, Dyscalculia, ADHD & Processing Disorders* (Oakland, CA: New Harbinger Publications, Inc., 2018).

Mertin, Mark, MD, *Mindful Parenting for ADHD: A Guide to Cultivating Calm, Reducing Stress, and Helping Children Thrive* (Oakland, CA: New Harbinger Publications, Inc., 2015).

Phelan, Thomas W., PhD, *All About ADHD: A Family Resource for Helping Your Child Succeed with ADHD* (Naperville, IL: Sourcebooks, 2017).

Rosier, Tamara, PhD, *Your Brain's Not Broken: Strategies for Navigating Your Emotions and Life with ADHD* (Grand Rapids: Revell, 2021).

Sonna, Linda, PhD, *The Everything Parent's Guide to Children with ADD/ADHD* (New York: F&W Publications, 2005).

Zylowska, L., et al., "Mindfulness Meditation Training in Adults and Adolescents with ADHD: A Feasibility Study." *Journal of Attention Disorders* 11, no. 6 (2008): 737–46.

Craving more from
SUZANNE WOODS FISHER?

Satisfy your sweet tooth with this
SNEAK PEEK of *The Sweet Life*

Available Now

1

Never ask a woman who is eating ice cream straight from the carton how she's doing.

—Anonymous

Needham, Massachusetts
Thursday, February 6

Dawn parked in front of her childhood home in Needham but couldn't make herself get out of the car. For this brief moment, the terrible news belonged only to her. As soon as she told someone, especially her mom, it would make it somehow more real. More true.

Maybe it wasn't real. She reviewed the conversation she'd had with Kevin last night. Was it possible that he'd suffered from premarital jitters? Just a case of cold feet. Cold, cold feet.

Tears flooded Dawn's eyes again. It wasn't just cold feet. Kevin said he wasn't sure he was in love with Dawn, not the way he thought he should be. Or the way he used to be. She looked around the car for a clean tissue, but all she could find were scrunched-up soggy ones. How in the world did she end up in a mess like this? Dawn Dixon was known as a levelheaded, objective, logical woman. Her nickname was Teflon Dawn. She could handle anything. Prepared for any crisis. Yet she'd missed Kevin's growing vacillation about getting married.

The front door opened and Mom stood at the threshold, the obvious question on her face. Why had Dawn come home, to Needham, on a weekday when she should've been at work in Boston? Dawn dreaded this conversation. Calling off the wedding, after all her mom had done to make it unique and one-of-a-kind, would devastate her too. Dawn thought of the hours her mother had spent making origami doves that would hang from the enormous and expensive rented tent.

Another image of Kevin popped into her head—one from just a few weeks ago. They were at the wedding venue to finalize some details. Dawn and her mom were talking to the wedding event planner. Like always, her mom had some new ideas, and the wedding event planner was listening with rapt, wide-eyed interest—Marnie Dixon had that effect on creative types. It was like opening a shaken can of soda pop and the fizz spilled everywhere. Dawn turned to ask Kevin a question, but he had slipped away. She found him close to the bay, facing the water. As she approached, he turned to her, his sunglasses hiding his eyes.

Something was off, she thought. "Are you feeling okay?"

"I'm fine. Just thinking about things."

Things. Like canceling their wedding. Their marriage. Their happily ever after. Those kinds of things.

Gag. Dawn felt queasy, thinking of what a cliché she'd become. Jilted. Just two months before the wedding. Maybe not left at the altar, but pretty darn close.

Mom stood on the threshold, arms folded against her chest. Dawn slowly got out of the car and closed the door. Steeling herself, she walked up the brick-lined path. "Mom," she said, her voice breaking. "There's something we have to talk about."

"She told you, didn't she?"

Dawn jerked her head up.

"I told her not to tell anyone. Blabbermouth. That's what she is. That's what I'm going to call her from now on. Maeve the Blabbermouth."

"Aunt Maeve?" Dawn scrunched up her face. "Maeve told me—"

"I didn't want anyone to know. At least not until after the wedding. I just wanted to get this surgery taken care of. I don't want you to worry, honey. It was caught early. I promise. That's the thing about breast cancer. Catch it quick and take care of it. So I did. And I have plenty of time before the wedding for treatment. The doctor promised. Come April twelfth, I'll be just fine. I hope Maeve didn't get it wrong and make it sound like something worse than it was. I'm sure she meant well, but she's in big trouble."

"You have . . . breast cancer?" Dawn's voice shook and broke and then stopped.

"Had. It's gone. I'm fine, honey. I promise."

For one dreadful, disorienting second, Dawn's mind emptied, stilled. Then denial roared in—loud and large. *No! No way. Not my mom.*

"Caught early. Taken care of. Gone." She snapped her fingers, like it was no big deal.

But it *was* a big deal. "When did you find out?"

"A month or so ago, I had a routine mammogram—and you know how much I hate going to doctors—but I went. And they called me back in." She shrugged. "That happens. I wasn't concerned. Not until they wanted the ultrasound. Then the biopsy."

"Biopsy?"

"Yes. On the day you were getting your makeup done for

the wedding. You didn't want me there, remember? You said I would get in the way."

"I said you would turn me into someone I didn't recognize."

"Well, it all worked out, because that was the day of the biopsy. And then things happened fast, honey. Surgeon, oncologist, boom. Surgery. They move fast when they find cancer."

"When?"

"A week ago."

"Mom . . ."

"I know, I know. Maybe I should have told you, but I just want this wedding to be perfect. I was going to tell you after you got back from the honeymoon. I promise. I'm not trying to hide anything from you."

"You had surgery and didn't tell me?"

"I left a letter for you that Maeve was supposed to give you . . . just in case something went wrong."

"But . . . how are you feeling?"

"Not bad. A little sore. Like I don't want anyone to accidentally bump into me kind of sore. But relieved. And grateful. I had good doctors who helped me make decisions."

"All alone? You didn't talk to anyone else?"

"I told Maeve about the surgery. And she took me to and from the hospital. She's brought me food and checked on me. I suppose I will forgive her, eventually. But I really didn't want you to know about any of this yet. I was so clear with her about that. What is the point of having a best friend if they go behind your back and tell your daughter that kind of news . . . right before her wedding?"

"Mom. Stop talking and listen to me. Kevin doesn't want to marry me. There isn't going to be a wedding."

Mom finally stopped talking.

There wasn't going to be a wedding. And her mom had cancer. Dawn and her mom stared at each other in a mixture of shock and disbelief.

There wasn't much in life that could knock Marnie Dixon down, but seeing her daughter sit at the kitchen table, head in hands, weeping, did the job. Her friend Maeve always said that mothers felt whatever pain their child felt, only magnified. Marnie jumped up, got a box of tissues to set on the table between them, and pulled out one for Dawn and another for her.

Dawn rarely cried, even as a little girl. When she was learning to walk, she would fall, pick herself up, and try again. That was Dawn. Philip used to say that their daughter was born accepting the fact that life would require grit and determination.

Dazed, Marnie dabbed her eyes, rose again, and went to get two cups of coffee. She filled them, then remembered they'd run out of coffee creamer. A brilliant idea struck. She opened the freezer and rummaged for a container of vanilla ice cream. She dropped a big spoonful of it into each mug and handed one to Dawn, who peered vaguely at the melting lumps.

"Everything's better with ice cream," Marnie said. She slipped into the chair next to her. "Start at the beginning. Tell me what happened." The timer on her phone went off and she jumped up to take her pain pills. Dawn sat at the kitchen table, watching her with worried eyes. "I'm fine, honey. I really am. This is just a little blip on the radar."

"Mom, please sit down."

Right. Marnie needed to settle. She sat in the chair opposite Dawn and put both hands around the warm coffee mug. "Let's talk about your wedding."

"I keep trying to tell you. There is no wedding."

"But . . . what are the chances that Kevin just has a bad case of pre-wedding jitters?" Dawn's eyes filled with tears again. That should have told Marnie, right there, all she needed to know. Those beautiful blue eyes of Dawn's, they were bottomless pools of sadness.

"Last night, Kevin came over to help me address wedding invitations. I was showing him how to put the stamp on just so." Dawn took a shaky breath, closing her eyes for a minute.

Marnie sighed. "Gorgeous stamps," she muttered. She'd designed them herself—two Eastern Bluebirds, building a nest—to complement the avian-themed wedding. Marnie loved birds.

"When I handed him the stamps, he held them in his hand and said he just couldn't do it. I didn't know what he was talking about, so I just showed him how to do it again. Then he said that he knew how to put a stamp on. What he couldn't do—" Her voice choked up. She reached for another tissue and dabbed at her eyes. "He said he couldn't marry me."

"Why? What reason did he give?"

"He said he didn't think he loved me. Not the way he thought he should."

"That's not possible! Kevin's loved you since the first time he laid eyes on you." Could there be another woman? Marnie didn't want to ask, didn't want to think it. After all, this was Kevin—nearly a son to her. He even spoke at Philip's memorial service—he was that much a part of their family tapestry. There was hardly a picture in the family albums that he wasn't in.

They'd known Kevin since he was fourteen years old, when his father accepted the call to be the senior pastor at their local church and moved his family to Needham. Kevin and Dawn met in youth group and shared a common circle of church friends. They started to date in their junior year of high school, went to the same college, dating steadily throughout all four years. They were the perfect couple, both immensely sensible and well suited. No drama, not ever. As Dawn and Kevin graduated from college, everyone expected they'd get engaged. Ever reasonable, they decided to wait a few years, to get work experience, live with friends in Boston, and not miss out on any young adult experience. That's exactly what they did. Two years passed, three, then five. Getting engaged was always the plan . . . someday.

But then Philip died, suddenly and unexpectedly, and everything changed. Everything. Kevin proposed, Dawn accepted, and elaborate wedding plans got underway.

Dawn picked up her mug and crossed the kitchen to the coffee-maker. She refilled her coffee and spooned more ice cream into the mug, then took a spoonful straight from the carton and ate it. Marnie noticed how Dawn's shoulders slumped in that way they had after Philip died, and her heart ached for her daughter. Dawn brooded, internalized every blessed thing, whereas Marnie shared every thought and feeling. Even now, Marnie had a dozen questions she wanted to ask but prudence kept her quiet. She needed to let Dawn reveal what she wanted to, and when. A lifetime of experience had taught her that if she asked too much, Dawn shut down.

"Looking back, I can see now that there were signs." Dawn returned to sit at the table, hands gripped tightly around the mug. "He never had any opinions about the wedding. I tried to get him interested, but he just kept deferring. He would say, 'You and your mom can make that call.'" She took a sip of coffee. "I thought he was just accommodating us, but now I realize he didn't want to be a part of it."

"So you think it was the choices of the wedding that caused this?" And if that were true, Marnie felt furious with him. He was a grown man, after all. He could have spoken up at any time.

On the heels of anger came guilt. The wedding, she admitted, was teetering toward over-the-top. Perhaps a tiny bit more than Dawn had asked for, definitely more than Kevin wanted. When they first got engaged, he said he'd always wanted a wedding on the beach with only family attending. Ridiculous! Imagine Dawn's wedding dress train dragged along the sand. For goodness' sakes, Dawn was an only child who had recently lost her father. Why shouldn't she have the wedding of her dreams?

Dawn stared into her mug. "I don't know. I just know that

things haven't been easy between us, not like they used to be, ever since . . ."

"Since when?"

She sighed and looked up. "That's what I don't know." She covered her face. "It's so humiliating. We have all the same friends. I will forever be known as the girl who was left at the altar."

"True friends aren't like that."

Dawn ran a hand through her hair. On a typical workday, her long red hair would be tightly pulled back and pinned, out of the way. She tried to look older than her years. Marnie thought that was silly. Dawn oozed such confidence and self-assurance that people had always thought she was a decade older than she was.

Today, though, wasn't a typical day. Dawn's thick tangled hair looked like it hadn't been combed recently. Dark circles rimmed her eyes. "This morning he sent a text asking to talk again tonight."

"Maybe—"

"No, Mom. No maybes. The wedding is off. That much, I'm sure of. I gave him the ring back."

Marnie's eyes slipped to Dawn's left hand. The ring—one that had belonged to Kevin's grandmother—was gone.

"We're only going to talk about how to divide up the cancelations. In his text, he said he would help call vendors. He'd make as many calls as needed."

Marnie sat back in her chair. "So he's really serious about this."

Dawn nodded. Another tear escaped and she wiped it off her cheek. "Dead serious."

Okay. Okay, then. Marnie jumped up and grabbed the wedding notebook. "I can handle everything, Dawn. You don't have to do a thing. Maeve can help. We'll take care of everything, sweetheart."

Dawn looked a little bewildered. "Hold it. Slow down. I know you can pivot on a dime, but I can't move quite that fast. Besides, Kevin is the one who is calling this wedding off. He offered to make the cancelations and I think we should let him." She leaned on her elbows. "Mom, you have cancer. We haven't even talked about that yet."

"Had cancer. It's gone." Marnie turned to a new page in the wedding binder. "I think you're right about letting Kevin make as many cancelation calls as possible. He shouldn't get off scot-free here."

"You're not going to talk about it?"

Marnie looked up. "It?"

"Cancer."

"No." She looked back down at the binder. "I'm not giving it any more space in my life."

Dawn sighed. "I'd better get to work." She rose.

Marnie's mouth went as round as an O. "Work? After such a traumatic event?"

"I'm in the middle of a big project. Don't worry. It's a good distraction." She paused. "Mom, are you really, really okay?"

"Well, I'm furious with Kevin."

"Not that. I meant . . . having cancer."

"*Had* cancer," Marnie said. "It's gone."

"Well, we're going to talk more about it. I'm glad you're recovering well from the surgery. Not so glad that you didn't tell me." She bent down and kissed Marnie on the top of her head. "Get some rest. I'll call you later."

"Promise?" There was a pleading note in her voice.

Dawn gave her a thumbs-up as she headed to the door. Marnie went and watched her leave. She felt as if her heart was breaking for Dawn. She wished she could take the pain away for her daughter, or take it on herself. But she couldn't. No mother could.

She knew she drove Dawn crazy some of the time. Most of

the time. To be honest, Dawn drove Marnie a little crazy too. In a nutshell, Dawn thought Marnie was too dramatic, and Marnie thought Dawn wasn't dramatic enough.

She supposed her uncharacteristically calm reaction to a diagnosis of cancer could be a shock in itself to Dawn. Frankly, Marnie was still in shock over it. She was careful about food. She exercised every single day. She did yoga. She had a deep and abiding faith in God that helped her cope with stress, with the tragedy of losing her husband. How in the world did Marnie Dixon have cancer? Scratch that. Had.

Having cancer was like having an unexpected and unwanted houseguest. Literally. Marnie didn't invite it, she didn't want it to stay, and she wanted it out as soon as she could evict it. It wasn't that she ignored the diagnosis—she faced it head on, underwent all the pre-op tests required before surgery (so many machines and needles! her poor little breast). She begged her surgeon for the earliest date for surgery that she could possibly give to her. *Get it out of me!* That's all Marnie could think about. *I have a wedding to put on! I have a life to live!* She could hardly wait to get on the other side of surgery, to wake up in the morning and soak in the awareness that the cancer was gone.

But like a clueless houseguest, cancer didn't get the hint. It left its mark, like a lingering odor. Whenever Marnie used to fry fish, the house would stink of it for days. That's what cancer did. It just stunk.

She knew that Dawn was upset she hadn't been told, but Marnie was still glad she'd listened to her gut instinct. They were so different that way. Dawn's guide in life was her black-and-white principles and Marnie respected that quality about her daughter. There was no one she'd rather trust with money, and she could see why Dawn had excelled in her chosen field of public accounting—which sounded astonishingly dull to Marnie. Dawn's work was all about reacting to what others had done. Looking for problems, checking for errors, bringing mistakes to light.

Marnie was led by intuition, by prayer. Things that were invisible, while principles were made of concrete. Philip was like Dawn in that way. Philip and Marnie's marriage had been a good one, but it wasn't without its bumps now and then. And whenever they had those inevitable rocky patches, those strong disagreements, it always boiled down to how they viewed the world. Philip's principles vs. Marnie's intuition. After thirty-two years of marriage, they had never quite solved that quagmire. And then he was gone.

She felt badly Dawn was upset that she hadn't told her about the surgery, but she kept quiet so the wedding could proceed without a hitch. And she had to admit that she did it for her own benefit. Getting a diagnosis of cancer thrust her into a world that she had always preferred to ignore. She had so much to learn about, so many decisions to make quickly, and then came the healing part. She needed the quiet. Even Maeve, dear Maeve, kept telling her stories of friends with cancer, and frankly, she just didn't want to hear them. Every single person was a distinct being and their medical situation was as unique as their fingerprints. That's why she stayed away from cancer stories. *No thank you.*

Marnie had thought once this health glitch was behind her, it would be smooth sailing. She plopped into Philip's favorite armchair with a sigh. No wedding? No Kevin in their lives?

Marnie's thoughts bounced to wondering how difficult it would be to cancel everything as quickly as possible. The wedding venue, the caterer, the florist. Could a wedding dress get returned? Doubtful. It would seem like a bad luck dress.

She closed her eyes, breathed in and out, a deep cleansing breath. In and out, in and out. *Everything will be okay. The Lord is sovereign. All things work together for good for those who love God.* Her mind clutched on every comforting Bible verse she could think of. *Breathe in and out, in and out. It will all turn out okay.*

She opened her eyes.

She wanted to kill Kevin.

2

Why does ice cream go with a broken heart? Because if you eat enough of it, it freezes the heart and numbs the pain for a bit.

—CC Hunter, author

Boston, Massachusetts
Thursday, February 6

Kevin wasn't dead, but it felt to Dawn like someone had died. The sickening feeling settled over her, the knowing that the path ahead was going to be a long, hard, bumpy road. Knowing she would survive this loss, but life would never be the same.

Dawn survived the workday by reminding herself of how she had gotten through those early weeks after her dad had died. She didn't need to figure out how to navigate the rest of her life without her dad, just that one day. She could make it one day at a time.

Around five o'clock, she received a text from Kevin asking when he could stop by her apartment to talk.

She paused before responding. Seeing him in person . . . she just couldn't handle it. Too high a risk of a hysterical break-down.

Dawn
Let's just talk on the phone. Call after 8.

Kevin
Oh. OK.

She waited to see if he had anything to add, then turned her phone on silent and put it in her purse. She finished the project she'd been working on, tidied up her office, and went home to shower, tried to eat something even though she had zero appetite, and prepared herself for Kevin's call. She couldn't even let herself think about Mom's breast cancer. She couldn't even go there, not with all the what-ifs and what might've happened.

The one bright spot in this horrible day was that her room-mate was away for a few days. Brynn was her best friend, as close to a sister as a friend could be, but Dawn wouldn't be able to hide anything from her, and she just couldn't handle trying to explain anything right now. She had no words to describe how her entire life had turned upside down in just twenty-four hours.

At eight o'clock sharp, Dawn's cell phone rang. Kevin's punc-tuality was something she'd always appreciated about him, but tonight it annoyed her. She let it ring a few times before she picked up. "Hello."

"Dawn, how are you? How did your day go?" He sounded genuinely concerned for her.

As her brain circled back to Kevin's "We're just not work-ing" statement from last night, she wondered again what the part was that hadn't been working, because so much of their relationship *did* work. "It was a busy day. Super busy. In fact, I still have something I have to finish. So, what exactly did you want to discuss?"

He saw beyond her smokescreen. "This is important too,

Dawn. If you can sit down for a moment and listen, I'll make it quick."

She plopped down on the sofa, holding the phone with one hand, rubbing her forehead with the other. "Shoot."

"I made some calls today and started the process. There are some vendors who are charging a fee. I'll cover all those costs, of course."

You bet you will, buddy.

"I'll send you an email with all the details about, well, specifics."

She noticed how carefully he avoided the words: canceling their wedding.

"Dawn, there's one thing I discovered today. To get the honeymoon package on the hotel, I had to pay it all up front. Nonrefundable. So, it's either forfeit the money or . . ."

If Kevin said he was going with someone else, Dawn would release a bloodcurdling scream. He knew how much the Cape meant to her. Her dad had once told her that the closest he'd been to Heaven was a spring day on Cape Cod. Dawn had never forgotten those words, and even planned for her wedding in April, just so she would have that chance for a heavenly honeymoon on the Cape.

". . . I thought that maybe . . . you could go. You know . . . take a friend. Take anyone you want to. I'd like you to go to Cape Cod, Dawn, and have a vacation. Take the package. It's already paid for. Please go. Go and enjoy yourself."

The first person who popped into Dawn's mind was her mother.

∽

NEEDHAM, MASSACHUSETTS
TUESDAY, APRIL 8

Two months had passed and Marnie was still in shock that Dawn had invited her along on the groomless honeymoon.

Three times she asked her if she was absolutely sure she wanted her to go, and three times Dawn said yes . . . and to please stop asking or she might change her mind.

Then Dawn surprised Marnie with a hug. "I think this would've made Dad happy. You know, the two of us, going together to a place he loved. His girls, together."

That's what Philip always called them. Marnie and Dawn were his girls.

Frankly, despite the bleak circumstances, Marnie couldn't remember ever feeling so excited about a vacation. She had just finished six weeks of radiation and was eager to forget the daily treatments. Eager to move on! And Cape Cod was a place she loved. When Dawn was little, they would spend a summer week camping on the Cape. That was before Philip started booking Dawn's summers at camps for gifted children, which weren't really camps at all. Science Camp, Engineering Camp, NASA Space Camp (Philip's favorite). Marnie thought those camps squelched Dawn's creative spark and what she really needed was an unscheduled summer of "sacred idleness."

Rubbish, Philip would say. She remembered one conversation in particular when Dawn was turning twelve years old. They were sitting at the breakfast table, drinking coffee, listening to a classical music station. "Do you hear, Philip? Do you hear those pauses in between the notes? They're necessary, to allow the ear to rest before the music starts up again and takes you to another place entirely. That's what Dawn needs this summer. A pause."

Philip scoffed that off. "You mean boredom. Marnie, you romanticize boredom. I was bored as a child. We had no money for anything. Not swim lessons, not tennis lessons, not anything. I would never let my own child face a summer of boredom." He was the eldest of five children, raised by a single mother. Too many to care for, he believed. That's why he was satisfied with only one child.

Marnie found another empty suitcase and heaved it onto her bed. Better too much of everything than not enough, she thought. She had high hopes for the week together with her daughter, whose heart and soul needed serious mending.

Early Sunday morning, the two women planned to drive down Route 6 to stay at the very ritzy Chatham Bars Inn. Marnie had never stayed in such a fancy hotel. Saturday, April twelfth, was the official (canceled) wedding day, and Marnie had wanted to do something special for Dawn, something to make her feel cherished. So she booked a spa day for her—the works!—and paid for Brynn, her longtime friend and apartment mate, to go too. They'd met at one of those camps Philip had found. Chess camp, she thought. Or coding. It was hard to remember.

She folded her new one-piece spandex bathing suit—called a Miraclesuit and Marnie hoped it would live up to its name. She was a big believer in miracles. Big ones, small ones, everyday ones. You just had to keep your eyes on the lookout for them. Not miss them. That was her theory on the topic, anyway. As she tucked it into her suitcase, she wondered again if Dawn regretted not bringing Brynn with her. Brynn would've been the logical choice of a traveling companion for Dawn. They could've played chess together on the beach.

But Marnie wasn't going to ask Dawn a fourth time.

She was over-the-moon excited for this trip, for her own sake as well as Dawn's. Marnie felt out of balance in her soul after that dreadful bout of cancer and desperately needed to restore harmony in her life, to find that settled center that had gone missing. She needed to step out of her own life and see it with fresh eyes. A pause from the music's frenetic pace, before it started up again and took her to an entirely new place.

Something wonderful was going to happen during this week on Cape Cod. She could just feel it, bone-deep.

Suzanne Woods Fisher is an award-winning, bestselling author of more than thirty books, including *The Moonlight School* and *A Season on the Wind*, as well as the Three Sisters Island, Nantucket Legacy, Amish Beginnings, The Bishop's Family, The Deacon's Family, and The Inn at Eagle Hill series. She is also the author of several nonfiction books about the Amish, including *Amish Peace* and *Amish Proverbs*. She lives in California. Learn more at www.suzannewoodsfisher.com and follow Suzanne on Facebook @SuzanneWoodsFisherAuthor and Twitter @suzannewfisher.

"Memorable characters, gorgeous Maine scenery, and plenty of family drama. I can't wait to visit Three Sisters Island again!"

—IRENE HANNON,
bestselling author of the beloved Hope Harbor series

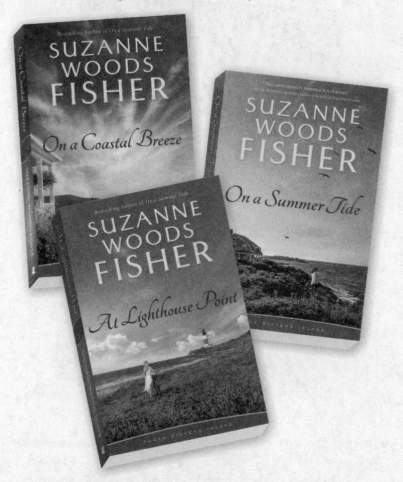

Following the lives of three sisters, this contemporary romance series from Suzanne Woods Fisher is sure to delight her fans and draw new ones.

"An unforgettable story about love and the transforming power of words and community. Deeply moving and uplifting!"

—LAURA FRANTZ,
Christy Award–winning author of *Tidewater Bride*

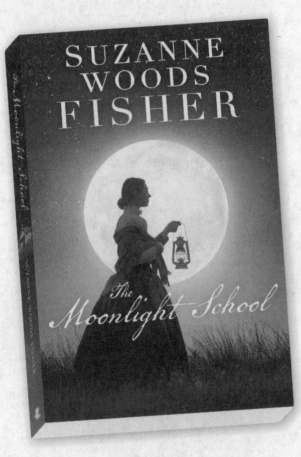

Based on true events, a young woman used to the finer things in life arrives in a small Appalachian town in 1911 to help her formidable cousin combat adult illiteracy by opening moonlight schools.

Revell
a division of Baker Publishing Group
www.RevellBooks.com

Available wherever books and ebooks are sold.

"*A Season on the Wind* overflows with warmth and conflict, laced with humor, and the possibility of rekindled love."

—**AMY CLIPSTON,**
bestselling author of *The Jam and Jelly Nook*

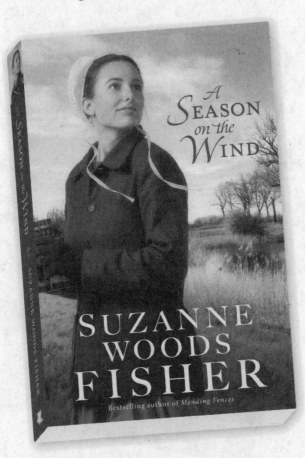

A rare bird draws Ben Zook back to his childhood home, the Amish community of Stoney Ridge—and back to Penny Weaver.

 Revell
a division of Baker Publishing Group
www.RevellBooks.com

Available wherever books and ebooks are sold.

Discover the mysteries of Stoney Ridge with the LANCASTER COUNTY SECRETS series

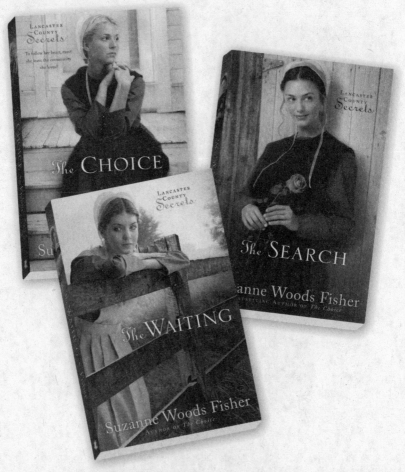

Revell
a division of Baker Publishing Group
www.RevellBooks.com

Available wherever books and ebooks are sold.

"There's just something unique and fresh about every Suzanne Woods Fisher book. Whatever the reason, I'm a fan."

—SHELLEY SHEPARD GRAY,
New York Times and *USA Today* bestselling author

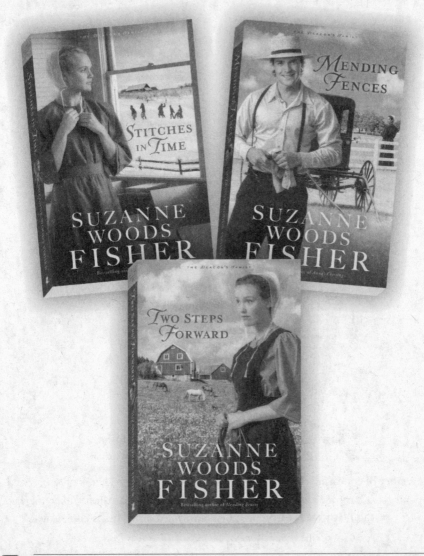

Bestselling author Suzanne Woods Fisher delivers her trademark twists, turns, and tender romance in this delightful and exciting visit to the quiet community of Stoney Ridge.

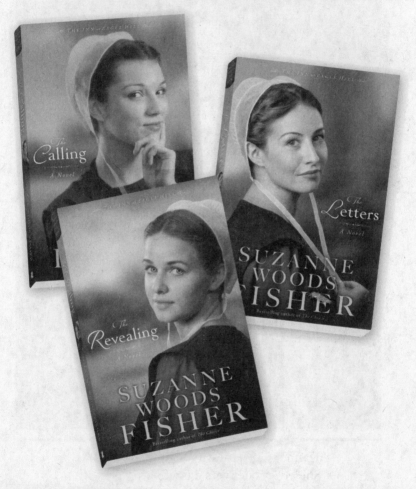

"Suzanne Woods Fisher weaves a cast of authentic characters, real-life problems, and a beautiful setting into a sweet and satisfying story."
—**LESLIE GOULD**, Christy Award–winning and bestselling author of *Adoring Addie*

a division of Baker Publishing Group
www.RevellBooks.com

Available wherever books and ebooks are sold.

Connect with SUZANNE

www.SuzanneWoodsFisher.com